image comics presents

# THE WALKING DEAD™

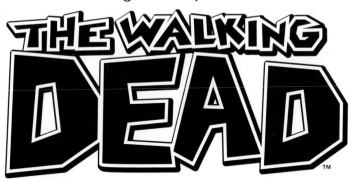

**ROBERT KIRKMAN**
CREATOR, WRITER

**CHARLIE ADLARD**
PENCILER

**STEFANO GAUDIANO**
INKER

**CLIFF RATHBURN**
GRAY TONES

**RUS WOOTON**
LETTERER

**CHARLIE ADLARD & DAVE STEWART**
COVER

**SEAN MACKIEWICZ**
EDITOR

For SKYBOUND ENTERTAINMENT
**Robert Kirkman** - Chairman
**David Alpert** - CEO
**Sean Mackiewicz** - Editorial Director
**Shawn Kirkham** - Senior VP Business Development
**Brian Huntington** - Online Editorial Director
**June Alian** - Publicity Director
**Jon Moisan** - Editor
**Arielle Basich** - Assistant Editor
**Andres Juarez** - Graphic Designer
**Paul Shin** - Business Development Assistant
**Johnny O'Dell** - Online Editorial Assistant
**Dan Petersen** - Operations Manager
**Nick Palmer** - Operations Coordinator

International inquiries: ag@sequentialrights.com
Licensing inquiries: contact@skybound.com
WWW.SKYBOUND.COM

**IMAGE COMICS, INC.**
**Robert Kirkman**—Chief Operating Officer
**Erik Larsen**—Chief Financial Officer
**Todd McFarlane**—President
**Marc Silvestri**—Chief Executive Officer
**Jim Valentino**—Vice-President

**Eric Stephenson**—Publisher
**Corey Murphy**—Director of Sales
**Jeff Boison**—Director of Publishing Planning & Book Trade Sales
**Chris Ross**—Director of Digital Sales
**Kat Salazar**—Director of PR & Marketing
**Branwyn Bigglestone**—Controller
**Drew Gill**—Art Director
**Brett Warnock**—Production Manager
**Meredith Wallace**—Print Manager
**Briah Skelly**—Publicist
**Aly Hoffman**— Conventions & Events Coordinator
**Sasha Head**—Sales & Marketing Production Designer
**David Brothers**—Branding Manager
**Melissa Gifford**—Content Manager
**Erika Schnatz**—Production Artist
**Ryan Brewer**—Production Artist
**Shanna Matuszak**—Production Artist
**Tricia Ramos**—Production Artist
**Vincent Kukua**—Production Artist
**Jeff Stang**—Direct Market Sales Representative
**Emilio Bautista**—Digital Sales Associate
**Leanna Caunter**—Accounting Assistant
**Chloe Ramos-Peterson**—Library Market Sales Representative
**IMAGECOMICS.COM**

THE WALKING DEAD, VOL. 27: THE WHISPERER WAR. First Printing. ISBN: 978-1-5343-0052-1. Published by Image Comics, Inc. Office of publication: 2701 NW Vaughn St., Ste. 780, Portland, OR 97210.  For information regarding the CPSIA on this printed material call: 203-595-3636 and provide reference # RICH – 719011. PRINTED IN THE USA

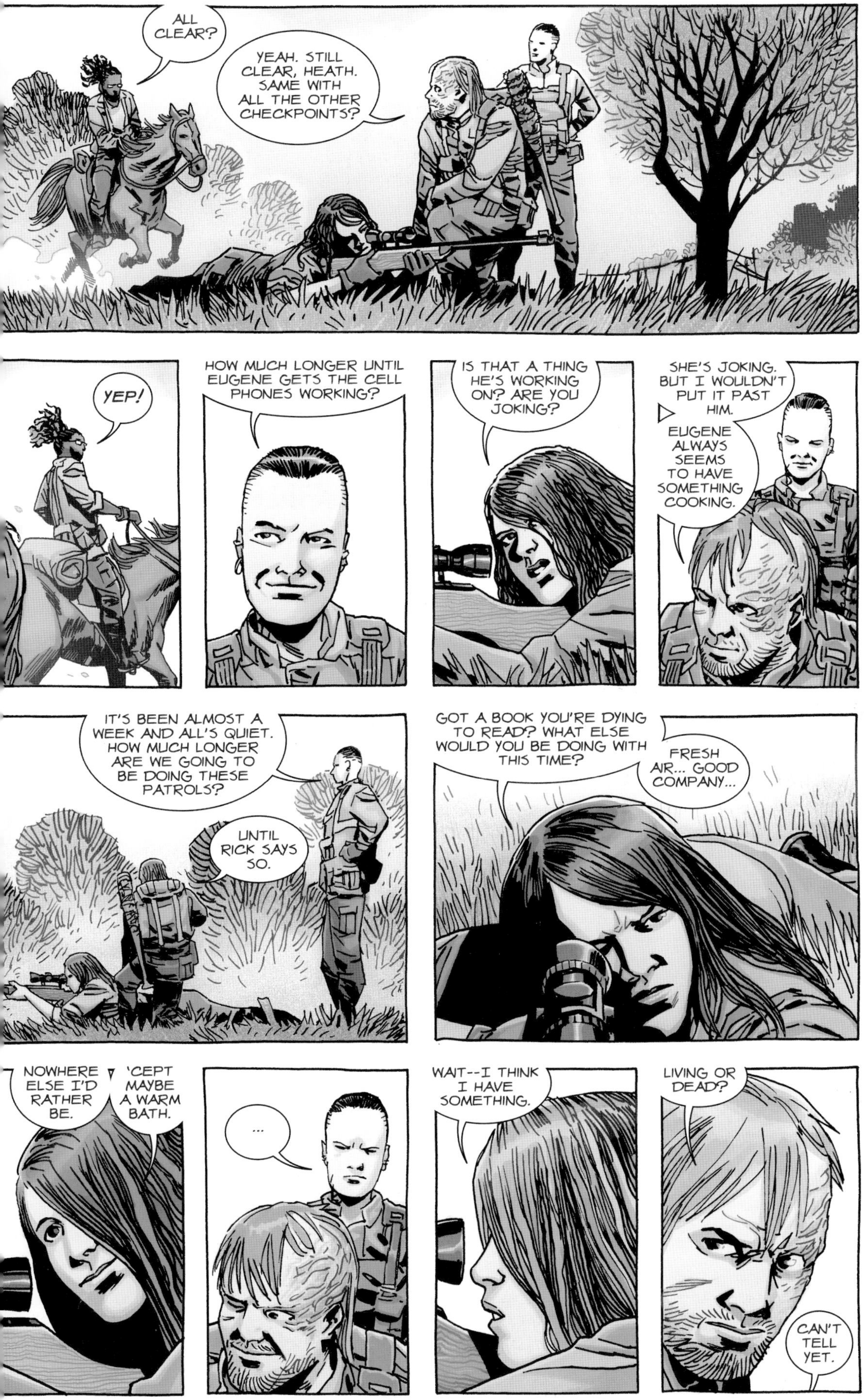
ALL CLEAR?
YEAH. STILL CLEAR, HEATH. SAME WITH ALL THE OTHER CHECKPOINTS?
YEP!
HOW MUCH LONGER UNTIL EUGENE GETS THE CELL PHONES WORKING?
IS THAT A THING HE'S WORKING ON? ARE YOU JOKING?
SHE'S JOKING. BUT I WOULDN'T PUT IT PAST HIM.
EUGENE ALWAYS SEEMS TO HAVE SOMETHING COOKING.
IT'S BEEN ALMOST A WEEK AND ALL'S QUIET. HOW MUCH LONGER ARE WE GOING TO BE DOING THESE PATROLS?
UNTIL RICK SAYS SO.
GOT A BOOK YOU'RE DYING TO READ? WHAT ELSE WOULD YOU BE DOING WITH THIS TIME?
FRESH AIR... GOOD COMPANY...
NOWHERE ELSE I'D RATHER BE.
'CEPT MAYBE A WARM BATH.
...
WAIT--I THINK I HAVE SOMETHING.
LIVING OR DEAD?
CAN'T TELL YET.

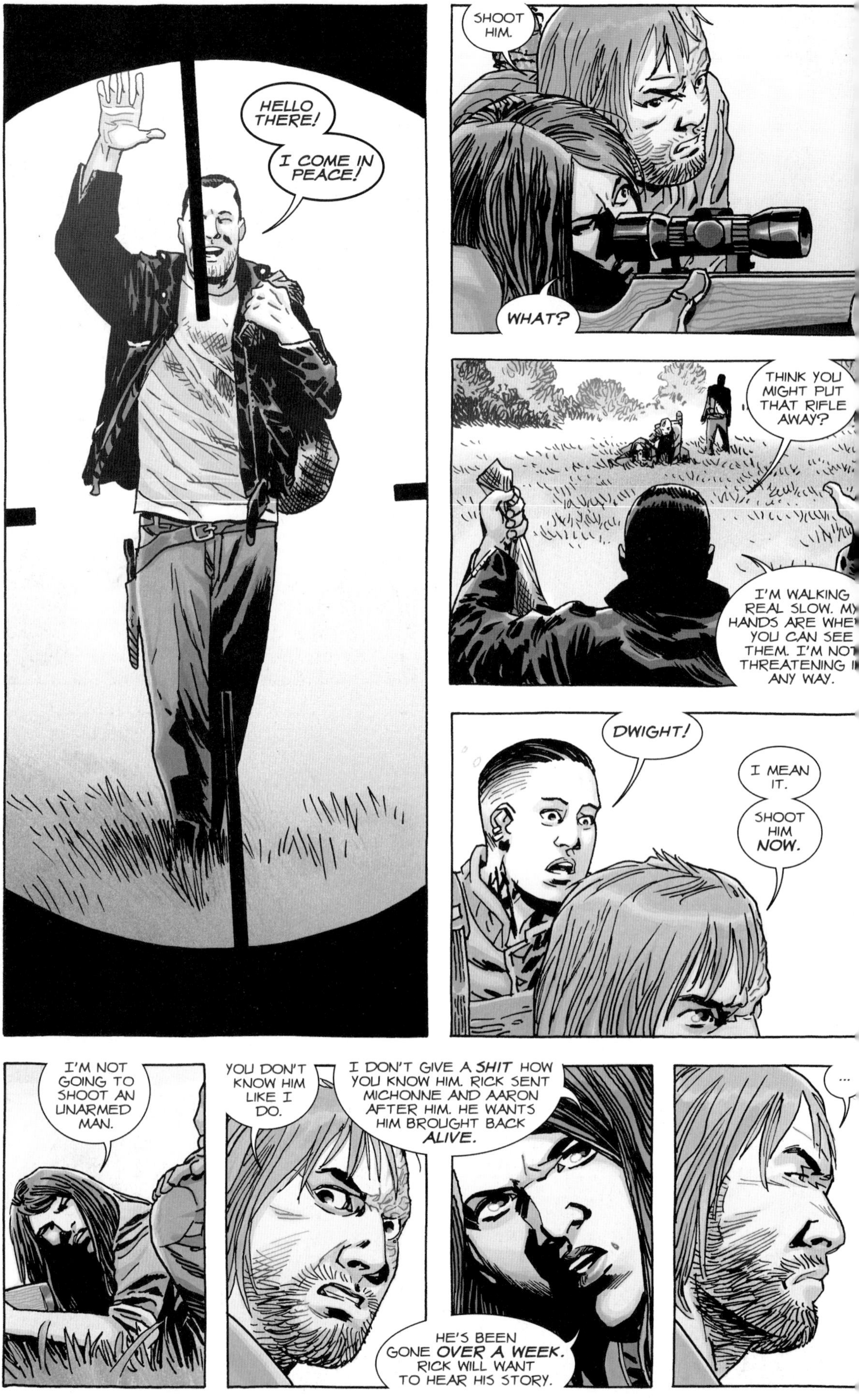
HELLO THERE!
I COME IN PEACE!
SHOOT HIM.
WHAT?
THINK YOU MIGHT PUT THAT RIFLE AWAY?
I'M WALKING REAL SLOW. MY HANDS ARE WHERE YOU CAN SEE THEM. I'M NOT THREATENING IN ANY WAY.
DWIGHT!
I MEAN IT.
SHOOT HIM NOW.
I'M NOT GOING TO SHOOT AN UNARMED MAN.
YOU DON'T KNOW HIM LIKE I DO.
I DON'T GIVE A SHIT HOW YOU KNOW HIM. RICK SENT MICHONNE AND AARON AFTER HIM. HE WANTS HIM BROUGHT BACK ALIVE.
HE'S BEEN GONE OVER A WEEK. RICK WILL WANT TO HEAR HIS STORY.
...

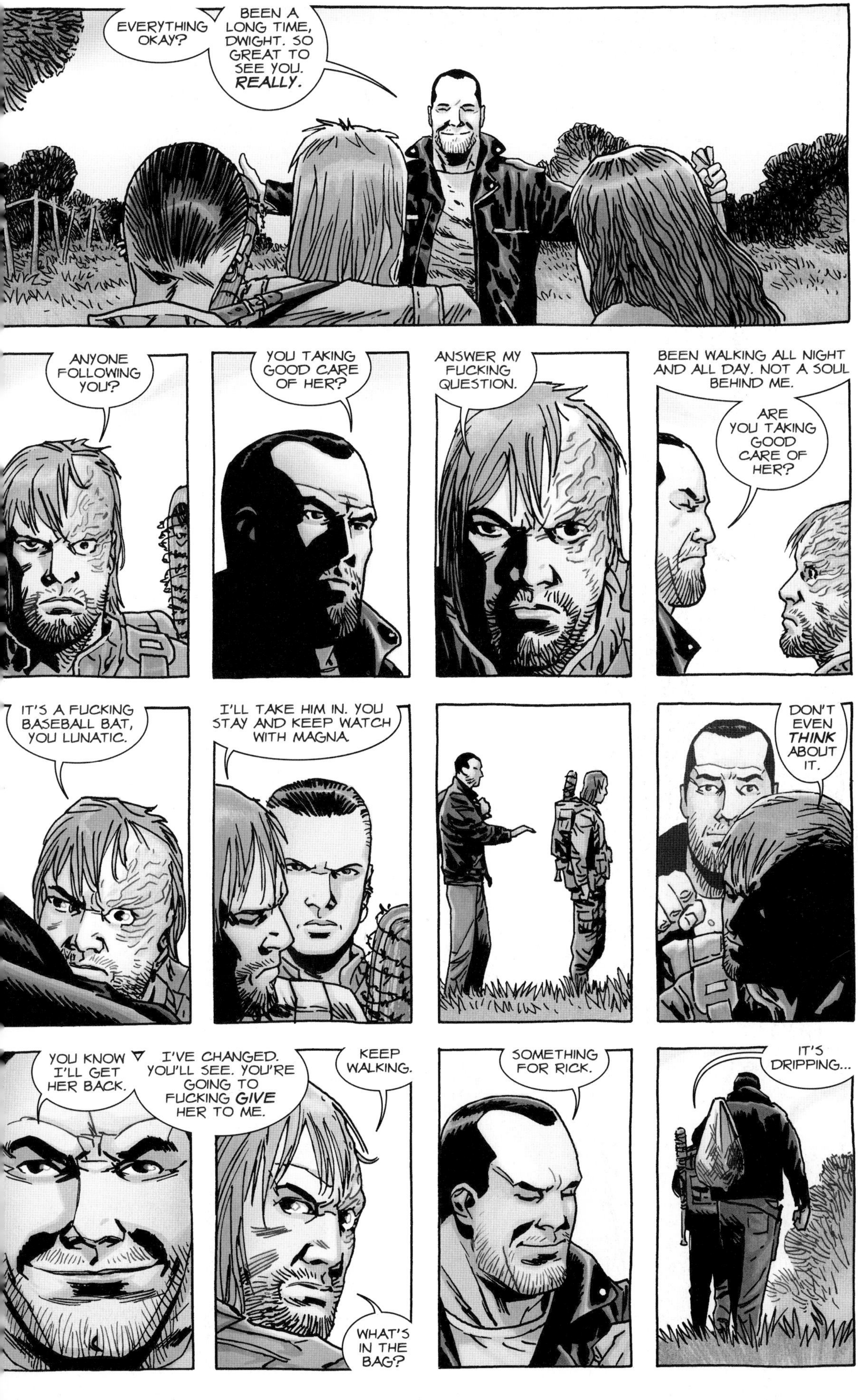

EVERYTHING OKAY?
BEEN A LONG TIME, DWIGHT. SO GREAT TO SEE YOU. *REALLY.*
ANYONE FOLLOWING YOU?
YOU TAKING GOOD CARE OF HER?
ANSWER MY FUCKING QUESTION.
BEEN WALKING ALL NIGHT AND ALL DAY. NOT A SOUL BEHIND ME.
ARE YOU TAKING GOOD CARE OF HER?
IT'S A FUCKING BASEBALL BAT, YOU LUNATIC.
I'LL TAKE HIM IN. YOU STAY AND KEEP WATCH WITH MAGNA.
DON'T EVEN *THINK* ABOUT IT.
YOU KNOW I'LL GET HER BACK.
I'VE CHANGED. YOU'LL SEE. YOU'RE GOING TO FUCKING *GIVE* HER TO ME.
KEEP WALKING.
WHAT'S IN THE BAG?
SOMETHING FOR RICK.
IT'S DRIPPING...

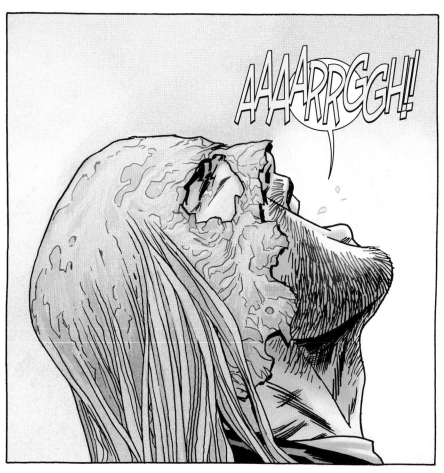

AAAARRGGH!!

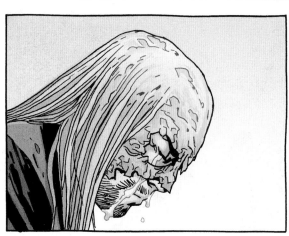

DID YOU FIND HER?

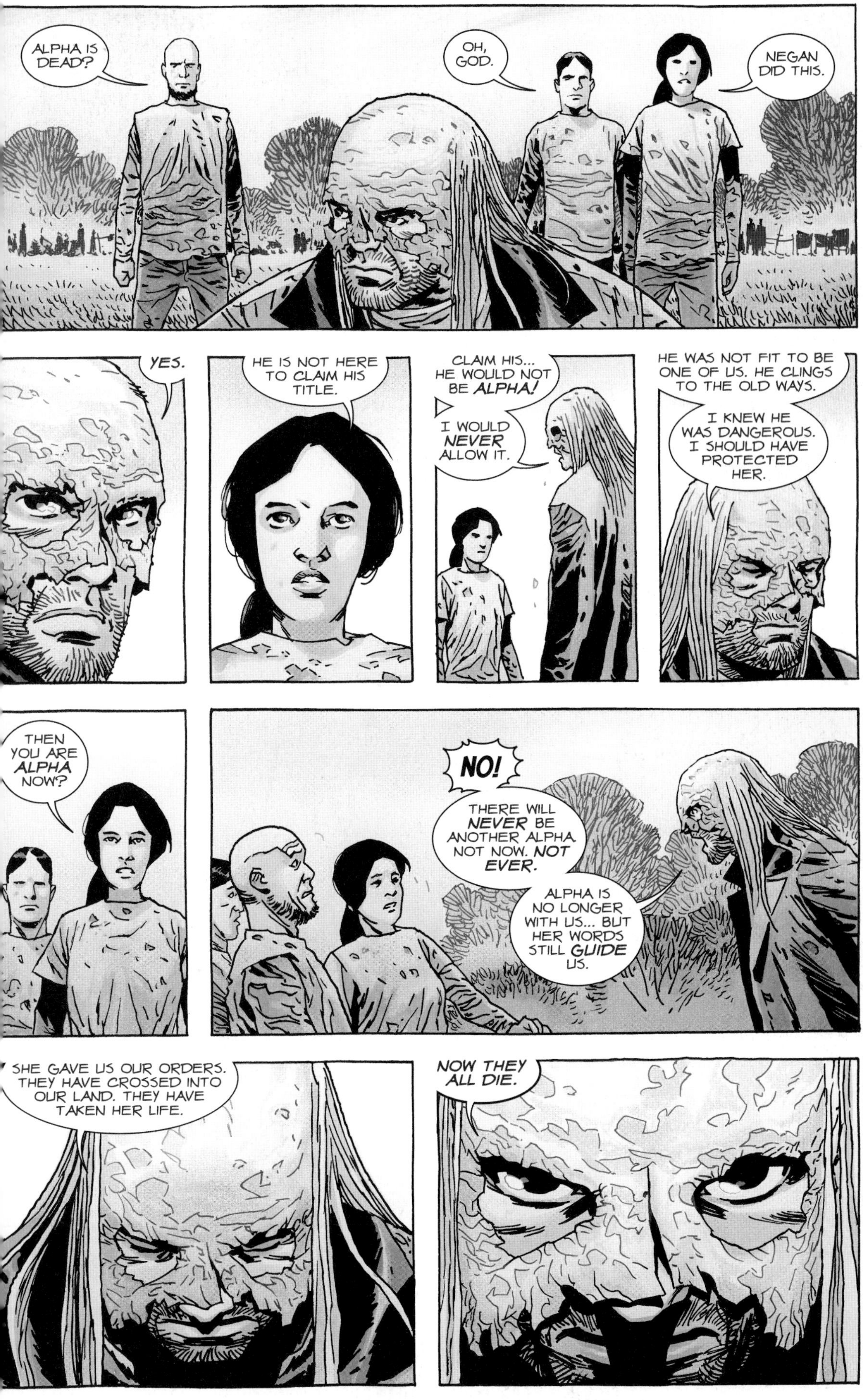
ALPHA IS DEAD?
OH, GOD.
NEGAN DID THIS.
YES.
HE IS NOT HERE TO CLAIM HIS TITLE.
CLAIM HIS... HE WOULD NOT BE ALPHA!
I WOULD NEVER ALLOW IT.
HE WAS NOT FIT TO BE ONE OF US. HE CLINGS TO THE OLD WAYS.
I KNEW HE WAS DANGEROUS. I SHOULD HAVE PROTECTED HER.
THEN YOU ARE ALPHA NOW?
NO!
THERE WILL NEVER BE ANOTHER ALPHA NOT NOW. NOT EVER.
ALPHA IS NO LONGER WITH US... BUT HER WORDS STILL GUIDE US.
SHE GAVE US OUR ORDERS. THEY HAVE CROSSED INTO OUR LAND. THEY HAVE TAKEN HER LIFE.
NOW THEY ALL DIE.

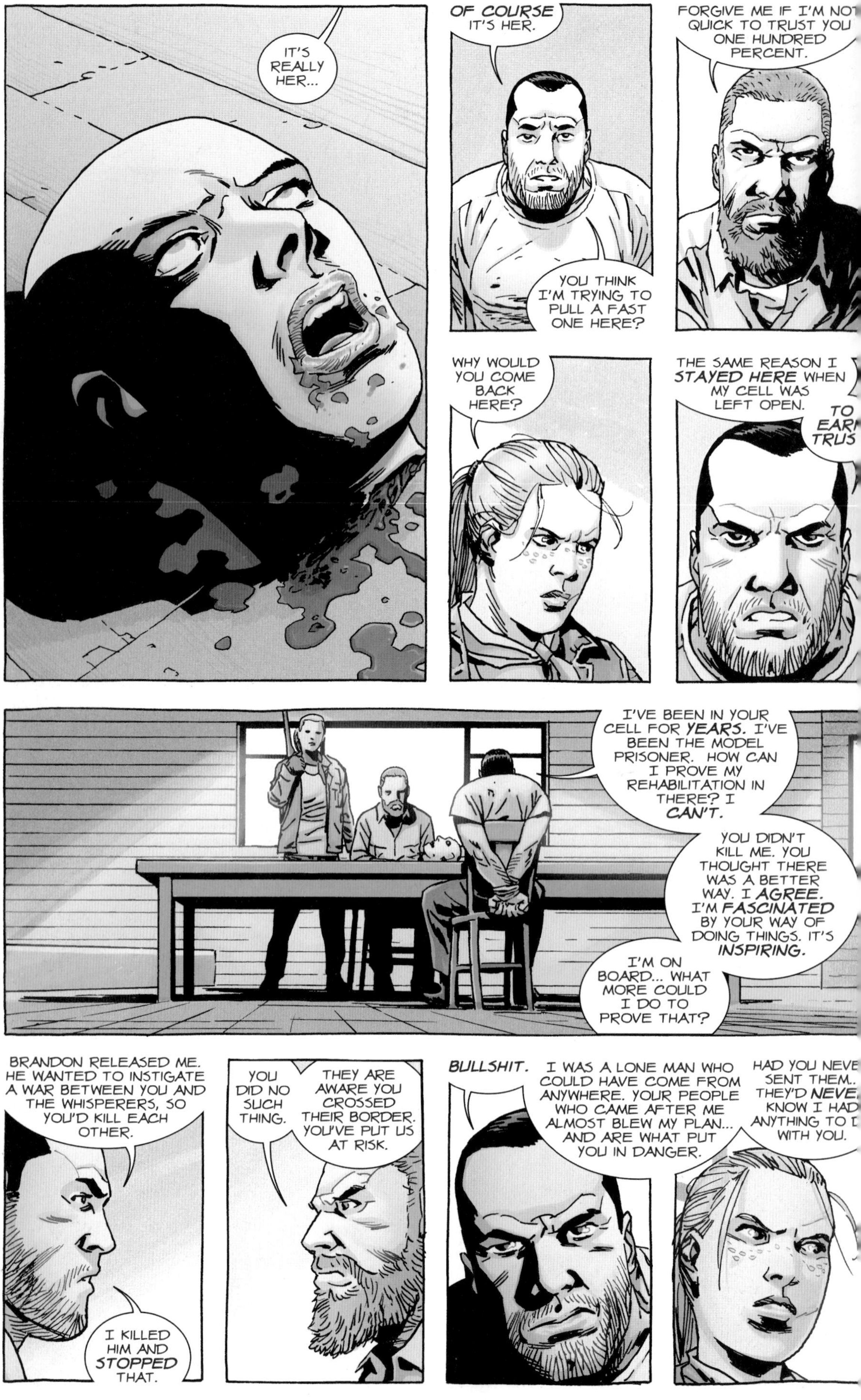
IT'S REALLY HER...
OF COURSE IT'S HER.
YOU THINK I'M TRYING TO PULL A FAST ONE HERE?
FORGIVE ME IF I'M NOT QUICK TO TRUST YOU ONE HUNDRED PERCENT.
WHY WOULD YOU COME BACK HERE?
THE SAME REASON I STAYED HERE WHEN MY CELL WAS LEFT OPEN.
TO EARN TRUS
I'VE BEEN IN YOUR CELL FOR YEARS. I'VE BEEN THE MODEL PRISONER. HOW CAN I PROVE MY REHABILITATION IN THERE? I CAN'T.
YOU DIDN'T KILL ME. YOU THOUGHT THERE WAS A BETTER WAY. I AGREE. I'M FASCINATED BY YOUR WAY OF DOING THINGS. IT'S INSPIRING.
I'M ON BOARD... WHAT MORE COULD I DO TO PROVE THAT?
BRANDON RELEASED ME. HE WANTED TO INSTIGATE A WAR BETWEEN YOU AND THE WHISPERERS, SO YOU'D KILL EACH OTHER.
I KILLED HIM AND STOPPED THAT.
YOU DID NO SUCH THING.
THEY ARE AWARE YOU CROSSED THEIR BORDER. YOU'VE PUT US AT RISK.
BULLSHIT.
I WAS A LONE MAN WHO COULD HAVE COME FROM ANYWHERE. YOUR PEOPLE WHO CAME AFTER ME ALMOST BLEW MY PLAN... AND ARE WHAT PUT YOU IN DANGER.
HAD YOU NEVE SENT THEM.. THEY'D NEVE KNOW I HAD ANYTHING TO D WITH YOU.

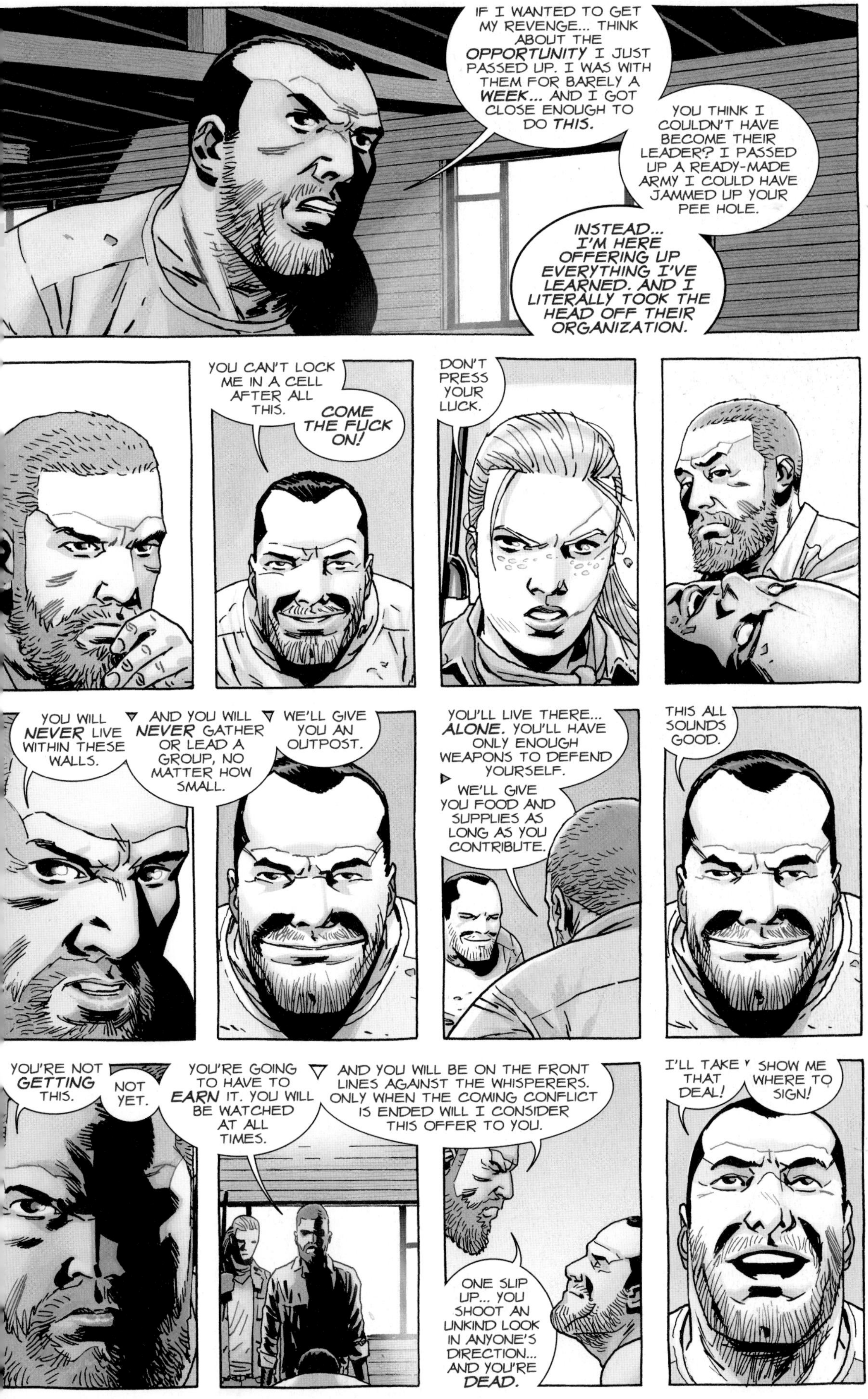
IF I WANTED TO GET MY REVENGE... THINK ABOUT THE OPPORTUNITY I JUST PASSED UP. I WAS WITH THEM FOR BARELY A WEEK... AND I GOT CLOSE ENOUGH TO DO THIS.
YOU THINK I COULDN'T HAVE BECOME THEIR LEADER? I PASSED UP A READY-MADE ARMY I COULD HAVE JAMMED UP YOUR PEE HOLE.
INSTEAD... I'M HERE OFFERING UP EVERYTHING I'VE LEARNED. AND I LITERALLY TOOK THE HEAD OFF THEIR ORGANIZATION.
YOU CAN'T LOCK ME IN A CELL AFTER ALL THIS.
COME THE FUCK ON!
DON'T PRESS YOUR LUCK.
YOU WILL NEVER LIVE WITHIN THESE WALLS.
AND YOU WILL NEVER GATHER OR LEAD A GROUP, NO MATTER HOW SMALL.
WE'LL GIVE YOU AN OUTPOST.
YOU'LL LIVE THERE... ALONE. YOU'LL HAVE ONLY ENOUGH WEAPONS TO DEFEND YOURSELF.
WE'LL GIVE YOU FOOD AND SUPPLIES AS LONG AS YOU CONTRIBUTE.
THIS ALL SOUNDS GOOD.
YOU'RE NOT GETTING THIS.
NOT YET.
YOU'RE GOING TO HAVE TO EARN IT. YOU WILL BE WATCHED AT ALL TIMES.
AND YOU WILL BE ON THE FRONT LINES AGAINST THE WHISPERERS. ONLY WHEN THE COMING CONFLICT IS ENDED WILL I CONSIDER THIS OFFER TO YOU.
ONE SLIP UP... YOU SHOOT AN UNKIND LOOK IN ANYONE'S DIRECTION... AND YOU'RE DEAD.
I'LL TAKE THAT DEAL!
SHOW ME WHERE TO SIGN!

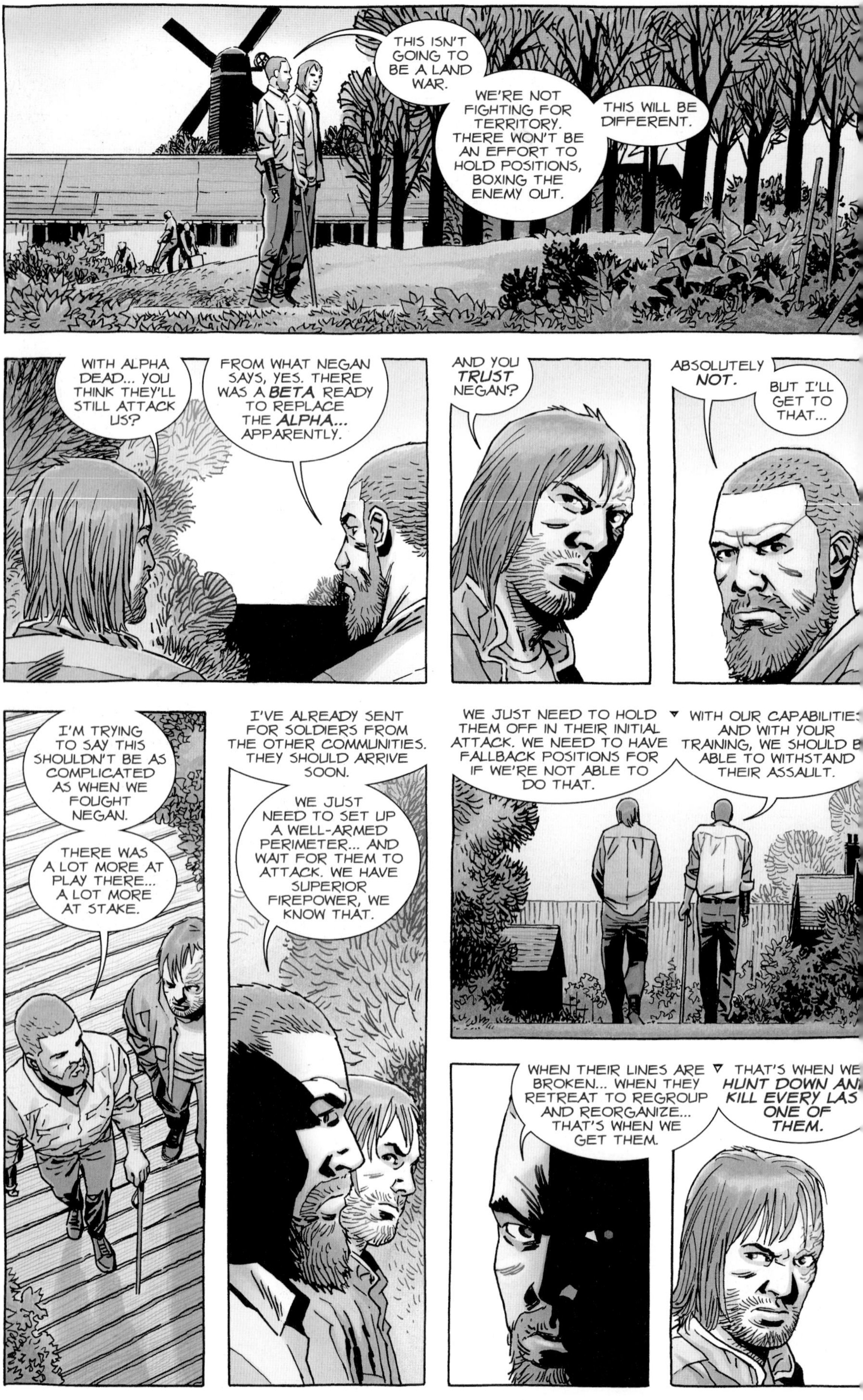
THIS ISN'T GOING TO BE A LAND WAR.
WE'RE NOT FIGHTING FOR TERRITORY. THERE WON'T BE AN EFFORT TO HOLD POSITIONS, BOXING THE ENEMY OUT.
THIS WILL BE DIFFERENT.
WITH ALPHA DEAD... YOU THINK THEY'LL STILL ATTACK US?
FROM WHAT NEGAN SAYS, YES. THERE WAS A BETA READY TO REPLACE THE ALPHA... APPARENTLY.
AND YOU TRUST NEGAN?
ABSOLUTELY NOT.
BUT I'LL GET TO THAT...
I'M TRYING TO SAY THIS SHOULDN'T BE AS COMPLICATED AS WHEN WE FOUGHT NEGAN.
THERE WAS A LOT MORE AT PLAY THERE... A LOT MORE AT STAKE.
I'VE ALREADY SENT FOR SOLDIERS FROM THE OTHER COMMUNITIES. THEY SHOULD ARRIVE SOON.
WE JUST NEED TO SET UP A WELL-ARMED PERIMETER... AND WAIT FOR THEM TO ATTACK. WE HAVE SUPERIOR FIREPOWER, WE KNOW THAT.
WE JUST NEED TO HOLD THEM OFF IN THEIR INITIAL ATTACK. WE NEED TO HAVE FALLBACK POSITIONS FOR IF WE'RE NOT ABLE TO DO THAT.
WITH OUR CAPABILITIE AND WITH YOUR TRAINING, WE SHOULD B ABLE TO WITHSTAND THEIR ASSAULT.
WHEN THEIR LINES ARE BROKEN... WHEN THEY RETREAT TO REGROUP AND REORGANIZE... THAT'S WHEN WE GET THEM.
THAT'S WHEN WE HUNT DOWN AN KILL EVERY LAS ONE OF THEM.

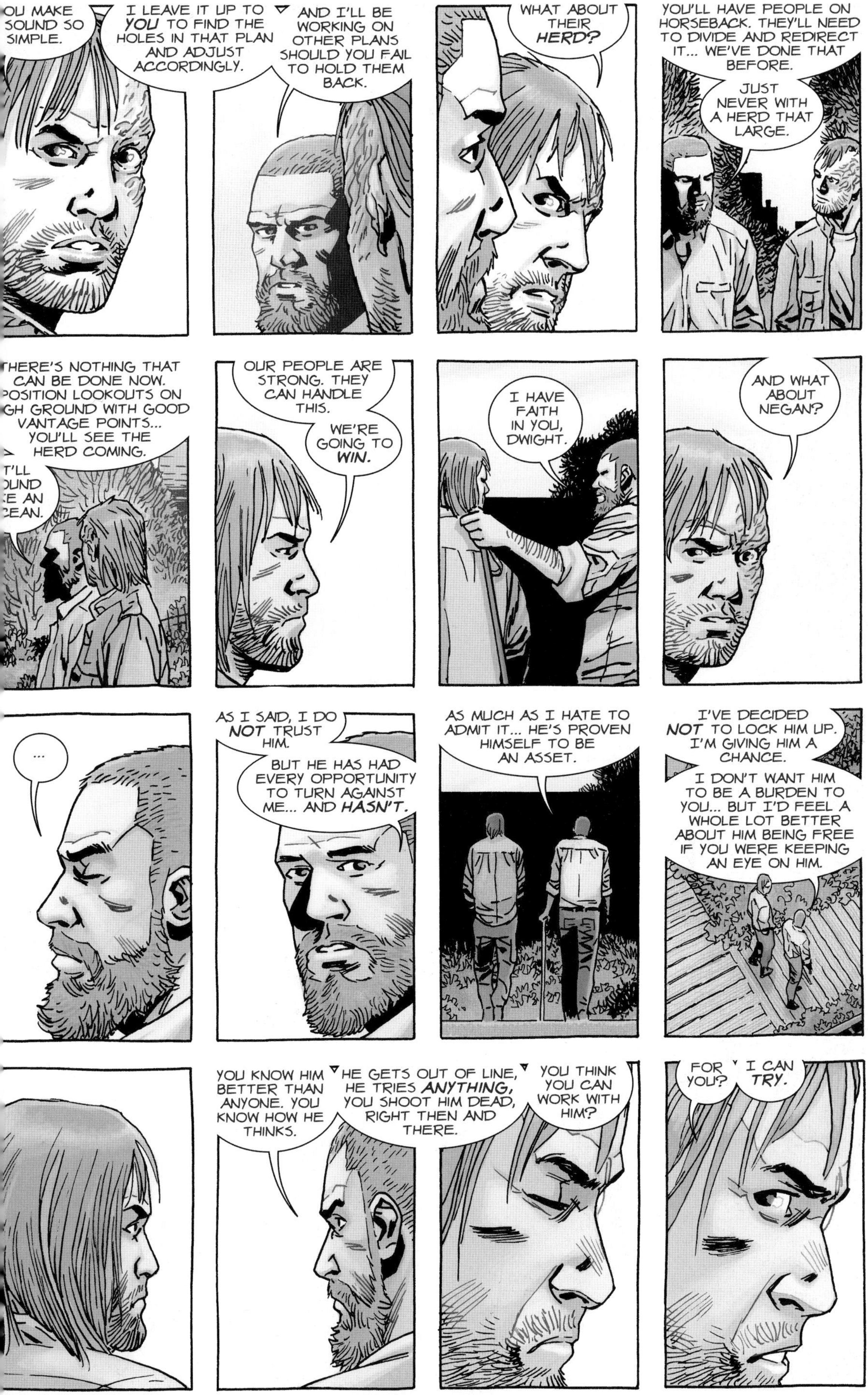
OU MAKE
SOUND SO
SIMPLE.
I LEAVE IT UP TO YOU TO FIND THE HOLES IN THAT PLAN AND ADJUST ACCORDINGLY.
AND I'LL BE WORKING ON OTHER PLANS SHOULD YOU FAIL TO HOLD THEM BACK.
WHAT ABOUT THEIR HERD?
YOU'LL HAVE PEOPLE ON HORSEBACK. THEY'LL NEED TO DIVIDE AND REDIRECT IT... WE'VE DONE THAT BEFORE.
JUST NEVER WITH A HERD THAT LARGE.
THERE'S NOTHING THAT CAN BE DONE NOW. POSITION LOOKOUTS ON GH GROUND WITH GOOD VANTAGE POINTS... YOU'LL SEE THE HERD COMING.
T'LL OUND E AN CEAN.
OUR PEOPLE ARE STRONG. THEY CAN HANDLE THIS.
WE'RE GOING TO WIN.
I HAVE FAITH IN YOU, DWIGHT.
AND WHAT ABOUT NEGAN?
...
AS I SAID, I DO NOT TRUST HIM.
BUT HE HAS HAD EVERY OPPORTUNITY TO TURN AGAINST ME... AND HASN'T.
AS MUCH AS I HATE TO ADMIT IT... HE'S PROVEN HIMSELF TO BE AN ASSET.
I'VE DECIDED NOT TO LOCK HIM UP. I'M GIVING HIM A CHANCE.
I DON'T WANT HIM TO BE A BURDEN TO YOU... BUT I'D FEEL A WHOLE LOT BETTER ABOUT HIM BEING FREE IF YOU WERE KEEPING AN EYE ON HIM.
YOU KNOW HIM BETTER THAN ANYONE. YOU KNOW HOW HE THINKS.
HE GETS OUT OF LINE, HE TRIES ANYTHING, YOU SHOOT HIM DEAD, RIGHT THEN AND THERE.
YOU THINK YOU CAN WORK WITH HIM?
FOR YOU?
I CAN TRY.

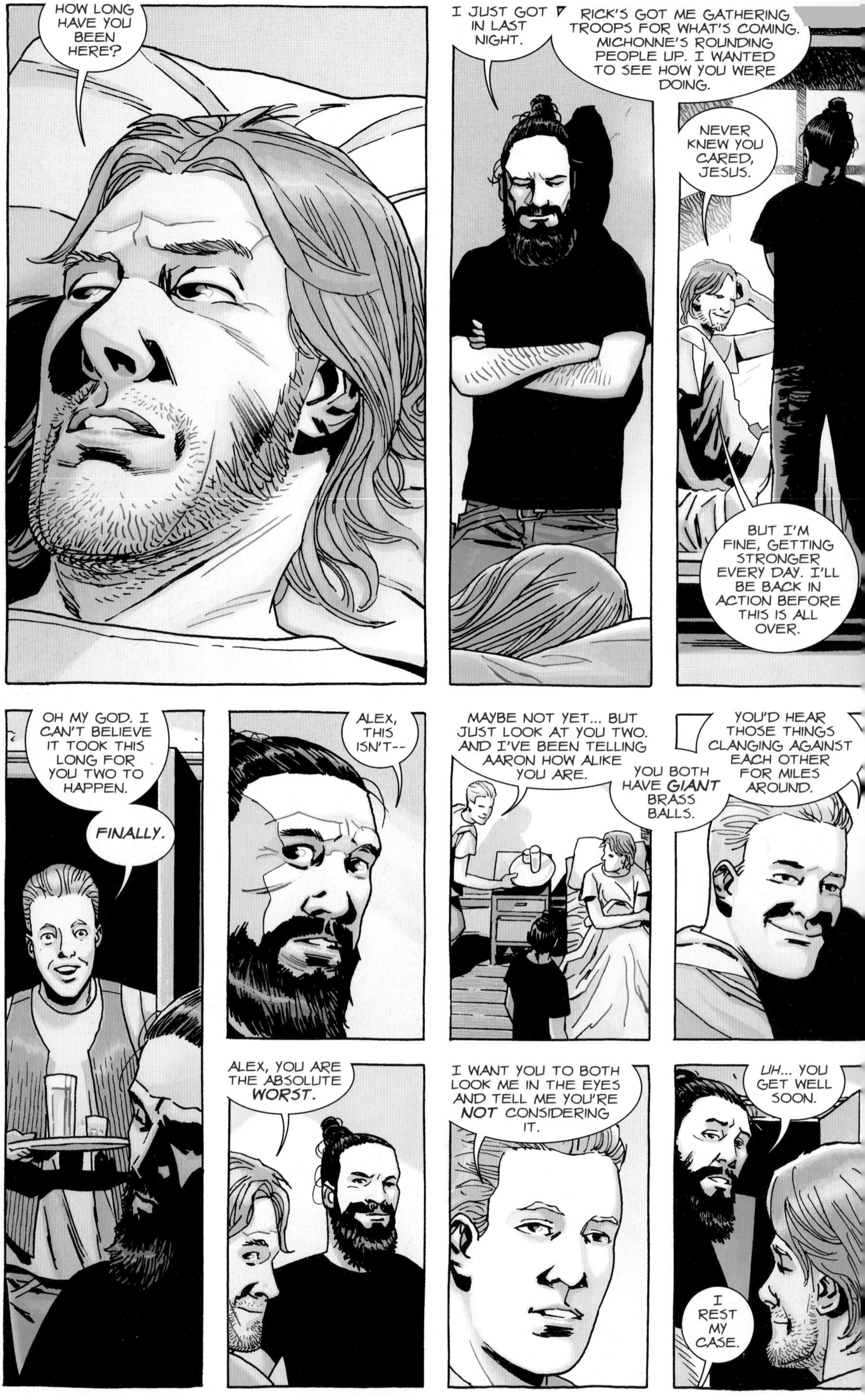
HOW LONG HAVE YOU BEEN HERE?
I JUST GOT IN LAST NIGHT.
RICK'S GOT ME GATHERING TROOPS FOR WHAT'S COMING. MICHONNE'S ROUNDING PEOPLE UP. I WANTED TO SEE HOW YOU WERE DOING.
NEVER KNEW YOU CARED, JESUS.
BUT I'M FINE, GETTING STRONGER EVERY DAY. I'LL BE BACK IN ACTION BEFORE THIS IS ALL OVER.
OH MY GOD. I CAN'T BELIEVE IT TOOK THIS LONG FOR YOU TWO TO HAPPEN.
FINALLY.
ALEX, THIS ISN'T--
MAYBE NOT YET... BUT JUST LOOK AT YOU TWO. AND I'VE BEEN TELLING AARON HOW ALIKE YOU ARE.
YOU BOTH HAVE GIANT BRASS BALLS.
YOU'D HEAR THOSE THINGS CLANGING AGAINST EACH OTHER FOR MILES AROUND.
ALEX, YOU ARE THE ABSOLUTE WORST.
I WANT YOU TO BOTH LOOK ME IN THE EYES AND TELL ME YOU'RE NOT CONSIDERING IT.
UH... YOU GET WELL SOON.
I REST MY CASE.

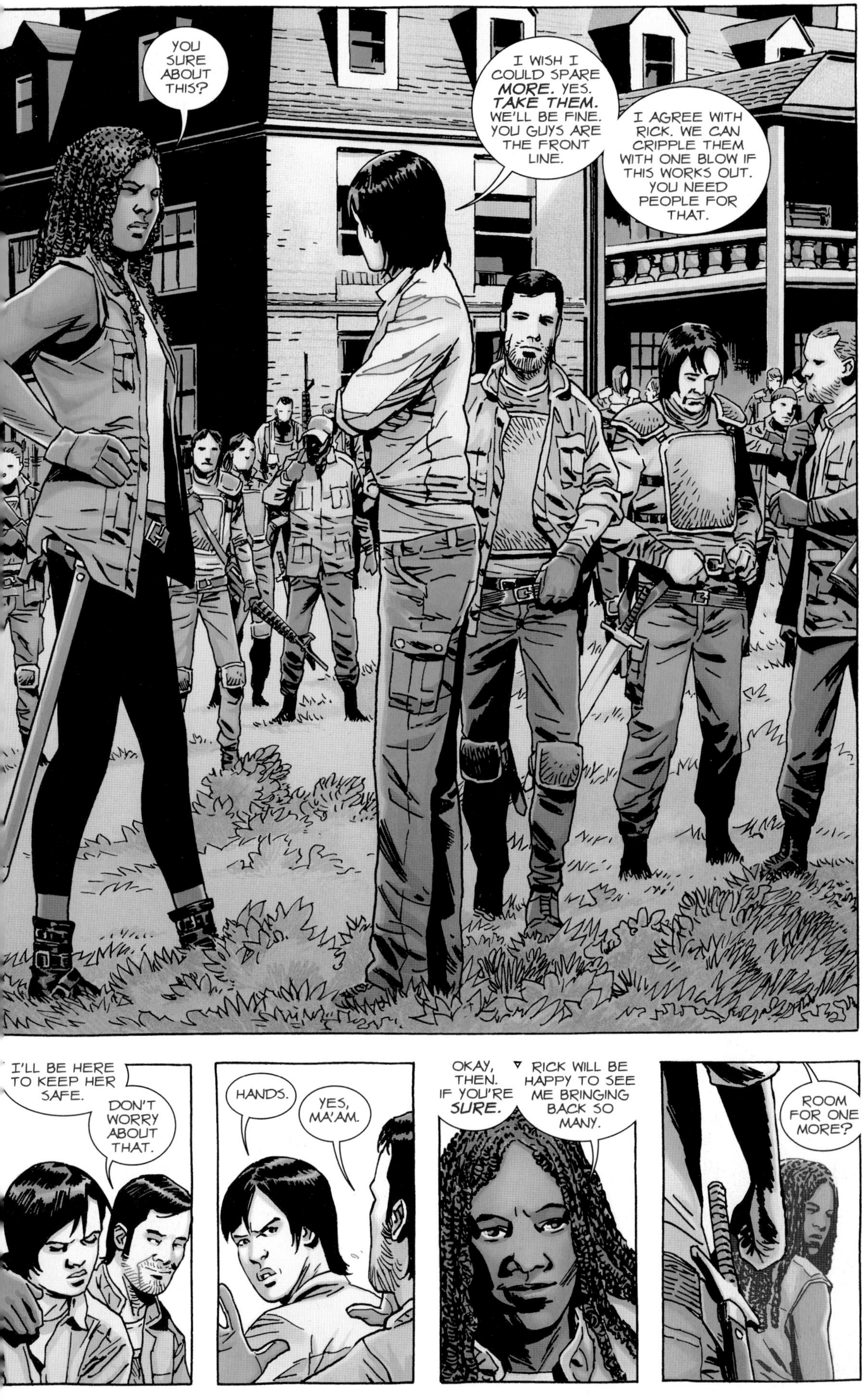
YOU SURE ABOUT THIS?
I WISH I COULD SPARE MORE. YES. TAKE THEM. WE'LL BE FINE. YOU GUYS ARE THE FRONT LINE.
I AGREE WITH RICK. WE CAN CRIPPLE THEM WITH ONE BLOW IF THIS WORKS OUT. YOU NEED PEOPLE FOR THAT.
I'LL BE HERE TO KEEP HER SAFE.
DON'T WORRY ABOUT THAT.
HANDS.
YES, MA'AM.
OKAY, THEN. IF YOU'RE SURE.
RICK WILL BE HAPPY TO SEE ME BRINGING BACK SO MANY.
ROOM FOR ONE MORE?

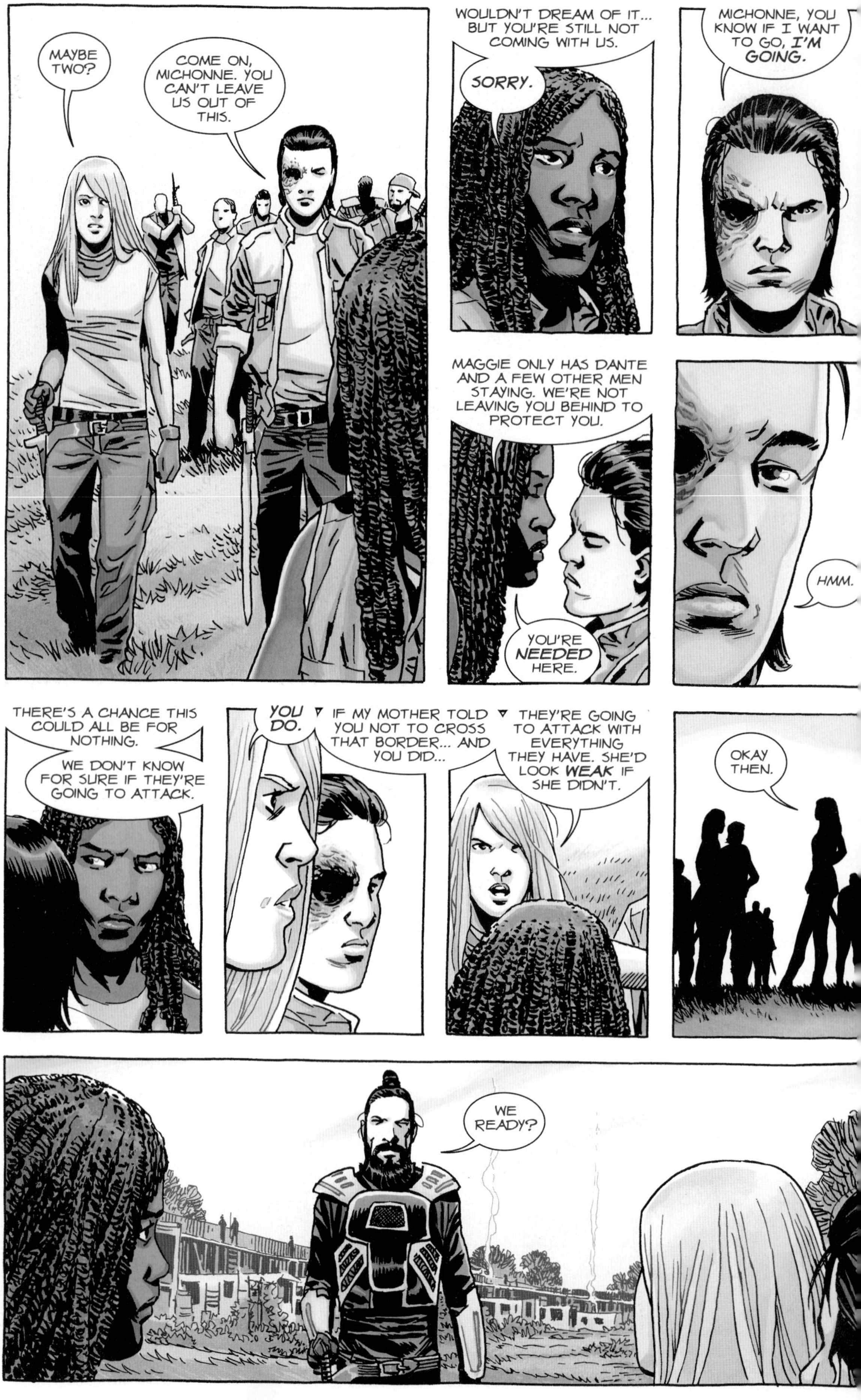
MAYBE TWO?
COME ON, MICHONNE. YOU CAN'T LEAVE US OUT OF THIS.
WOULDN'T DREAM OF IT... BUT YOU'RE STILL NOT COMING WITH US.
SORRY.
MICHONNE, YOU KNOW IF I WANT TO GO, I'M GOING.
MAGGIE ONLY HAS DANTE AND A FEW OTHER MEN STAYING. WE'RE NOT LEAVING YOU BEHIND TO PROTECT YOU.
YOU'RE NEEDED HERE.
HMM.
THERE'S A CHANCE THIS COULD ALL BE FOR NOTHING.
WE DON'T KNOW FOR SURE IF THEY'RE GOING TO ATTACK.
YOU DO.
IF MY MOTHER TOLD YOU NOT TO CROSS THAT BORDER... AND YOU DID...
THEY'RE GOING TO ATTACK WITH EVERYTHING THEY HAVE. SHE'D LOOK WEAK IF SHE DIDN'T.
OKAY THEN.
WE READY?

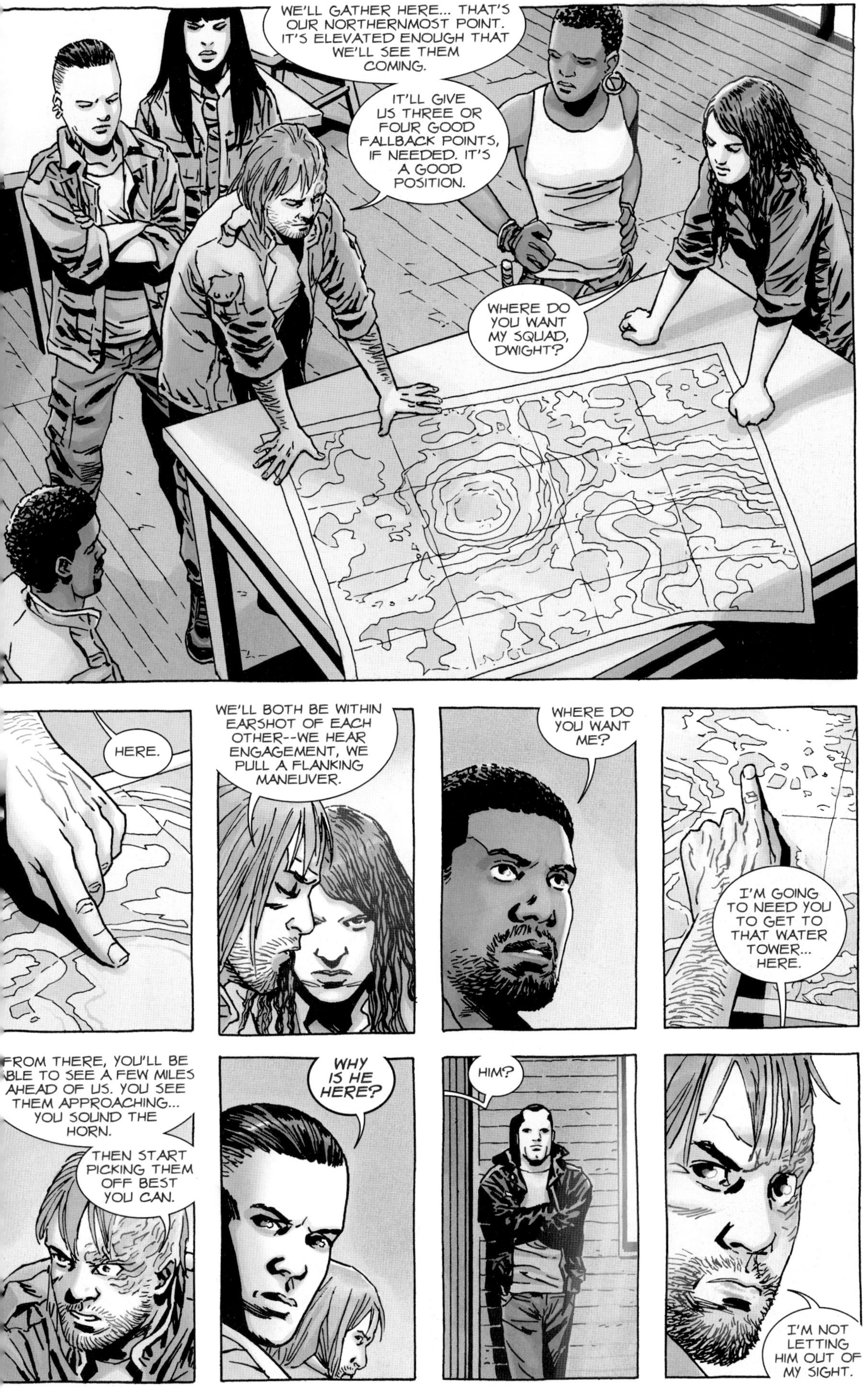
WE'LL GATHER HERE... THAT'S OUR NORTHERNMOST POINT. IT'S ELEVATED ENOUGH THAT WE'LL SEE THEM COMING.
IT'LL GIVE US THREE OR FOUR GOOD FALLBACK POINTS, IF NEEDED. IT'S A GOOD POSITION.
WHERE DO YOU WANT MY SQUAD, DWIGHT?
HERE.
WE'LL BOTH BE WITHIN EARSHOT OF EACH OTHER--WE HEAR ENGAGEMENT, WE PULL A FLANKING MANEUVER.
WHERE DO YOU WANT ME?
I'M GOING TO NEED YOU TO GET TO THAT WATER TOWER... HERE.
FROM THERE, YOU'LL BE BLE TO SEE A FEW MILES AHEAD OF US. YOU SEE THEM APPROACHING... YOU SOUND THE HORN.
THEN START PICKING THEM OFF BEST YOU CAN.
*WHY IS HE HERE?*
HIM?
I'M NOT LETTING HIM OUT OF MY SIGHT.

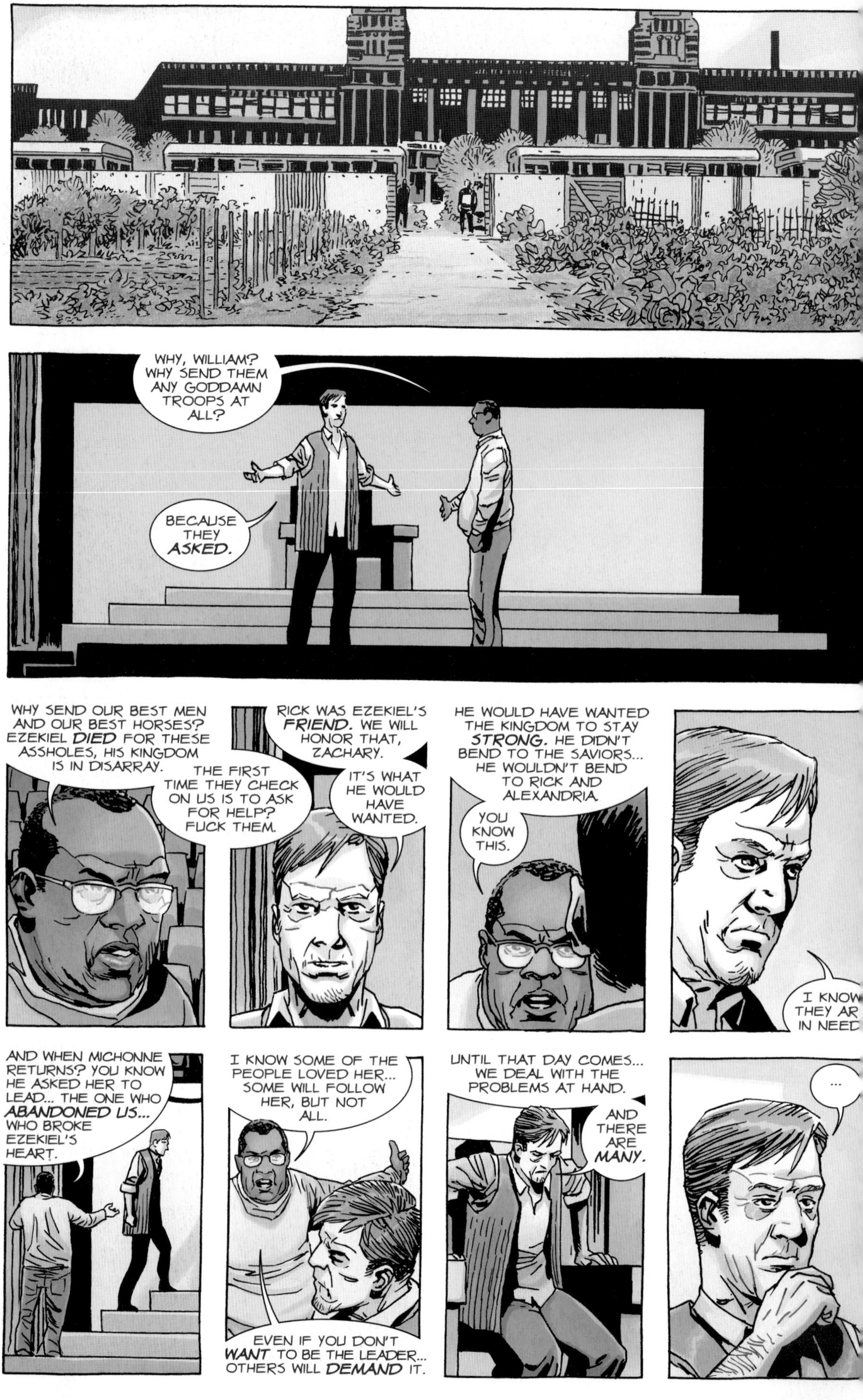
WHY, WILLIAM? WHY SEND THEM ANY GODDAMN TROOPS AT ALL?
BECAUSE THEY ASKED.
WHY SEND OUR BEST MEN AND OUR BEST HORSES? EZEKIEL DIED FOR THESE ASSHOLES, HIS KINGDOM IS IN DISARRAY.
THE FIRST TIME THEY CHECK ON US IS TO ASK FOR HELP? FUCK THEM.
RICK WAS EZEKIEL'S FRIEND. WE WILL HONOR THAT, ZACHARY.
IT'S WHAT HE WOULD HAVE WANTED.
HE WOULD HAVE WANTED THE KINGDOM TO STAY STRONG. HE DIDN'T BEND TO THE SAVIORS... HE WOULDN'T BEND TO RICK AND ALEXANDRIA.
YOU KNOW THIS.
I KNOW THEY AR IN NEED
AND WHEN MICHONNE RETURNS? YOU KNOW HE ASKED HER TO LEAD... THE ONE WHO ABANDONED US... WHO BROKE EZEKIEL'S HEART.
I KNOW SOME OF THE PEOPLE LOVED HER... SOME WILL FOLLOW HER, BUT NOT ALL.
EVEN IF YOU DON'T WANT TO BE THE LEADER... OTHERS WILL DEMAND IT.
UNTIL THAT DAY COMES... WE DEAL WITH THE PROBLEMS AT HAND.
AND THERE ARE MANY.
...

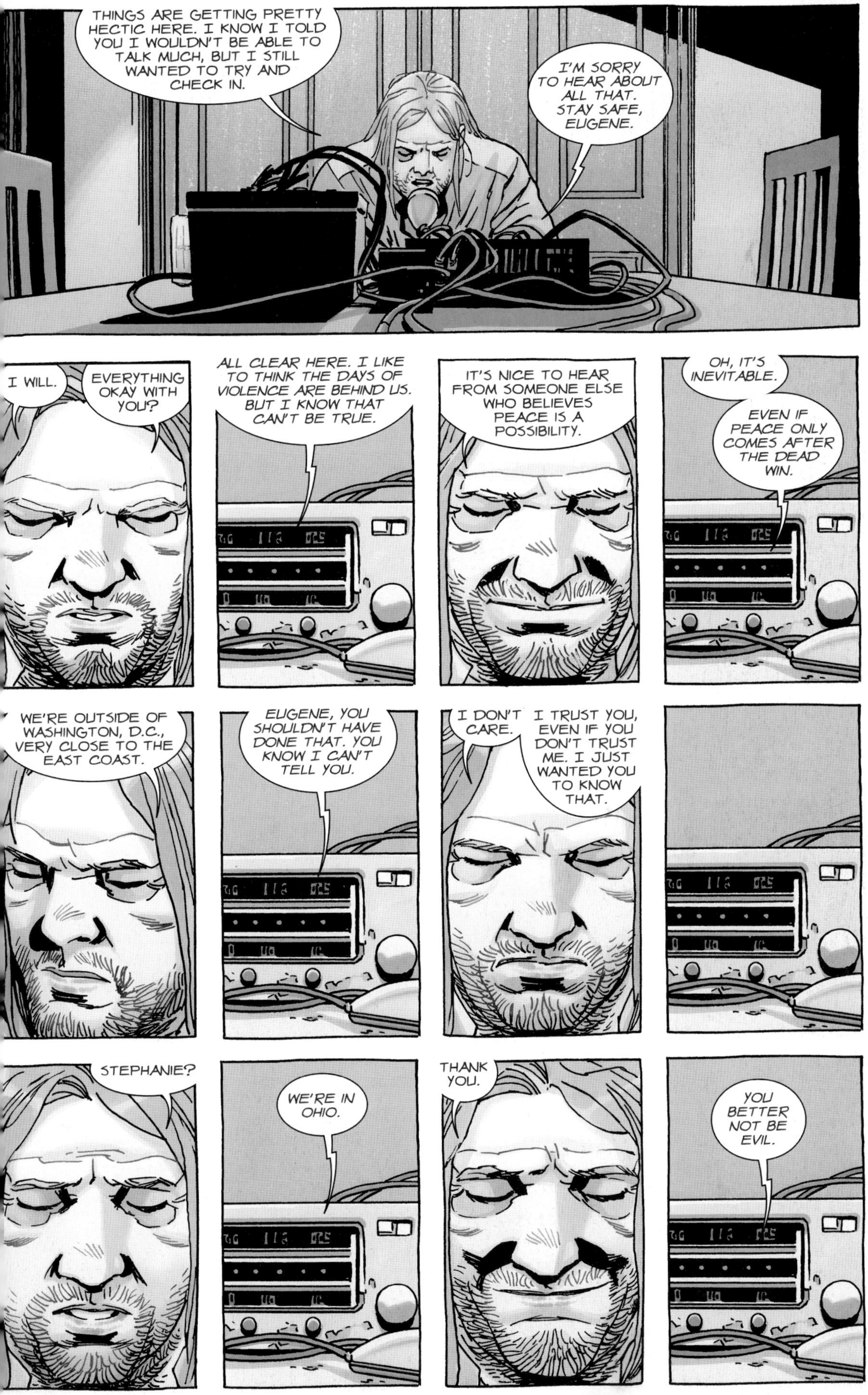

THINGS ARE GETTING PRETTY HECTIC HERE. I KNOW I TOLD YOU I WOULDN'T BE ABLE TO TALK MUCH, BUT I STILL WANTED TO TRY AND CHECK IN.
I'M SORRY TO HEAR ABOUT ALL THAT. STAY SAFE, EUGENE.
I WILL.
EVERYTHING OKAY WITH YOU?
ALL CLEAR HERE. I LIKE TO THINK THE DAYS OF VIOLENCE ARE BEHIND US. BUT I KNOW THAT CAN'T BE TRUE.
IT'S NICE TO HEAR FROM SOMEONE ELSE WHO BELIEVES PEACE IS A POSSIBILITY.
OH, IT'S INEVITABLE.
EVEN IF PEACE ONLY COMES AFTER THE DEAD WIN.
WE'RE OUTSIDE OF WASHINGTON, D.C., VERY CLOSE TO THE EAST COAST.
EUGENE, YOU SHOULDN'T HAVE DONE THAT. YOU KNOW I CAN'T TELL YOU.
I DON'T CARE.
I TRUST YOU, EVEN IF YOU DON'T TRUST ME. I JUST WANTED YOU TO KNOW THAT.
STEPHANIE?
WE'RE IN OHIO.
THANK YOU.
YOU BETTER NOT BE EVIL.

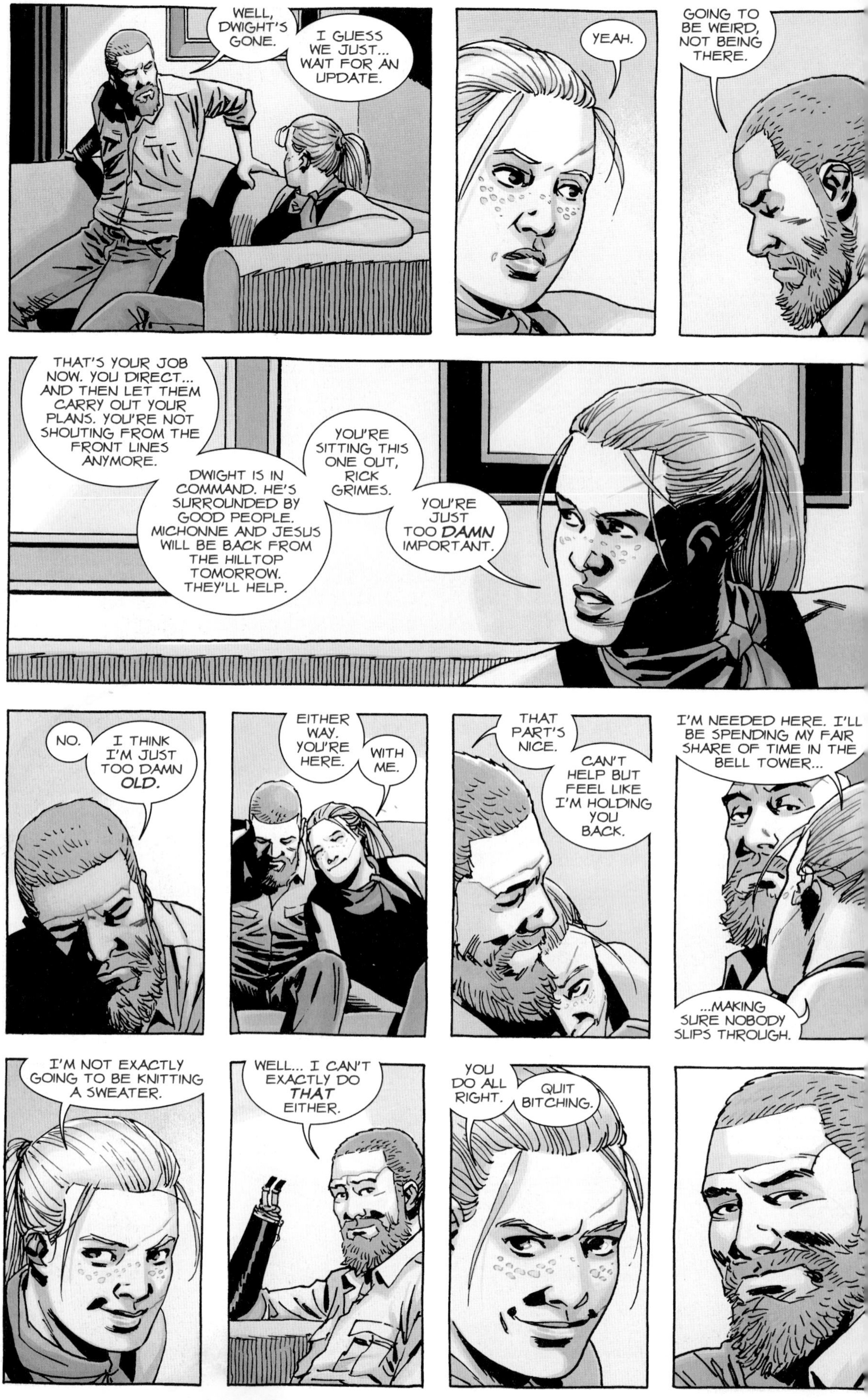
WELL, DWIGHT'S GONE.
I GUESS WE JUST... WAIT FOR AN UPDATE.
YEAH.
GOING TO BE WEIRD, NOT BEING THERE.
THAT'S YOUR JOB NOW. YOU DIRECT... AND THEN LET THEM CARRY OUT YOUR PLANS. YOU'RE NOT SHOUTING FROM THE FRONT LINES ANYMORE.
DWIGHT IS IN COMMAND. HE'S SURROUNDED BY GOOD PEOPLE. MICHONNE AND JESUS WILL BE BACK FROM THE HILLTOP TOMORROW. THEY'LL HELP.
YOU'RE SITTING THIS ONE OUT, RICK GRIMES.
YOU'RE JUST TOO DAMN IMPORTANT.
NO.
I THINK I'M JUST TOO DAMN OLD.
EITHER WAY. YOU'RE HERE.
WITH ME.
THAT PART'S NICE.
CAN'T HELP BUT FEEL LIKE I'M HOLDING YOU BACK.
I'M NEEDED HERE. I'LL BE SPENDING MY FAIR SHARE OF TIME IN THE BELL TOWER...
...MAKING SURE NOBODY SLIPS THROUGH.
I'M NOT EXACTLY GOING TO BE KNITTING A SWEATER.
WELL... I CAN'T EXACTLY DO THAT EITHER.
YOU DO ALL RIGHT.
QUIT BITCHING.

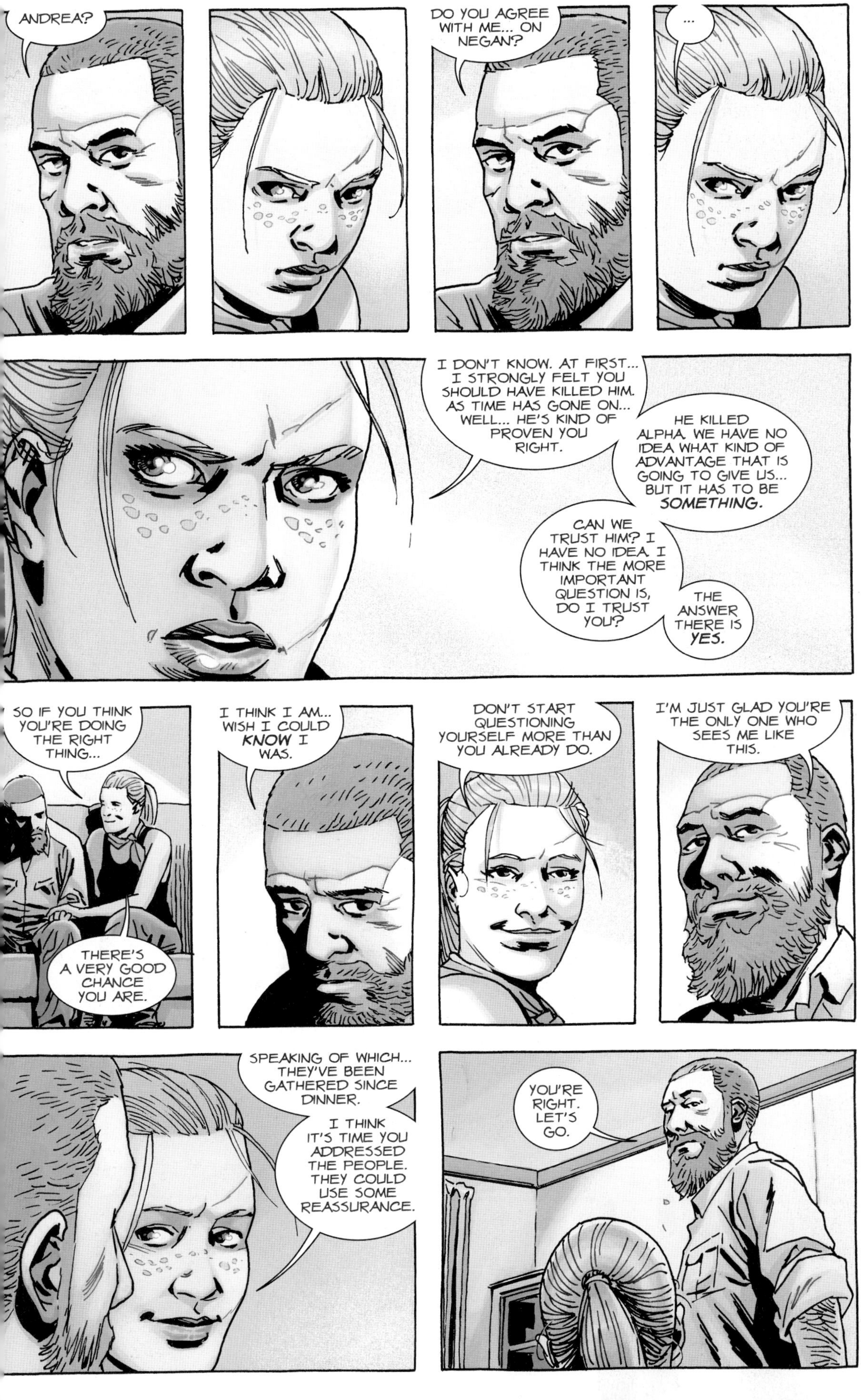

ANDREA?
DO YOU AGREE WITH ME... ON NEGAN?
...
I DON'T KNOW. AT FIRST... I STRONGLY FELT YOU SHOULD HAVE KILLED HIM. AS TIME HAS GONE ON... WELL... HE'S KIND OF PROVEN YOU RIGHT.
HE KILLED ALPHA. WE HAVE NO IDEA WHAT KIND OF ADVANTAGE THAT IS GOING TO GIVE US... BUT IT HAS TO BE SOMETHING.
CAN WE TRUST HIM? I HAVE NO IDEA. I THINK THE MORE IMPORTANT QUESTION IS, DO I TRUST YOU?
THE ANSWER THERE IS YES.
SO IF YOU THINK YOU'RE DOING THE RIGHT THING...
THERE'S A VERY GOOD CHANCE YOU ARE.
I THINK I AM... WISH I COULD KNOW I WAS.
DON'T START QUESTIONING YOURSELF MORE THAN YOU ALREADY DO.
I'M JUST GLAD YOU'RE THE ONLY ONE WHO SEES ME LIKE THIS.
SPEAKING OF WHICH... THEY'VE BEEN GATHERED SINCE DINNER.
I THINK IT'S TIME YOU ADDRESSED THE PEOPLE. THEY COULD USE SOME REASSURANCE.
YOU'RE RIGHT. LET'S GO.

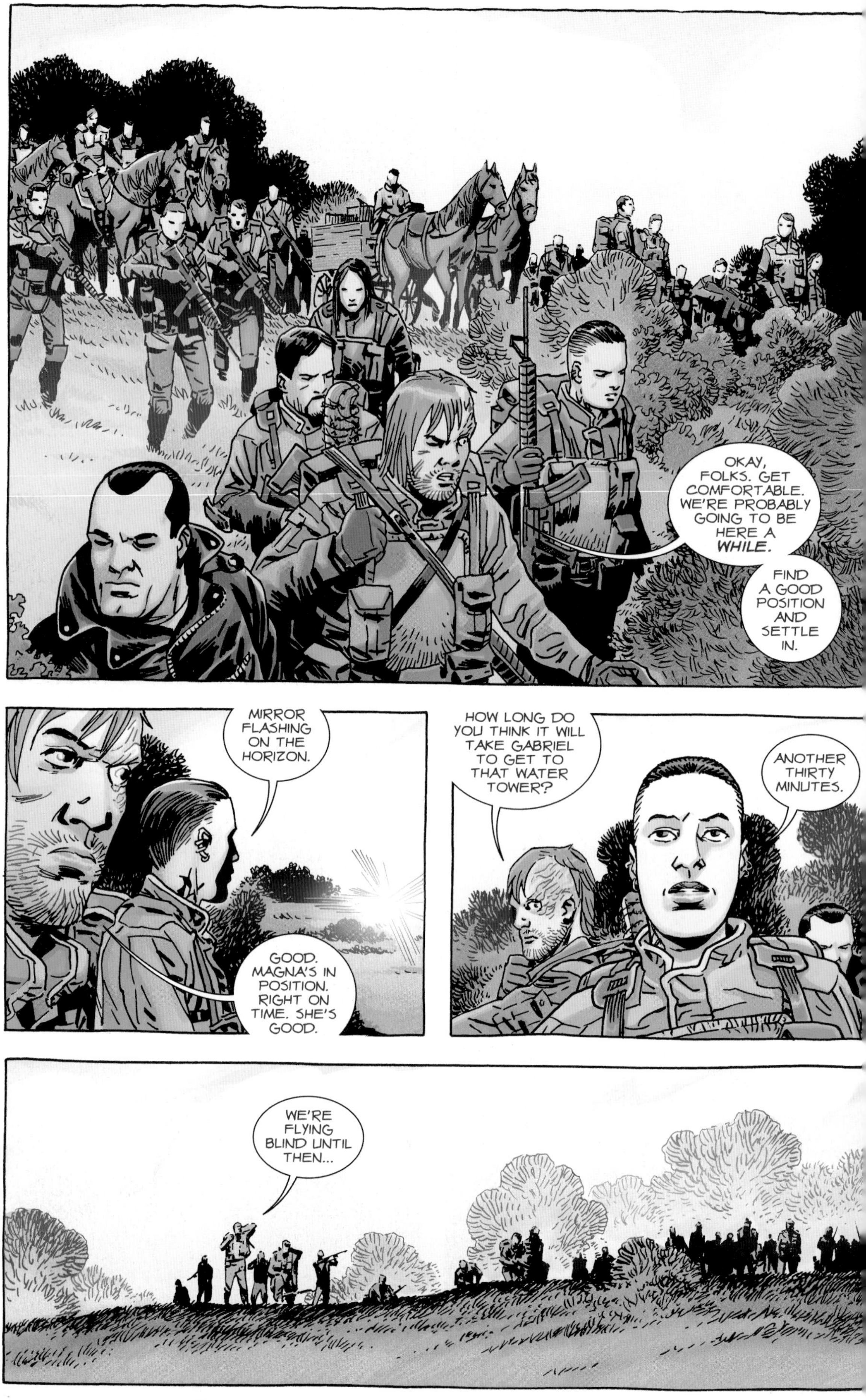
OKAY, FOLKS. GET COMFORTABLE. WE'RE PROBABLY GOING TO BE HERE A *WHILE.*
FIND A GOOD POSITION AND SETTLE IN.
MIRROR FLASHING ON THE HORIZON.
GOOD. MAGNA'S IN POSITION. RIGHT ON TIME. SHE'S GOOD.
HOW LONG DO YOU THINK IT WILL TAKE GABRIEL TO GET TO THAT WATER TOWER?
ANOTHER THIRTY MINUTES.
WE'RE FLYING BLIND UNTIL THEN...

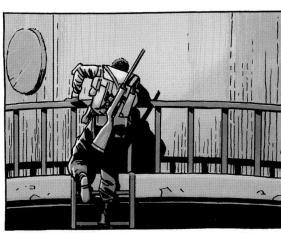

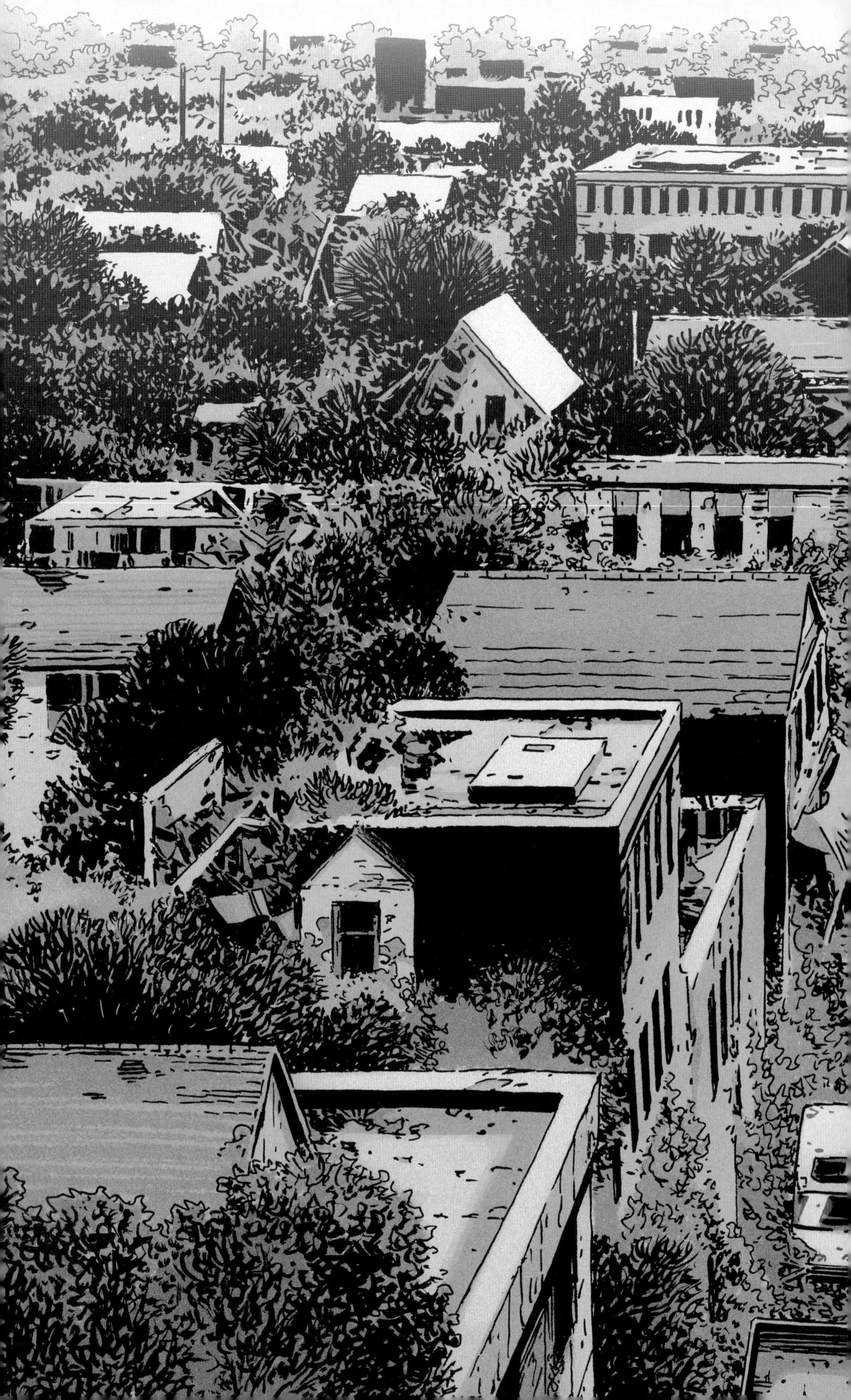

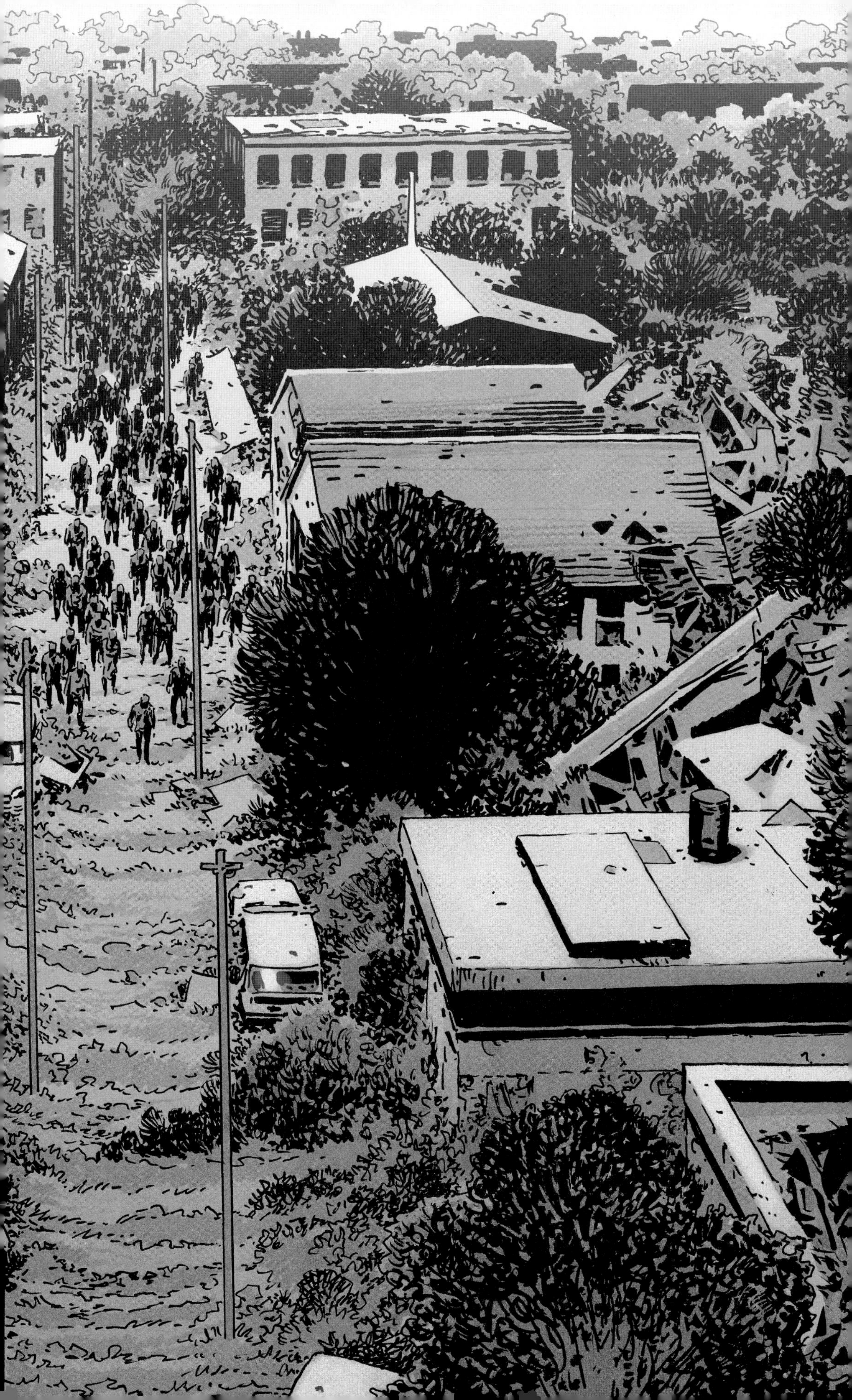

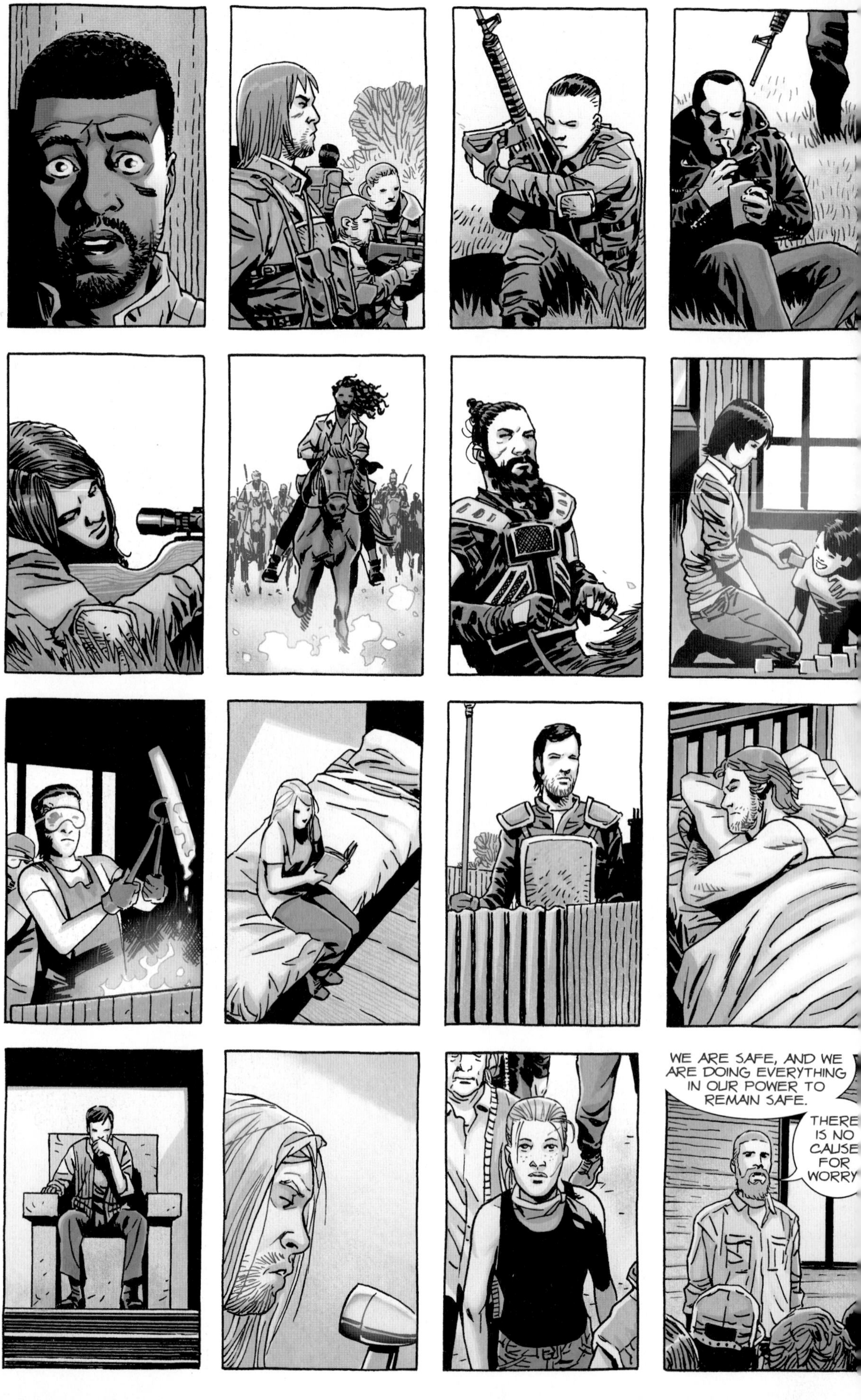
WE ARE SAFE, AND WE ARE DOING EVERYTHING IN OUR POWER TO REMAIN SAFE.
THERE IS NO CAUSE FOR WORRY

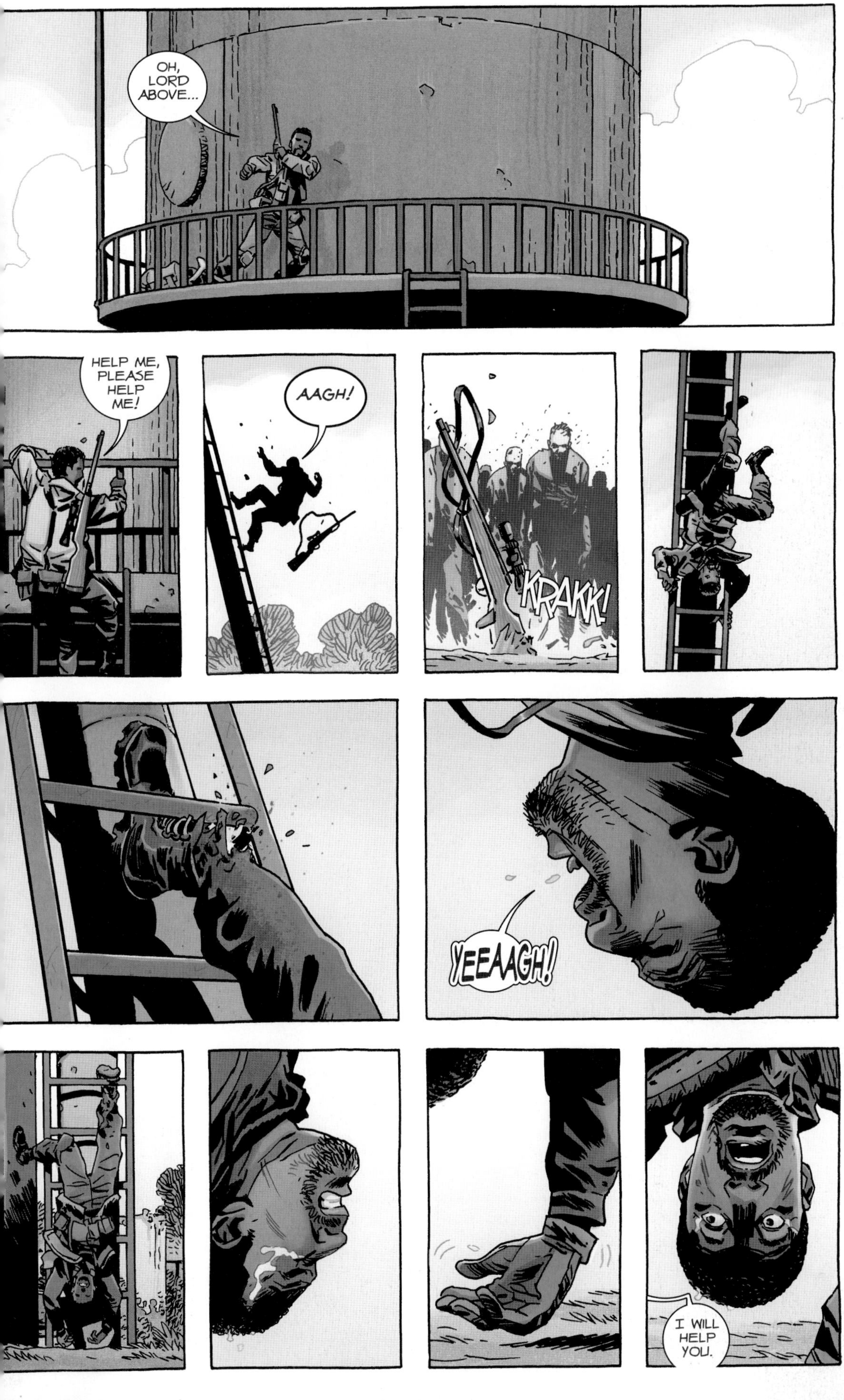
OH, LORD ABOVE...
HELP ME, PLEASE HELP ME!
AAGH!
KRAKK!
YEEAAGH!
I WILL HELP YOU.

I RELEASE YOU.

≈GUCKK!≈

YOU SHOULD HAVE WHISPERED...

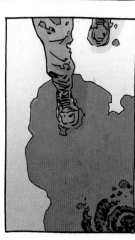

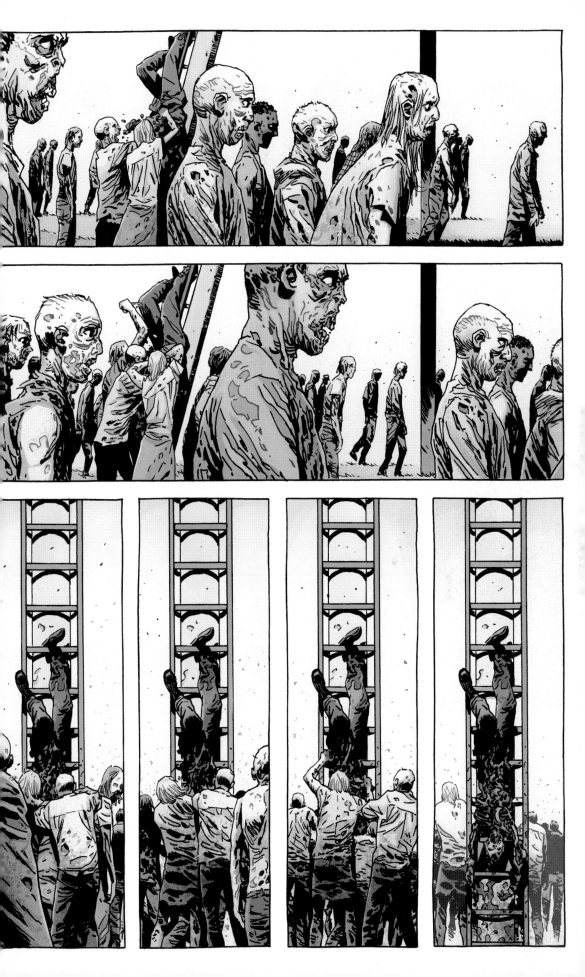

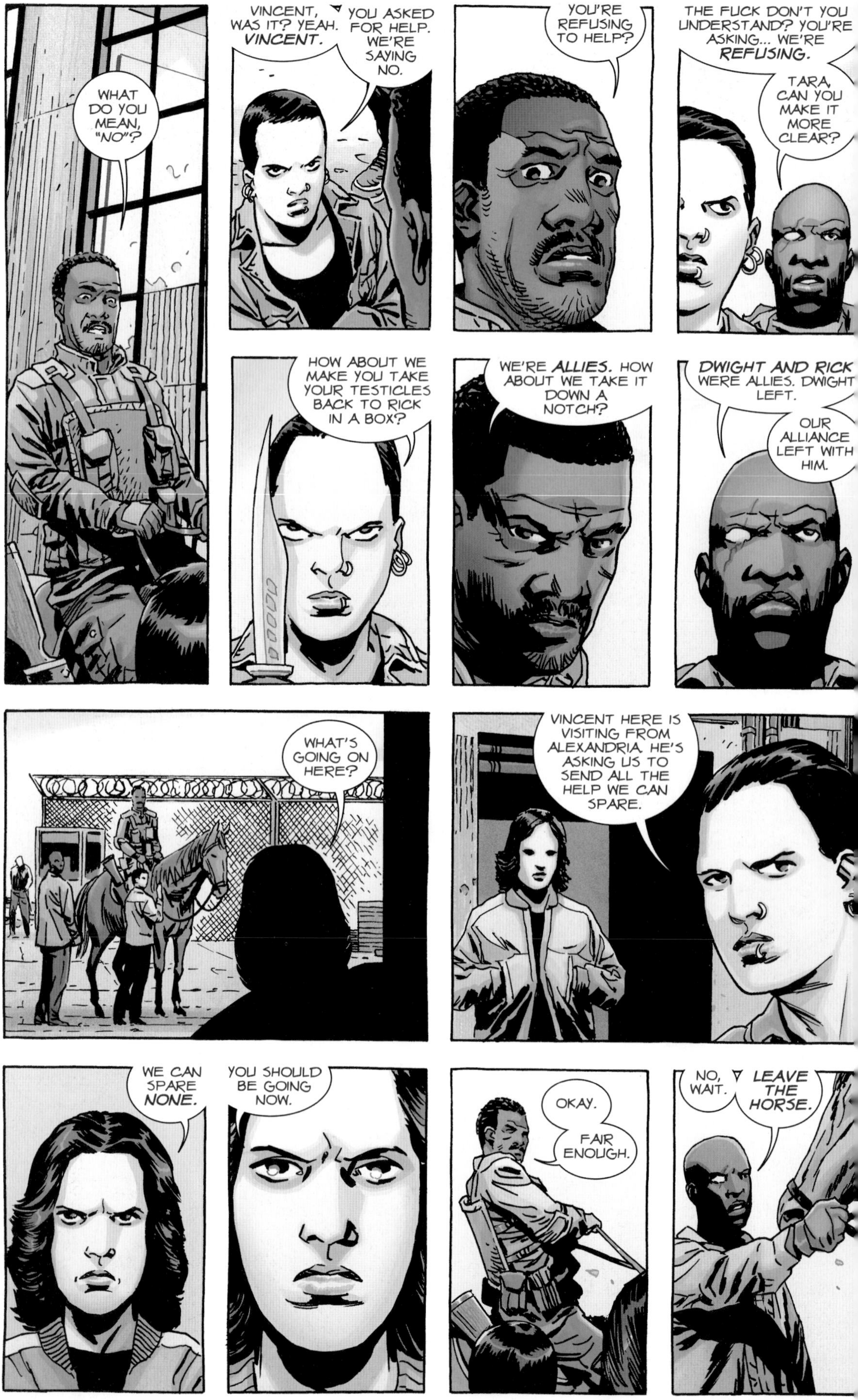

WHAT DO YOU MEAN, "NO"?
VINCENT, WAS IT? YEAH. VINCENT.
YOU ASKED FOR HELP. WE'RE SAYING NO.
YOU'RE REFUSING TO HELP?
THE FUCK DON'T YOU UNDERSTAND? YOU'RE ASKING... WE'RE REFUSING.
TARA, CAN YOU MAKE IT MORE CLEAR?
HOW ABOUT WE MAKE YOU TAKE YOUR TESTICLES BACK TO RICK IN A BOX?
WE'RE ALLIES. HOW ABOUT WE TAKE IT DOWN A NOTCH?
DWIGHT AND RICK WERE ALLIES. DWIGHT LEFT.
OUR ALLIANCE LEFT WITH HIM.
WHAT'S GOING ON HERE?
VINCENT HERE IS VISITING FROM ALEXANDRIA. HE'S ASKING US TO SEND ALL THE HELP WE CAN SPARE.
WE CAN SPARE NONE.
YOU SHOULD BE GOING NOW.
OKAY.
FAIR ENOUGH.
NO, WAIT.
LEAVE THE HORSE.

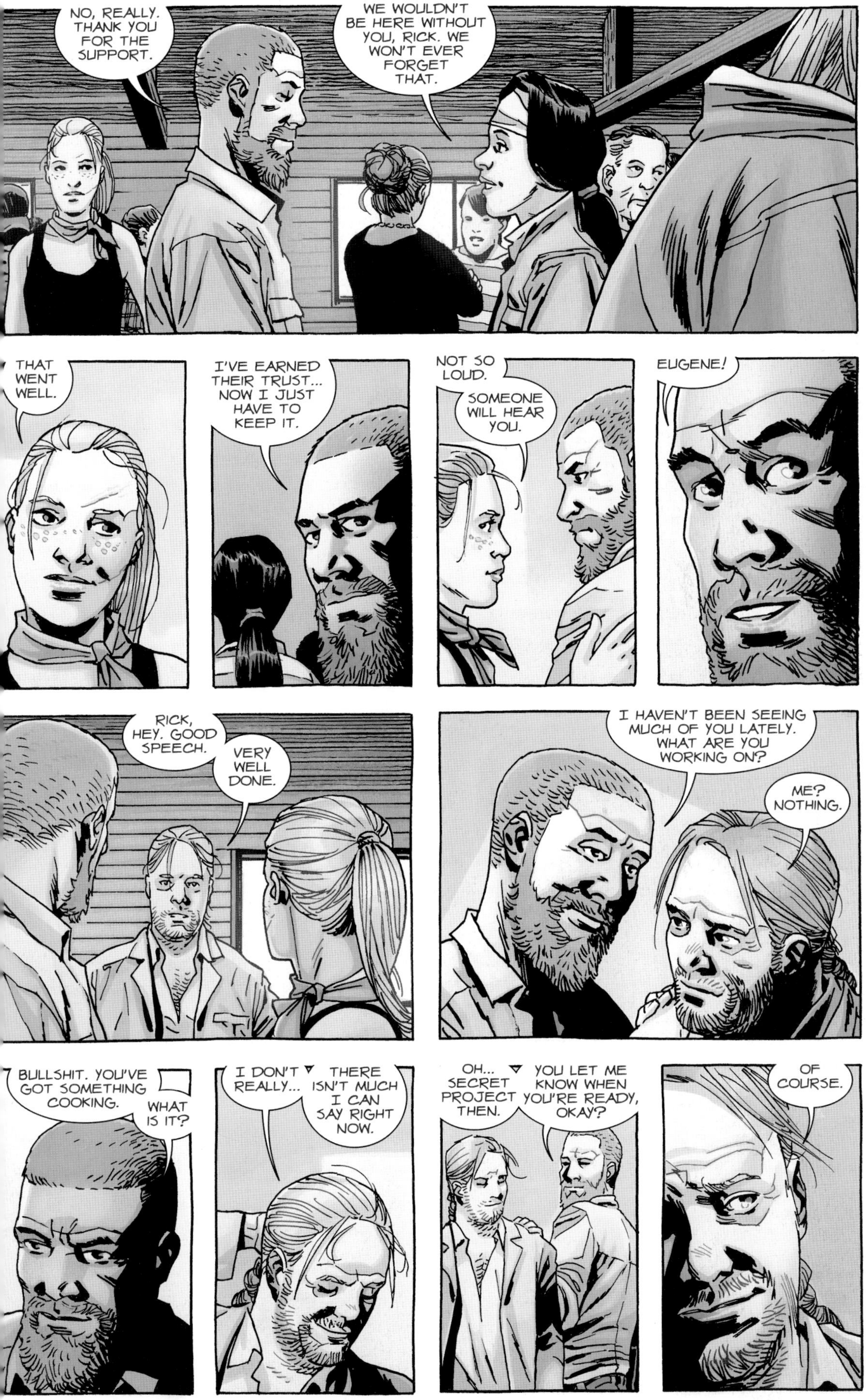
NO, REALLY. THANK YOU FOR THE SUPPORT.
WE WOULDN'T BE HERE WITHOUT YOU, RICK. WE WON'T EVER FORGET THAT.
THAT WENT WELL.
I'VE EARNED THEIR TRUST... NOW I JUST HAVE TO KEEP IT.
NOT SO LOUD.
SOMEONE WILL HEAR YOU.
EUGENE!
RICK, HEY. GOOD SPEECH.
VERY WELL DONE.
I HAVEN'T BEEN SEEING MUCH OF YOU LATELY. WHAT ARE YOU WORKING ON?
ME? NOTHING.
BULLSHIT. YOU'VE GOT SOMETHING COOKING.
WHAT IS IT?
I DON'T REALLY...
THERE ISN'T MUCH I CAN SAY RIGHT NOW.
OH... SECRET PROJECT THEN.
YOU LET ME KNOW WHEN YOU'RE READY, OKAY?
OF COURSE.

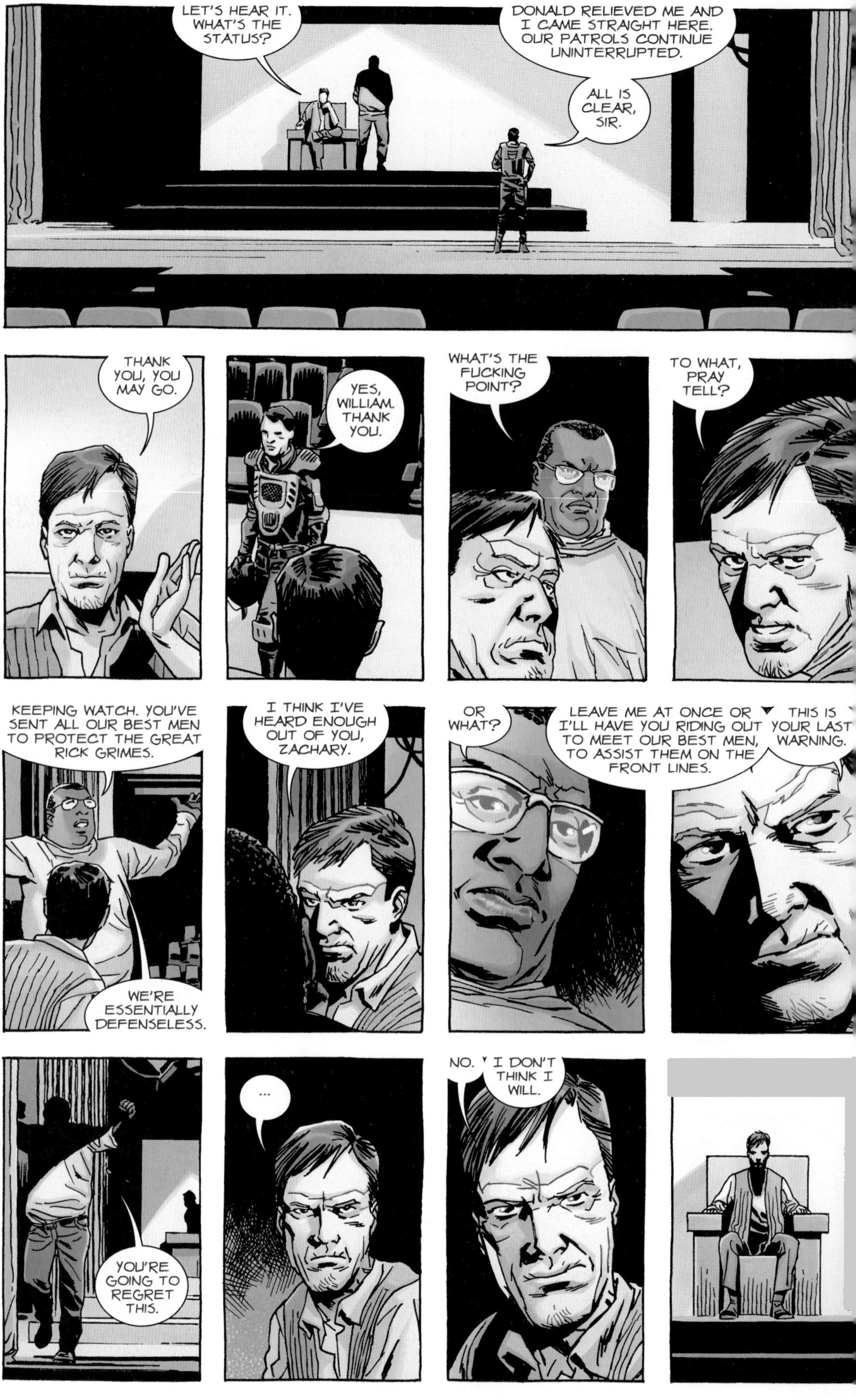
LET'S HEAR IT. WHAT'S THE STATUS?
DONALD RELIEVED ME AND I CAME STRAIGHT HERE. OUR PATROLS CONTINUE UNINTERRUPTED.
ALL IS CLEAR, SIR.
THANK YOU, YOU MAY GO.
YES, WILLIAM. THANK YOU.
WHAT'S THE FUCKING POINT?
TO WHAT, PRAY TELL?
KEEPING WATCH. YOU'VE SENT ALL OUR BEST MEN TO PROTECT THE GREAT RICK GRIMES.
WE'RE ESSENTIALLY DEFENSELESS.
I THINK I'VE HEARD ENOUGH OUT OF YOU, ZACHARY.
OR WHAT?
LEAVE ME AT ONCE OR I'LL HAVE YOU RIDING OUT TO MEET OUR BEST MEN, TO ASSIST THEM ON THE FRONT LINES.
THIS IS YOUR LAST WARNING.
YOU'RE GOING TO REGRET THIS.
...
NO.
I DON'T THINK I WILL.

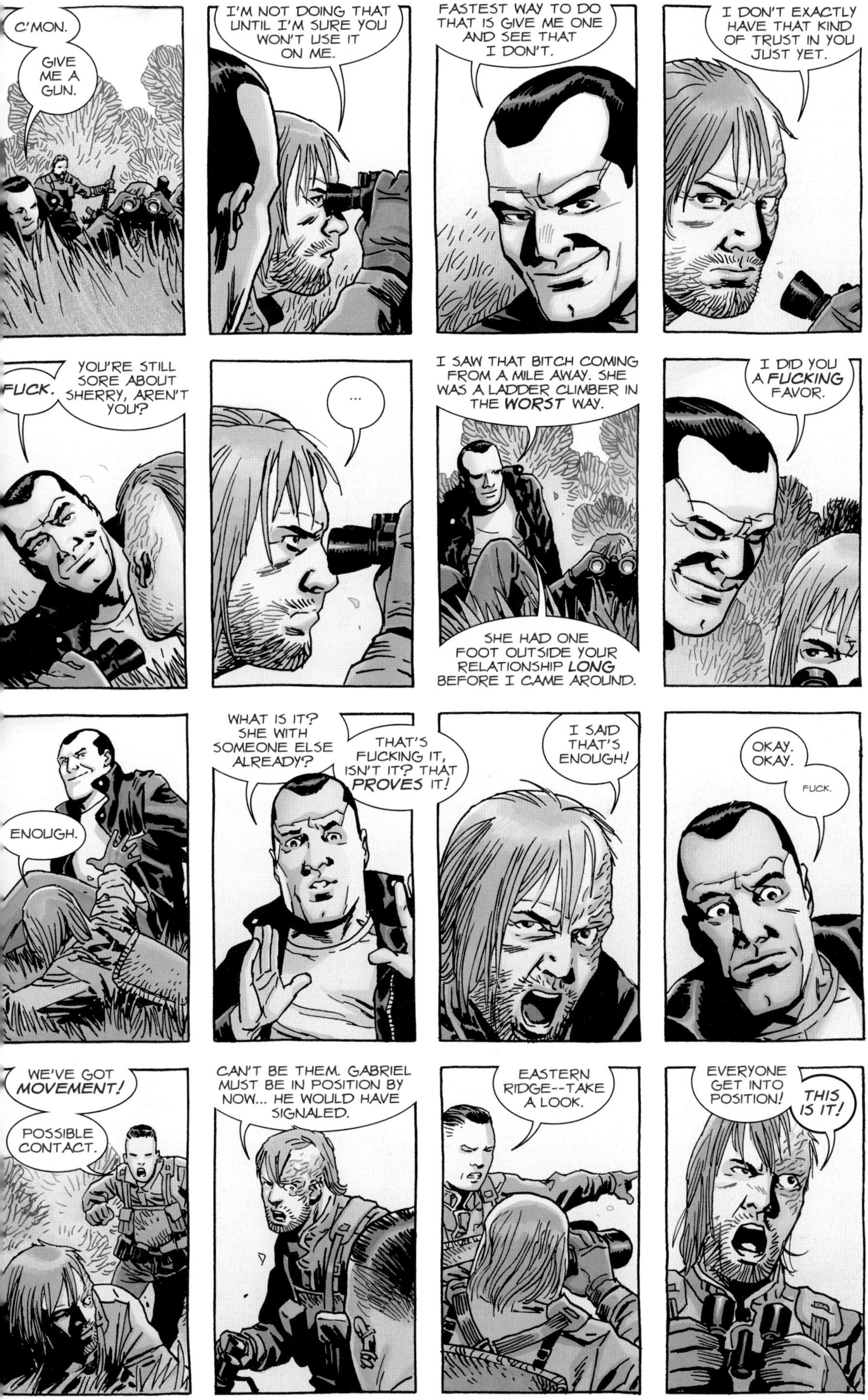
C'MON.
GIVE ME A GUN.
I'M NOT DOING THAT UNTIL I'M SURE YOU WON'T USE IT ON ME.
FASTEST WAY TO DO THAT IS GIVE ME ONE AND SEE THAT I DON'T.
I DON'T EXACTLY HAVE THAT KIND OF TRUST IN YOU JUST YET.
FUCK.
YOU'RE STILL SORE ABOUT SHERRY, AREN'T YOU?
...
I SAW THAT BITCH COMING FROM A MILE AWAY. SHE WAS A LADDER CLIMBER IN THE WORST WAY.
SHE HAD ONE FOOT OUTSIDE YOUR RELATIONSHIP LONG BEFORE I CAME AROUND.
I DID YOU A FUCKING FAVOR.
ENOUGH.
WHAT IS IT? SHE WITH SOMEONE ELSE ALREADY?
THAT'S FUCKING IT, ISN'T IT? THAT PROVES IT!
I SAID THAT'S ENOUGH!
OKAY. OKAY.
FUCK.
WE'VE GOT MOVEMENT!
POSSIBLE CONTACT.
CAN'T BE THEM. GABRIEL MUST BE IN POSITION BY NOW... HE WOULD HAVE SIGNALED.
EASTERN RIDGE--TAKE A LOOK.
EVERYONE GET INTO POSITION!
THIS IS IT!

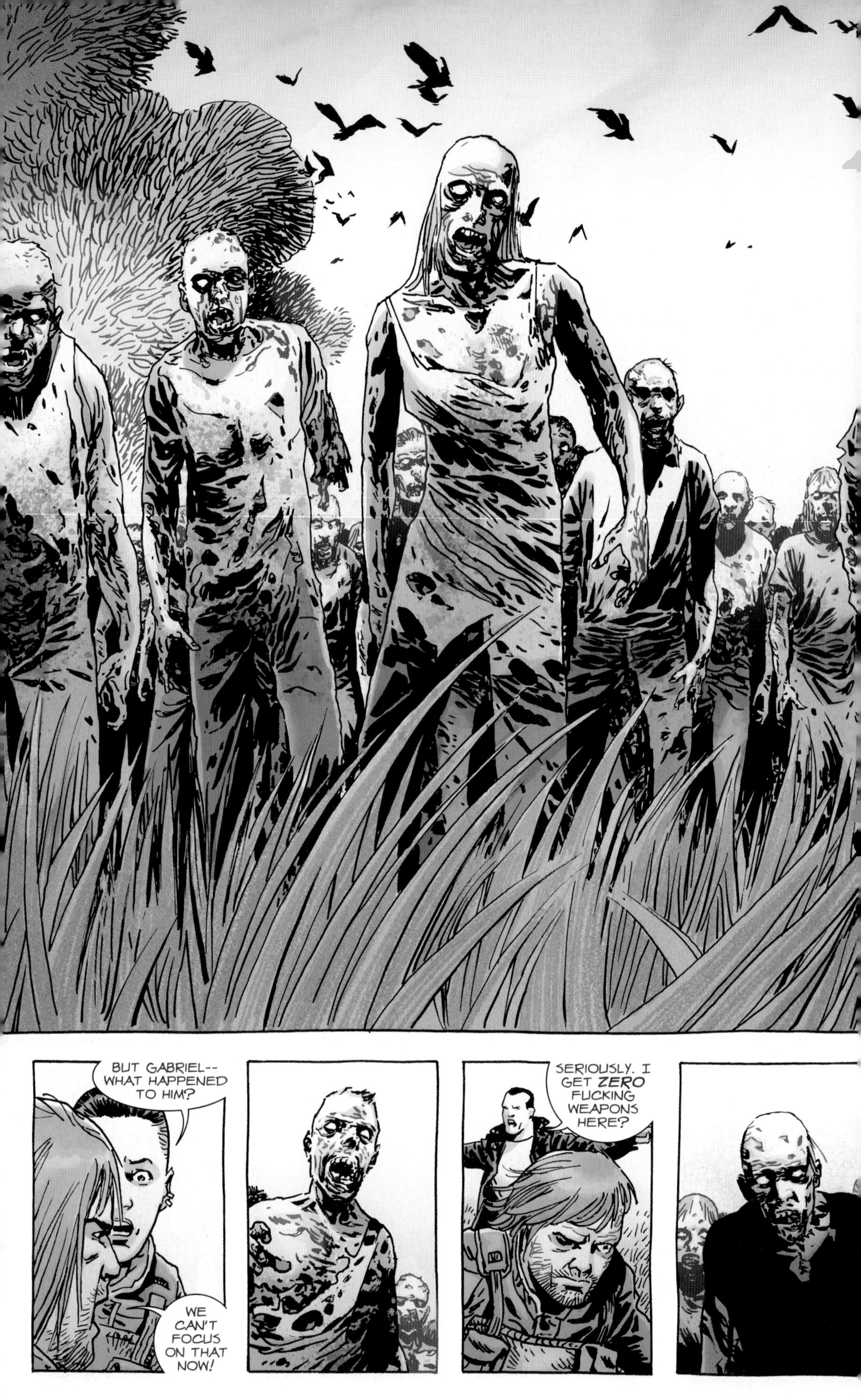
BUT GABRIEL-- WHAT HAPPENED TO HIM?
WE CAN'T FOCUS ON THAT NOW!
SERIOUSLY. I GET ZERO FUCKING WEAPONS HERE?

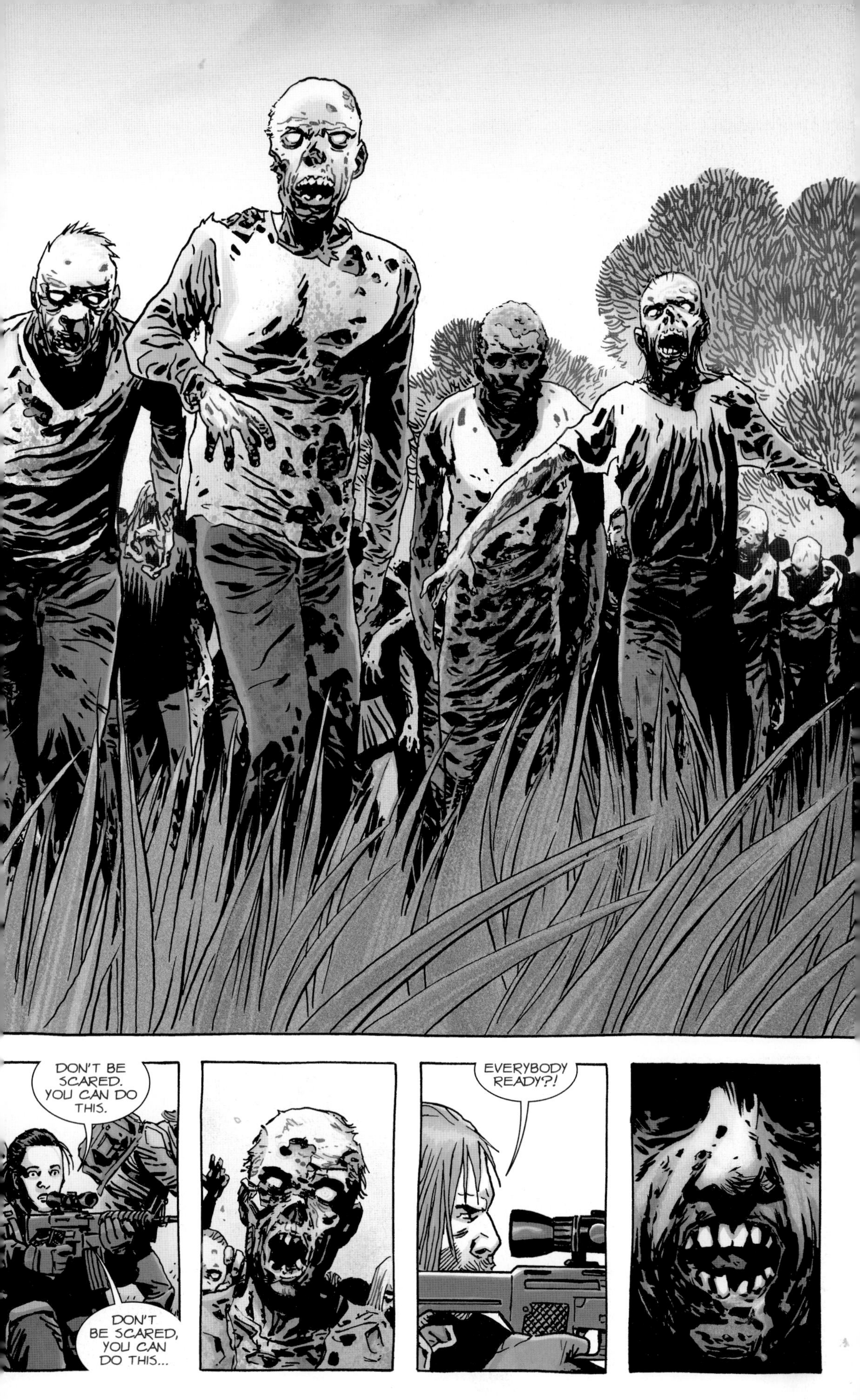

DON'T BE SCARED. YOU CAN DO THIS.
DON'T BE SCARED, YOU CAN DO THIS...
EVERYBODY READY?!

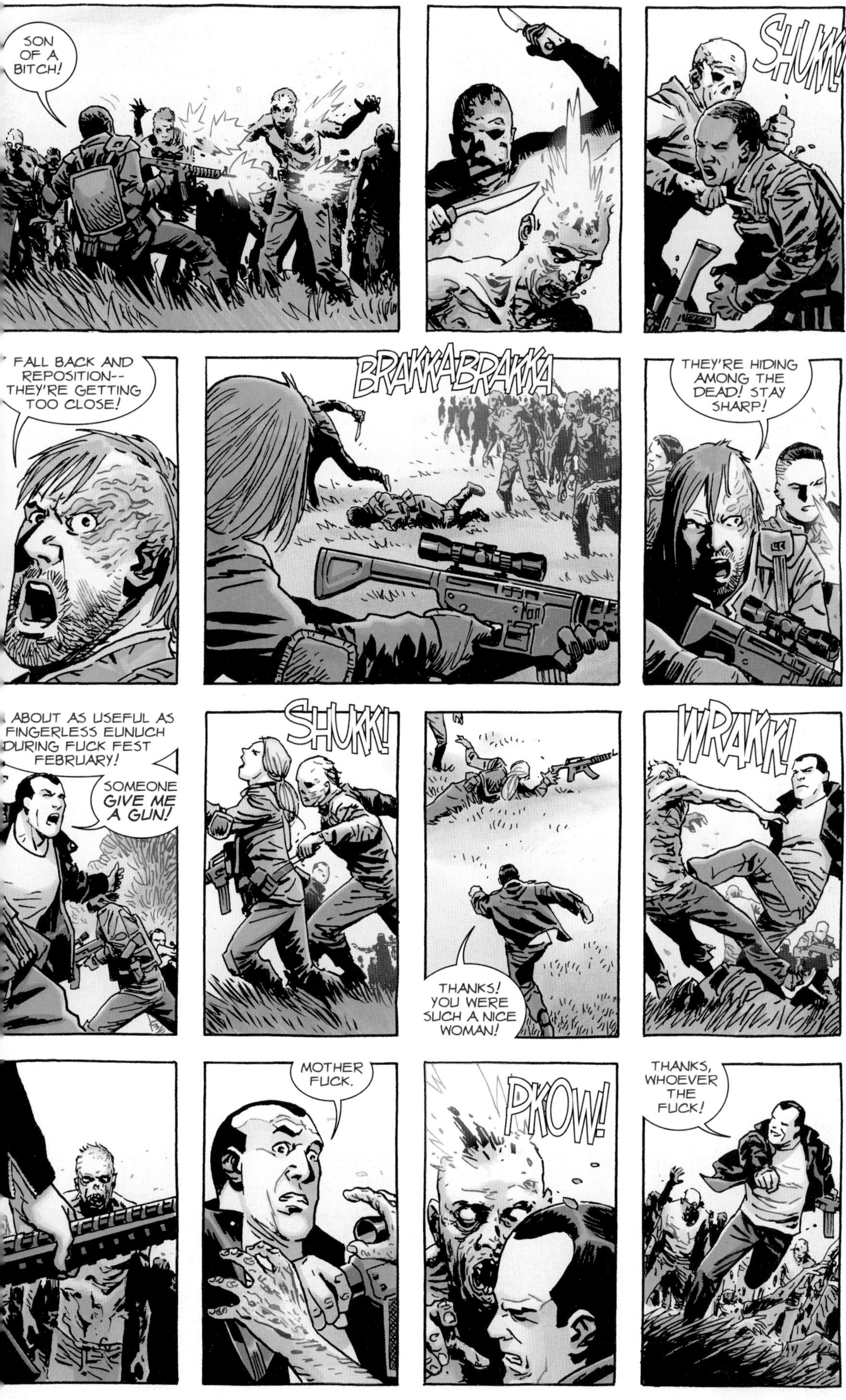
SON OF A BITCH!
SHUKK!
FALL BACK AND REPOSITION-- THEY'RE GETTING TOO CLOSE!
BRAKKABRAKKA
THEY'RE HIDING AMONG THE DEAD! STAY SHARP!
ABOUT AS USEFUL AS FINGERLESS EUNUCH DURING FUCK FEST FEBRUARY!
SOMEONE GIVE ME A GUN!
SHUKK!
THANKS! YOU WERE SUCH A NICE WOMAN!
WRAKK!
MOTHER FUCK.
PKOW!
THANKS, WHOEVER THE FUCK!

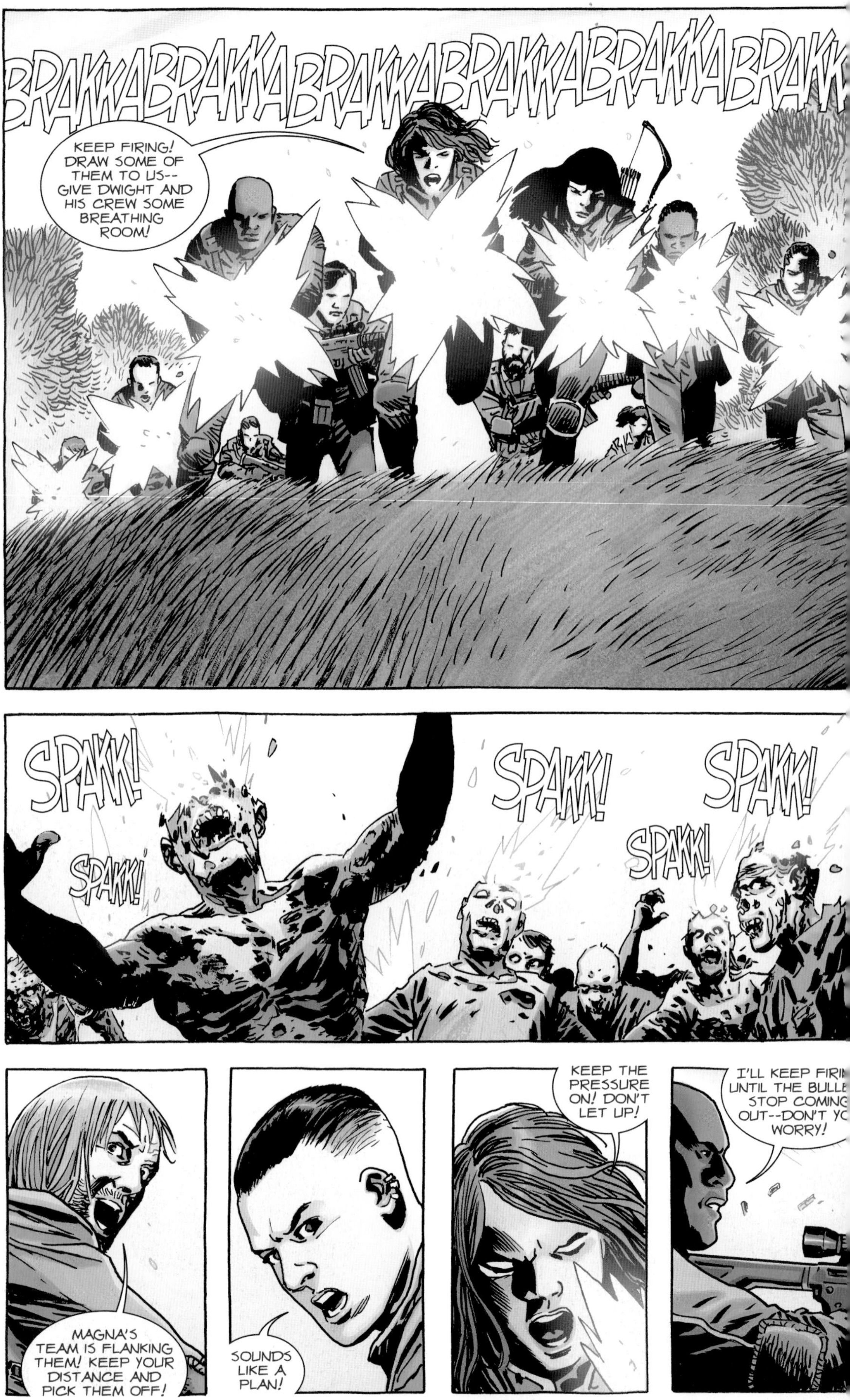
BRAKKABRAKKABRAKKABRAKKABRAKKABRAKK
KEEP FIRING! DRAW SOME OF THEM TO US-- GIVE DWIGHT AND HIS CREW SOME BREATHING ROOM!
SPAKK!
SPAKK!
SPAKK!
SPAKK!
SPAKK!
MAGNA'S TEAM IS FLANKING THEM! KEEP YOUR DISTANCE AND PICK THEM OFF!
SOUNDS LIKE A PLAN!
KEEP THE PRESSURE ON! DON'T LET UP!
I'LL KEEP FIRI
UNTIL THE BULL
STOP COMING
OUT--DON'T Y
WORRY!

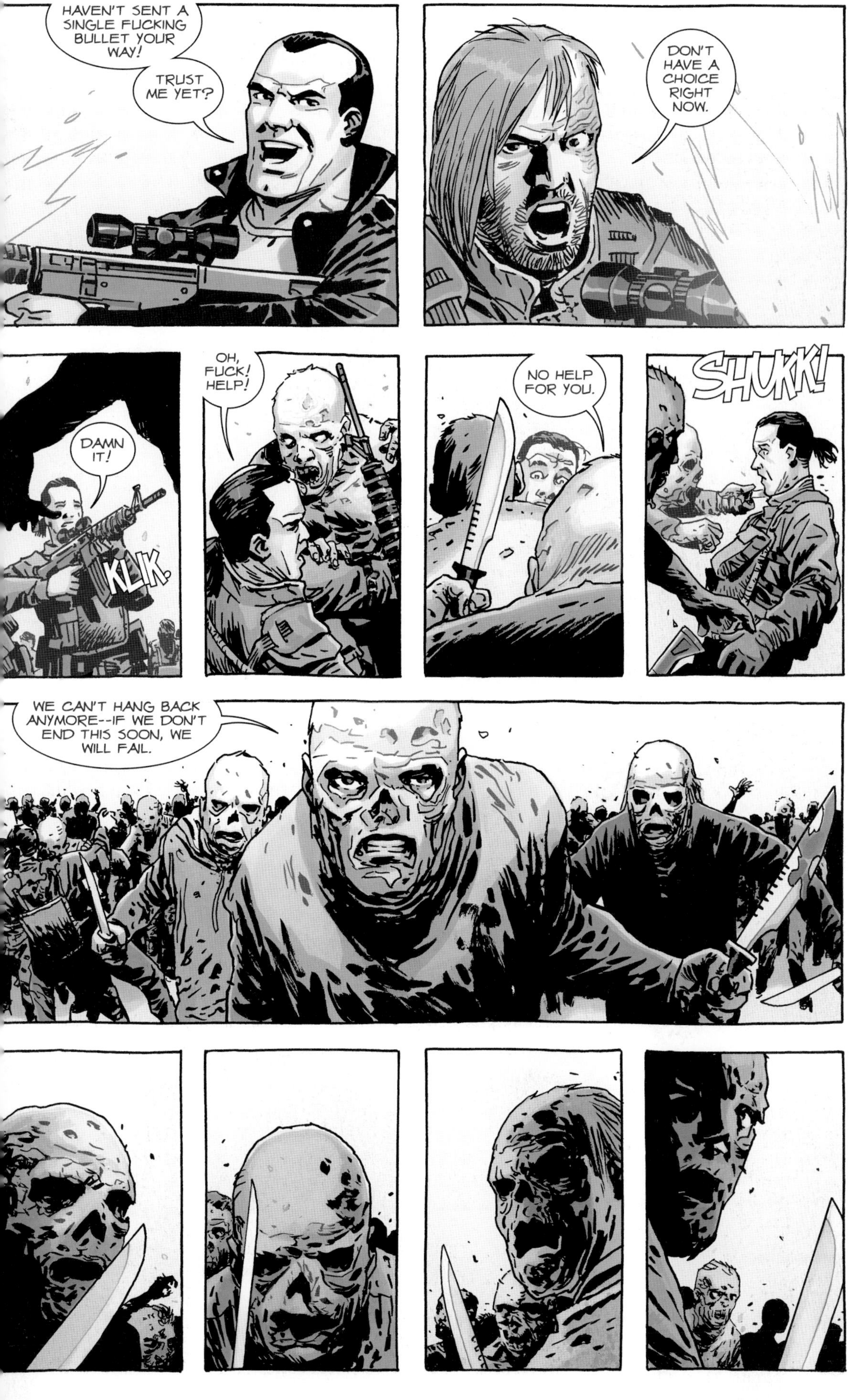
HAVEN'T SENT A SINGLE FUCKING BULLET YOUR WAY!
TRUST ME YET?
DON'T HAVE A CHOICE RIGHT NOW.
DAMN IT!
KLIK.
OH, FUCK! HELP!
NO HELP FOR YOU.
SHUKK!
WE CAN'T HANG BACK ANYMORE--IF WE DON'T END THIS SOON, WE WILL FAIL.

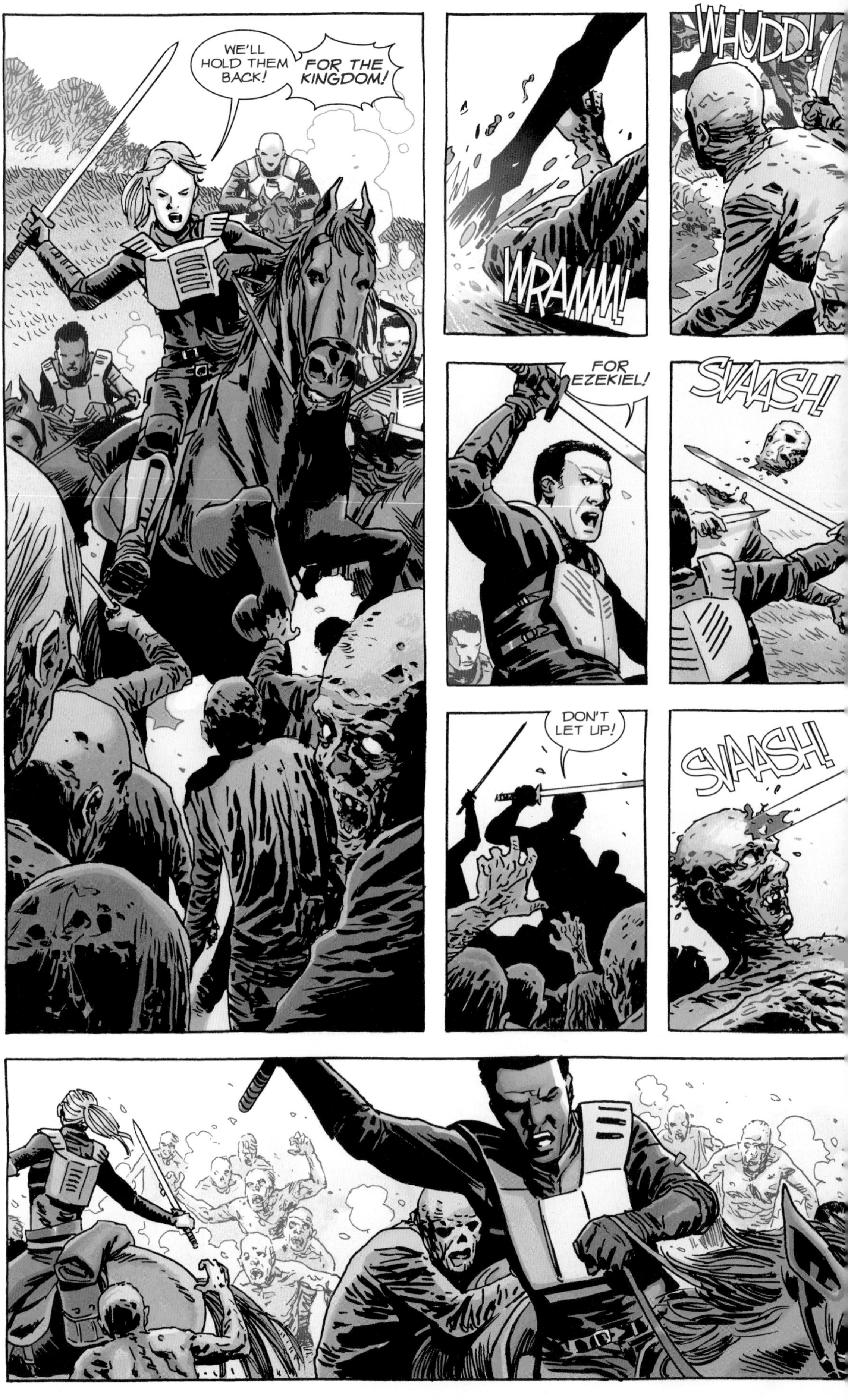
WE'LL HOLD THEM BACK!
FOR THE KINGDOM!
WRAMM!
WHUDD!
FOR EZEKIEL!
SVAASH!
DON'T LET UP!
SVAASH!

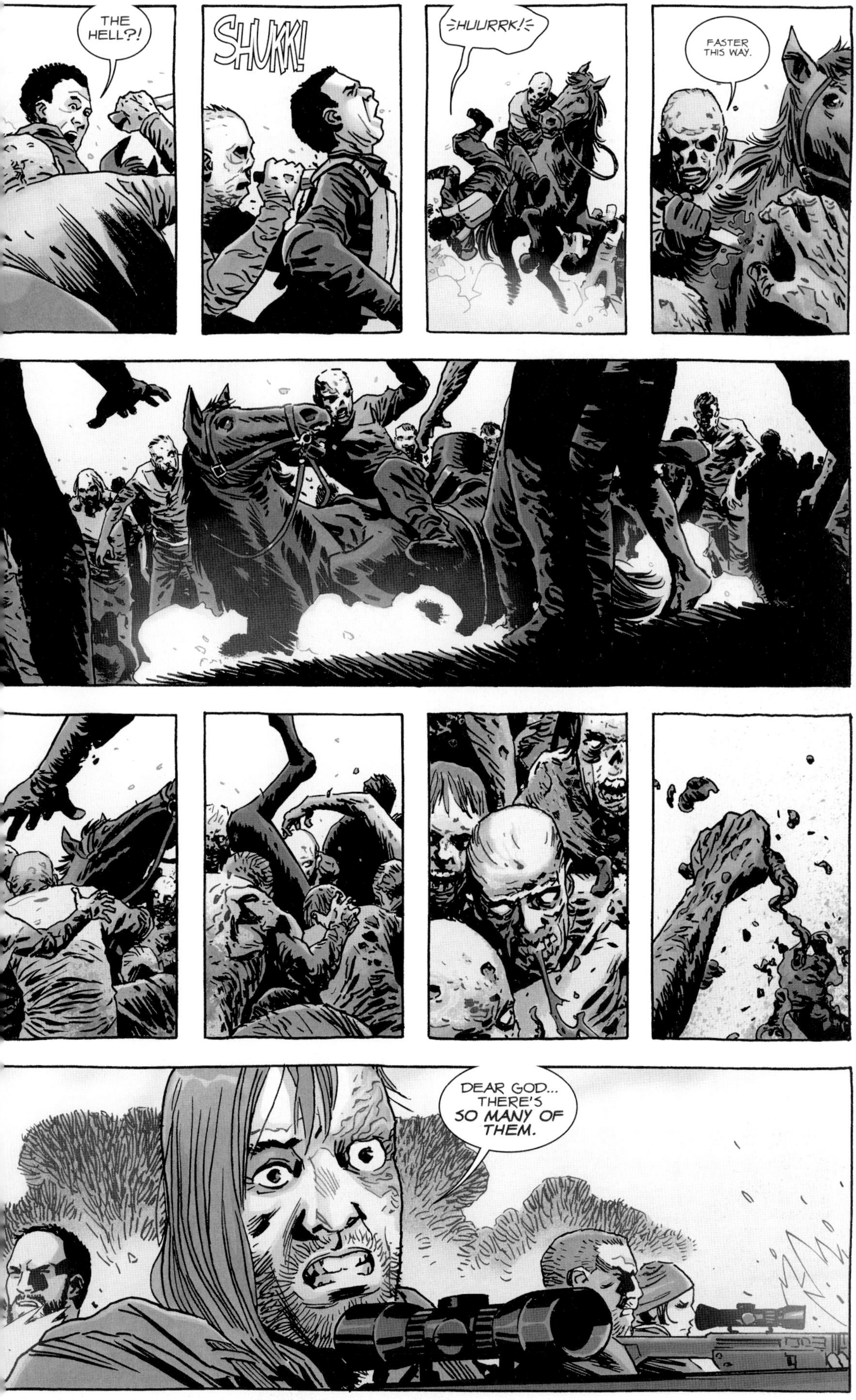
THE HELL?!
SHUKK!
HUURRK!
FASTER THIS WAY.
DEAR GOD... THERE'S SO MANY OF THEM.

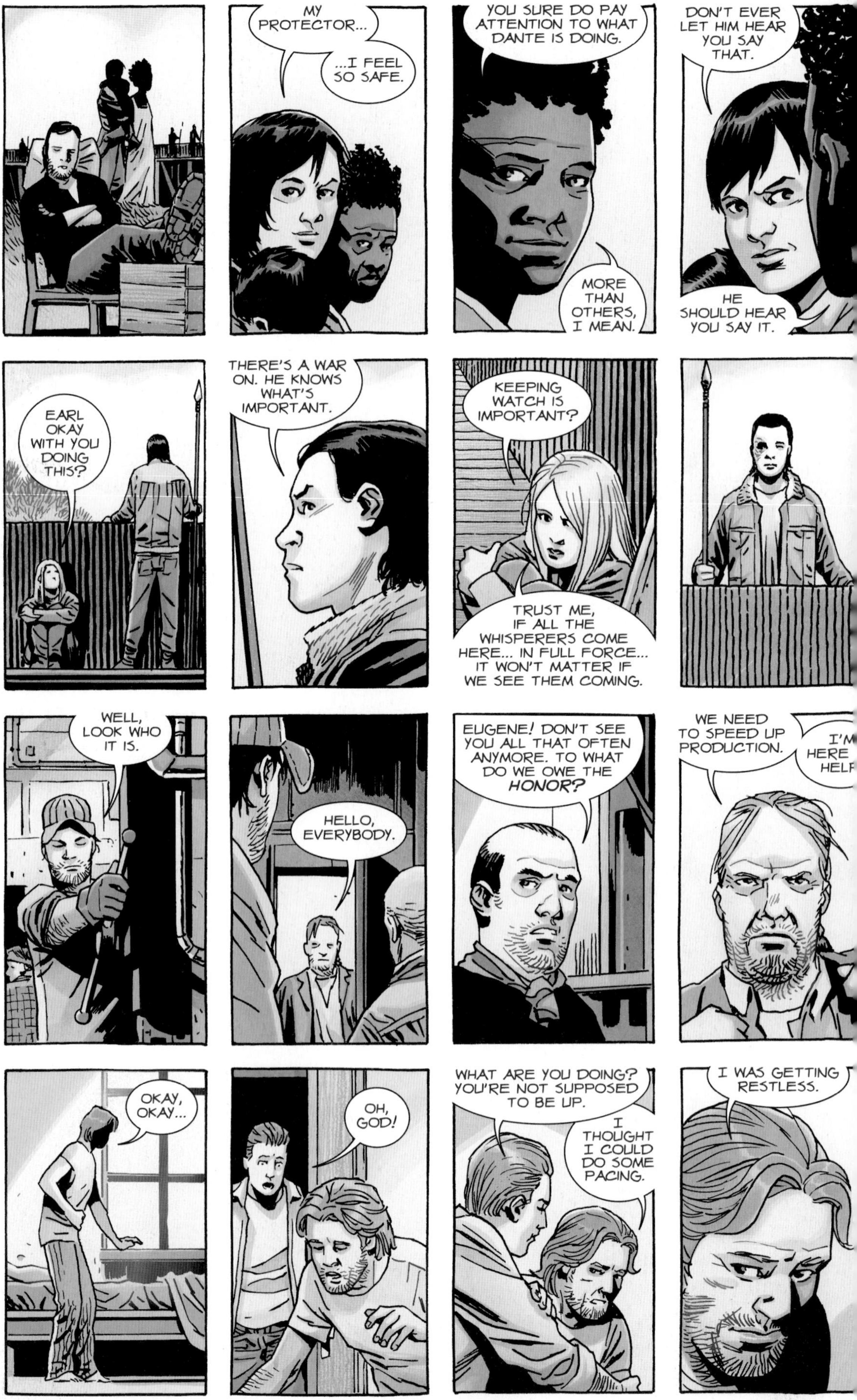

MY PROTECTOR...
...I FEEL SO SAFE.
YOU SURE DO PAY ATTENTION TO WHAT DANTE IS DOING.
MORE THAN OTHERS, I MEAN.
DON'T EVER LET HIM HEAR YOU SAY THAT.
HE SHOULD HEAR YOU SAY IT.
EARL OKAY WITH YOU DOING THIS?
THERE'S A WAR ON. HE KNOWS WHAT'S IMPORTANT.
KEEPING WATCH IS IMPORTANT?
TRUST ME, IF ALL THE WHISPERERS COME HERE... IN FULL FORCE... IT WON'T MATTER IF WE SEE THEM COMING.
WELL, LOOK WHO IT IS.
HELLO, EVERYBODY.
EUGENE! DON'T SEE YOU ALL THAT OFTEN ANYMORE. TO WHAT DO WE OWE THE HONOR?
WE NEED TO SPEED UP PRODUCTION.
OKAY, OKAY...
OH, GOD!
WHAT ARE YOU DOING? YOU'RE NOT SUPPOSED TO BE UP.
I THOUGHT I COULD DO SOME PACING.
I WAS GETTING RESTLESS.

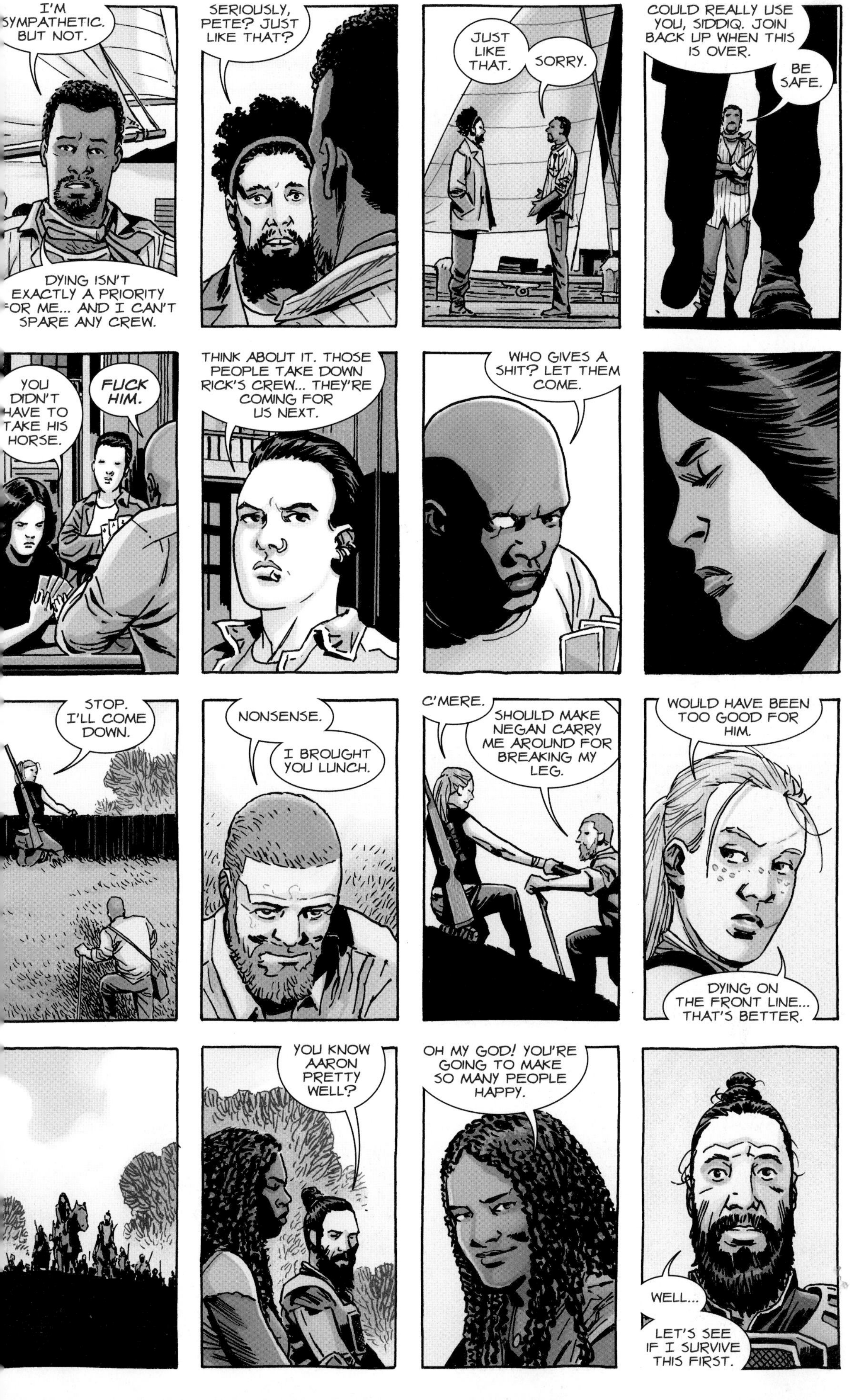

I'M SYMPATHETIC. BUT NOT.
DYING ISN'T EXACTLY A PRIORITY FOR ME... AND I CAN'T SPARE ANY CREW.
SERIOUSLY, PETE? JUST LIKE THAT?
JUST LIKE THAT.
SORRY.
COULD REALLY USE YOU, SIDDIQ. JOIN BACK UP WHEN THIS IS OVER.
BE SAFE.
YOU DIDN'T HAVE TO TAKE HIS HORSE.
FUCK HIM.
THINK ABOUT IT. THOSE PEOPLE TAKE DOWN RICK'S CREW... THEY'RE COMING FOR US NEXT.
WHO GIVES A SHIT? LET THEM COME.
STOP. I'LL COME DOWN.
NONSENSE.
I BROUGHT YOU LUNCH.
C'MERE.
SHOULD MAKE NEGAN CARRY ME AROUND FOR BREAKING MY LEG.
WOULD HAVE BEEN TOO GOOD FOR HIM.
DYING ON THE FRONT LINE... THAT'S BETTER.
YOU KNOW AARON PRETTY WELL?
OH MY GOD! YOU'RE GOING TO MAKE SO MANY PEOPLE HAPPY.
WELL...
LET'S SEE IF I SURVIVE THIS FIRST.

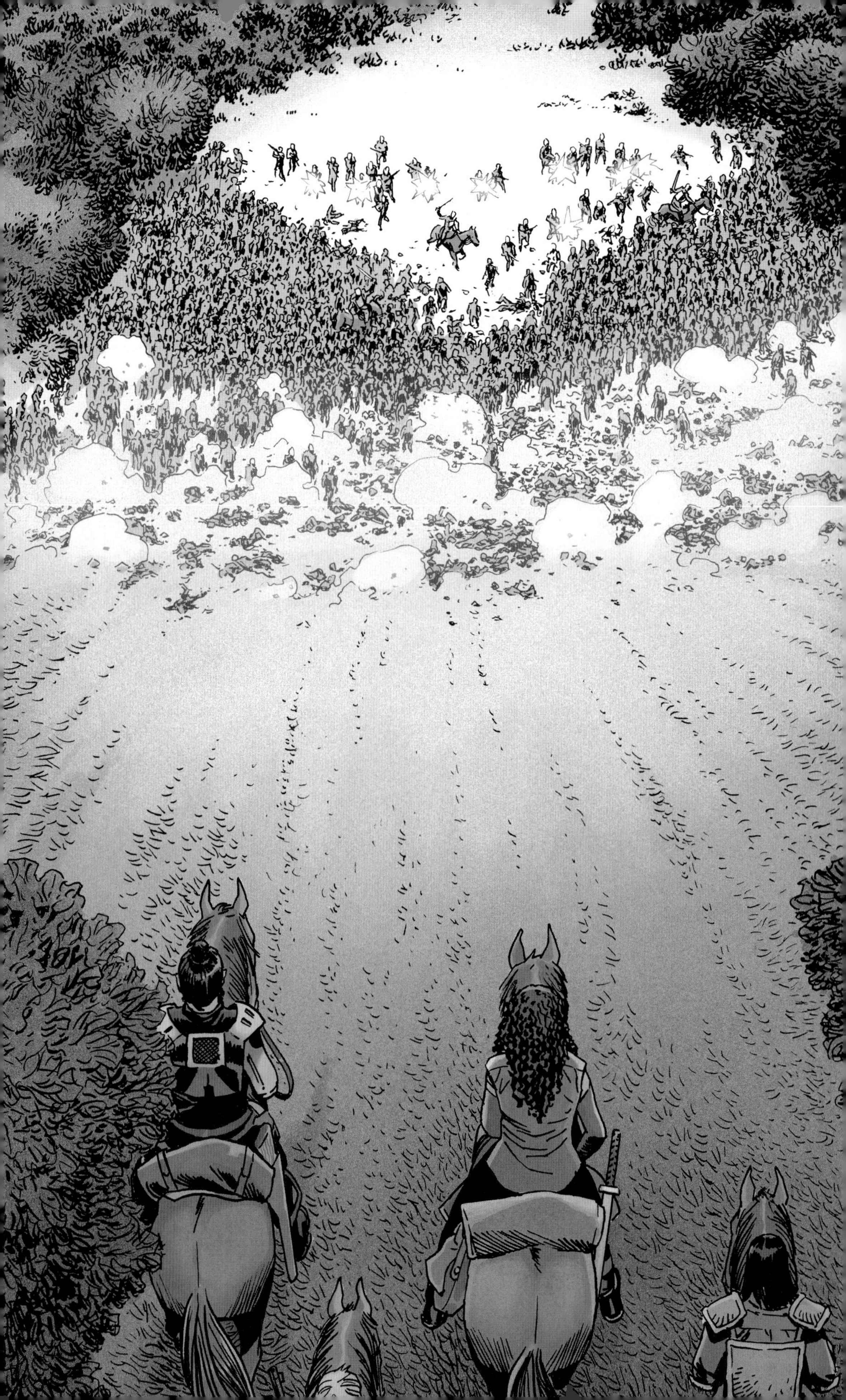

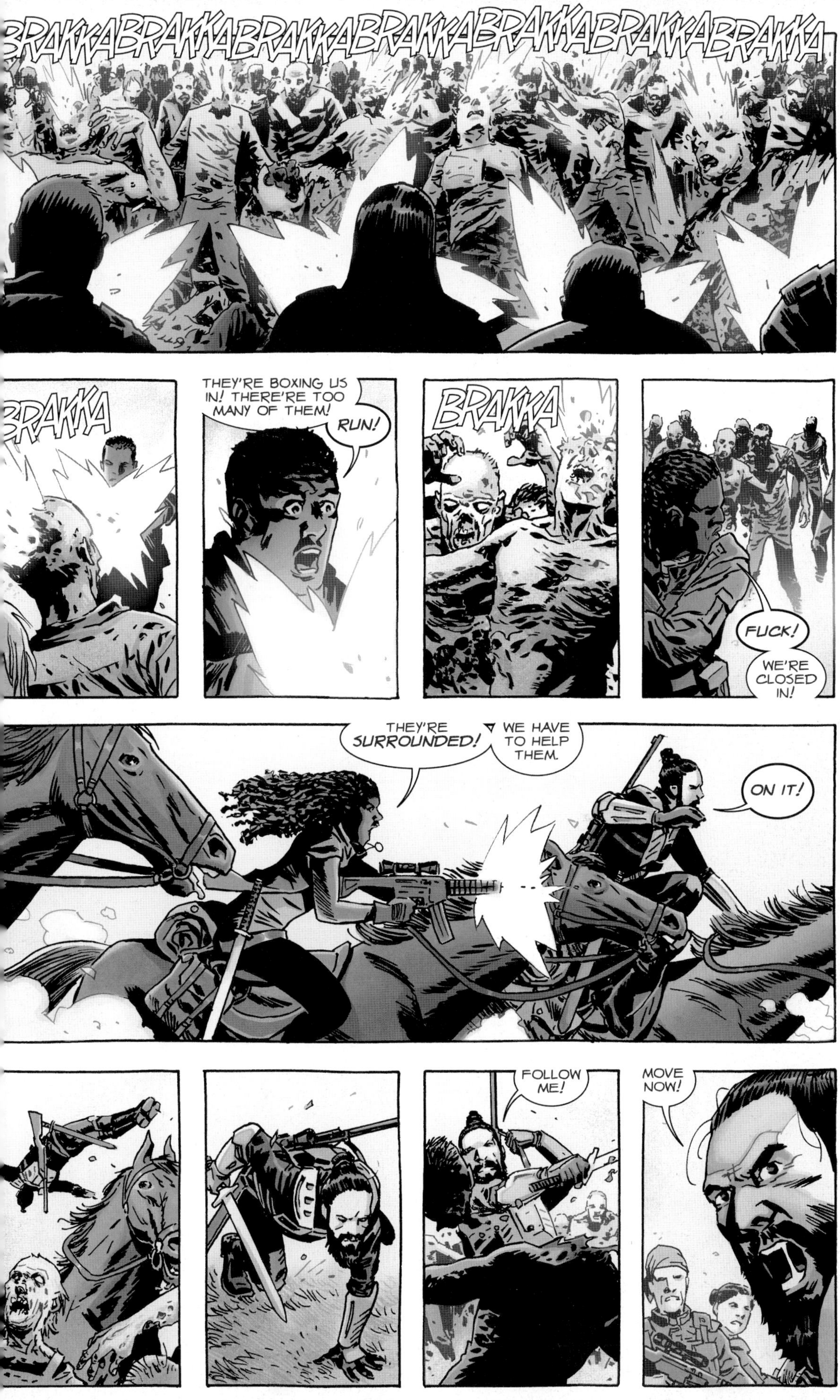
BRAKKABRAKKABRAKKABRAKKABRAKKABRAKKABRAKKA
BRAKKA
THEY'RE BOXING US IN! THERE'RE TOO MANY OF THEM!
RUN!
BRAKKA
FUCK!
WE'RE CLOSED IN!
THEY'RE SURROUNDED!
WE HAVE TO HELP THEM.
ON IT!
FOLLOW ME!
MOVE NOW!

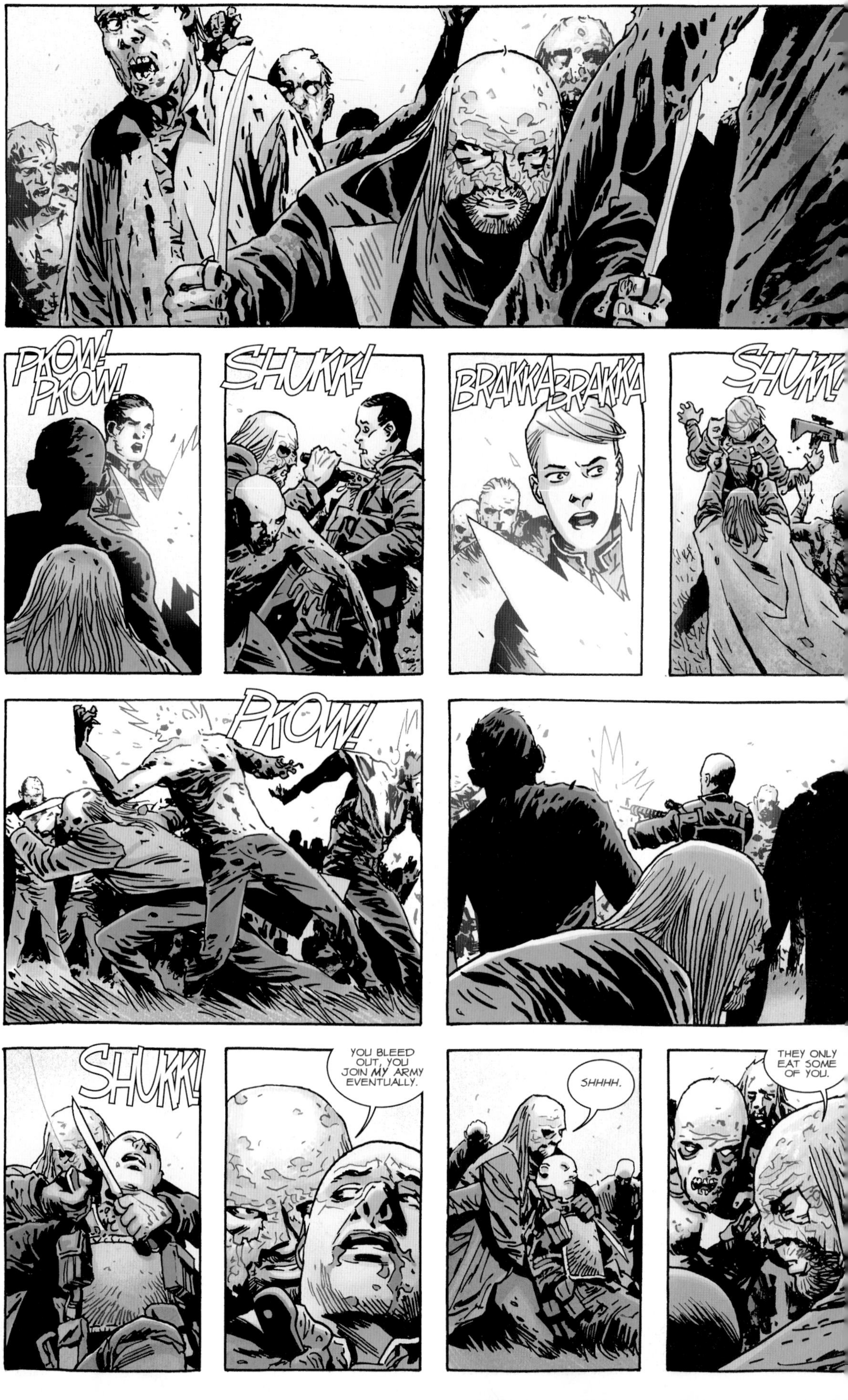
PKOW! PKOW!
SHUKK!
BRAKKABRAKKA
SHUKK!
PKOW!
SHUKK!
YOU BLEED OUT, YOU JOIN MY ARMY EVENTUALLY.
SHHHH.
THEY ONLY EAT SOME OF YOU.

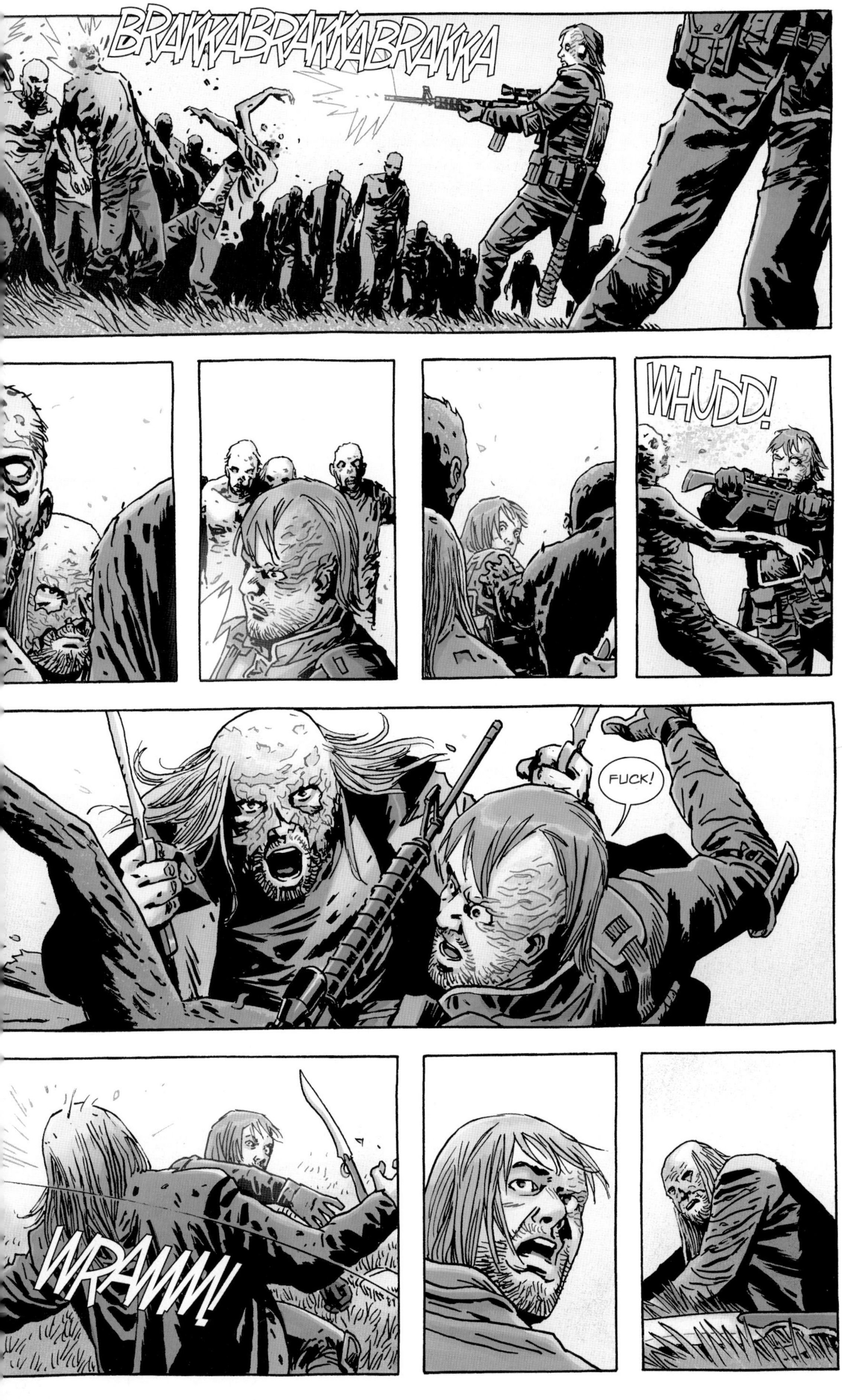
BRAKKABRAKKABRAKKA
WHUDD!
FUCK!
WRAMM!

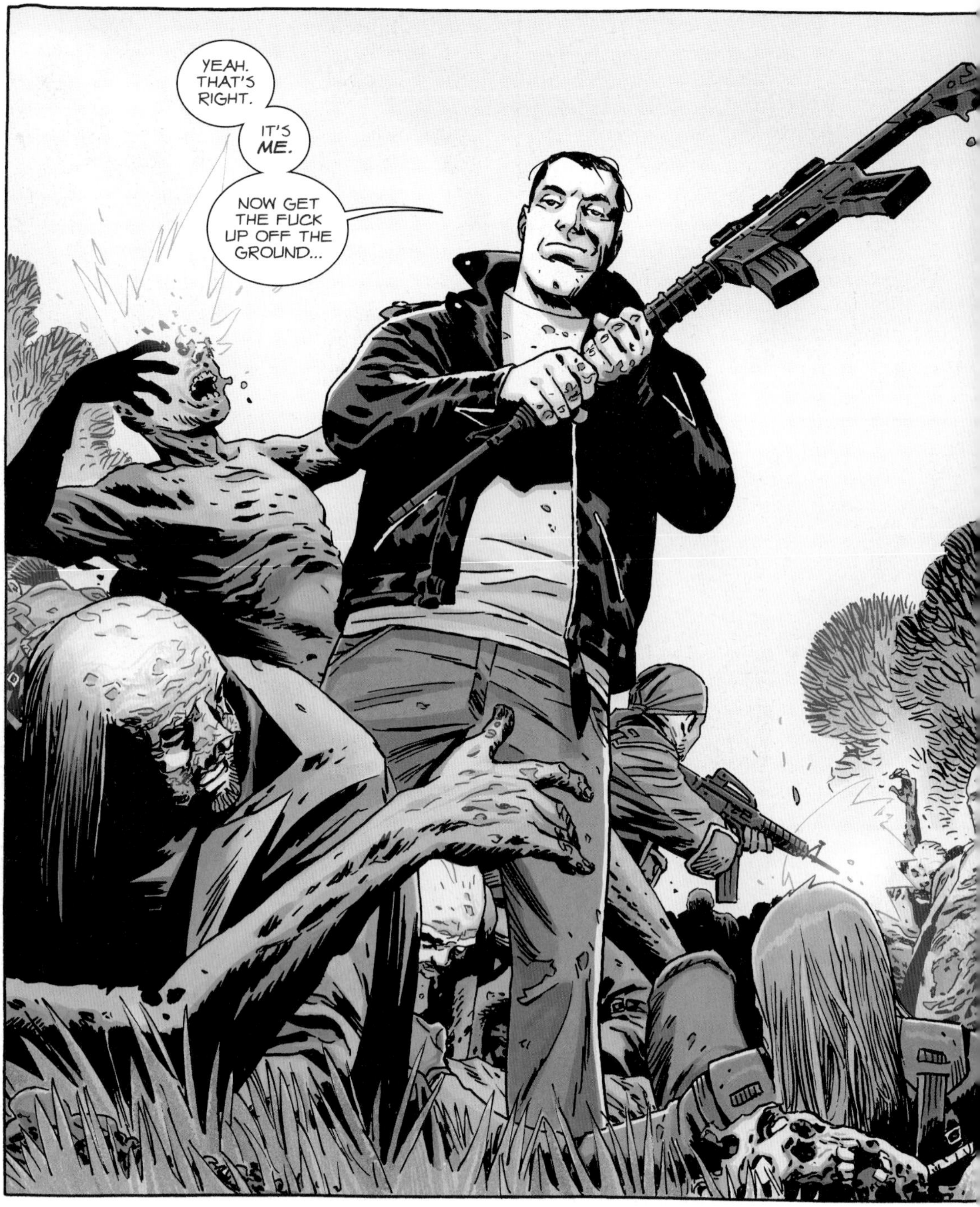
YEAH. THAT'S RIGHT.
IT'S *ME.*
NOW GET THE FUCK UP OFF THE GROUND...

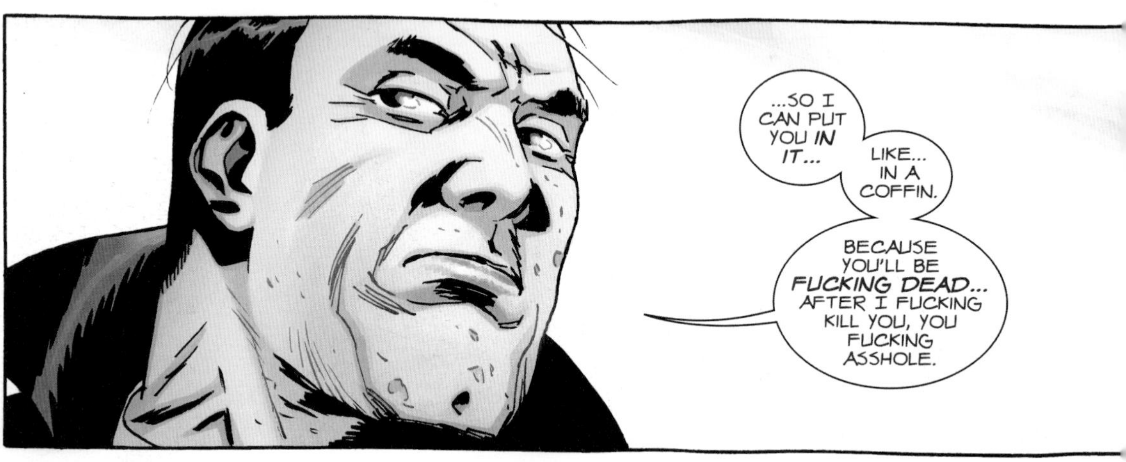
...SO I CAN PUT YOU *IN IT...*
LIKE... IN A COFFIN.
BECAUSE YOU'LL BE *FUCKING DEAD...* AFTER I FUCKING KILL YOU, YOU FUCKING ASSHOLE.

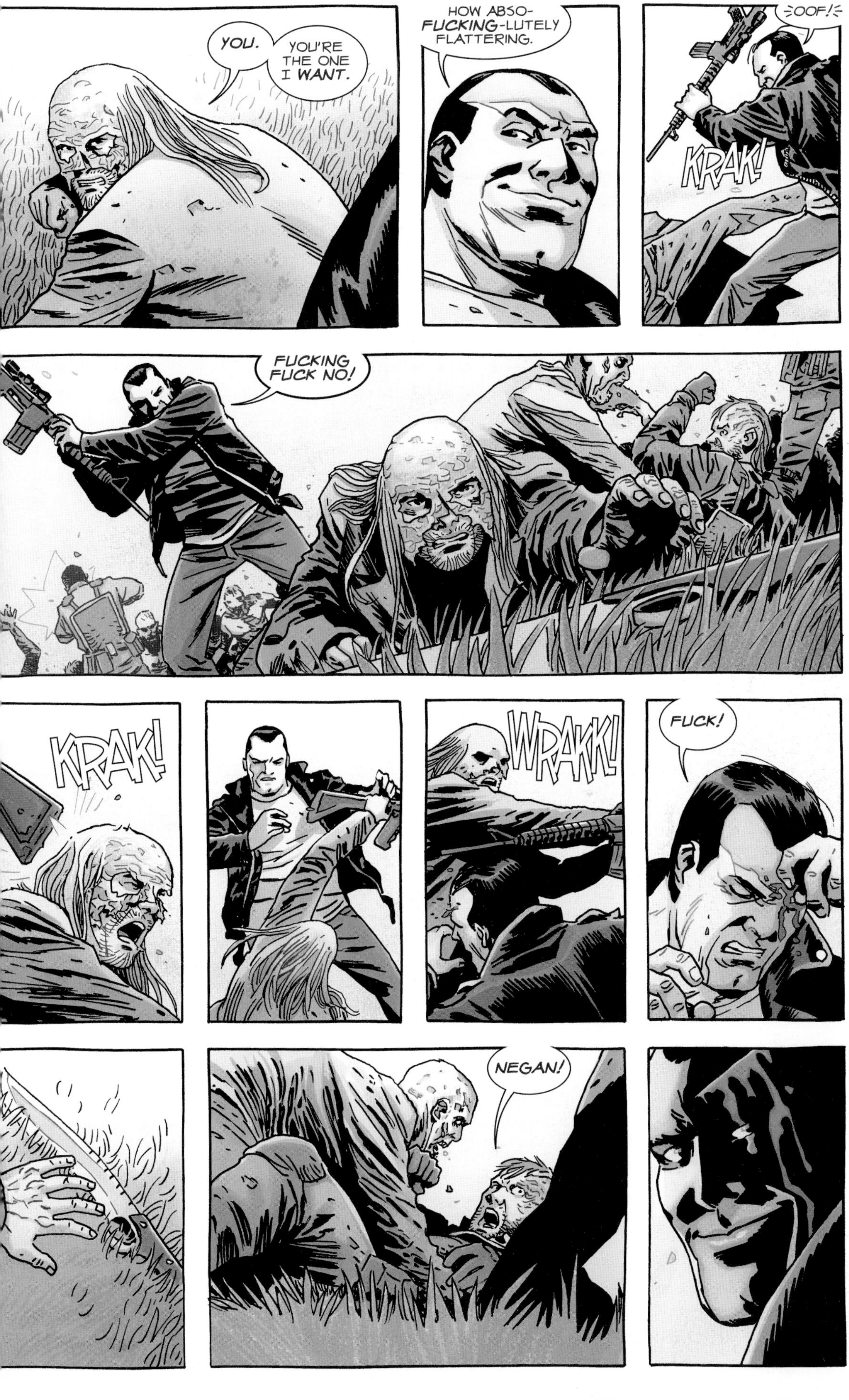
YOU.
YOU'RE THE ONE I WANT.
HOW ABSO-FUCKING-LUTELY FLATTERING.
OOF!
KRAK!
FUCKING FUCK NO!
KRAK!
WRAKK!
FUCK!
NEGAN!

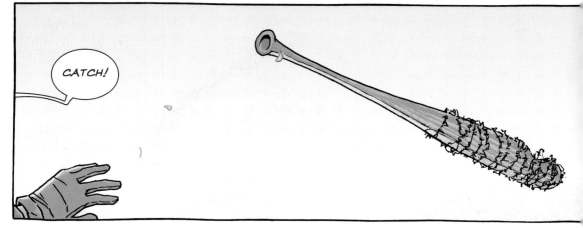

CATCH!

WELCOME HOME, BABY.

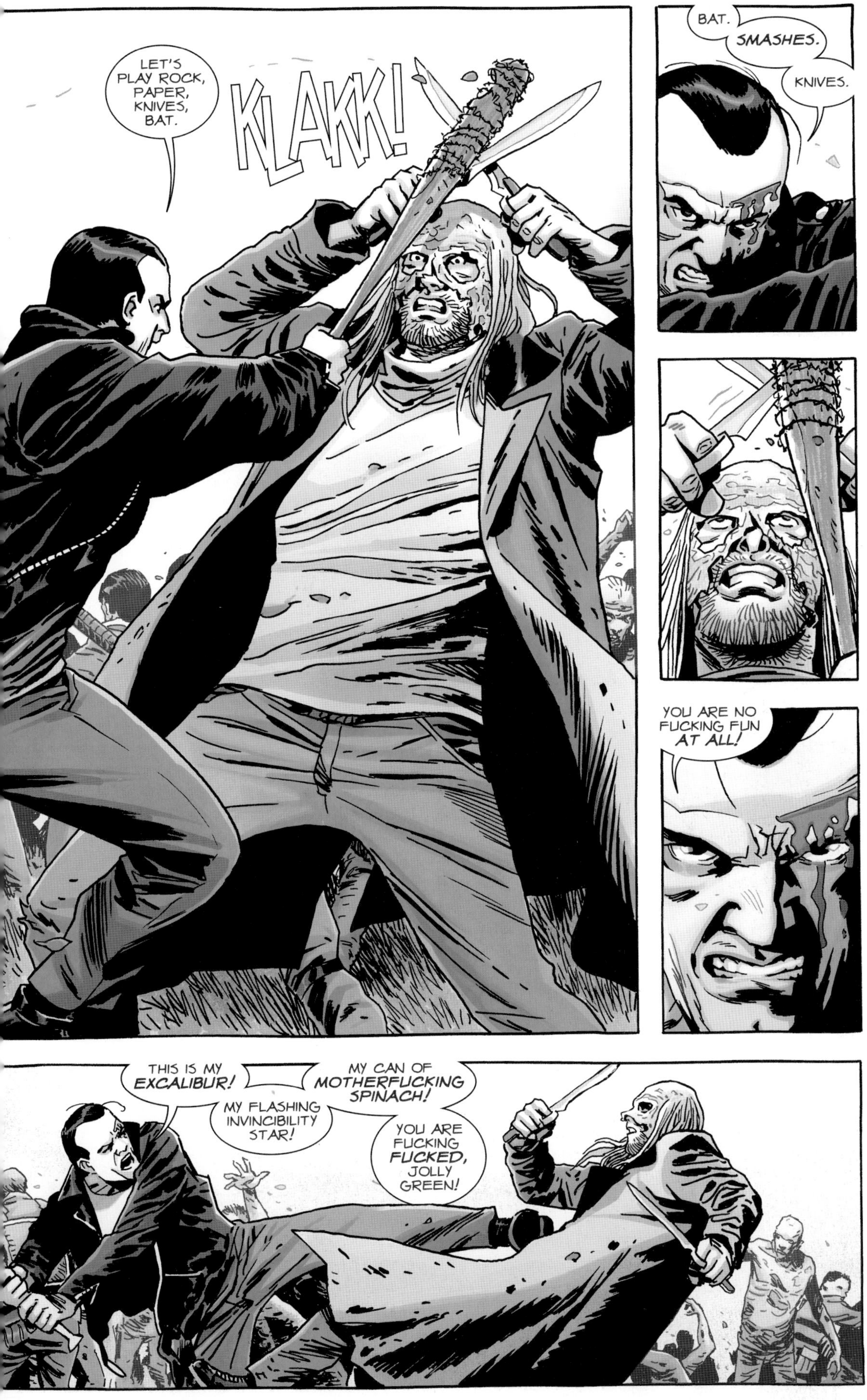
LET'S PLAY ROCK, PAPER, KNIVES, BAT.
KLAKK!
BAT.
SMASHES.
KNIVES.
YOU ARE NO FUCKING FUN AT ALL!
THIS IS MY EXCALIBUR!
MY FLASHING INVINCIBILITY STAR!
MY CAN OF MOTHERFUCKING SPINACH!
YOU ARE FUCKING FUCKED, JOLLY GREEN!

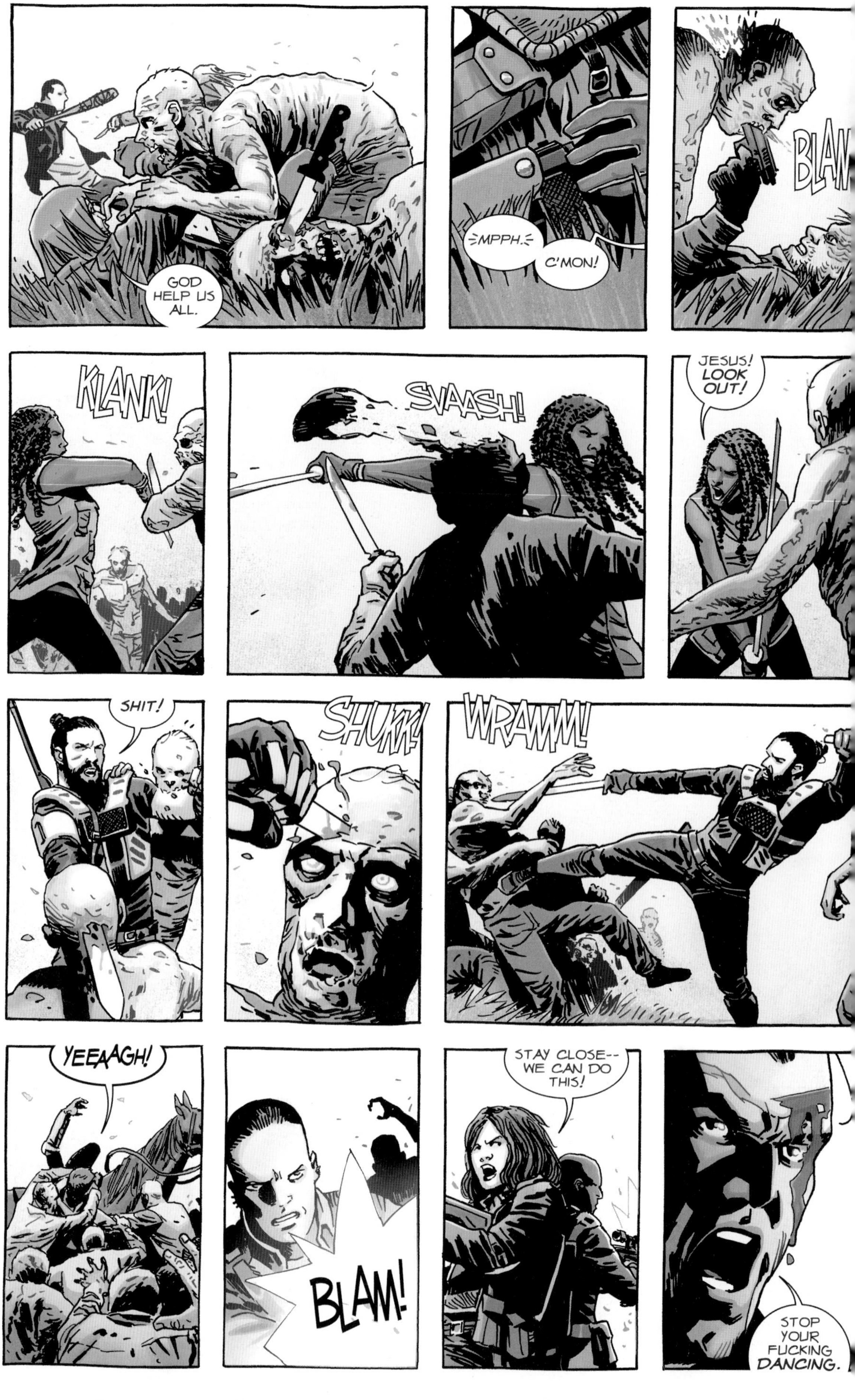
GOD HELP US ALL.
MPPH.
C'MON!
BLAM
KLANK!
SVAASH!
JESUS! LOOK OUT!
SHIT!
SHUKK!
WRANNN!
YEEAAGH!
BLAM!
STAY CLOSE-- WE CAN DO THIS!
STOP YOUR FUCKING DANCING.

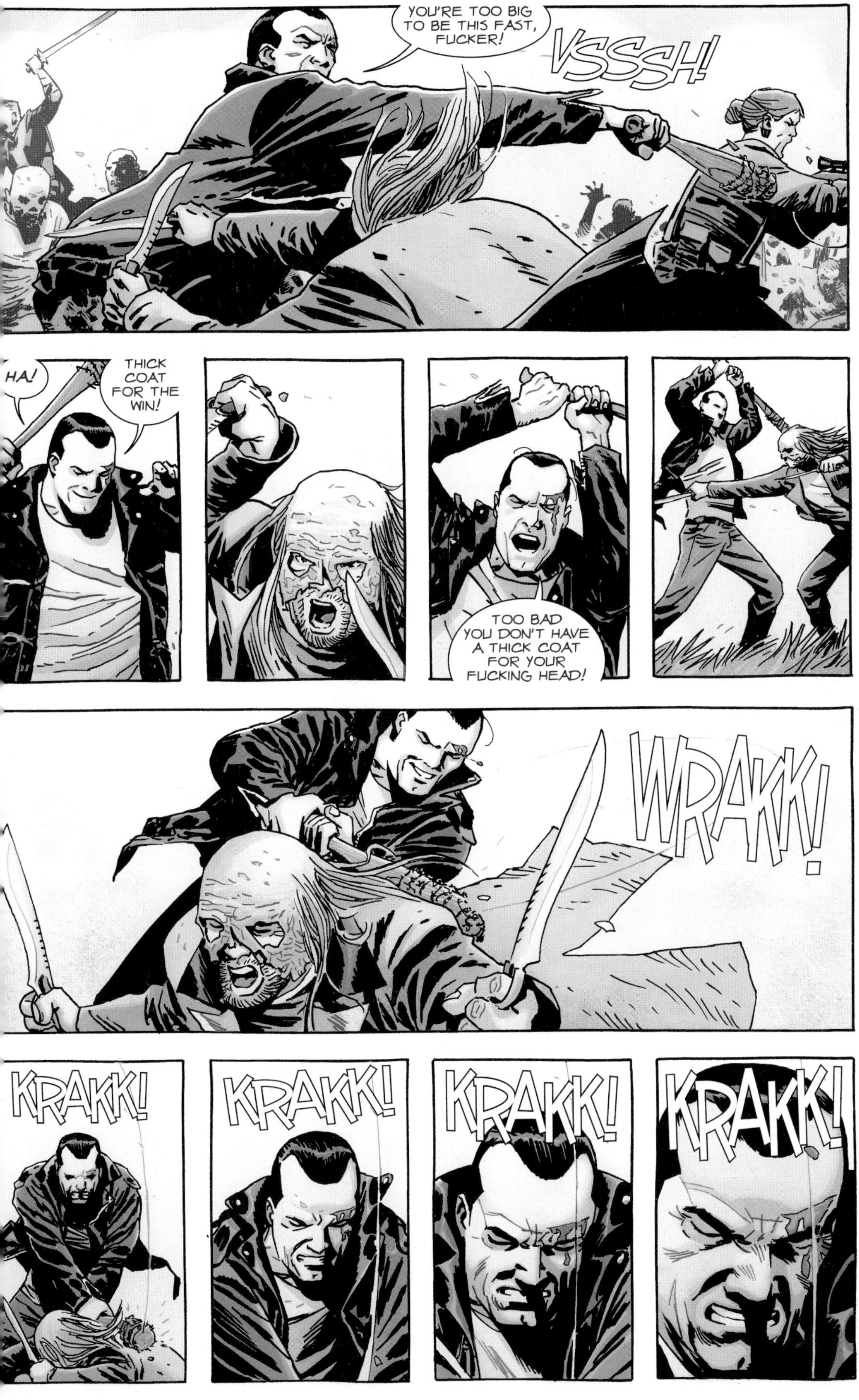

YOU'RE TOO BIG TO BE THIS FAST, FUCKER!
VSSSH!
HA!
THICK COAT FOR THE WIN!
TOO BAD YOU DON'T HAVE A THICK COAT FOR YOUR FUCKING HEAD!
WRAKK!
KRAKK!
KRAKK!
KRAKK!
KRAKK!

**KRIIIKK!**

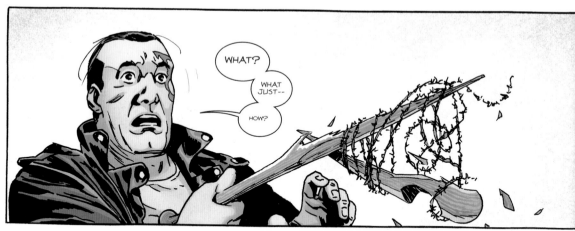

WHAT?

WHAT JUST--

HOW?

**NOOOOO!**

YOU!

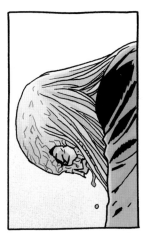

YOU FUCKING BROKE HER!

YOU BROKE LUCILLE!!

AAAARGGH!!

FUCK!

NO!

BETA LIVES.

HIS STRENGTH WILL NEVER BE QUESTIONED.

NO!

NO!

HE'S FUCKING MINE!

BRING HIM BACK!

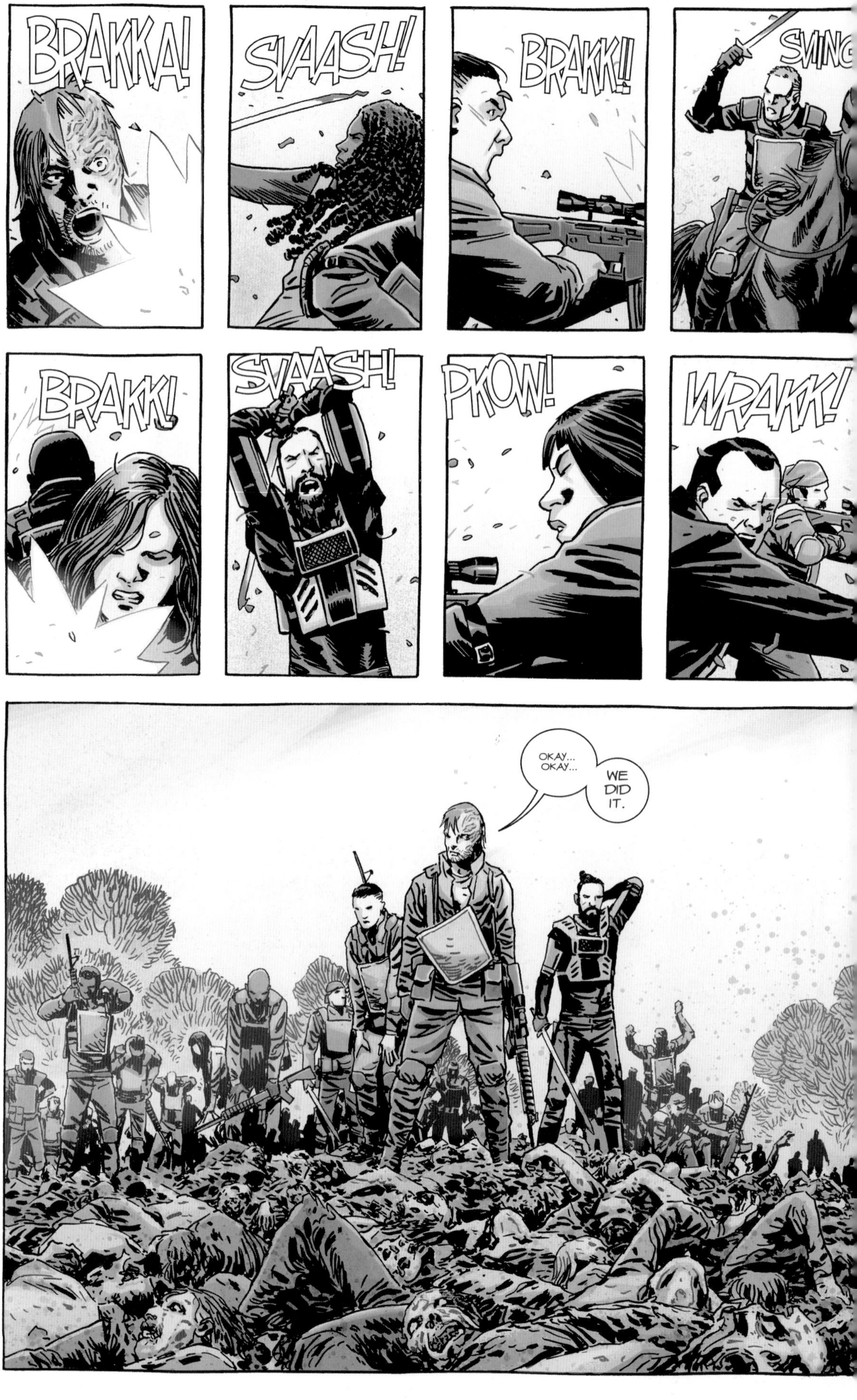
BRAKKA!
SVAASH!
BRAKK!!
SVING
BRAKK!
SVAASH!
PKOW!
WRAKK!
OKAY... OKAY...
WE DID IT.

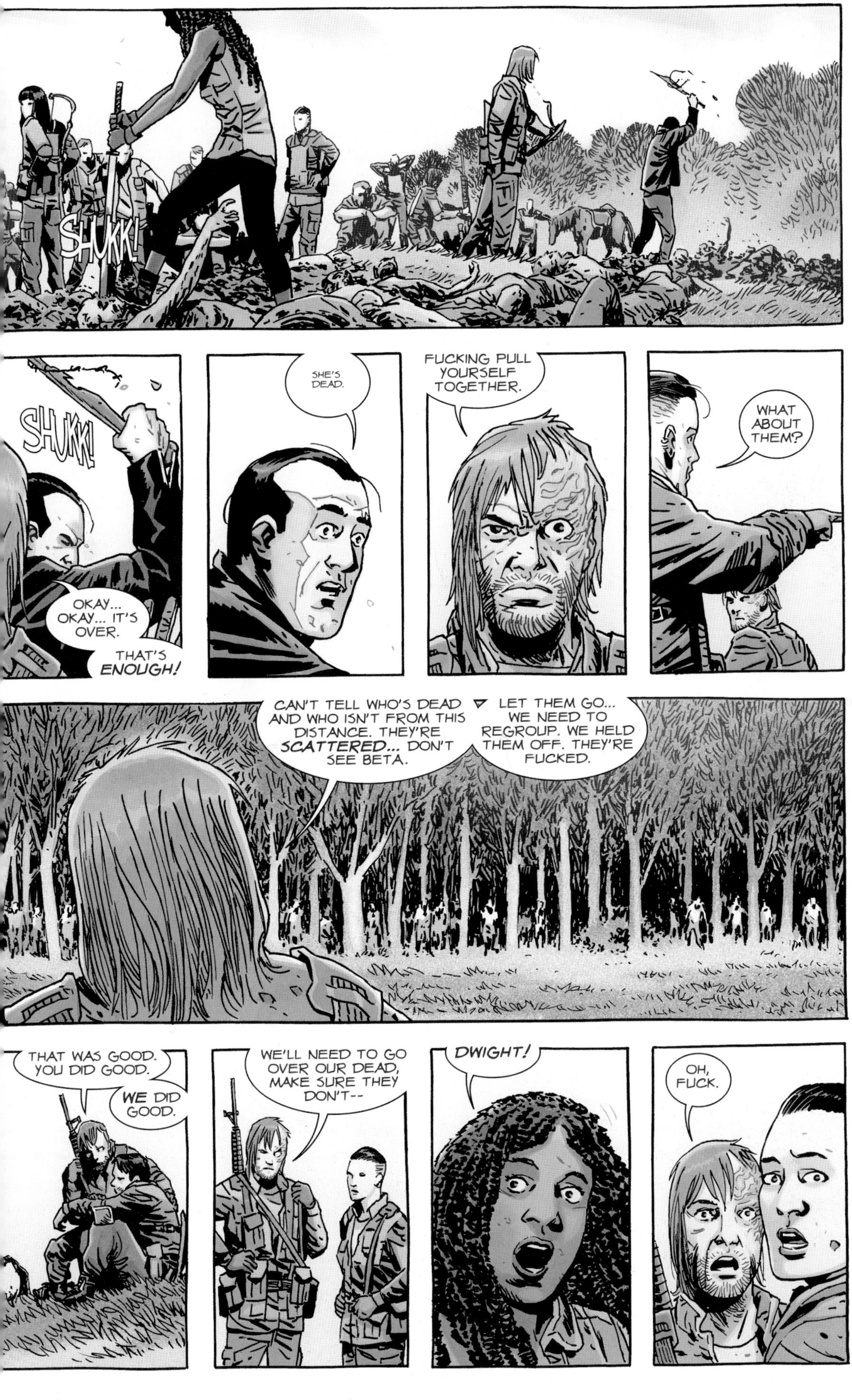
SHUKK!
SHUKK!
OKAY... OKAY... IT'S OVER.
THAT'S ENOUGH!
SHE'S DEAD.
FUCKING PULL YOURSELF TOGETHER.
WHAT ABOUT THEM?
CAN'T TELL WHO'S DEAD AND WHO ISN'T FROM THIS DISTANCE. THEY'RE SCATTERED... DON'T SEE BETA.
LET THEM GO... WE NEED TO REGROUP. WE HELD THEM OFF. THEY'RE FUCKED.
THAT WAS GOOD. YOU DID GOOD.
WE DID GOOD.
WE'LL NEED TO GO OVER OUR DEAD, MAKE SURE THEY DON'T--
DWIGHT!
OH, FUCK.

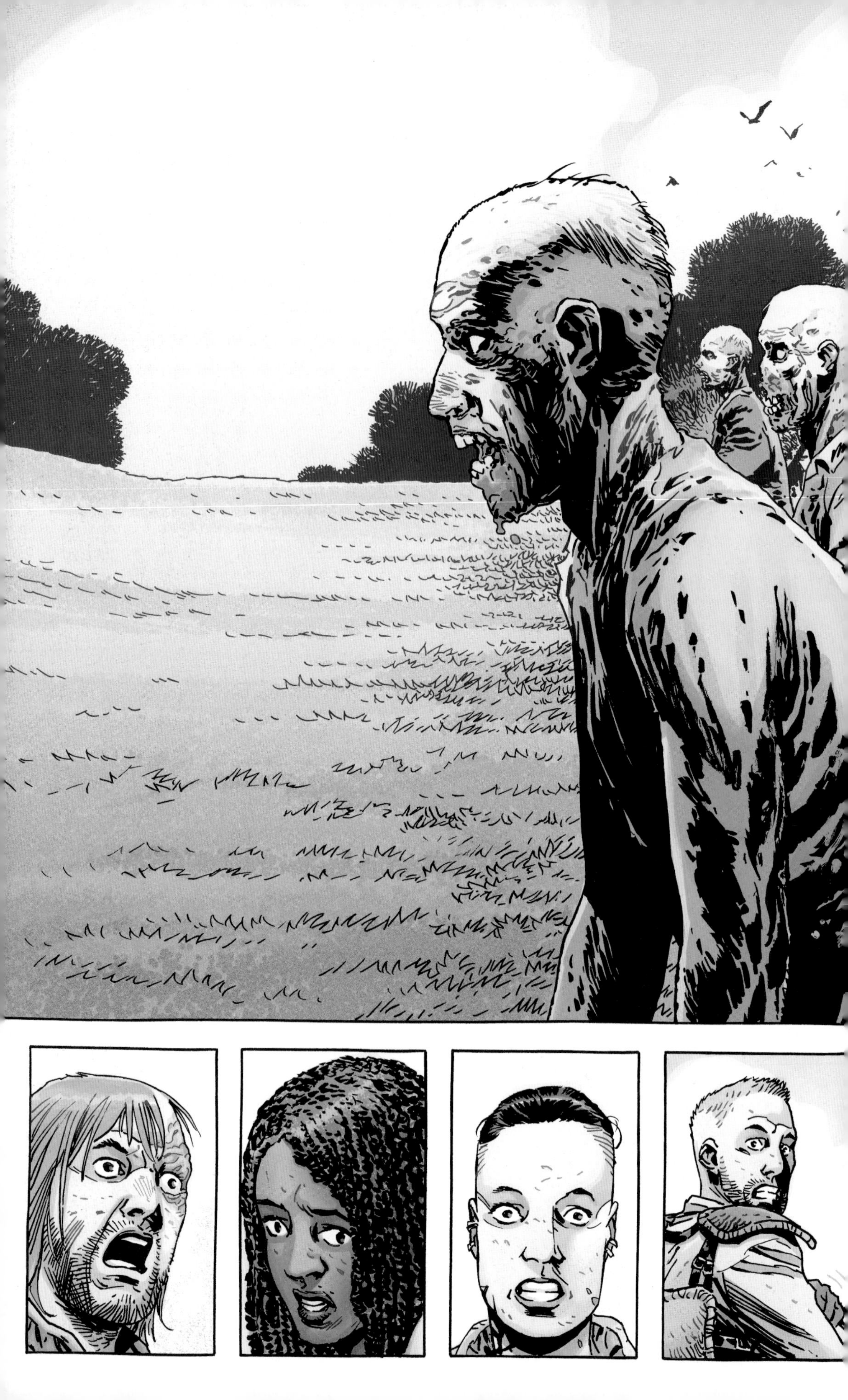

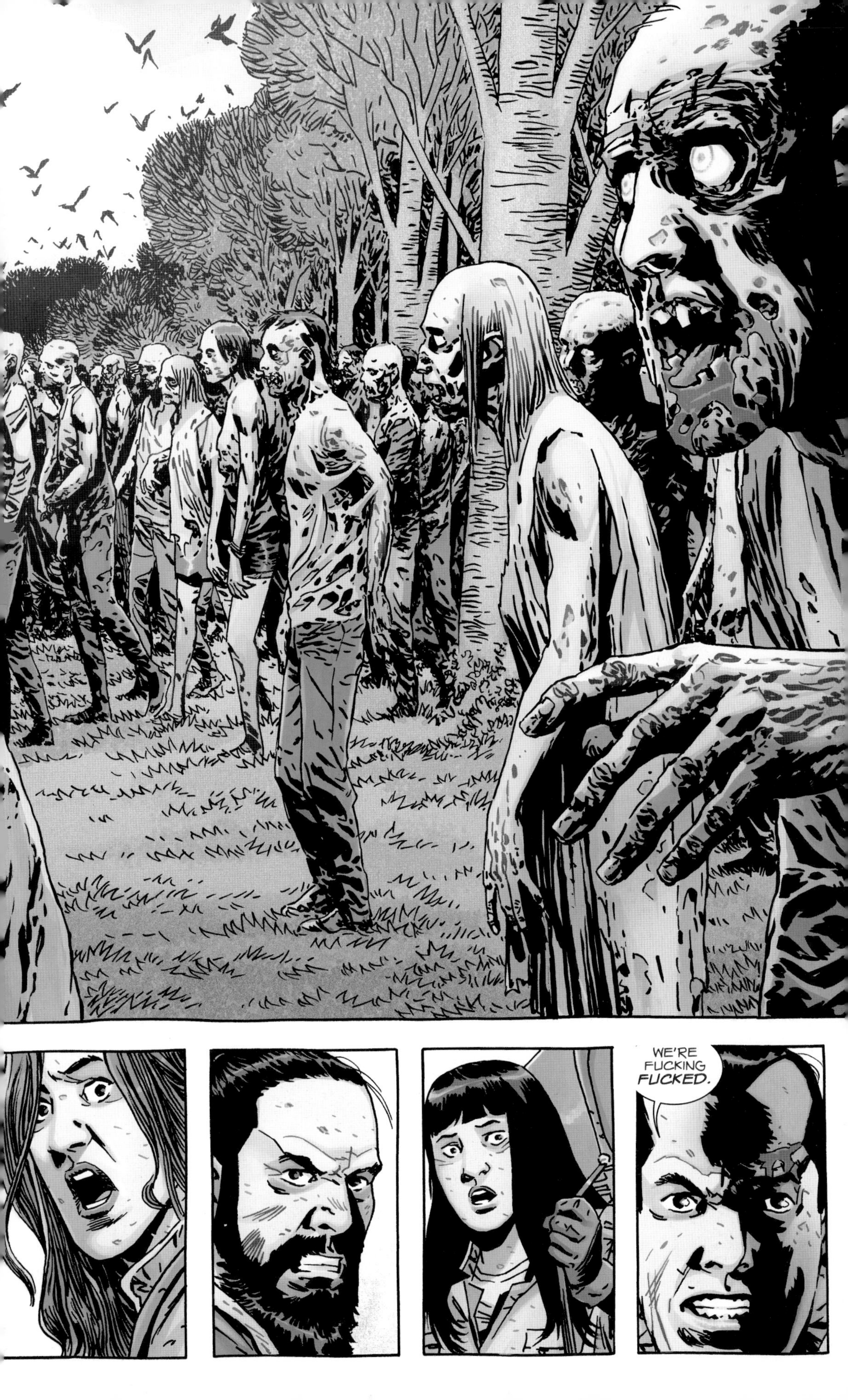
WE'RE FUCKING FUCKED.

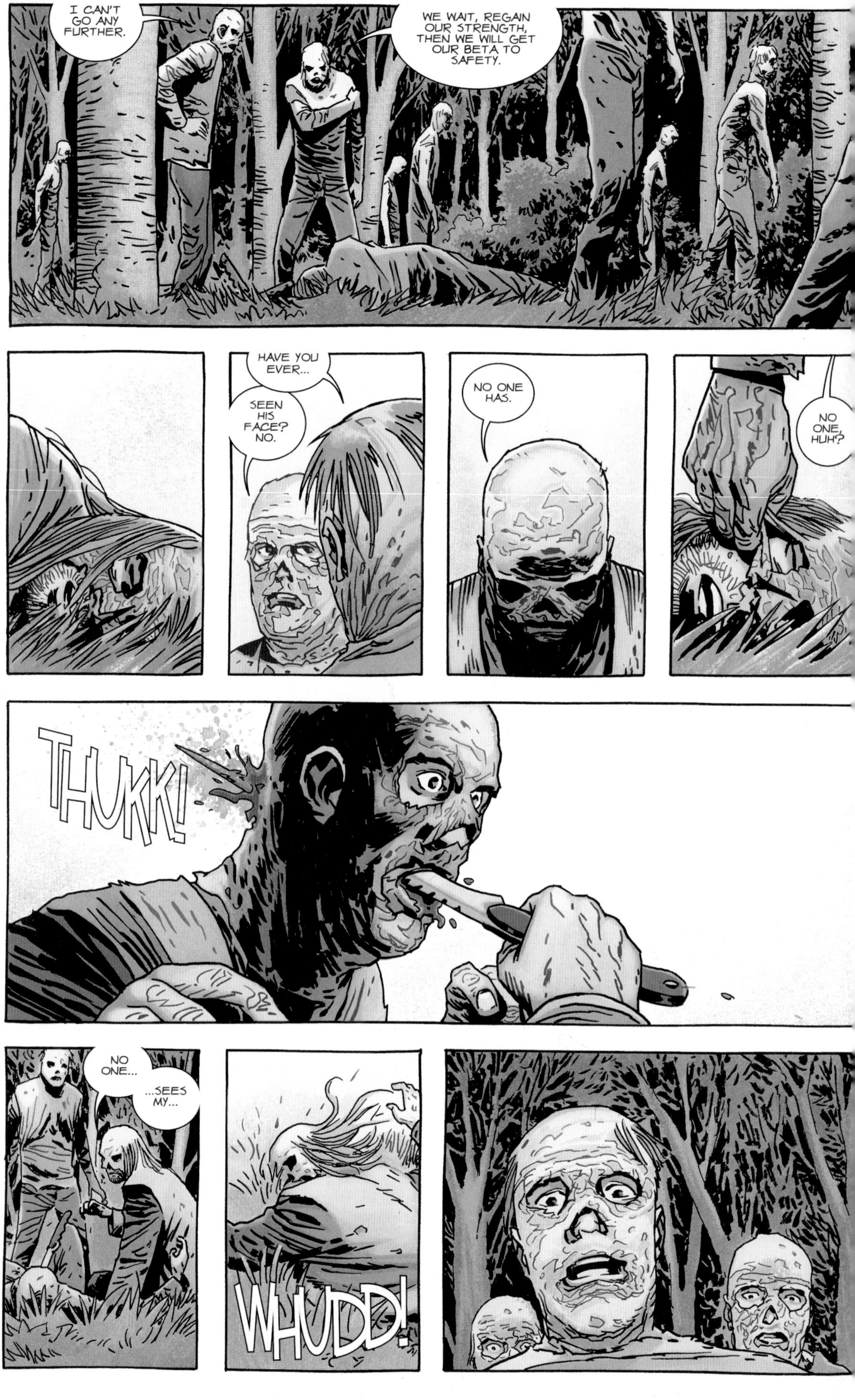
I CAN'T GO ANY FURTHER.
WE WAIT, REGAIN OUR STRENGTH, THEN WE WILL GET OUR BETA TO SAFETY.
HAVE YOU EVER...
SEEN HIS FACE? NO.
NO ONE HAS.
NO ONE, HUH?
THUKK!
NO ONE...
...SEES MY...
WHUDD!

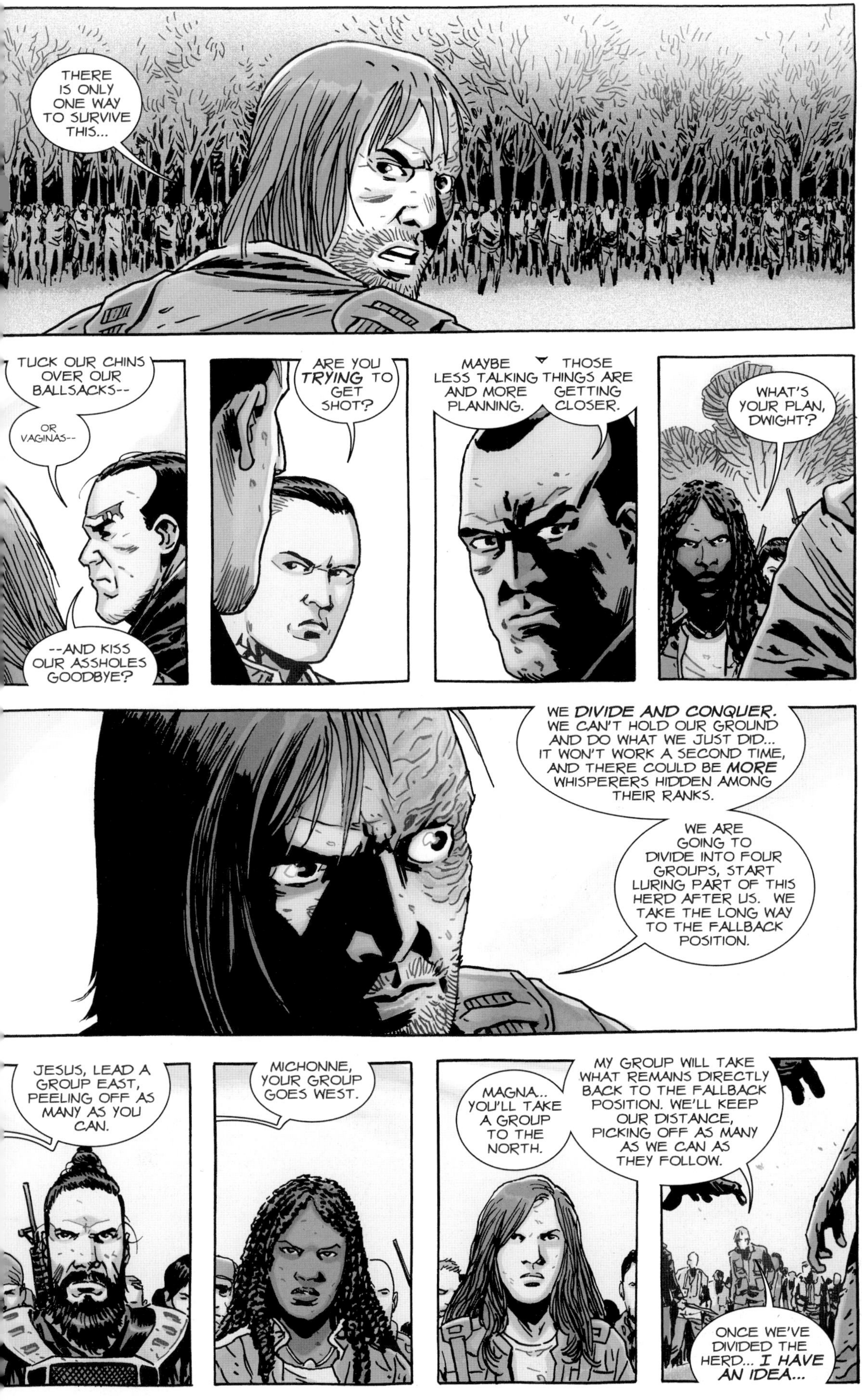
THERE IS ONLY ONE WAY TO SURVIVE THIS...
TUCK OUR CHINS OVER OUR BALLSACKS--
OR VAGINAS--
--AND KISS OUR ASSHOLES GOODBYE?
ARE YOU *TRYING* TO GET SHOT?
MAYBE LESS TALKING AND MORE PLANNING.
THOSE THINGS ARE GETTING CLOSER.
WHAT'S YOUR PLAN, DWIGHT?
WE *DIVIDE AND CONQUER.* WE CAN'T HOLD OUR GROUND AND DO WHAT WE JUST DID... IT WON'T WORK A SECOND TIME, AND THERE COULD BE *MORE* WHISPERERS HIDDEN AMONG THEIR RANKS.
WE ARE GOING TO DIVIDE INTO FOUR GROUPS, START LURING PART OF THIS HERD AFTER US. WE TAKE THE LONG WAY TO THE FALLBACK POSITION.
JESUS, LEAD A GROUP EAST, PEELING OFF AS MANY AS YOU CAN.
MICHONNE, YOUR GROUP GOES WEST.
MAGNA... YOU'LL TAKE A GROUP TO THE NORTH.
MY GROUP WILL TAKE WHAT REMAINS DIRECTLY BACK TO THE FALLBACK POSITION. WE'LL KEEP OUR DISTANCE, PICKING OFF AS MANY AS WE CAN AS THEY FOLLOW.
ONCE WE'VE DIVIDED THE HERD... *I HAVE AN IDEA...*

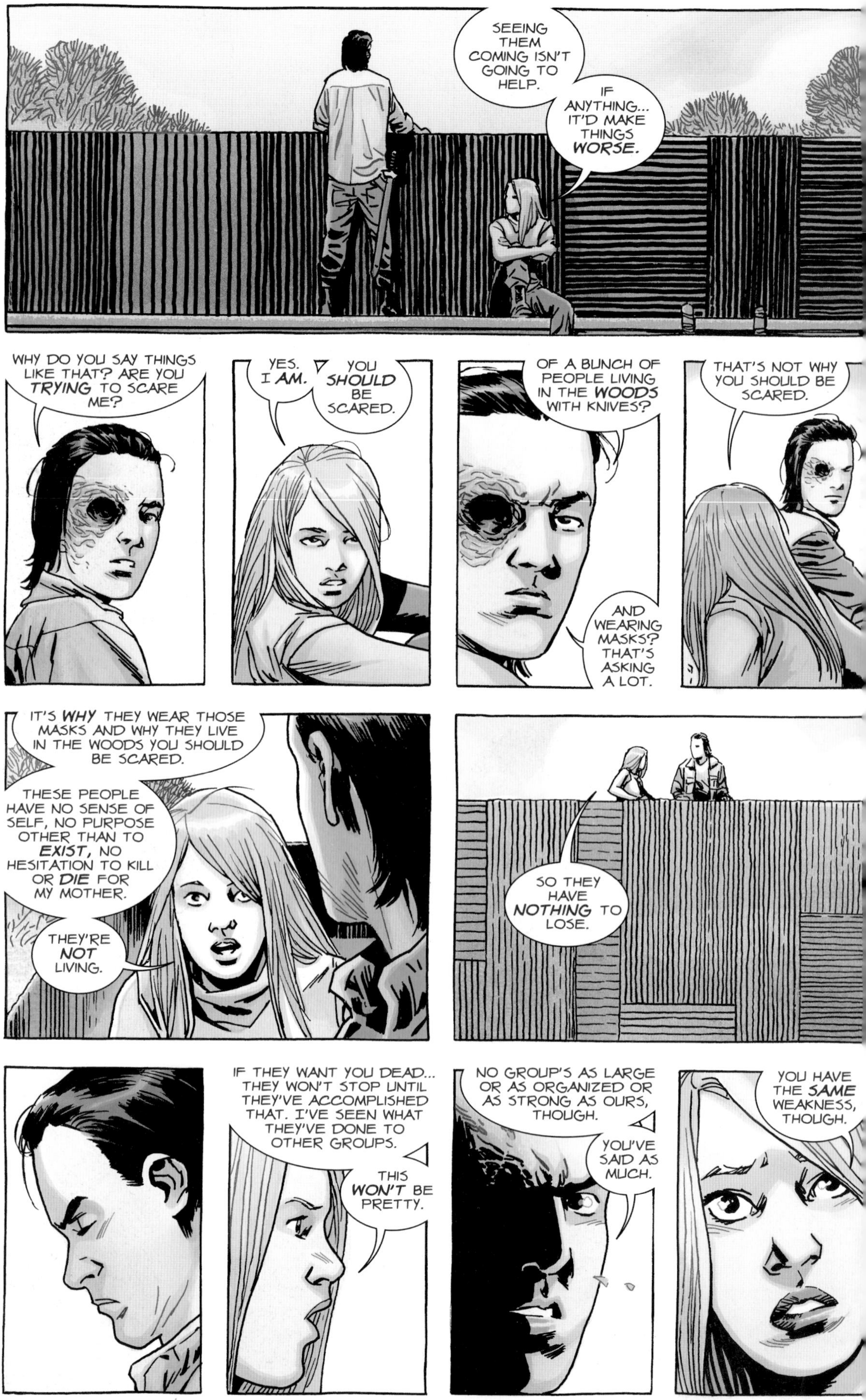
SEEING THEM COMING ISN'T GOING TO HELP.
IF ANYTHING... IT'D MAKE THINGS WORSE.
WHY DO YOU SAY THINGS LIKE THAT? ARE YOU TRYING TO SCARE ME?
YES. I AM.
YOU SHOULD BE SCARED.
OF A BUNCH OF PEOPLE LIVING IN THE WOODS WITH KNIVES?
AND WEARING MASKS? THAT'S ASKING A LOT.
THAT'S NOT WHY YOU SHOULD BE SCARED.
IT'S WHY THEY WEAR THOSE MASKS AND WHY THEY LIVE IN THE WOODS YOU SHOULD BE SCARED.
THESE PEOPLE HAVE NO SENSE OF SELF, NO PURPOSE OTHER THAN TO EXIST, NO HESITATION TO KILL OR DIE FOR MY MOTHER.
THEY'RE NOT LIVING.
SO THEY HAVE NOTHING TO LOSE.
IF THEY WANT YOU DEAD... THEY WON'T STOP UNTIL THEY'VE ACCOMPLISHED THAT. I'VE SEEN WHAT THEY'VE DONE TO OTHER GROUPS.
THIS WON'T BE PRETTY.
NO GROUP'S AS LARGE OR AS ORGANIZED OR AS STRONG AS OURS, THOUGH.
YOU'VE SAID AS MUCH.
YOU HAVE THE SAME WEAKNESS, THOUGH.

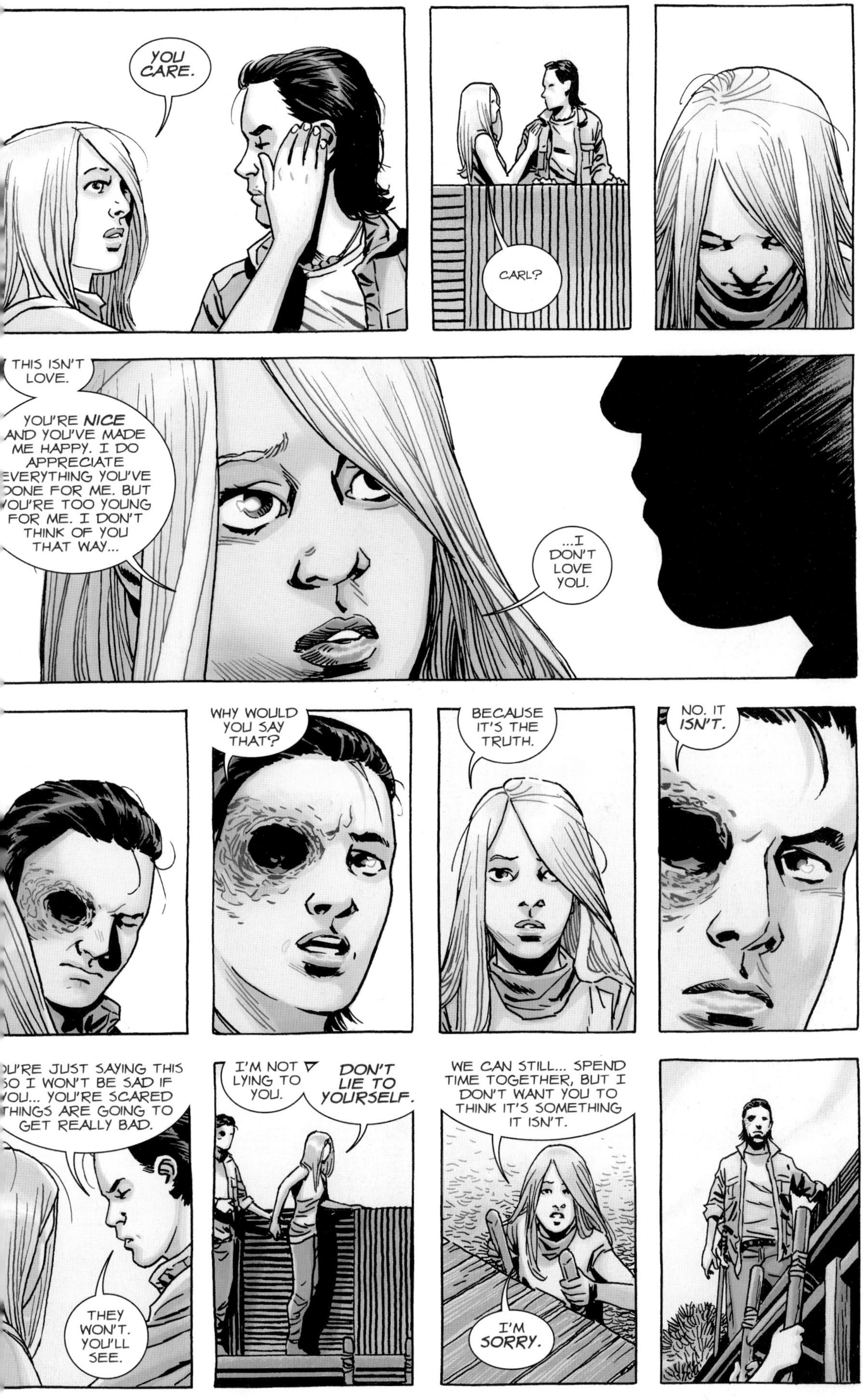
YOU CARE.
CARL?
THIS ISN'T LOVE.
YOU'RE NICE AND YOU'VE MADE ME HAPPY. I DO APPRECIATE EVERYTHING YOU'VE DONE FOR ME. BUT YOU'RE TOO YOUNG FOR ME. I DON'T THINK OF YOU THAT WAY...
...I DON'T LOVE YOU.
WHY WOULD YOU SAY THAT?
BECAUSE IT'S THE TRUTH.
NO. IT ISN'T.
YOU'RE JUST SAYING THIS SO I WON'T BE SAD IF YOU... YOU'RE SCARED THINGS ARE GOING TO GET REALLY BAD.
THEY WON'T. YOU'LL SEE.
I'M NOT LYING TO YOU.
DON'T LIE TO YOURSELF.
WE CAN STILL... SPEND TIME TOGETHER, BUT I DON'T WANT YOU TO THINK IT'S SOMETHING IT ISN'T.
I'M SORRY.

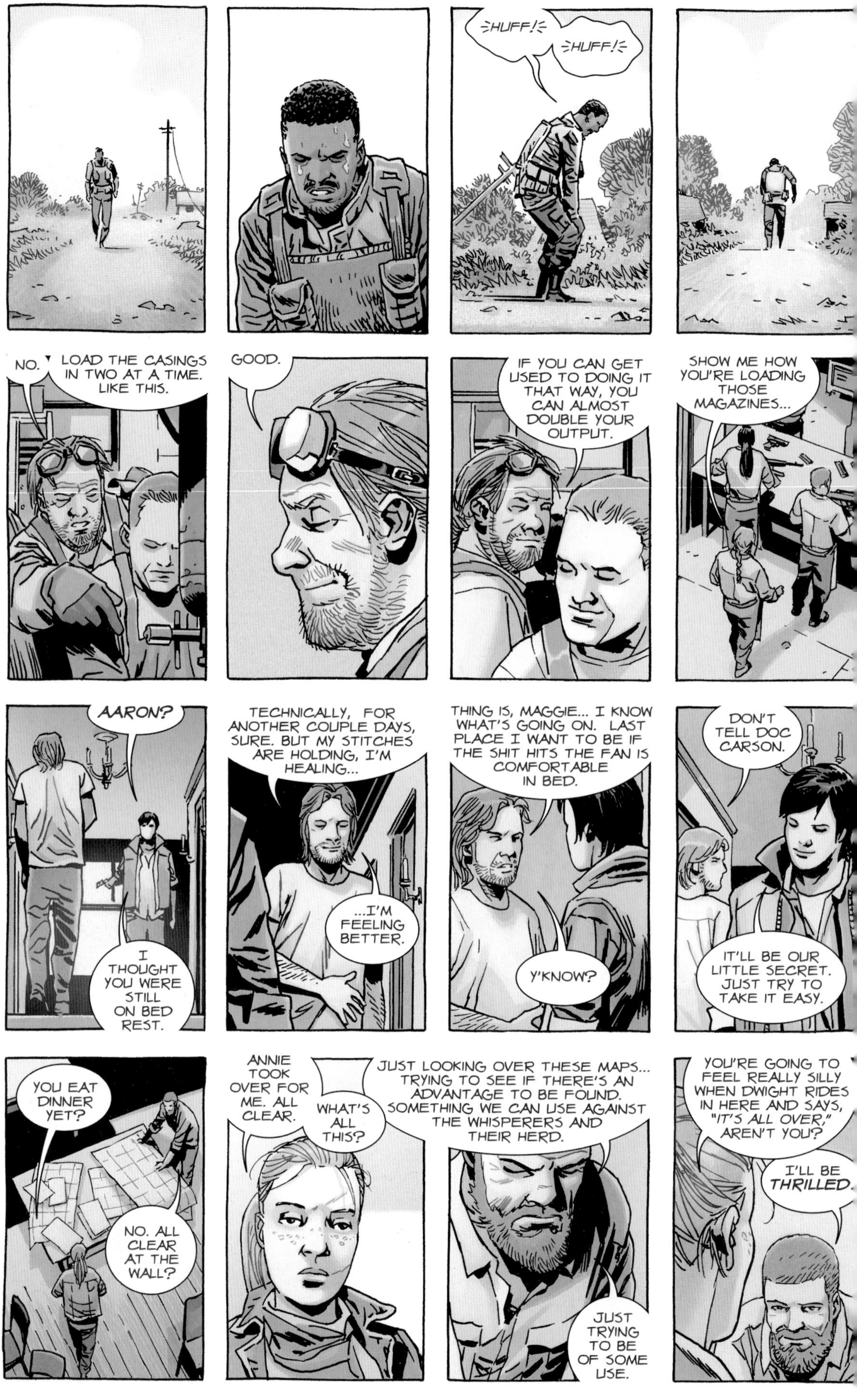

≈HUFF!≈
≈HUFF!≈
NO.
LOAD THE CASINGS IN TWO AT A TIME. LIKE THIS.
GOOD.
IF YOU CAN GET USED TO DOING IT THAT WAY, YOU CAN ALMOST DOUBLE YOUR OUTPUT.
SHOW ME HOW YOU'RE LOADING THOSE MAGAZINES...
AARON?
I THOUGHT YOU WERE STILL ON BED REST.
TECHNICALLY, FOR ANOTHER COUPLE DAYS, SURE. BUT MY STITCHES ARE HOLDING, I'M HEALING...
...I'M FEELING BETTER.
THING IS, MAGGIE... I KNOW WHAT'S GOING ON. LAST PLACE I WANT TO BE IF THE SHIT HITS THE FAN IS COMFORTABLE IN BED.
Y'KNOW?
DON'T TELL DOC CARSON.
IT'LL BE OUR LITTLE SECRET. JUST TRY TO TAKE IT EASY.
YOU EAT DINNER YET?
NO. ALL CLEAR AT THE WALL?
ANNIE TOOK OVER FOR ME. ALL CLEAR.
WHAT'S ALL THIS?
JUST LOOKING OVER THESE MAPS... TRYING TO SEE IF THERE'S AN ADVANTAGE TO BE FOUND. SOMETHING WE CAN USE AGAINST THE WHISPERERS AND THEIR HERD.
JUST TRYING TO BE OF SOME USE.
YOU'RE GOING TO FEEL REALLY SILLY WHEN DWIGHT RIDES IN HERE AND SAYS, "IT'S ALL OVER," AREN'T YOU?
I'LL BE THRILLED.

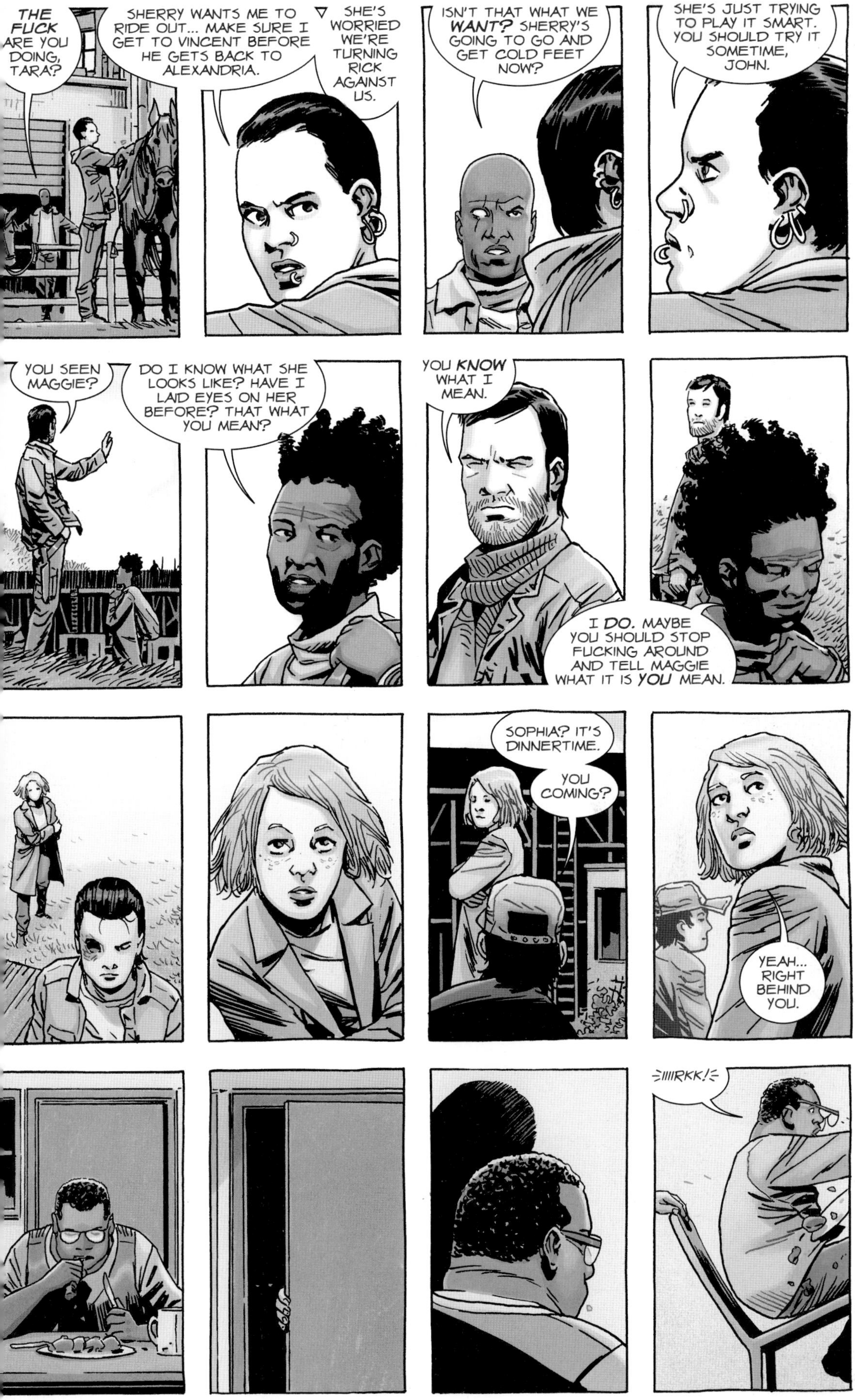
THE FUCK ARE YOU DOING, TARA?
SHERRY WANTS ME TO RIDE OUT... MAKE SURE I GET TO VINCENT BEFORE HE GETS BACK TO ALEXANDRIA.
SHE'S WORRIED WE'RE TURNING RICK AGAINST US.
ISN'T THAT WHAT WE WANT? SHERRY'S GOING TO GO AND GET COLD FEET NOW?
SHE'S JUST TRYING TO PLAY IT SMART. YOU SHOULD TRY IT SOMETIME, JOHN.
YOU SEEN MAGGIE?
DO I KNOW WHAT SHE LOOKS LIKE? HAVE I LAID EYES ON HER BEFORE? THAT WHAT YOU MEAN?
YOU KNOW WHAT I MEAN.
I DO. MAYBE YOU SHOULD STOP FUCKING AROUND AND TELL MAGGIE WHAT IT IS YOU MEAN.
SOPHIA? IT'S DINNERTIME.
YOU COMING?
YEAH... RIGHT BEHIND YOU.
IIIIRKK!

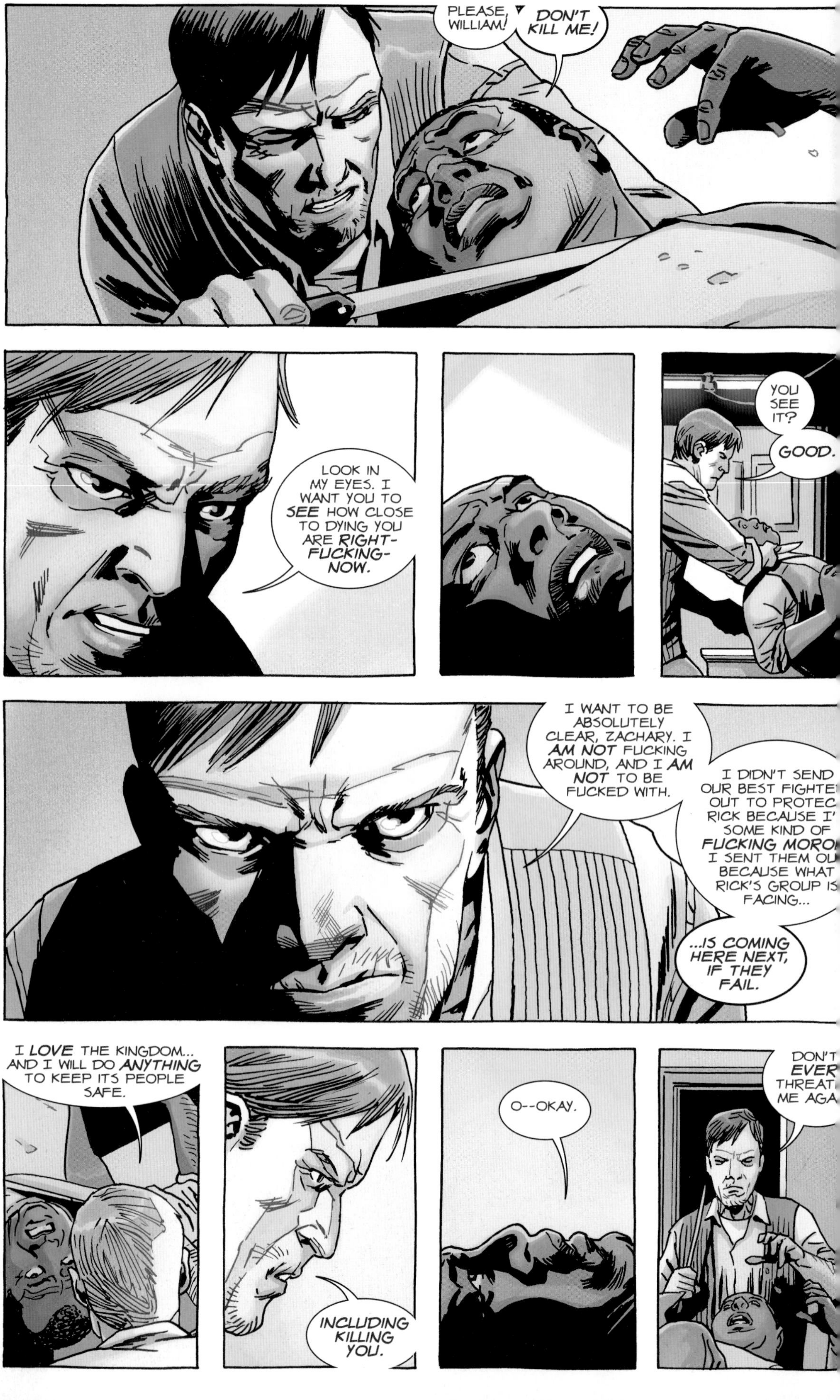

PLEASE, WILLIAM!
DON'T KILL ME!
LOOK IN MY EYES. I WANT YOU TO SEE HOW CLOSE TO DYING YOU ARE RIGHT-FUCKING-NOW.
YOU SEE IT?
GOOD.
I WANT TO BE ABSOLUTELY CLEAR, ZACHARY. I AM NOT FUCKING AROUND, AND I AM NOT TO BE FUCKED WITH.
I DIDN'T SEND OUR BEST FIGHTE OUT TO PROTEC RICK BECAUSE I' SOME KIND OF FUCKING MORO I SENT THEM OU BECAUSE WHAT RICK'S GROUP IS FACING...
...IS COMING HERE NEXT, IF THEY FAIL.
I LOVE THE KINGDOM... AND I WILL DO ANYTHING TO KEEP ITS PEOPLE SAFE.
INCLUDING KILLING YOU.
O--OKAY.
DON'T EVER THREAT ME AGA

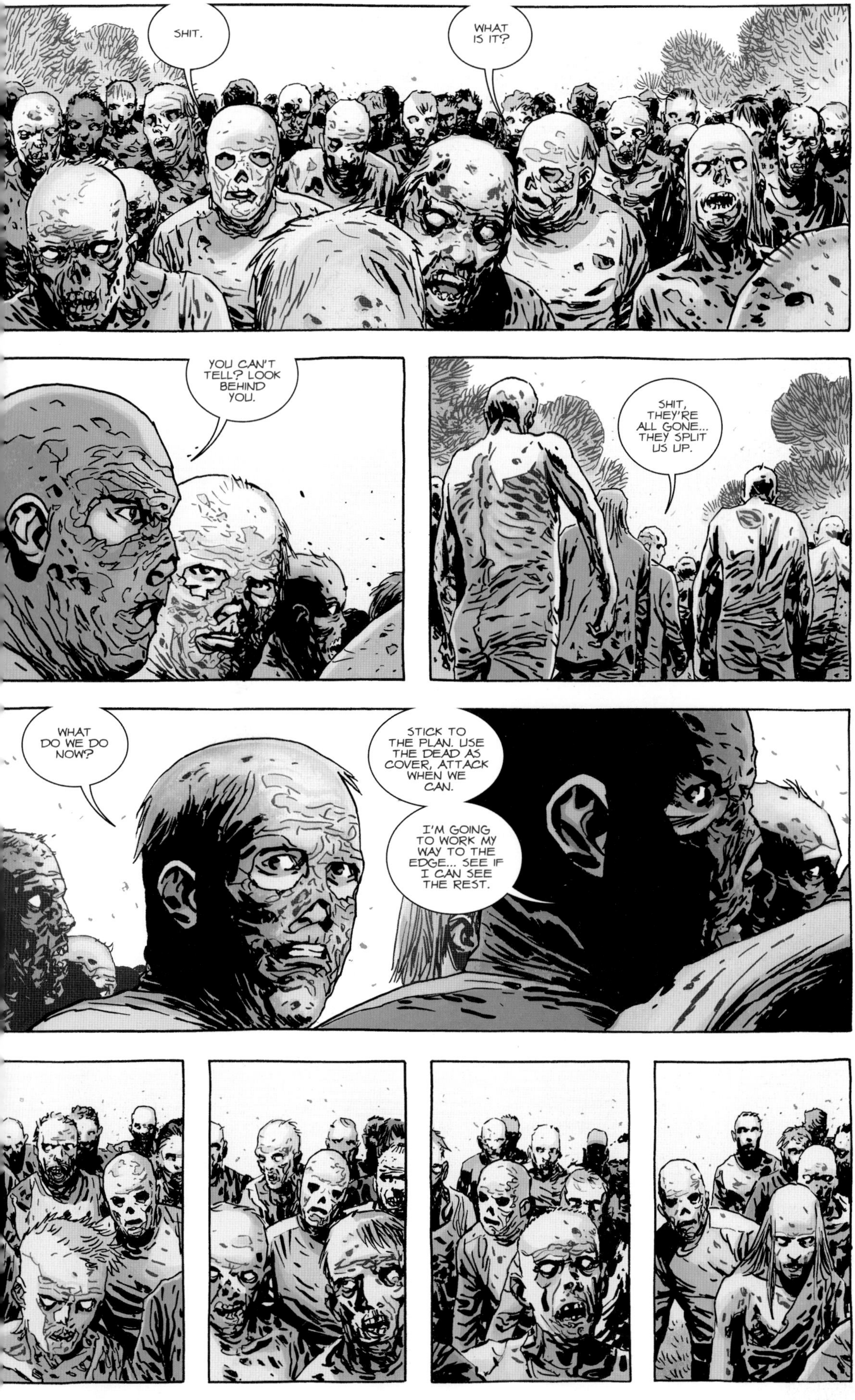
SHIT.
WHAT IS IT?
YOU CAN'T TELL? LOOK BEHIND YOU.
SHIT, THEY'RE ALL GONE... THEY SPLIT US UP.
WHAT DO WE DO NOW?
STICK TO THE PLAN. USE THE DEAD AS COVER, ATTACK WHEN WE CAN.
I'M GOING TO WORK MY WAY TO THE EDGE... SEE IF I CAN SEE THE REST.

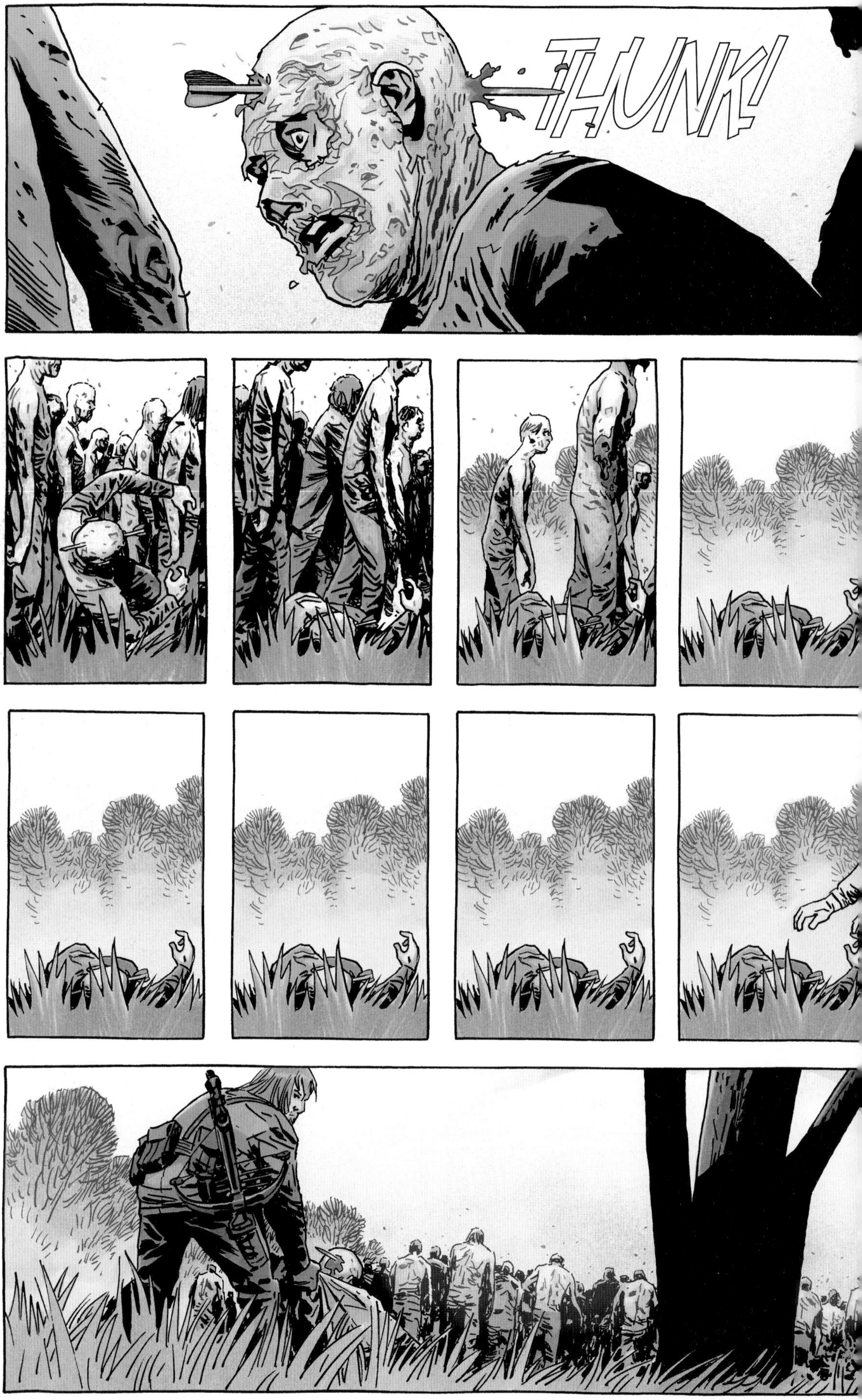
THUNK!

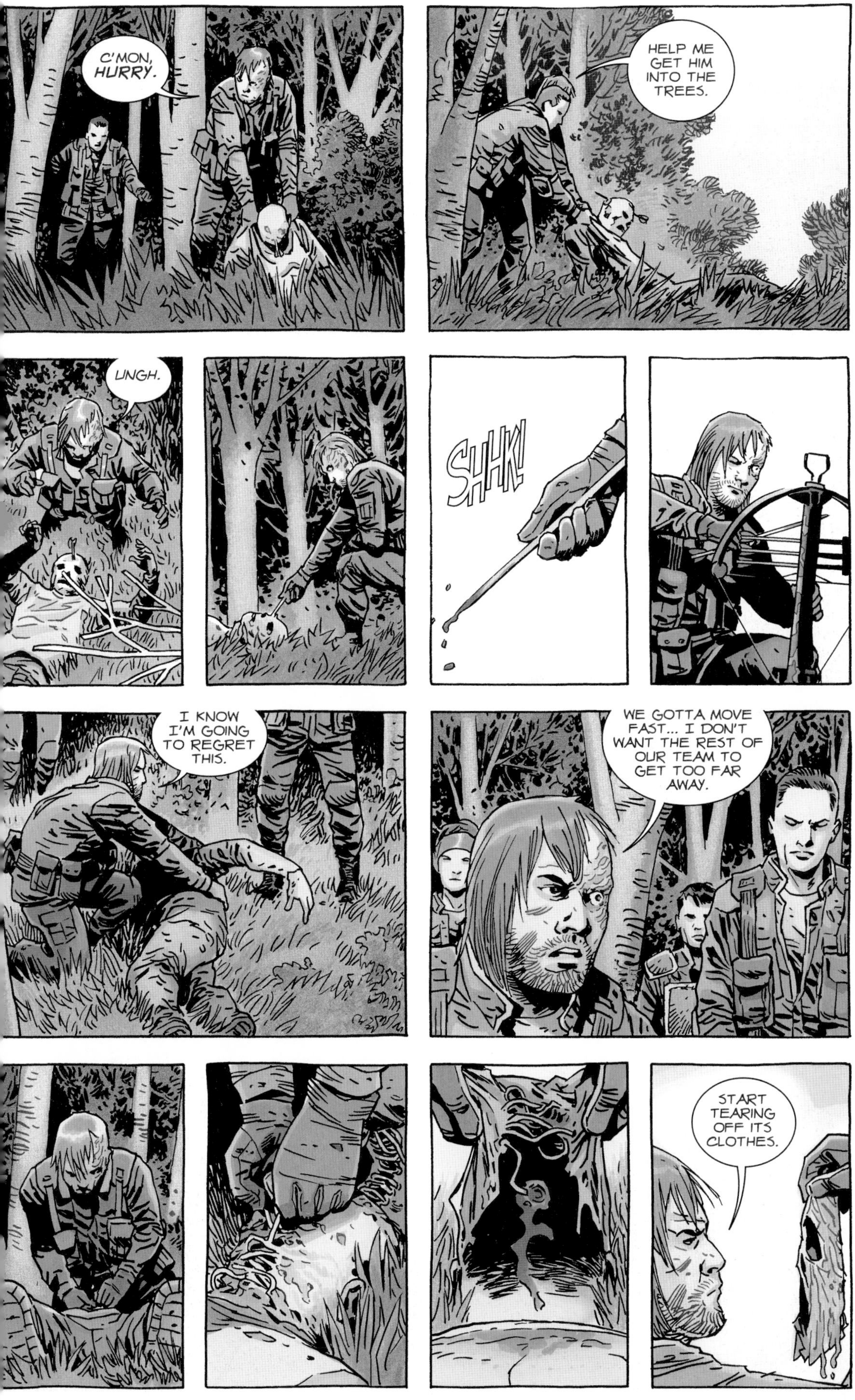
C'MON, HURRY.
HELP ME GET HIM INTO THE TREES.
UNGH.
SHHK!
I KNOW I'M GOING TO REGRET THIS.
WE GOTTA MOVE FAST... I DON'T WANT THE REST OF OUR TEAM TO GET TOO FAR AWAY.
START TEARING OFF ITS CLOTHES.

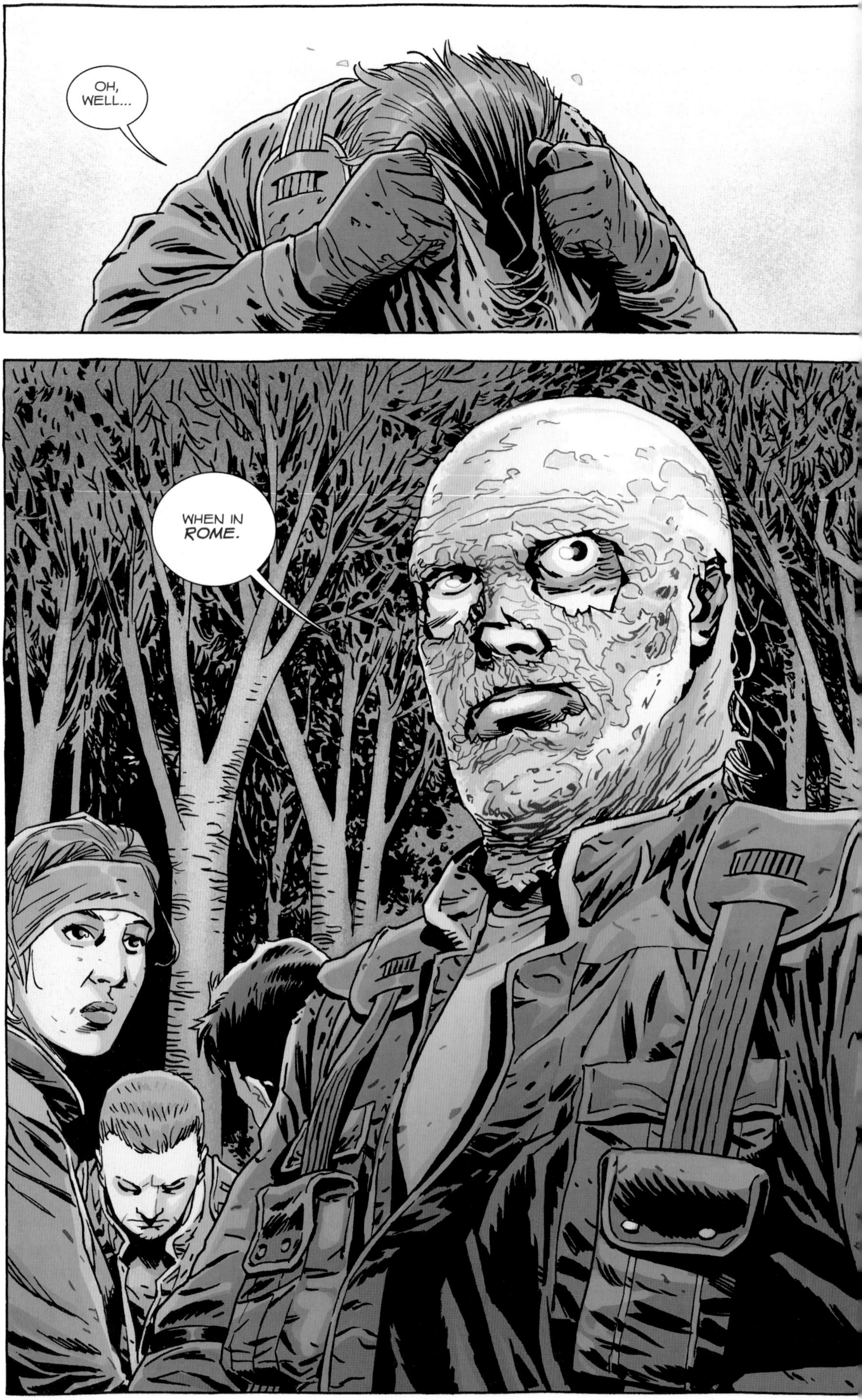
OH, WELL...
WHEN IN ROME.

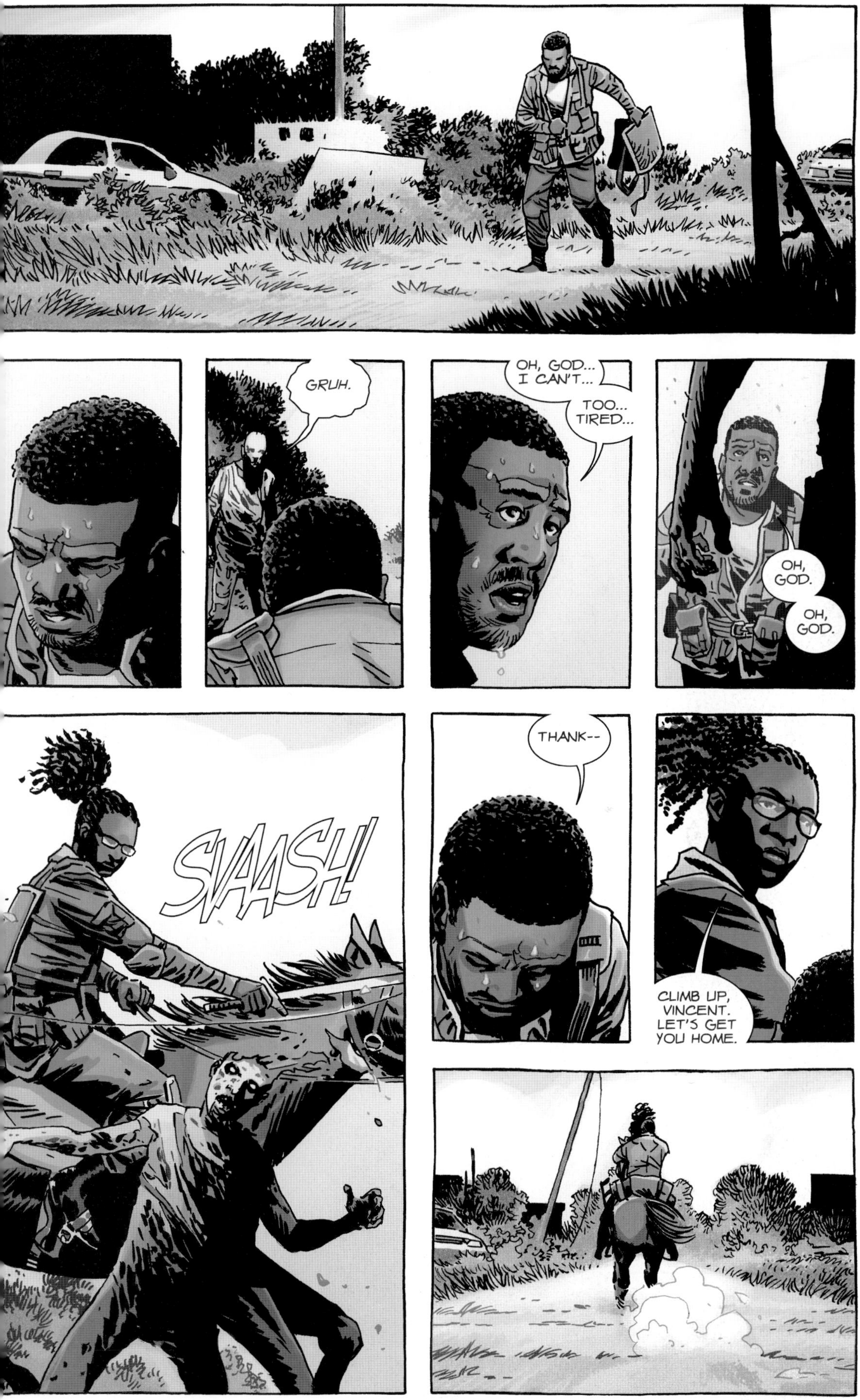
GRUH.
OH, GOD... I CAN'T...
TOO... TIRED...
OH, GOD.
OH, GOD.
SVAASH!
THANK--
CLIMB UP, VINCENT. LET'S GET YOU HOME.

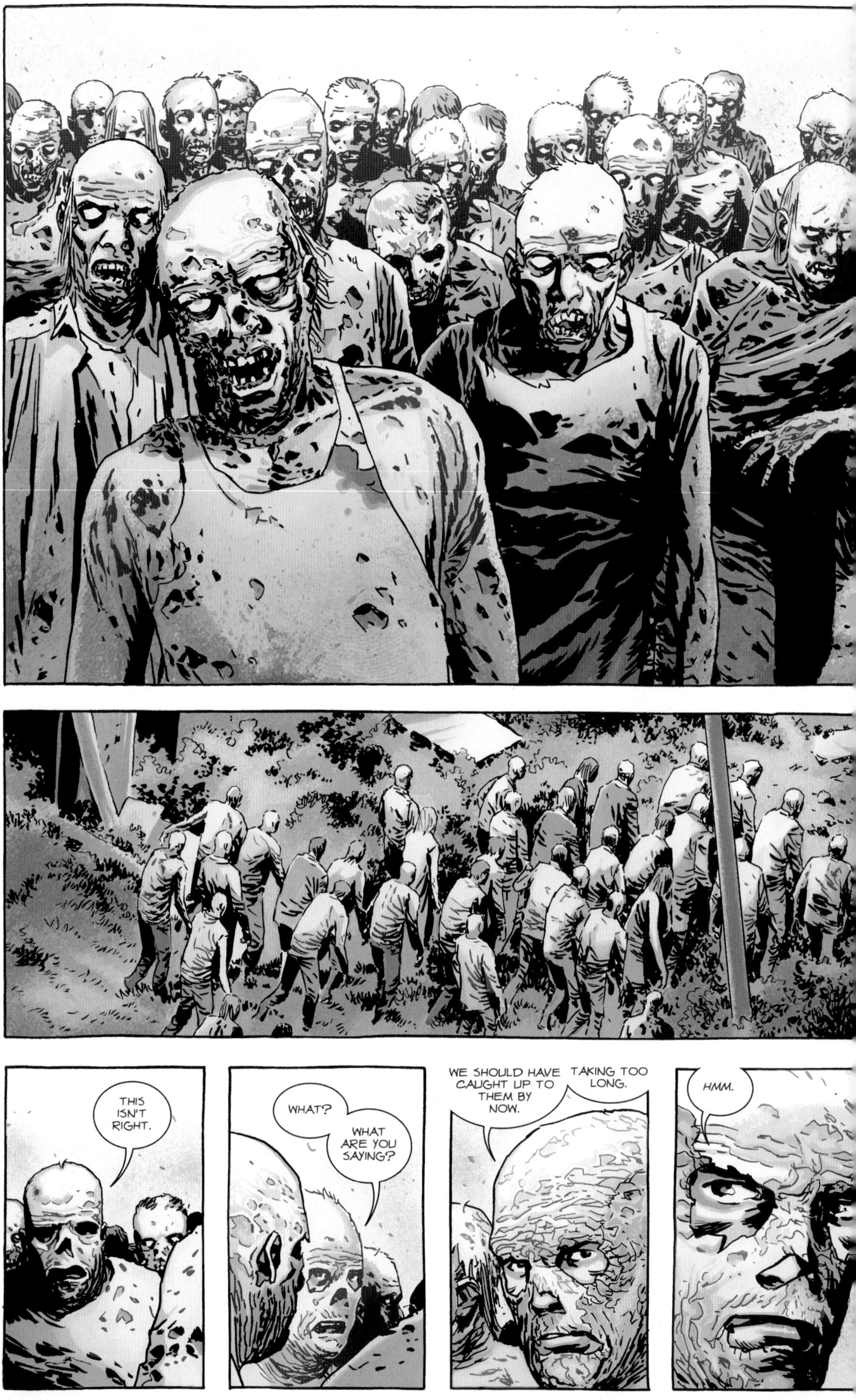
THIS ISN'T RIGHT.
WHAT?
WHAT ARE YOU SAYING?
WE SHOULD HAVE CAUGHT UP TO THEM BY NOW.
TAKING TOO LONG.
HMM.

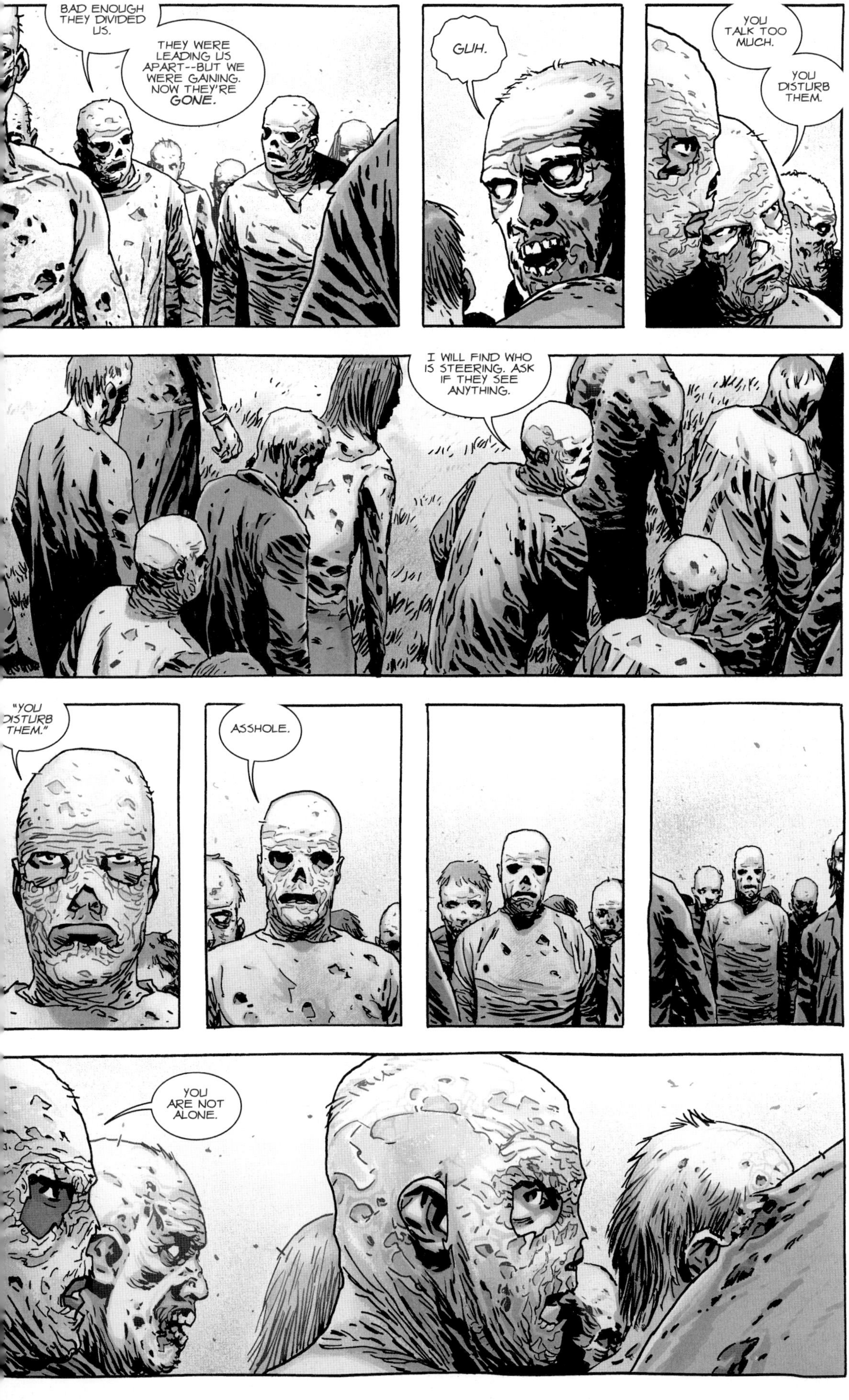
BAD ENOUGH THEY DIVIDED US.
THEY WERE LEADING US APART--BUT WE WERE GAINING. NOW THEY'RE GONE.
GUH.
YOU TALK TOO MUCH.
YOU DISTURB THEM.
I WILL FIND WHO IS STEERING. ASK IF THEY SEE ANYTHING.
"YOU DISTURB THEM."
ASSHOLE.
YOU ARE NOT ALONE.

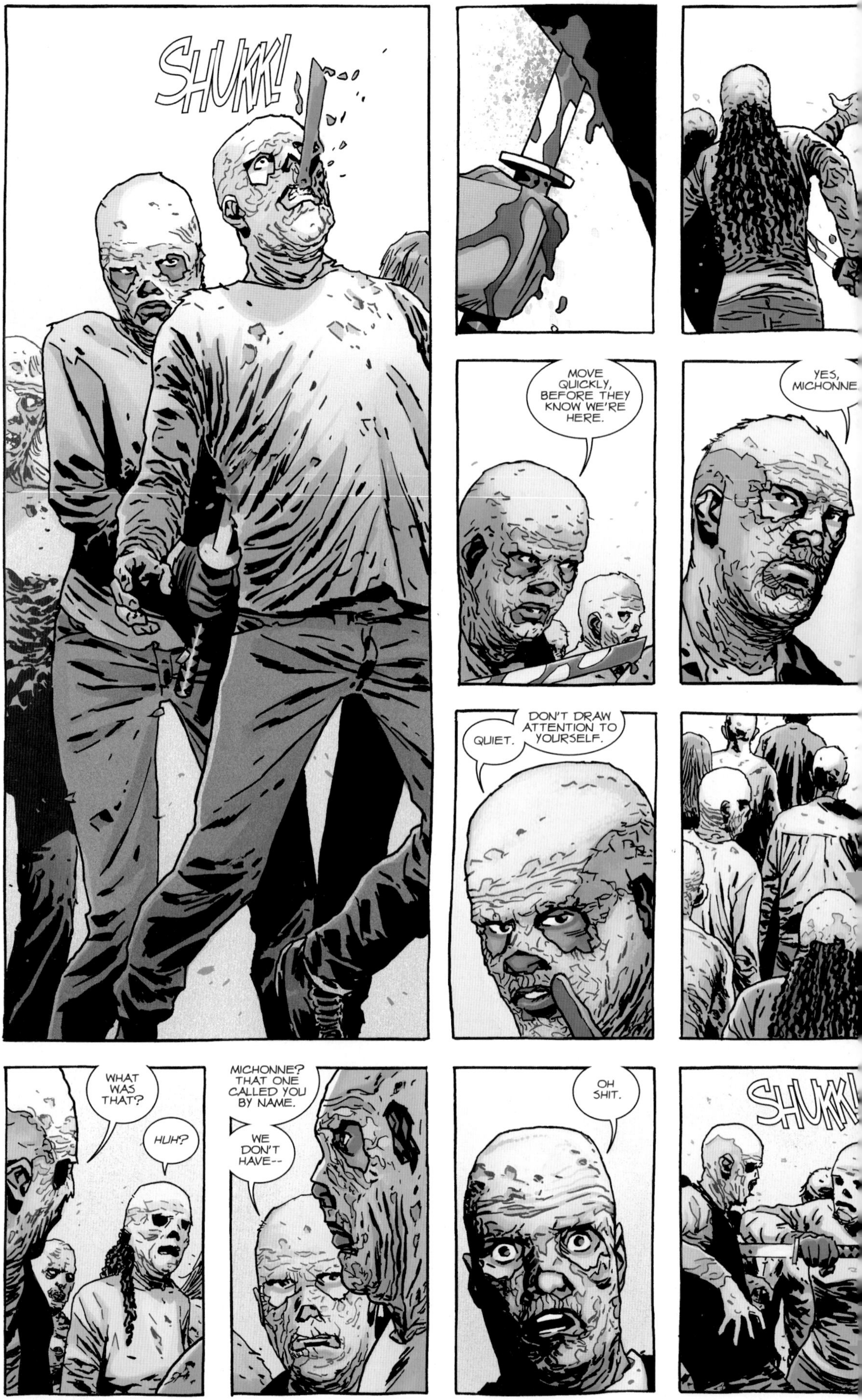
SHUKK!
MOVE QUICKLY, BEFORE THEY KNOW WE'RE HERE.
YES, MICHONNE.
QUIET.
DON'T DRAW ATTENTION TO YOURSELF.
WHAT WAS THAT?
HUH?
MICHONNE? THAT ONE CALLED YOU BY NAME.
WE DON'T HAVE--
OH SHIT.
SHUKK!

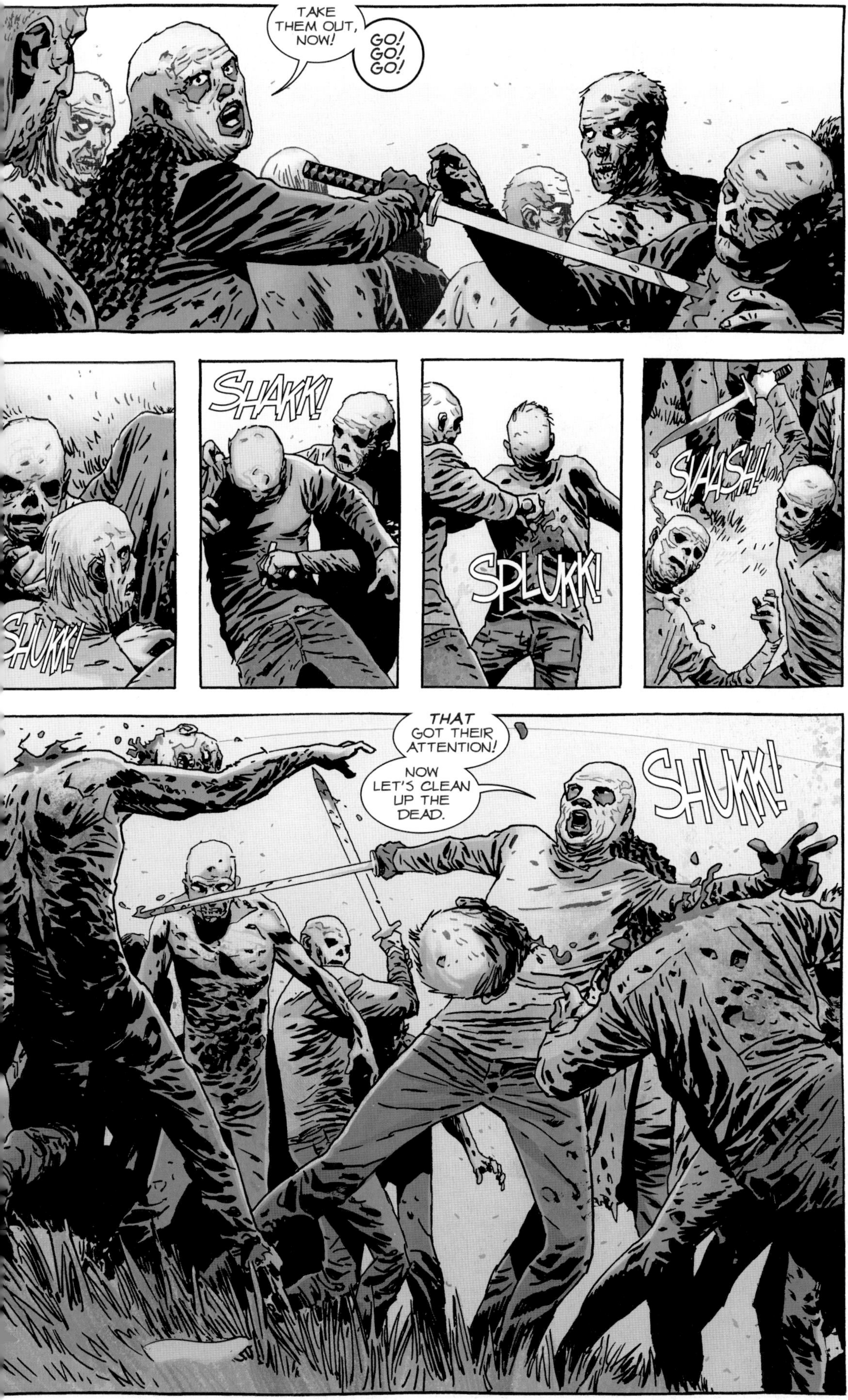
TAKE THEM OUT, NOW!
GO! GO! GO!
SHUKK!
SHAKK!
SPLUKK!
SLAASH!
THAT GOT THEIR ATTENTION!
NOW LET'S CLEAN UP THE DEAD.
SHUKK!

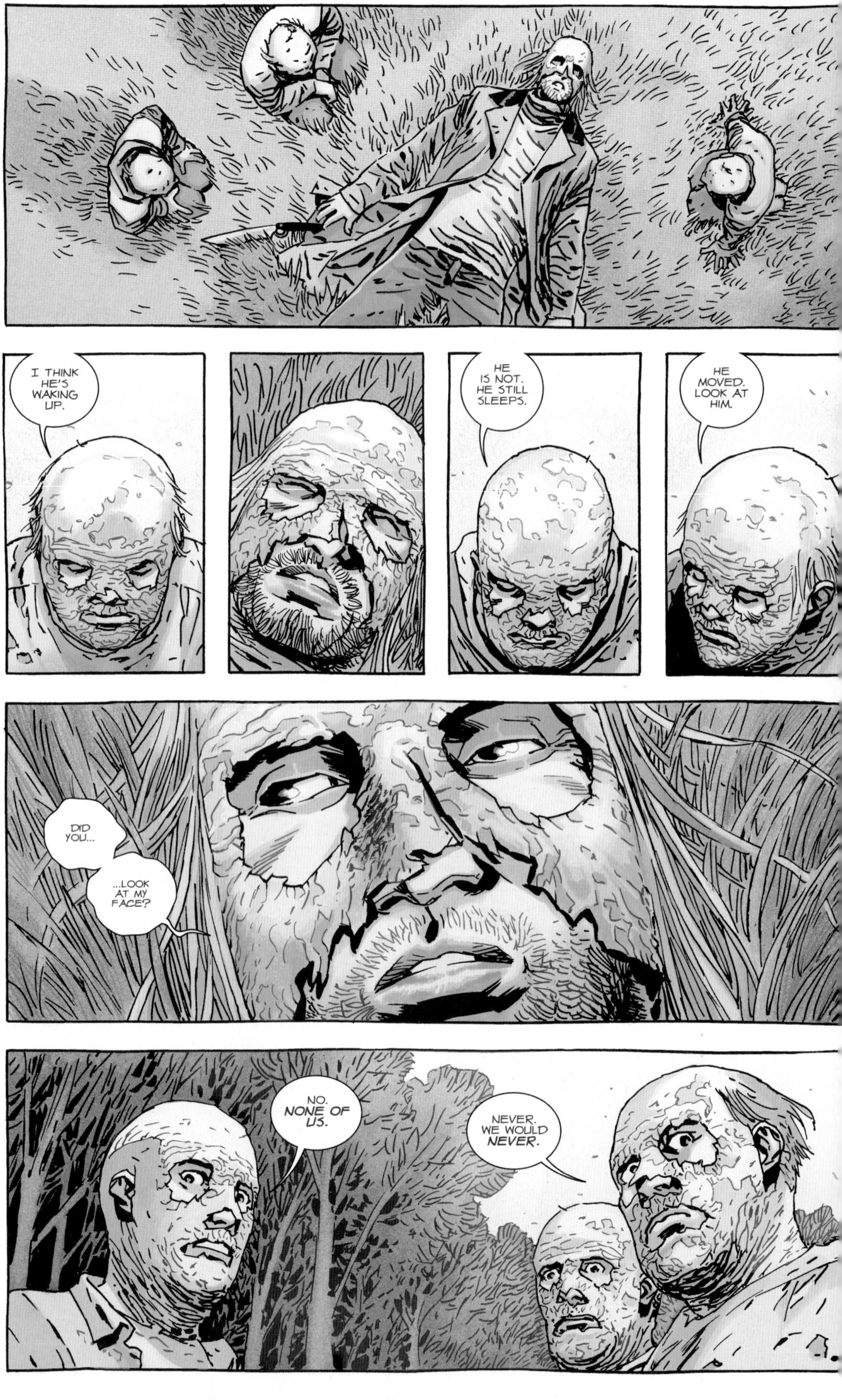

I THINK HE'S WAKING UP.
HE IS NOT. HE STILL SLEEPS.
HE MOVED. LOOK AT HIM.
DID YOU...
...LOOK AT MY FACE?
NO. NONE OF US.
NEVER. WE WOULD NEVER.

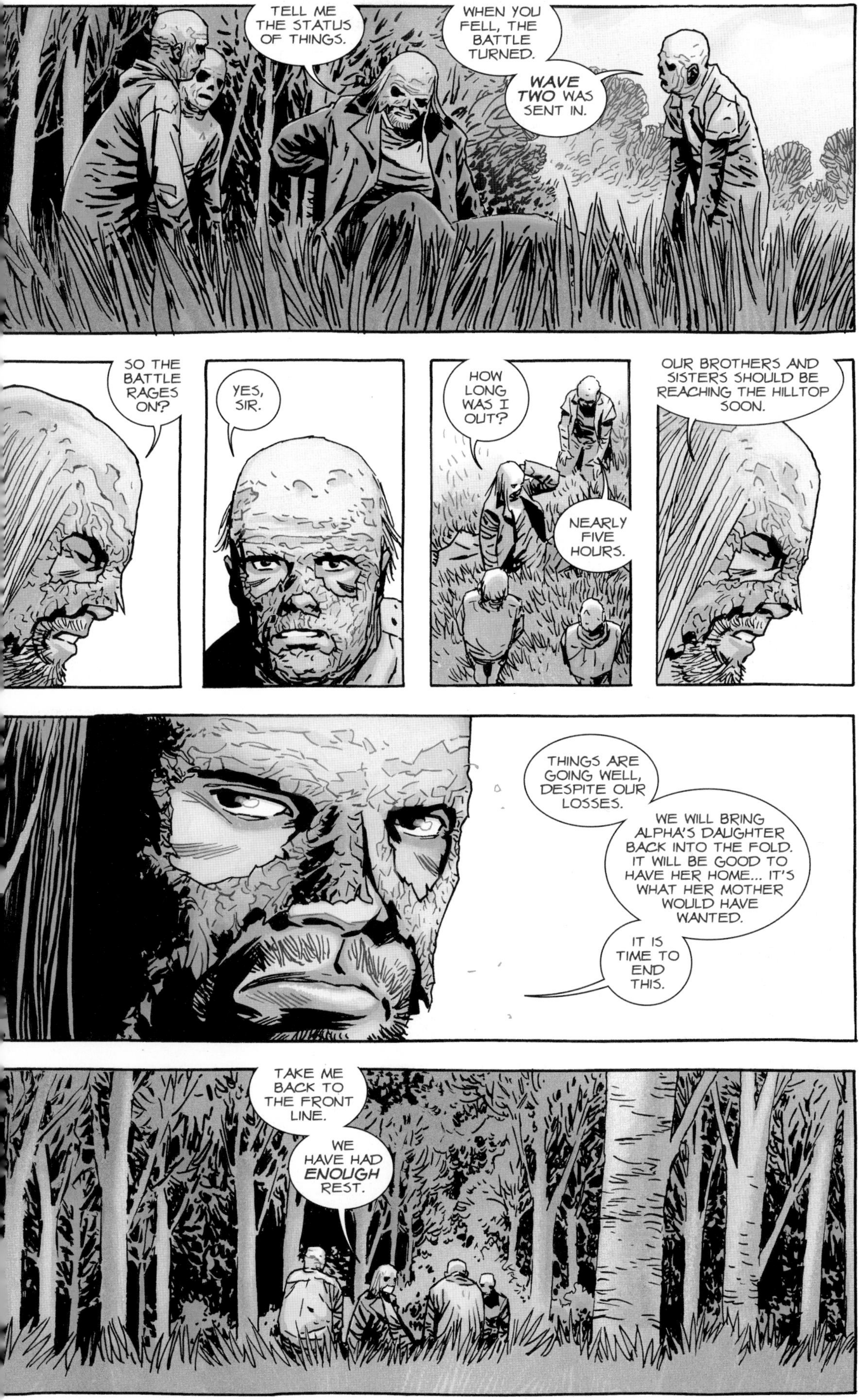
TELL ME THE STATUS OF THINGS.
WHEN YOU FELL, THE BATTLE TURNED.
*WAVE TWO* WAS SENT IN.
SO THE BATTLE RAGES ON?
YES, SIR.
HOW LONG WAS I OUT?
NEARLY FIVE HOURS.
OUR BROTHERS AND SISTERS SHOULD BE REACHING THE HILLTOP SOON.
THINGS ARE GOING WELL, DESPITE OUR LOSSES.
WE WILL BRING ALPHA'S DAUGHTER BACK INTO THE FOLD. IT WILL BE GOOD TO HAVE HER HOME... IT'S WHAT HER MOTHER WOULD HAVE WANTED.
IT IS TIME TO END THIS.
TAKE ME BACK TO THE FRONT LINE.
WE HAVE HAD *ENOUGH* REST.

I KNOW THIS BRIDGE.

THE HILLTOP IS CLOSE.

VERY GOOD. BE READY.

WE ARE READY.

WE A ARE

WHAT HAPPENED TO YOU?

RICK SENT ME TO THE SANCTUARY... TO ASK THE SAVIORS FOR HELP AGAINST THE WHISPERERS.

THEY TOOK MY HORSE.

RICK'S NOT GOING TO BE HAPPY ABOUT THAT.

NO... SEEMS ONE WAR MAY BE BEGINNING BEFORE ANOTHER ENDS.

YOU'VE BEEN BUSY.

JUST DOING MY PART. WHAT LITTLE I CAN.

I HEAR YOU THERE. WE'RE WELL-STOCKED?

YES... AND BETTER STOCKED BY THE MINUTE.

LET'S HO WE DON NEED I

YOU WALK A HELL OF A LOT FASTER THAN I THOUGHT YOU COULD, VINCENT.

FUCK.

TOO LATE

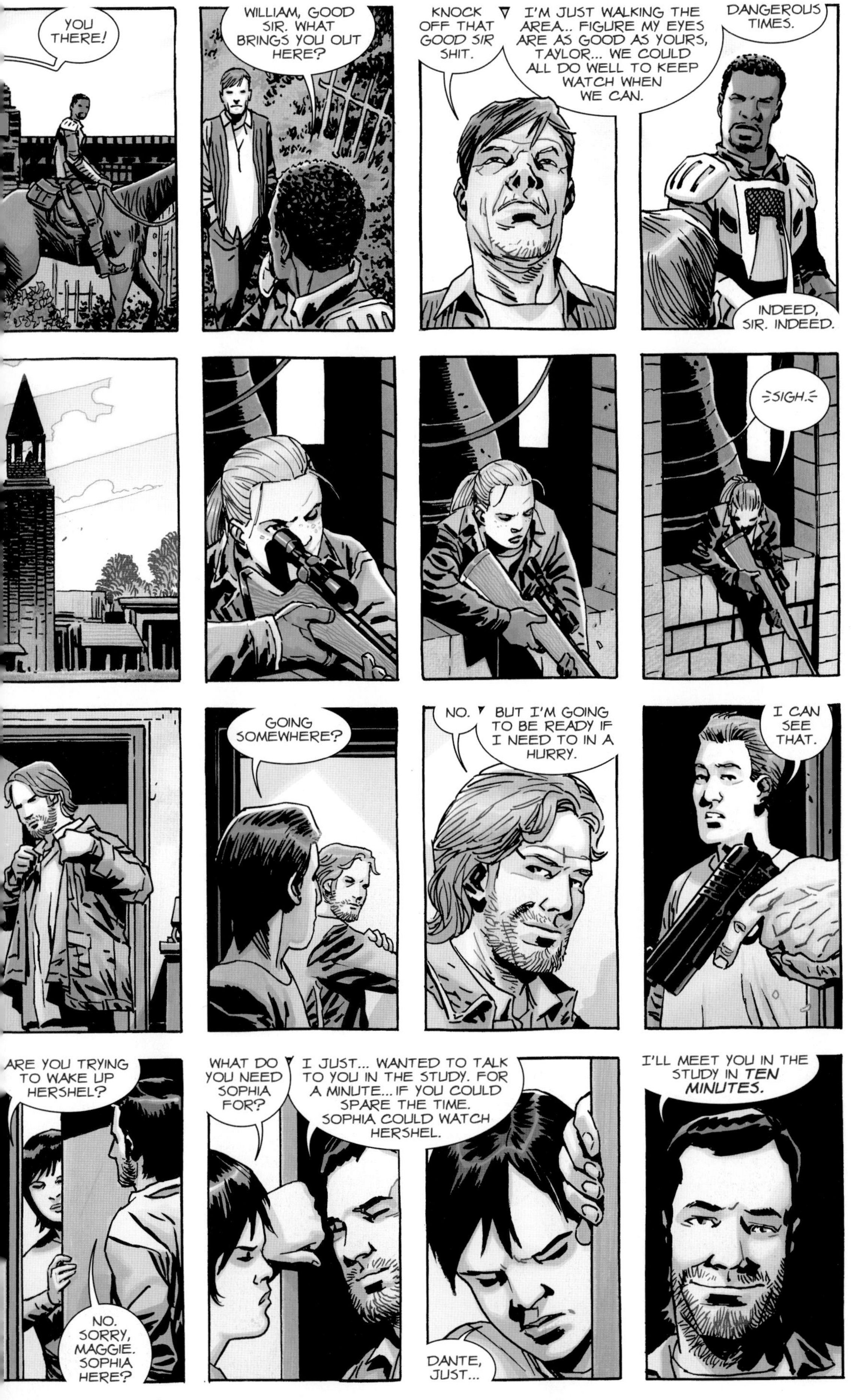

YOU THERE!
WILLIAM, GOOD SIR. WHAT BRINGS YOU OUT HERE?
KNOCK OFF THAT GOOD SIR SHIT.
I'M JUST WALKING THE AREA... FIGURE MY EYES ARE AS GOOD AS YOURS, TAYLOR... WE COULD ALL DO WELL TO KEEP WATCH WHEN WE CAN.
DANGEROUS TIMES.
INDEED, SIR. INDEED.
SIGH.
GOING SOMEWHERE?
NO.
BUT I'M GOING TO BE READY IF I NEED TO IN A HURRY.
I CAN SEE THAT.
ARE YOU TRYING TO WAKE UP HERSHEL?
NO. SORRY, MAGGIE. SOPHIA HERE?
WHAT DO YOU NEED SOPHIA FOR?
I JUST... WANTED TO TALK TO YOU IN THE STUDY. FOR A MINUTE... IF YOU COULD SPARE THE TIME. SOPHIA COULD WATCH HERSHEL.
DANTE, JUST...
I'LL MEET YOU IN THE STUDY IN TEN MINUTES.

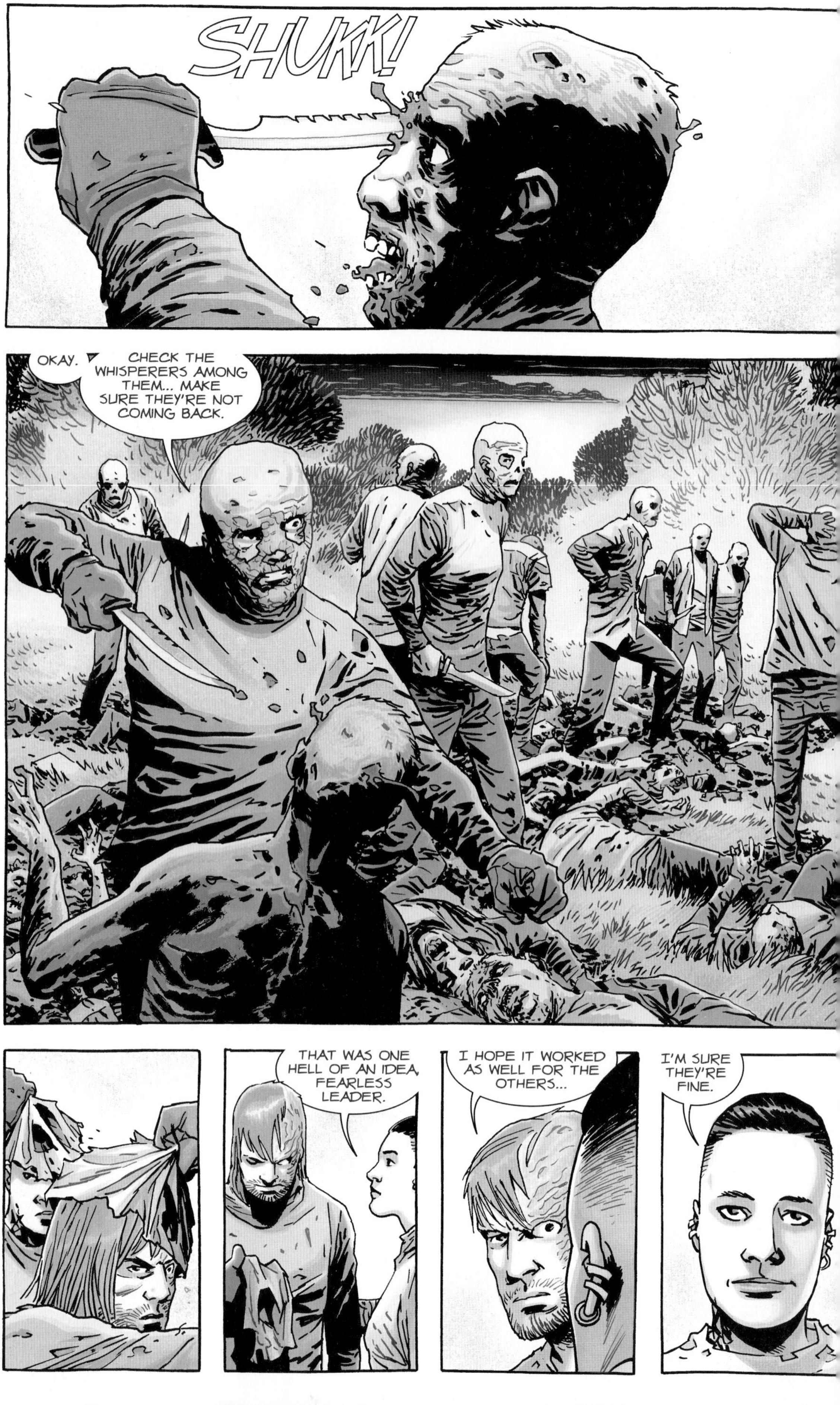
SHUKK!
OKAY.
CHECK THE WHISPERERS AMONG THEM... MAKE SURE THEY'RE NOT COMING BACK.
THAT WAS ONE HELL OF AN IDEA, FEARLESS LEADER.
I HOPE IT WORKED AS WELL FOR THE OTHERS...
I'M SURE THEY'RE FINE.

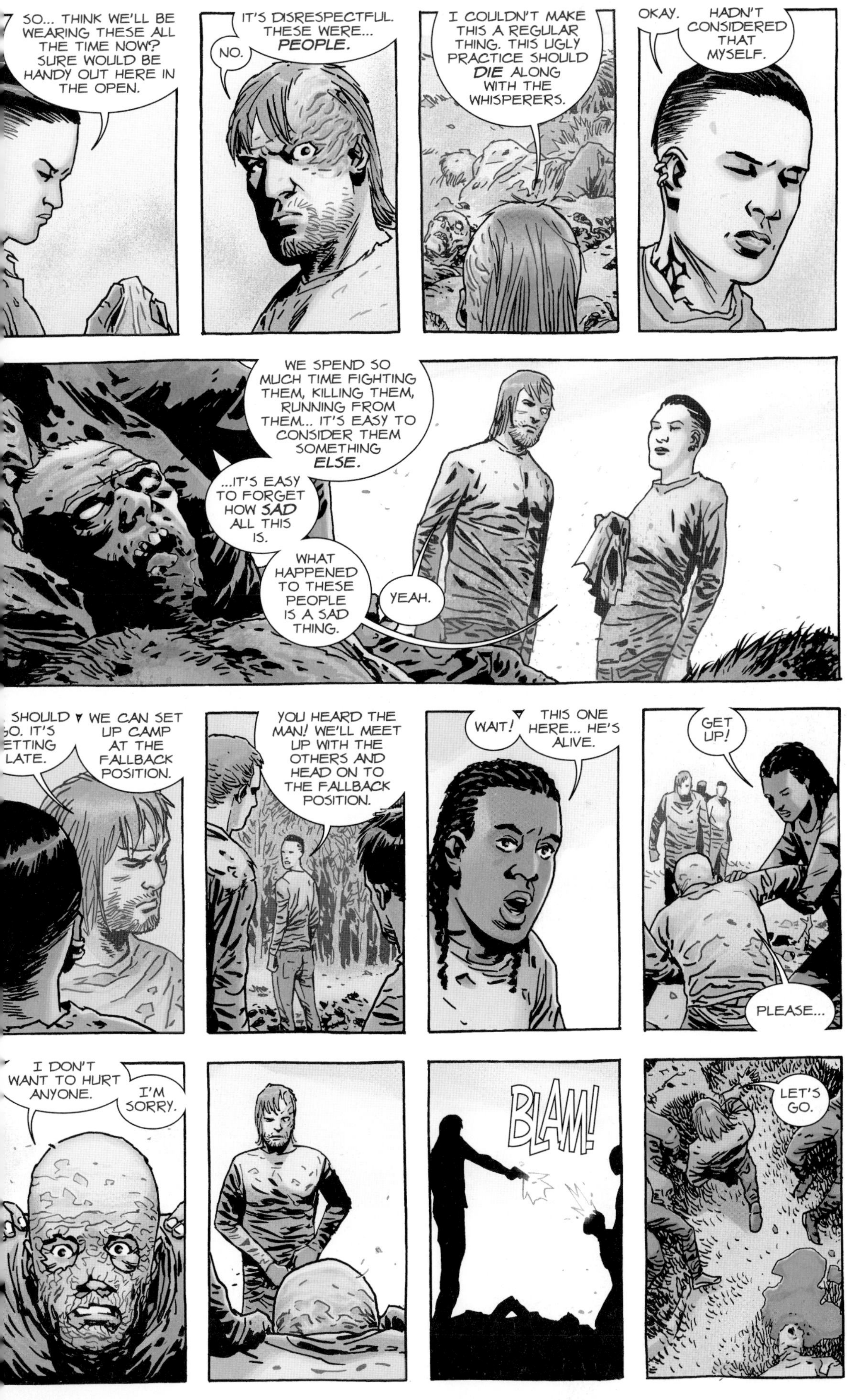

SO... THINK WE'LL BE WEARING THESE ALL THE TIME NOW? SURE WOULD BE HANDY OUT HERE IN THE OPEN.
NO.
IT'S DISRESPECTFUL. THESE WERE... PEOPLE.
I COULDN'T MAKE THIS A REGULAR THING. THIS UGLY PRACTICE SHOULD DIE ALONG WITH THE WHISPERERS.
OKAY.
HADN'T CONSIDERED THAT MYSELF.
WE SPEND SO MUCH TIME FIGHTING THEM, KILLING THEM, RUNNING FROM THEM... IT'S EASY TO CONSIDER THEM SOMETHING ELSE.
...IT'S EASY TO FORGET HOW SAD ALL THIS IS.
WHAT HAPPENED TO THESE PEOPLE IS A SAD THING.
YEAH.
SHOULD GO. IT'S ETTING LATE.
WE CAN SET UP CAMP AT THE FALLBACK POSITION.
YOU HEARD THE MAN! WE'LL MEET UP WITH THE OTHERS AND HEAD ON TO THE FALLBACK POSITION.
WAIT!
THIS ONE HERE... HE'S ALIVE.
GET UP!
PLEASE...
I DON'T WANT TO HURT ANYONE.
I'M SORRY.
BLAM!
LET'S GO.

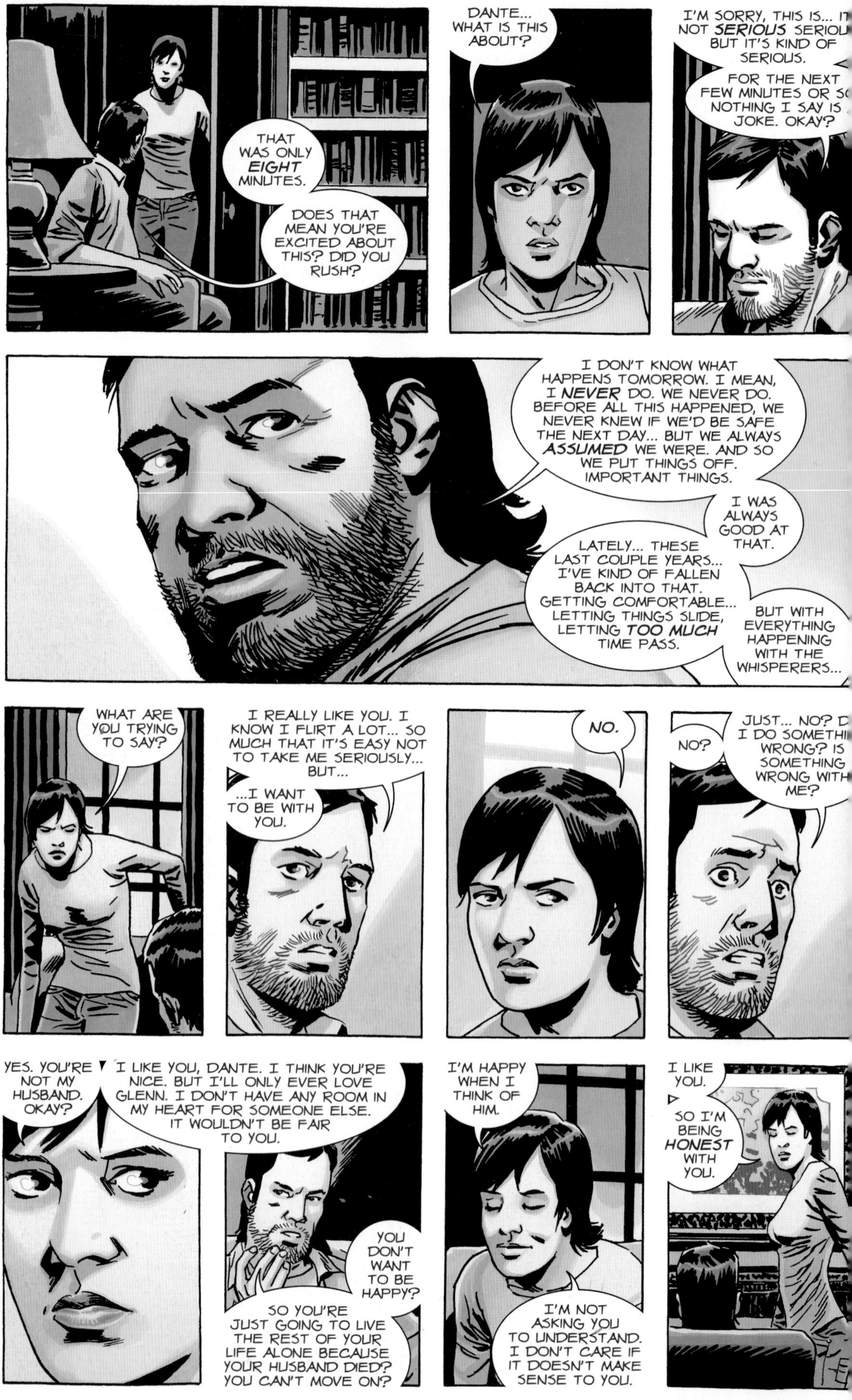
THAT WAS ONLY EIGHT MINUTES.
DOES THAT MEAN YOU'RE EXCITED ABOUT THIS? DID YOU RUSH?
DANTE... WHAT IS THIS ABOUT?
I'M SORRY, THIS IS... IT NOT SERIOUS SERIOU BUT IT'S KIND OF SERIOUS.
FOR THE NEXT FEW MINUTES OR SO NOTHING I SAY IS JOKE. OKAY?
I DON'T KNOW WHAT HAPPENS TOMORROW. I MEAN, I NEVER DO. WE NEVER DO. BEFORE ALL THIS HAPPENED, WE NEVER KNEW IF WE'D BE SAFE THE NEXT DAY... BUT WE ALWAYS ASSUMED WE WERE. AND SO WE PUT THINGS OFF. IMPORTANT THINGS.
I WAS ALWAYS GOOD AT THAT.
LATELY... THESE LAST COUPLE YEARS... I'VE KIND OF FALLEN BACK INTO THAT. GETTING COMFORTABLE... LETTING THINGS SLIDE, LETTING TOO MUCH TIME PASS.
BUT WITH EVERYTHING HAPPENING WITH THE WHISPERERS...
WHAT ARE YOU TRYING TO SAY?
I REALLY LIKE YOU. I KNOW I FLIRT A LOT... SO MUCH THAT IT'S EASY NOT TO TAKE ME SERIOUSLY... BUT...
...I WANT TO BE WITH YOU.
NO.
NO?
JUST... NO? DID I DO SOMETHING WRONG? IS SOMETHING WRONG WITH ME?
YES. YOU'RE NOT MY HUSBAND. OKAY?
I LIKE YOU, DANTE. I THINK YOU'RE NICE. BUT I'LL ONLY EVER LOVE GLENN. I DON'T HAVE ANY ROOM IN MY HEART FOR SOMEONE ELSE. IT WOULDN'T BE FAIR TO YOU.
YOU DON'T WANT TO BE HAPPY?
SO YOU'RE JUST GOING TO LIVE THE REST OF YOUR LIFE ALONE BECAUSE YOUR HUSBAND DIED? YOU CAN'T MOVE ON?
I'M HAPPY WHEN I THINK OF HIM.
I'M NOT ASKING YOU TO UNDERSTAND. I DON'T CARE IF IT DOESN'T MAKE SENSE TO YOU.
I LIKE YOU.
SO I'M BEING HONEST WITH YOU.

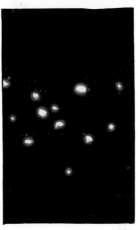

WHAT
IN--?

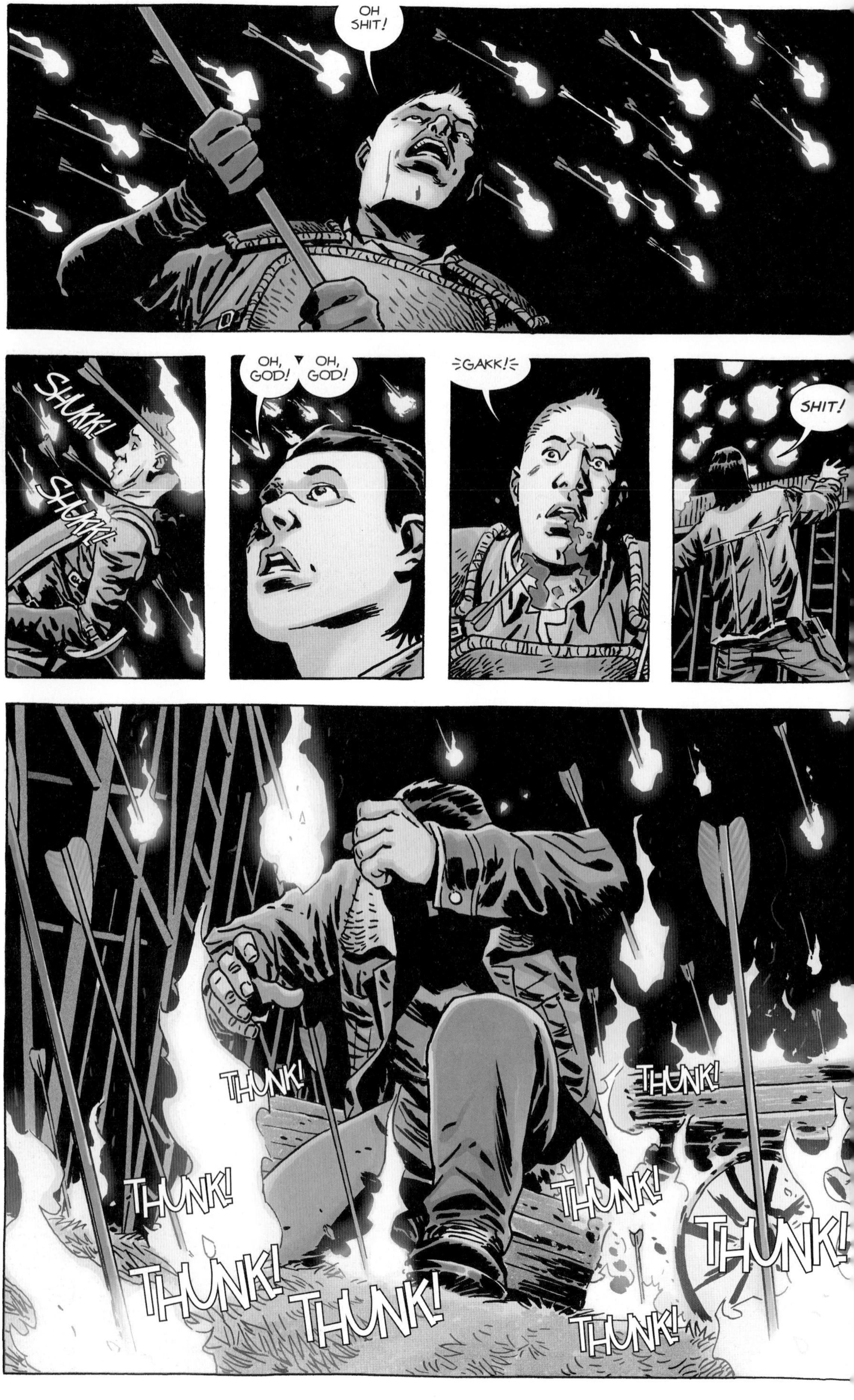
OH SHIT!
SHUKK!
SHUKK!
OH, GOD!
OH, GOD!
GAKK!
SHIT!
THUNK!
THUNK!
THUNK!
THUNK!
THUNK!
THUNK!
THUNK!
THUNK!

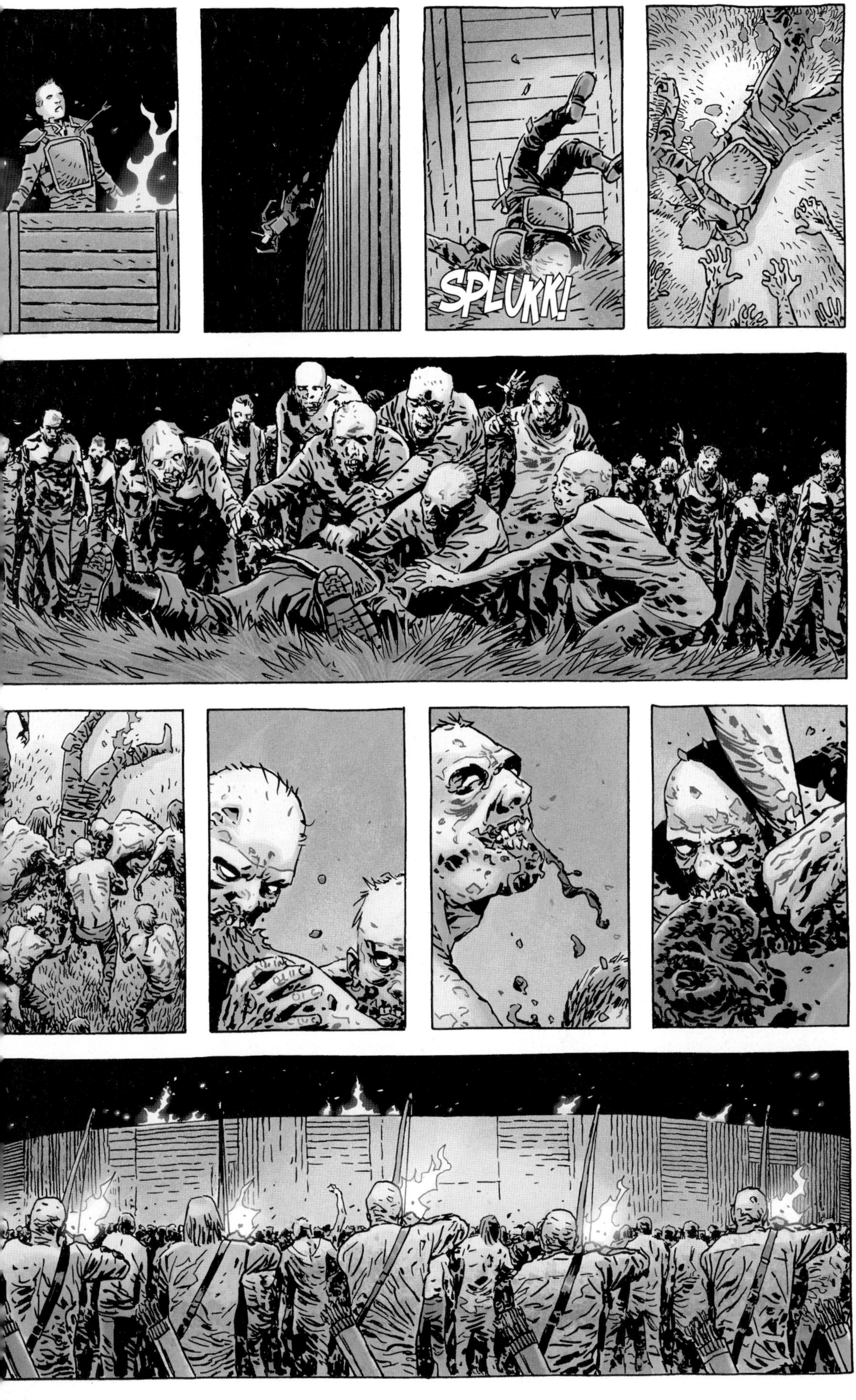
SPLUKK!

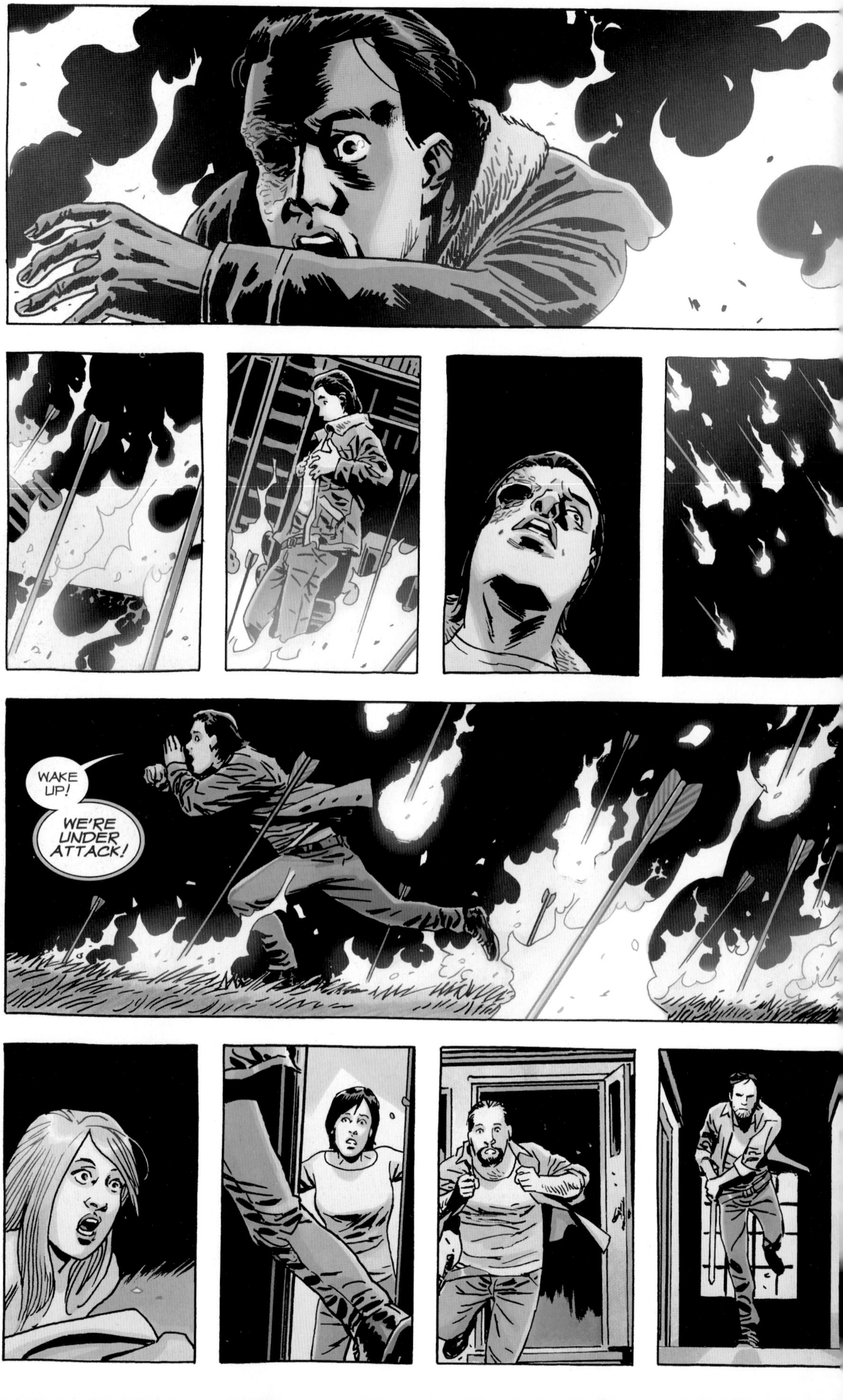
WAKE UP!
WE'RE UNDER ATTACK!

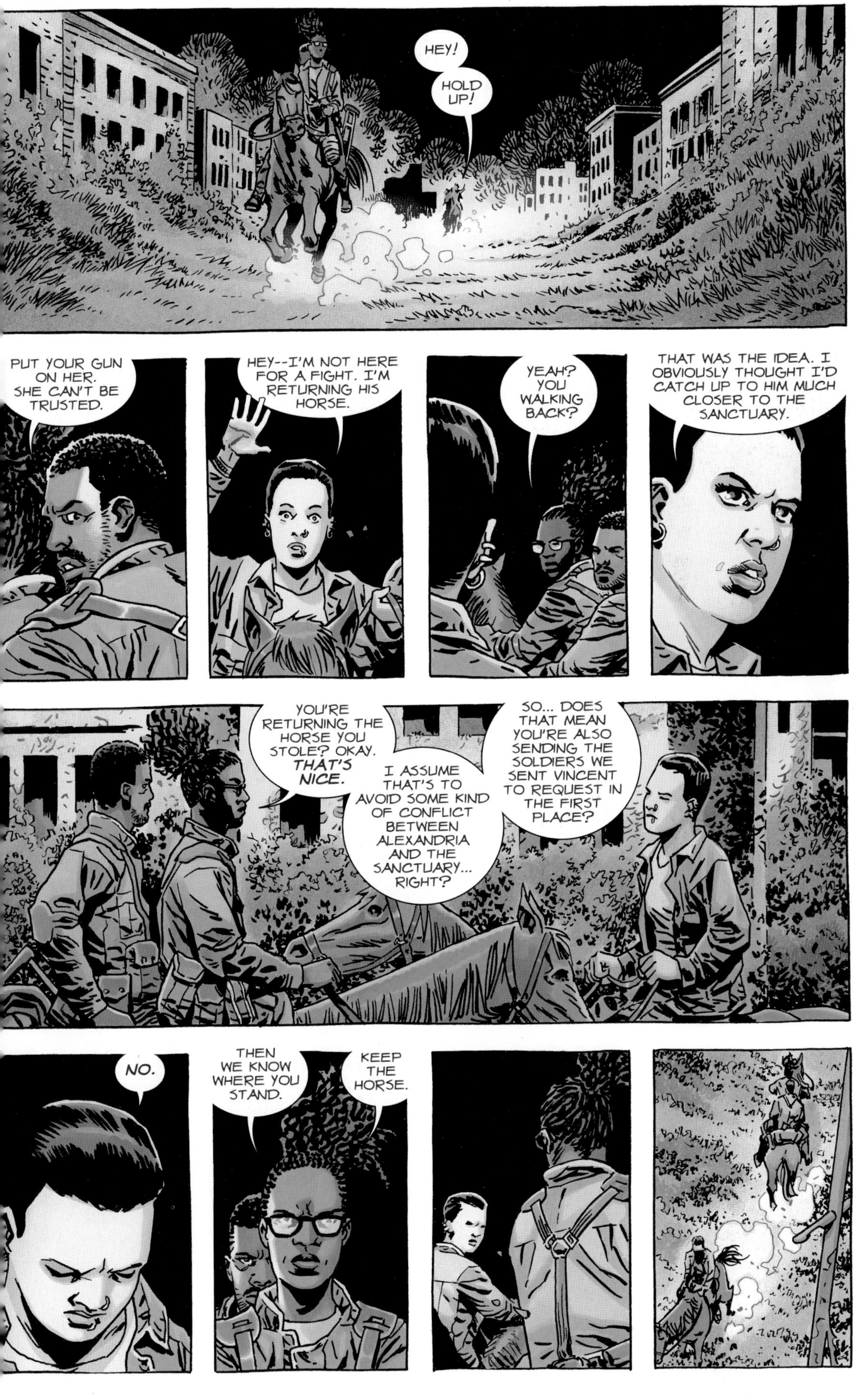
HEY!
HOLD UP!
PUT YOUR GUN ON HER. SHE CAN'T BE TRUSTED.
HEY--I'M NOT HERE FOR A FIGHT. I'M RETURNING HIS HORSE.
YEAH? YOU WALKING BACK?
THAT WAS THE IDEA. I OBVIOUSLY THOUGHT I'D CATCH UP TO HIM MUCH CLOSER TO THE SANCTUARY.
YOU'RE RETURNING THE HORSE YOU STOLE? OKAY. THAT'S NICE.
I ASSUME THAT'S TO AVOID SOME KIND OF CONFLICT BETWEEN ALEXANDRIA AND THE SANCTUARY... RIGHT?
SO... DOES THAT MEAN YOU'RE ALSO SENDING THE SOLDIERS WE SENT VINCENT TO REQUEST IN THE FIRST PLACE?
NO.
THEN WE KNOW WHERE YOU STAND.
KEEP THE HORSE.

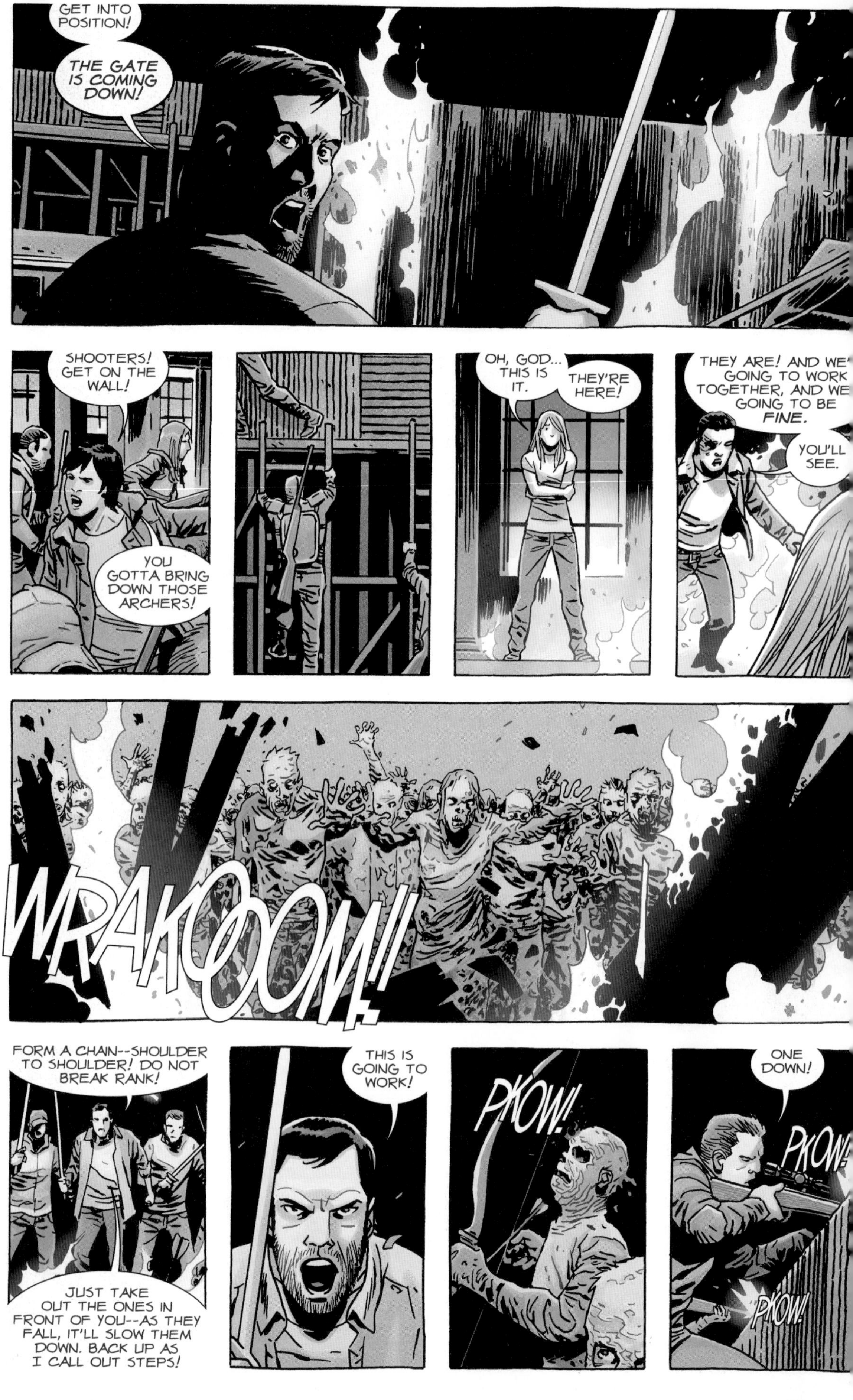
GET INTO POSITION!
THE GATE IS COMING DOWN!
SHOOTERS! GET ON THE WALL!
YOU GOTTA BRING DOWN THOSE ARCHERS!
OH, GOD... THIS IS IT.
THEY'RE HERE!
THEY ARE! AND WE' GOING TO WORK TOGETHER, AND WE GOING TO BE FINE.
YOU'LL SEE.
WRAKOOOM!!
FORM A CHAIN--SHOULDER TO SHOULDER! DO NOT BREAK RANK!
JUST TAKE OUT THE ONES IN FRONT OF YOU--AS THEY FALL, IT'LL SLOW THEM DOWN. BACK UP AS I CALL OUT STEPS!
THIS IS GOING TO WORK!
PKOW!
ONE DOWN!
PKOW!
PKOW!

SHUKK!!

FIRE!

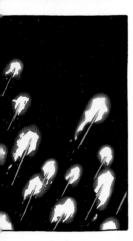

SHUKK!

THUNK!

THUNK! THUNK!

THUNK!

OH, GOD!

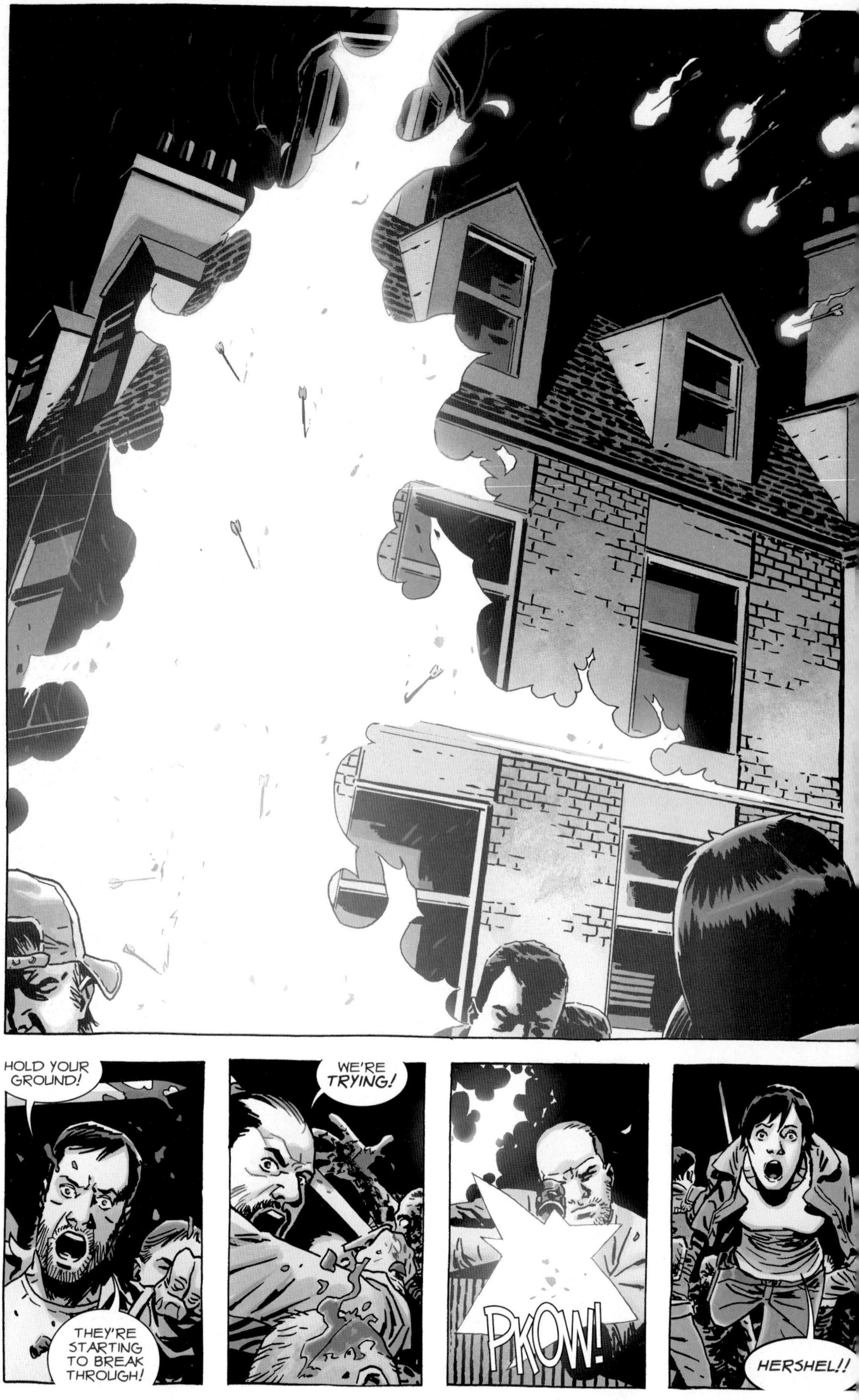
HOLD YOUR GROUND!
THEY'RE STARTING TO BREAK THROUGH!
WE'RE TRYING!
PKOW!
HERSHEL!!

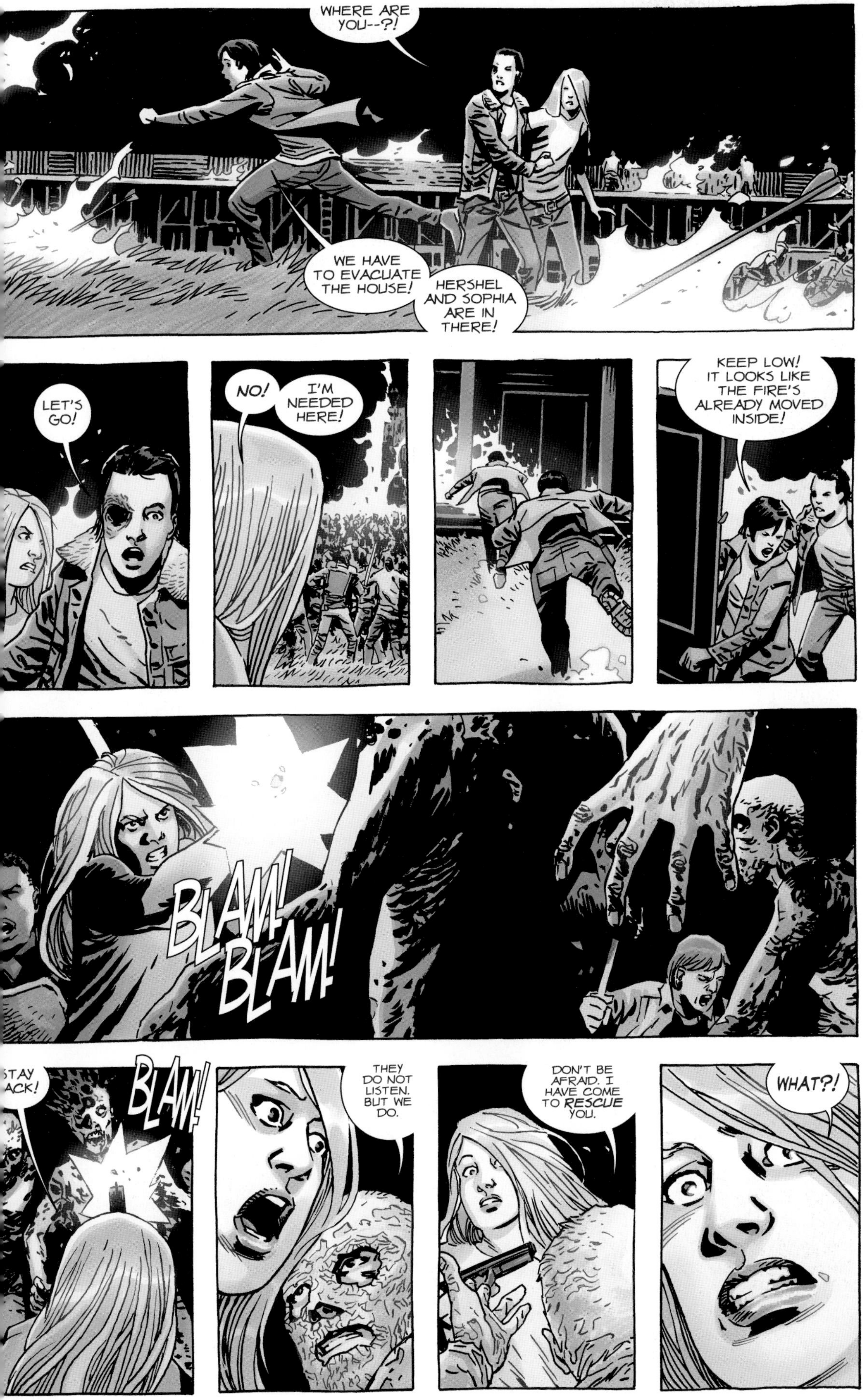
WHERE ARE YOU--?!
WE HAVE TO EVACUATE THE HOUSE!
HERSHEL AND SOPHIA ARE IN THERE!
LET'S GO!
NO!
I'M NEEDED HERE!
KEEP LOW! IT LOOKS LIKE THE FIRE'S ALREADY MOVED INSIDE!
BLAM! BLAM!
STAY BACK!
BLAM!
THEY DO NOT LISTEN. BUT WE DO.
DON'T BE AFRAID. I HAVE COME TO RESCUE YOU.
WHAT?!

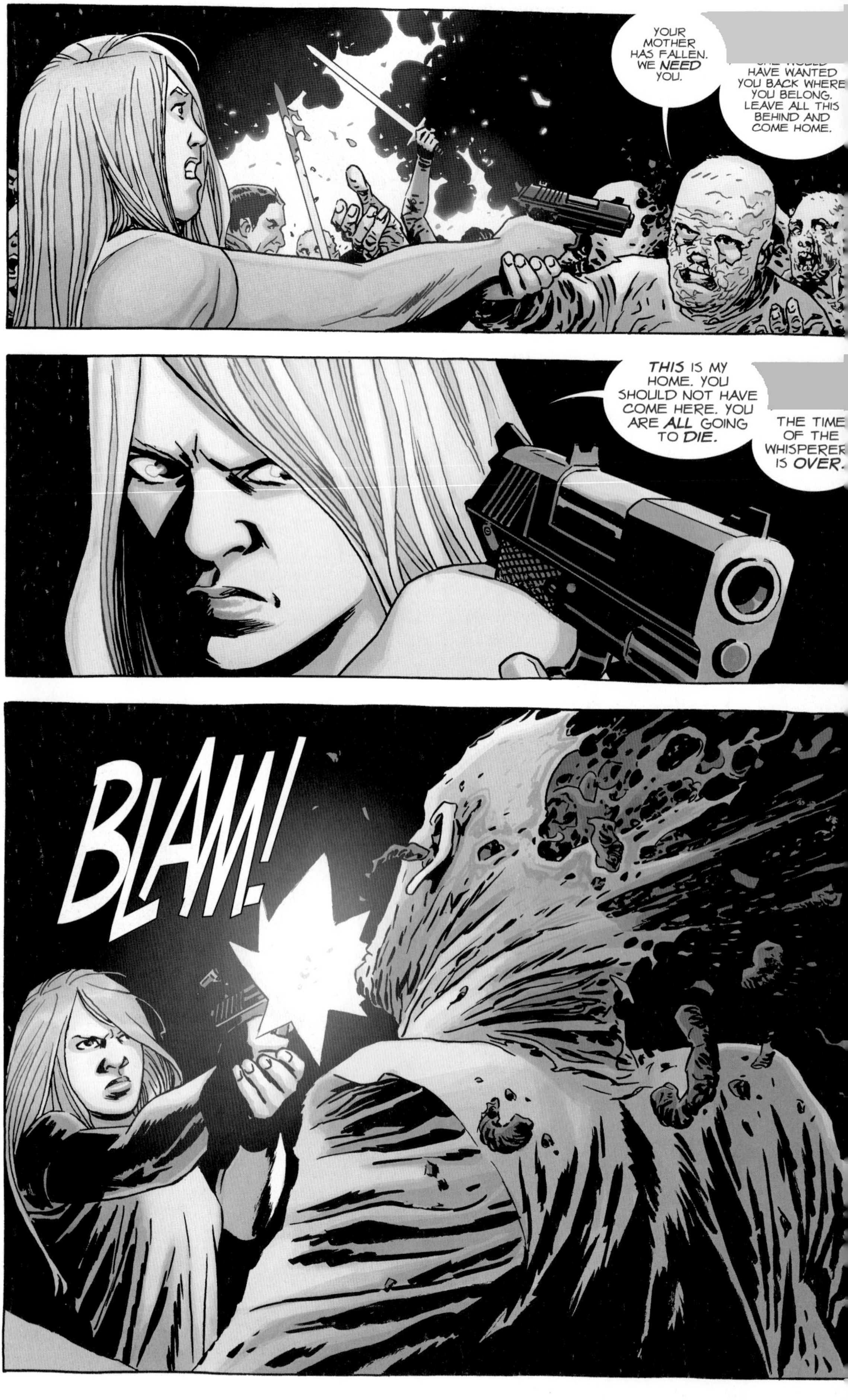

YOUR MOTHER HAS FALLEN. WE **NEED** YOU.
HAVE WANTED YOU BACK WHERE YOU BELONG. LEAVE ALL THIS BEHIND AND COME HOME.
***THIS*** IS MY HOME. YOU SHOULD NOT HAVE COME HERE. YOU ARE ***ALL*** GOING TO ***DIE.***
THE TIME OF THE WHISPERER IS ***OVER.***
BLAM!

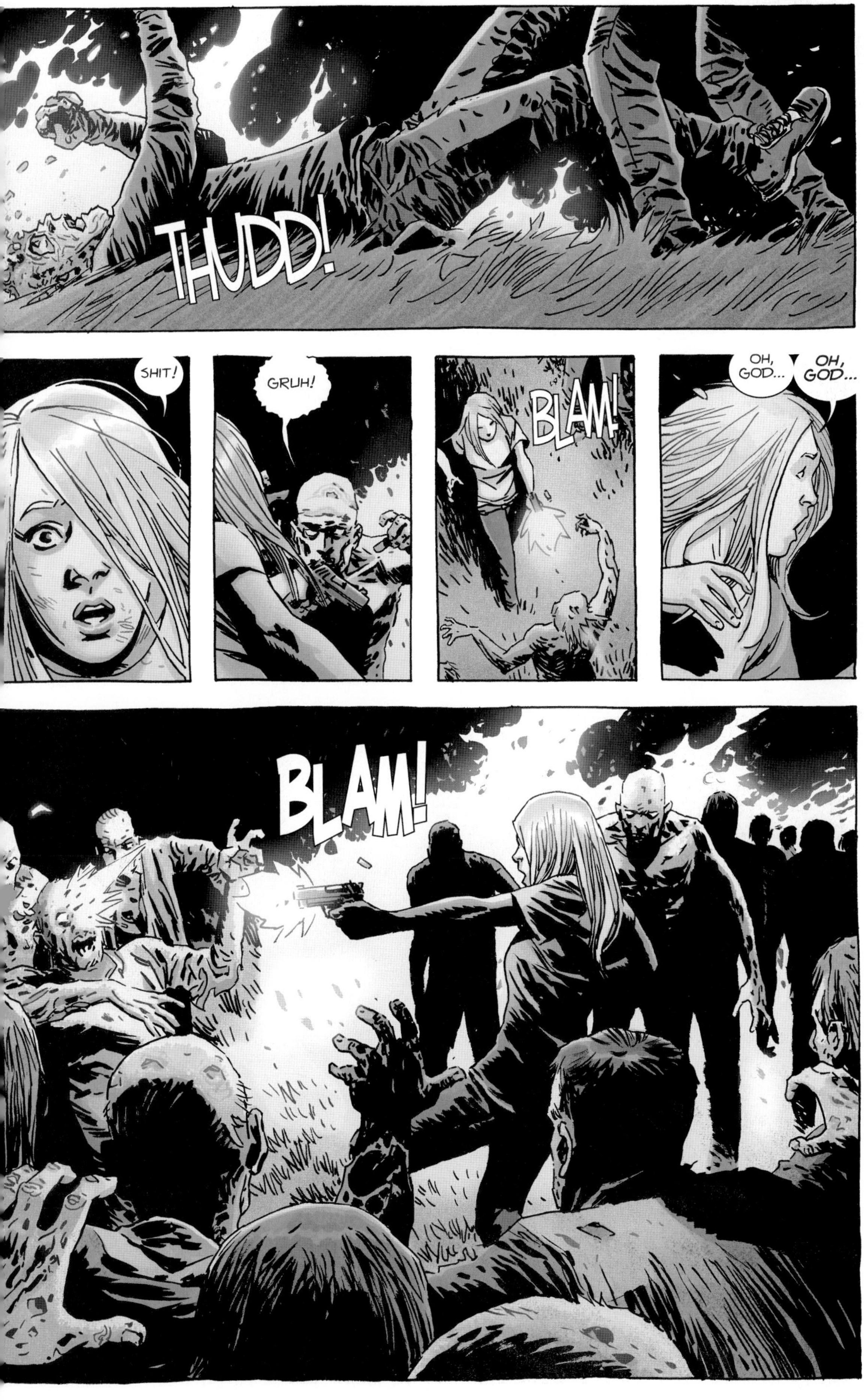
THUDD!
SHIT!
GRUH!
BLAM!
OH, GOD...
OH, GOD...
BLAM!

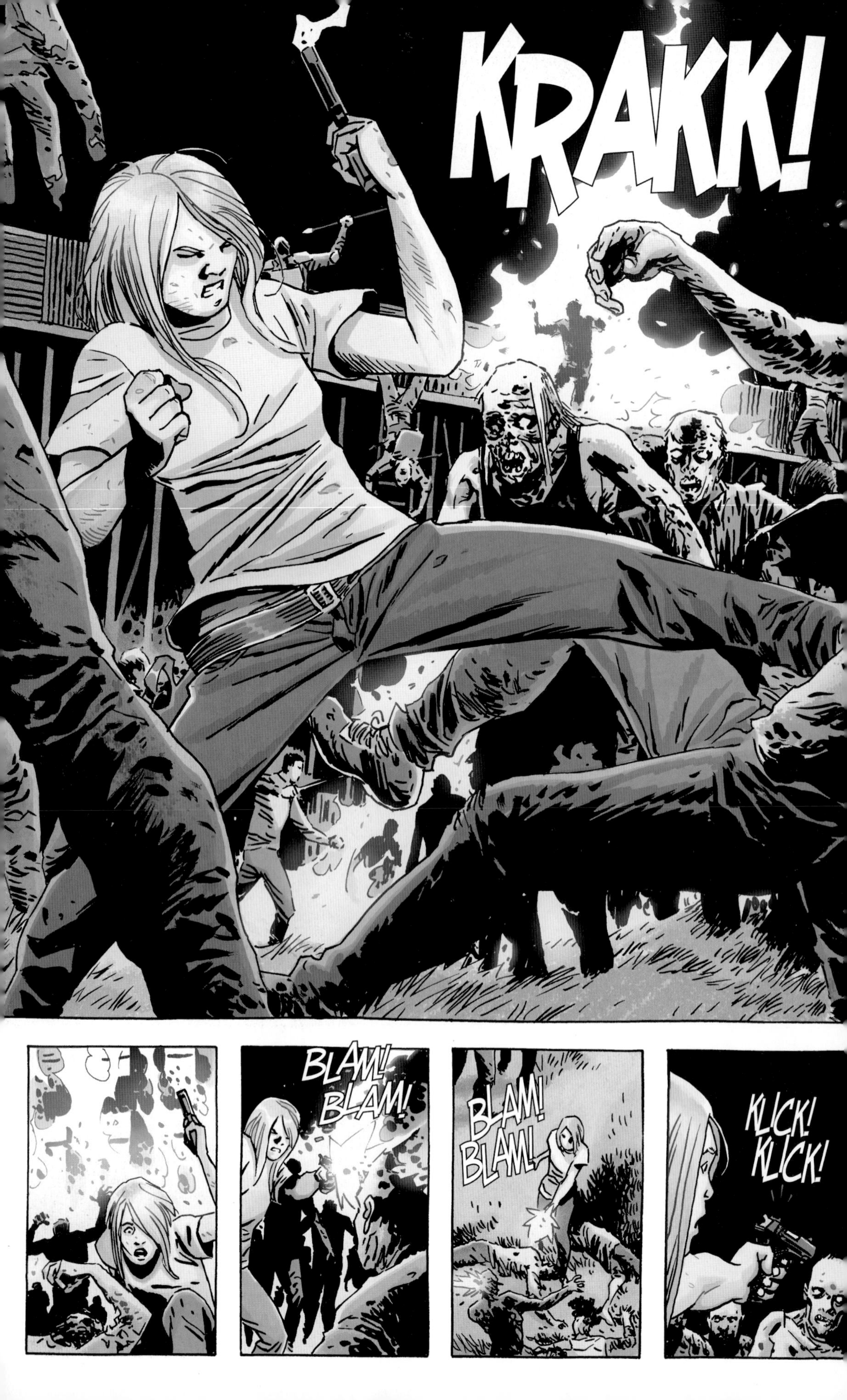
KRAKK!
BLAM! BLAM!
BLAM! BLAM!
KLICK! KLICK!

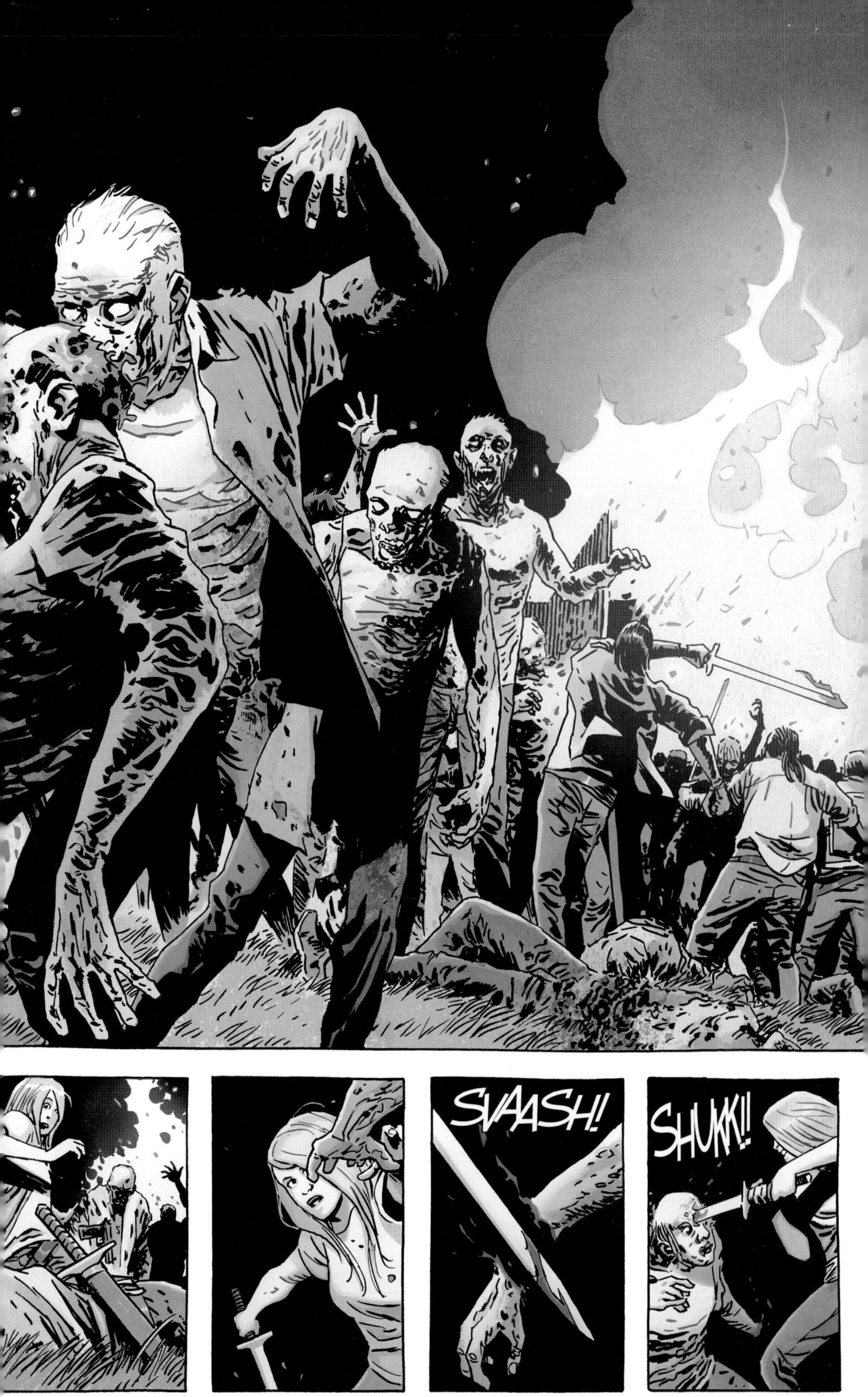
SVAASH!
SHUKK!!

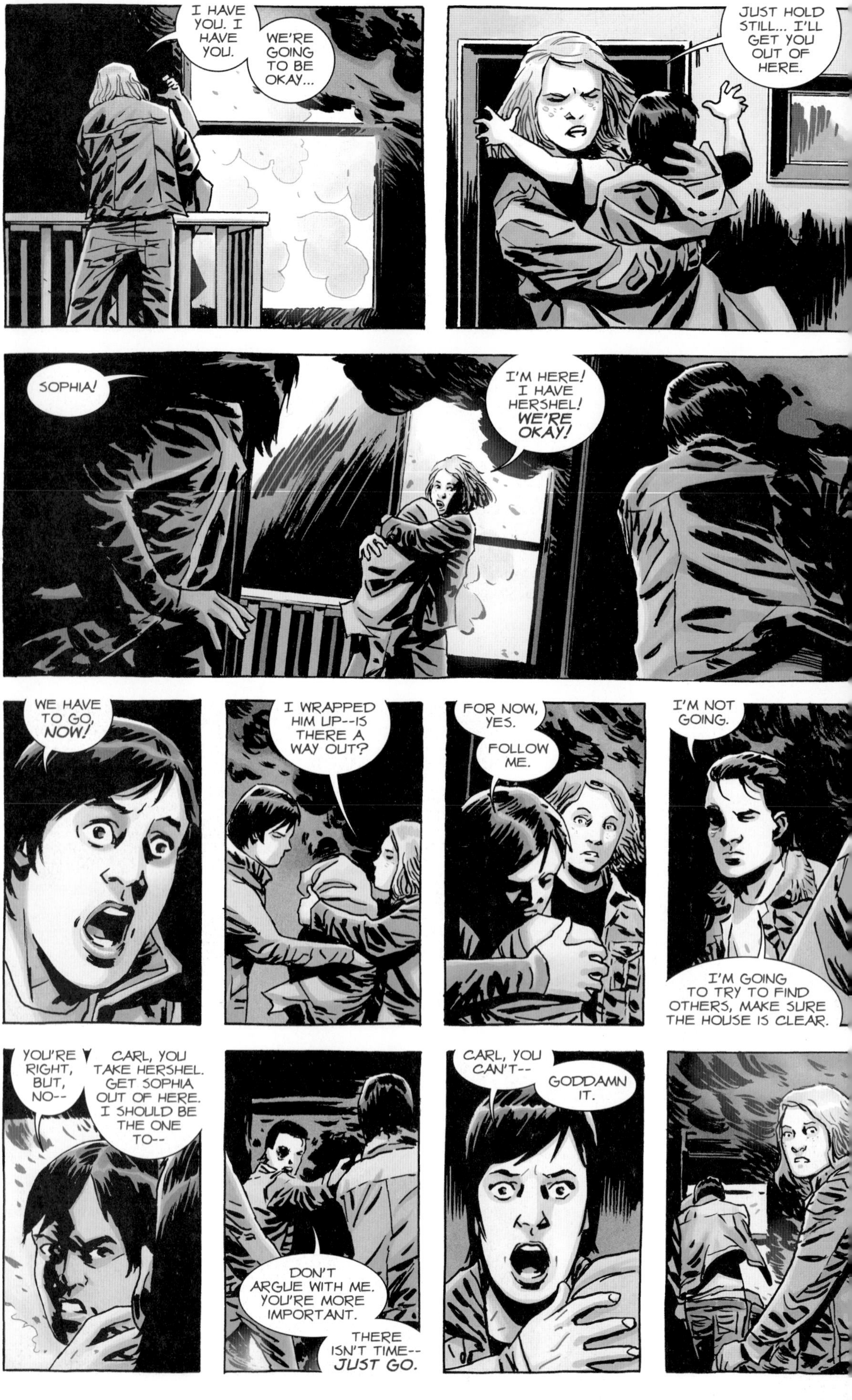
I HAVE YOU. I HAVE YOU.
WE'RE GOING TO BE OKAY...
JUST HOLD STILL... I'LL GET YOU OUT OF HERE.
SOPHIA!
I'M HERE! I HAVE HERSHEL! WE'RE OKAY!
WE HAVE TO GO, NOW!
I WRAPPED HIM UP--IS THERE A WAY OUT?
FOR NOW, YES.
FOLLOW ME.
I'M NOT GOING.
I'M GOING TO TRY TO FIND OTHERS, MAKE SURE THE HOUSE IS CLEAR.
YOU'RE RIGHT, BUT, NO--
CARL, YOU TAKE HERSHEL. GET SOPHIA OUT OF HERE. I SHOULD BE THE ONE TO--
DON'T ARGUE WITH ME. YOU'RE MORE IMPORTANT.
THERE ISN'T TIME-- JUST GO.
CARL, YOU CAN'T--
GODDAMN IT.

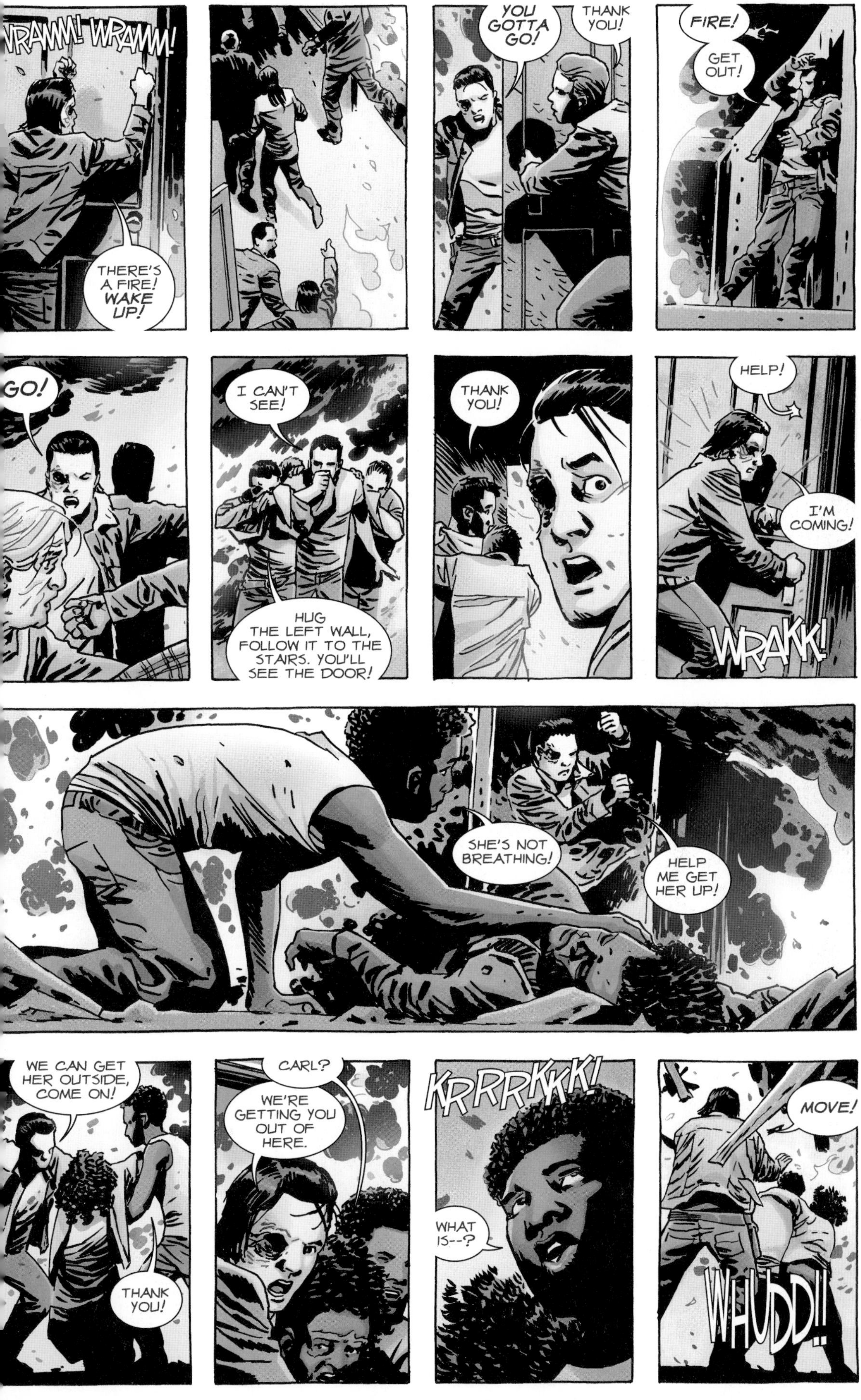
WRAMM! WRAMM!
THERE'S A FIRE! WAKE UP!
YOU GOTTA GO!
THANK YOU!
FIRE!
GET OUT!
GO!
I CAN'T SEE!
HUG THE LEFT WALL, FOLLOW IT TO THE STAIRS. YOU'LL SEE THE DOOR!
THANK YOU!
HELP!
I'M COMING!
WRAKK!
SHE'S NOT BREATHING!
HELP ME GET HER UP!
WE CAN GET HER OUTSIDE, COME ON!
THANK YOU!
CARL?
WE'RE GETTING YOU OUT OF HERE.
KRRRKKK!
WHAT IS--?
MOVE!
WHUDD!!

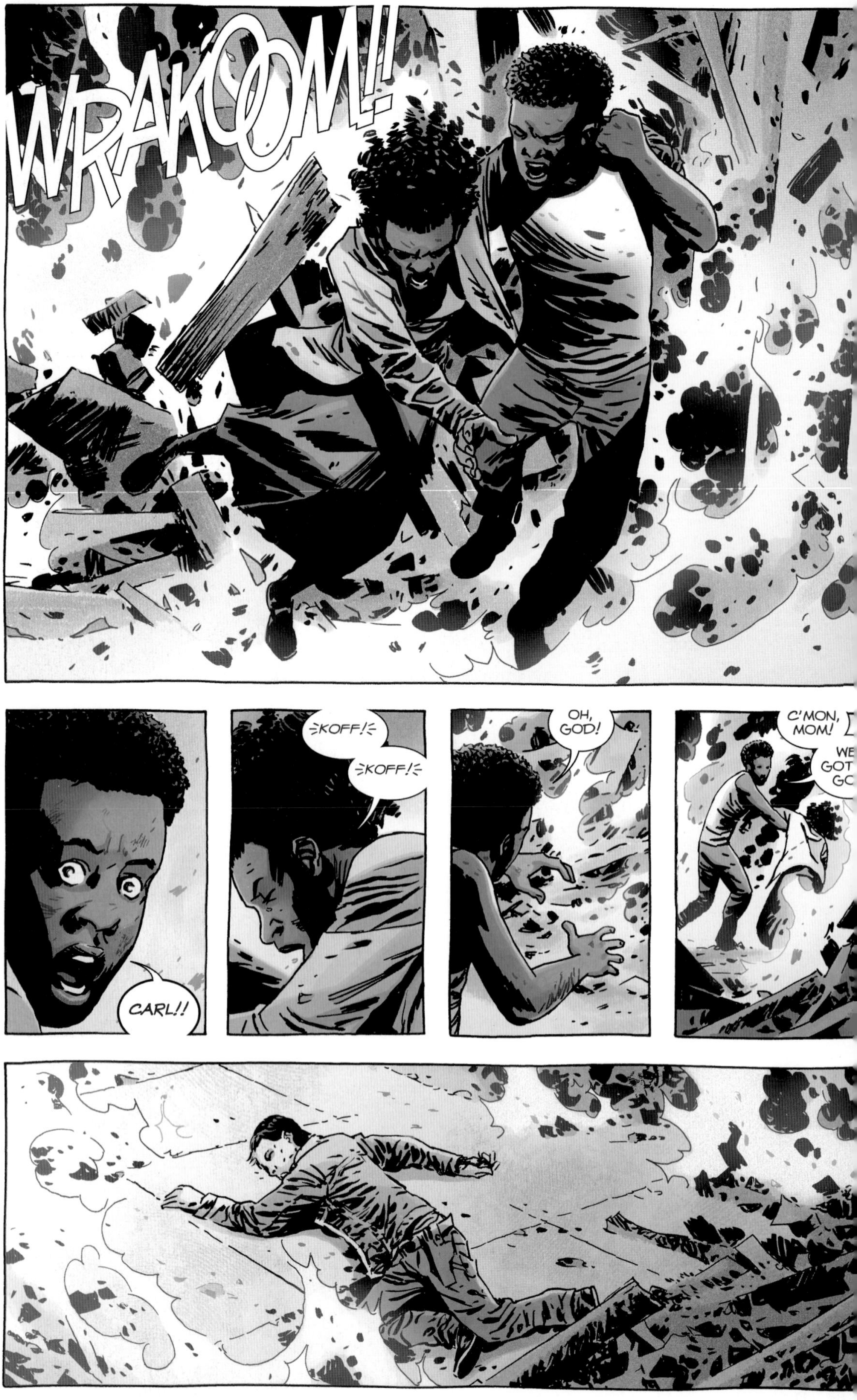
WRAKOOM!!
CARL!!
KOFF!
KOFF!
OH, GOD!
C'MON, MOM!
WE GOT GO

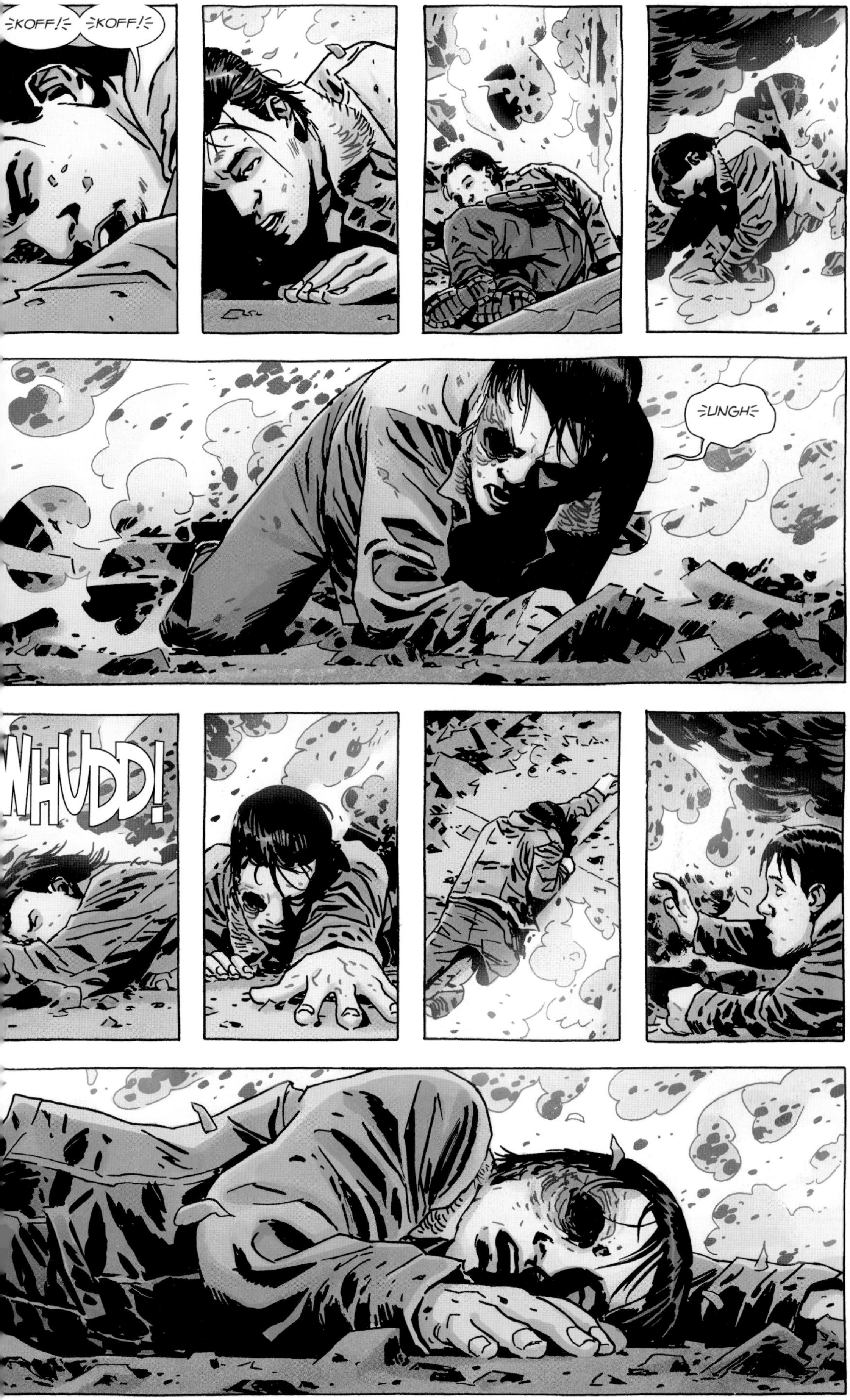
KOFF!
KOFF!
UNGH
WHUDD!

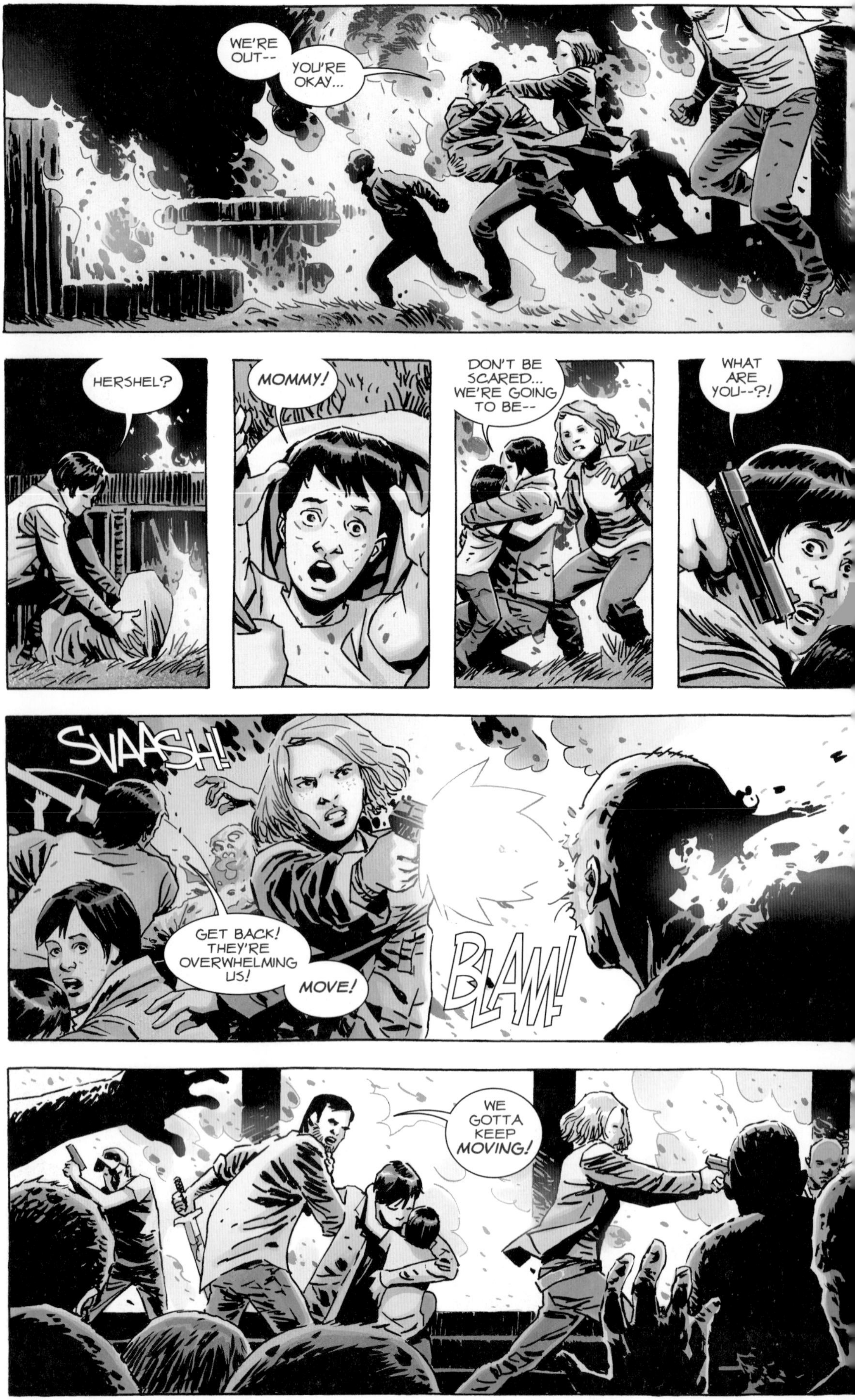
WE'RE OUT--
YOU'RE OKAY...
HERSHEL?
MOMMY!
DON'T BE SCARED... WE'RE GOING TO BE--
WHAT ARE YOU--?!
SVAASH!
GET BACK! THEY'RE OVERWHELMING US!
MOVE!
BLAM!
WE GOTTA KEEP MOVING!

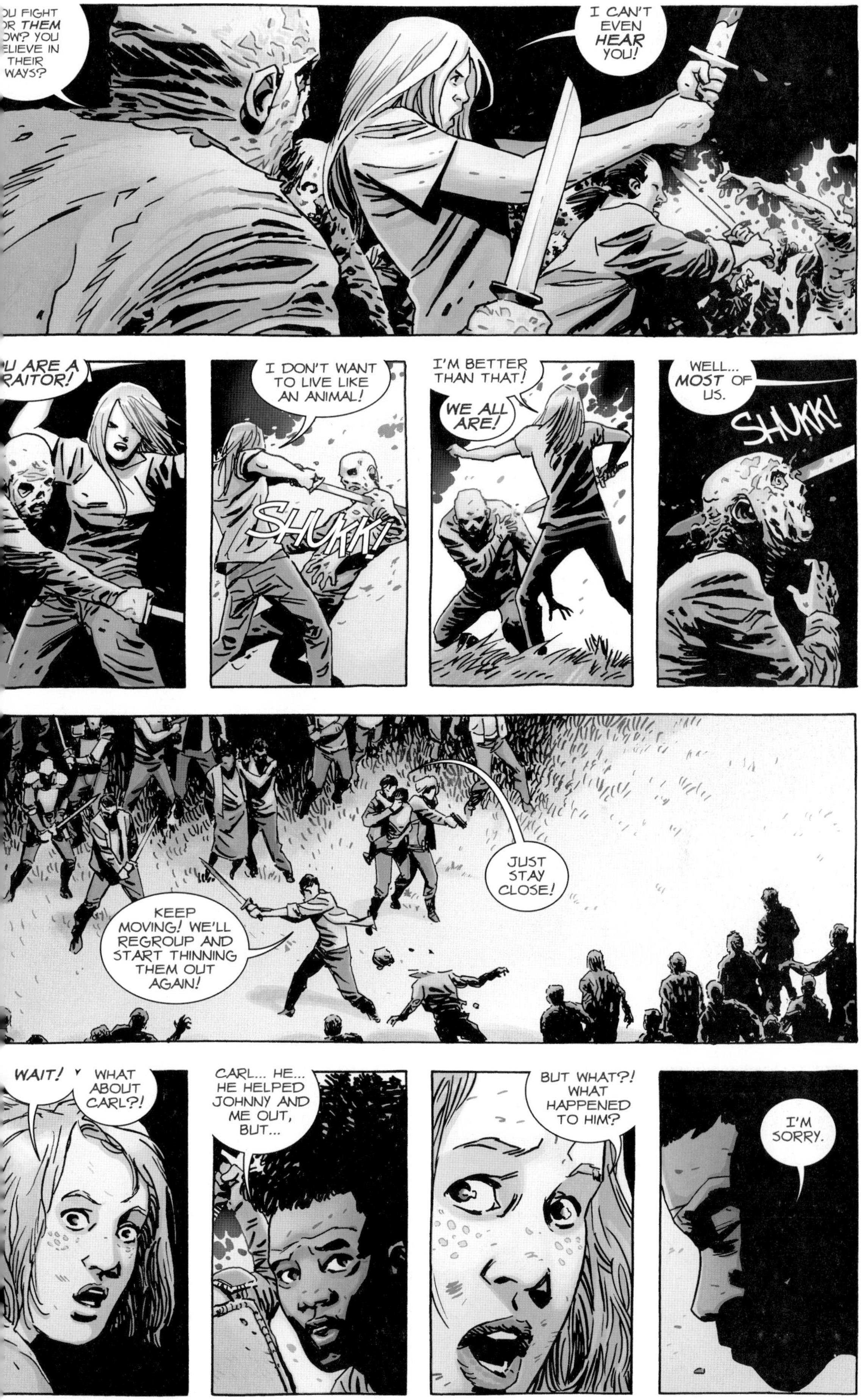
OU FIGHT OR THEM OW? YOU ELIEVE IN THEIR WAYS?
I CAN'T EVEN HEAR YOU!
U ARE A RAITOR!
I DON'T WANT TO LIVE LIKE AN ANIMAL!
SHUKK!
I'M BETTER THAN THAT!
WE ALL ARE!
WELL... MOST OF US.
SHUKK!
JUST STAY CLOSE!
KEEP MOVING! WE'LL REGROUP AND START THINNING THEM OUT AGAIN!
WAIT!
WHAT ABOUT CARL?!
CARL... HE... HE HELPED JOHNNY AND ME OUT, BUT...
BUT WHAT?! WHAT HAPPENED TO HIM?
I'M SORRY.

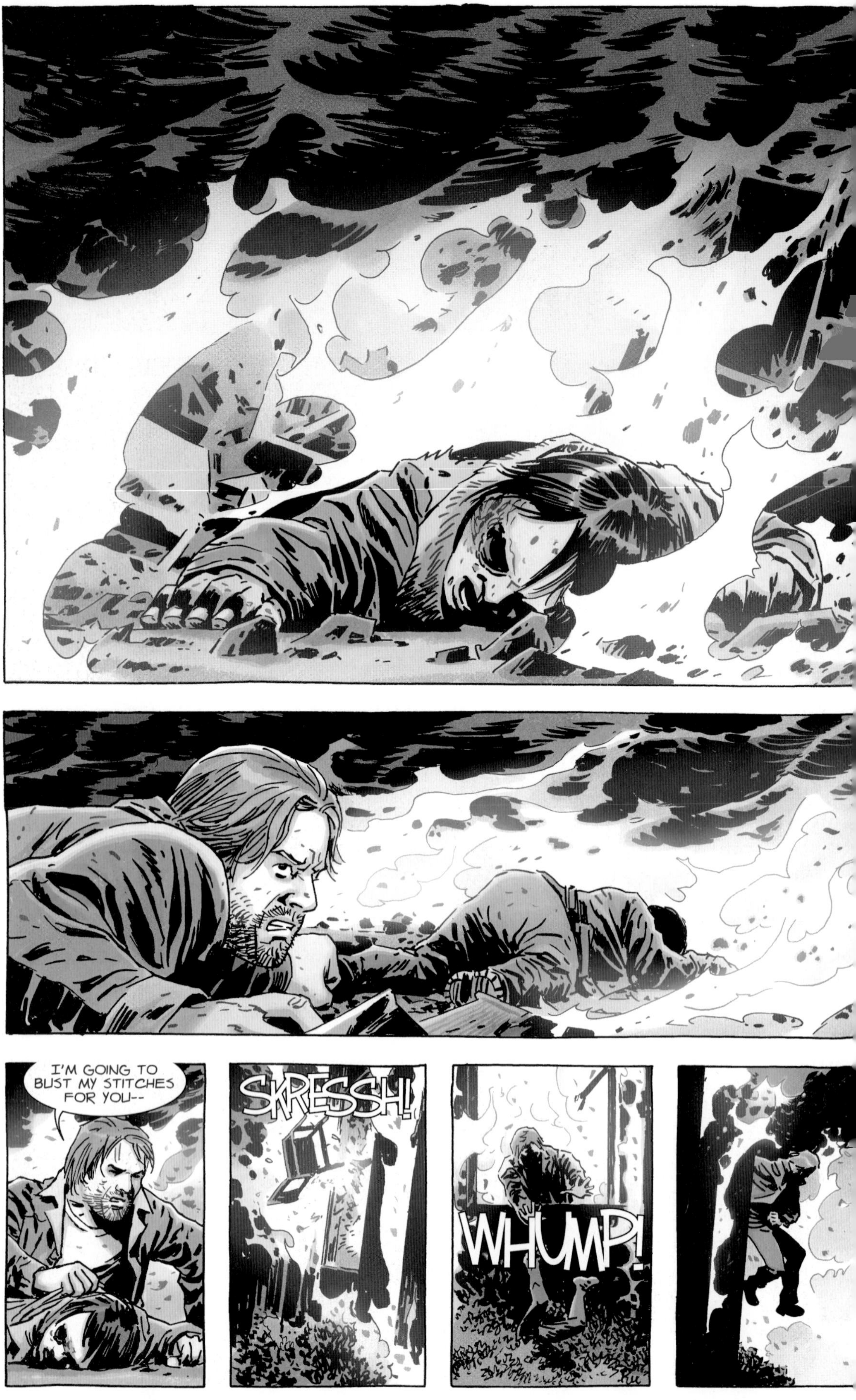

I'M GOING TO BUST MY STITCHES FOR YOU--
SKRESSH!
WHUMP!

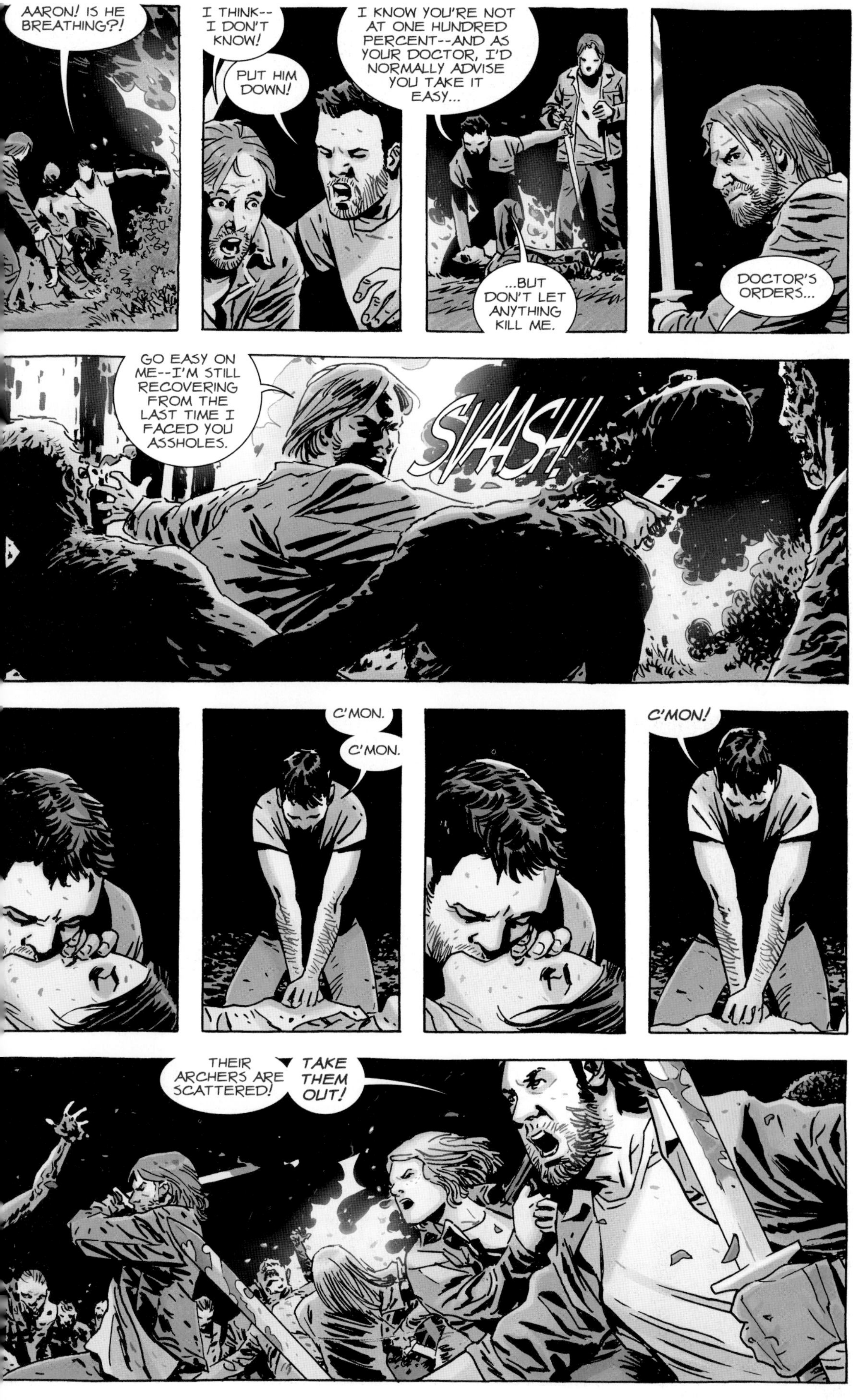
AARON! IS HE BREATHING?!
I THINK-- I DON'T KNOW!
PUT HIM DOWN!
I KNOW YOU'RE NOT AT ONE HUNDRED PERCENT--AND AS YOUR DOCTOR, I'D NORMALLY ADVISE YOU TAKE IT EASY...
...BUT DON'T LET ANYTHING KILL ME.
DOCTOR'S ORDERS...
GO EASY ON ME--I'M STILL RECOVERING FROM THE LAST TIME I FACED YOU ASSHOLES.
SHAASH!
C'MON.
C'MON.
C'MON!
THEIR ARCHERS ARE SCATTERED!
TAKE THEM OUT!

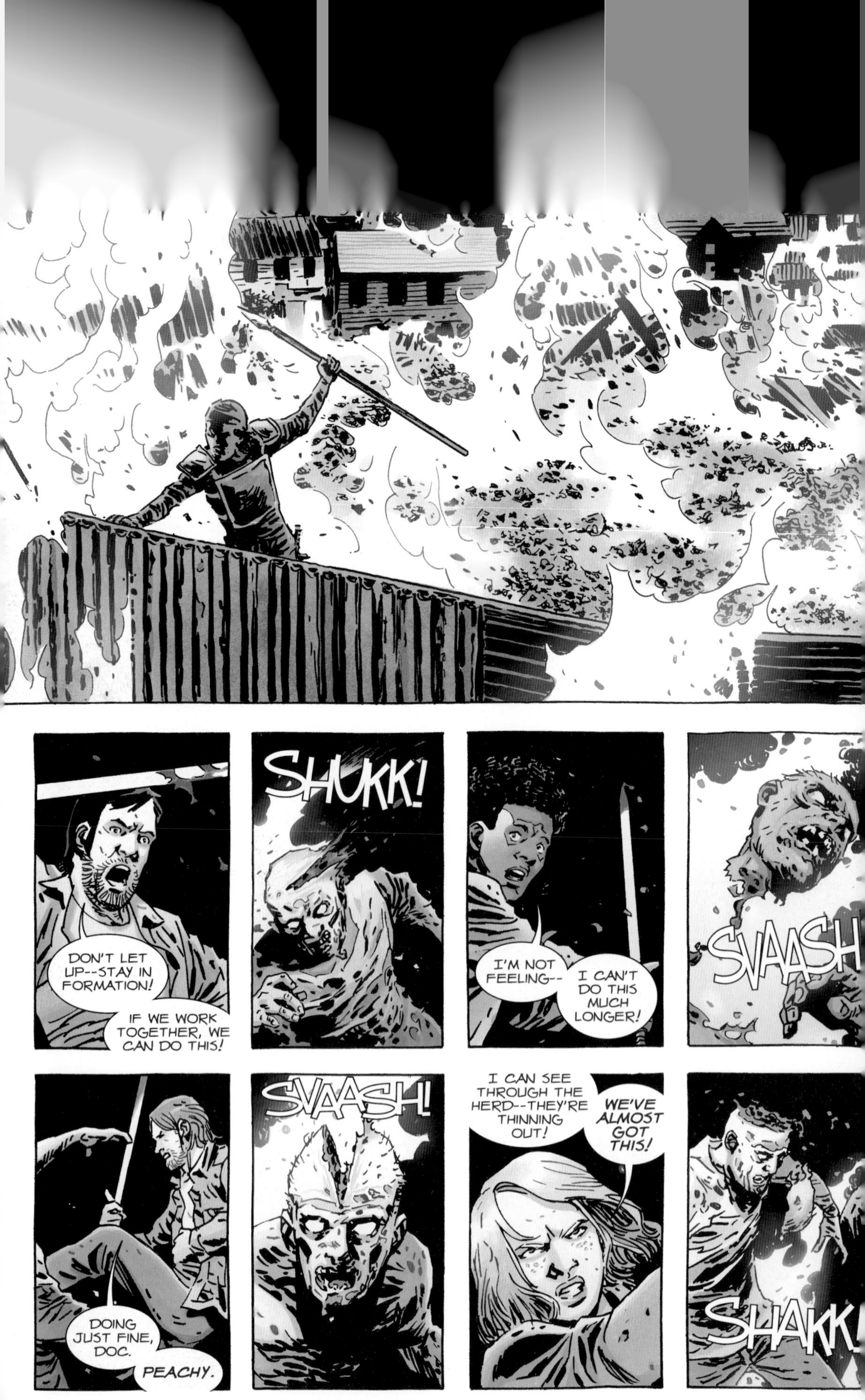

DON'T LET UP--STAY IN FORMATION!
IF WE WORK TOGETHER, WE CAN DO THIS!
SHUKK!
I'M NOT FEELING--
I CAN'T DO THIS MUCH LONGER!
SVAASH
DOING JUST FINE, DOC.
PEACHY.
SVAASH!
I CAN SEE THROUGH THE HERD--THEY'RE THINNING OUT!
WE'VE ALMOST GOT THIS!
SHAKK!

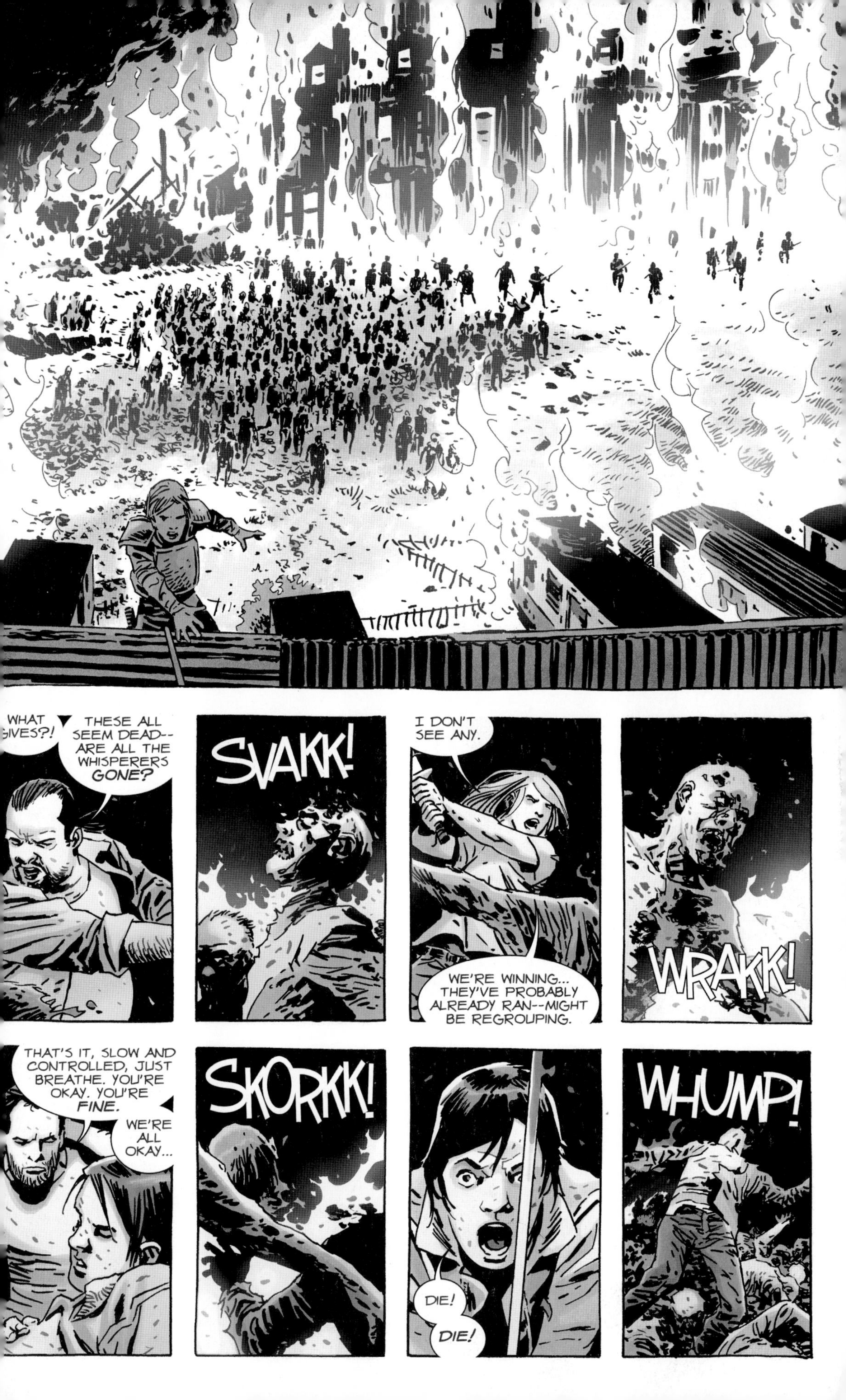
WHAT GIVES?!
THESE ALL SEEM DEAD-- ARE ALL THE WHISPERERS GONE?
SVAKK!
I DON'T SEE ANY.
WE'RE WINNING... THEY'VE PROBABLY ALREADY RAN--MIGHT BE REGROUPING.
WRAKK!
THAT'S IT, SLOW AND CONTROLLED, JUST BREATHE. YOU'RE OKAY. YOU'RE FINE.
WE'RE ALL OKAY...
SKORKK!
DIE!
DIE!
WHUMP!

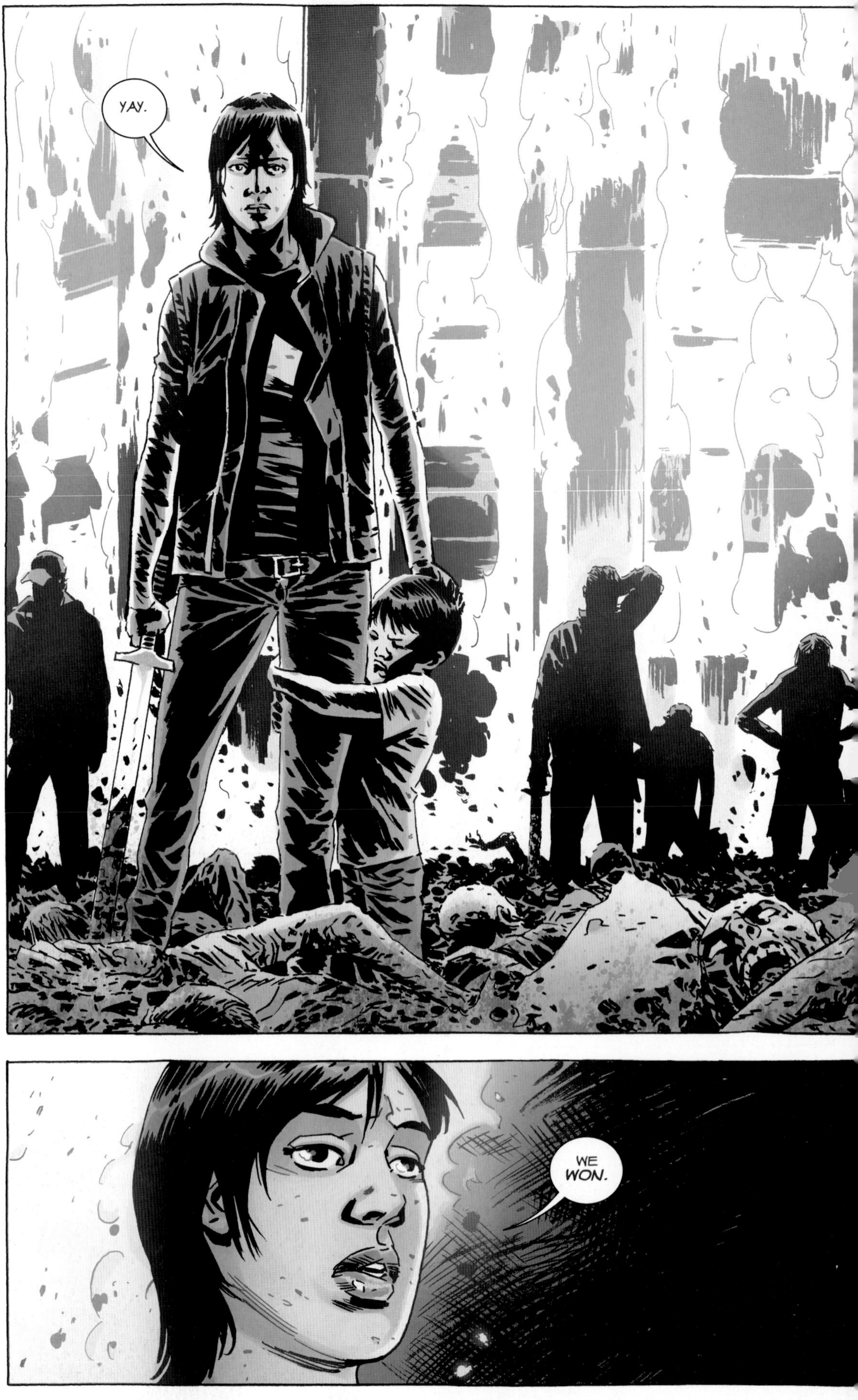
YAY.
WE WON.

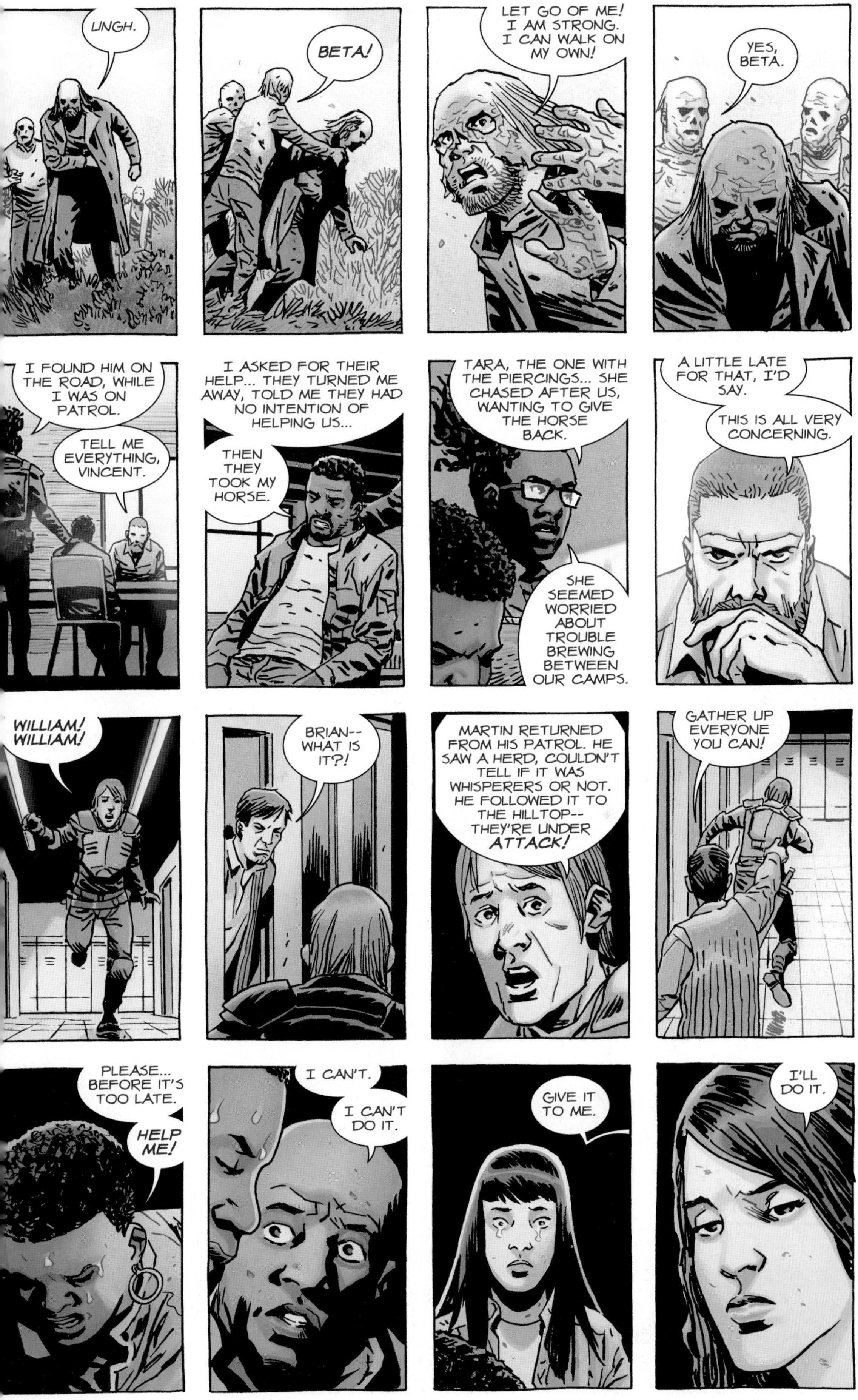
UNGH.
BETA!
LET GO OF ME! I AM STRONG. I CAN WALK ON MY OWN!
YES, BETA.
I FOUND HIM ON THE ROAD, WHILE I WAS ON PATROL.
TELL ME EVERYTHING, VINCENT.
I ASKED FOR THEIR HELP... THEY TURNED ME AWAY, TOLD ME THEY HAD NO INTENTION OF HELPING US...
THEN THEY TOOK MY HORSE.
TARA, THE ONE WITH THE PIERCINGS... SHE CHASED AFTER US, WANTING TO GIVE THE HORSE BACK.
SHE SEEMED WORRIED ABOUT TROUBLE BREWING BETWEEN OUR CAMPS.
A LITTLE LATE FOR THAT, I'D SAY.
THIS IS ALL VERY CONCERNING.
WILLIAM! WILLIAM!
BRIAN-- WHAT IS IT?!
MARTIN RETURNED FROM HIS PATROL. HE SAW A HERD, COULDN'T TELL IF IT WAS WHISPERERS OR NOT. HE FOLLOWED IT TO THE HILLTOP-- THEY'RE UNDER ATTACK!
GATHER UP EVERYONE YOU CAN!
PLEASE... BEFORE IT'S TOO LATE.
HELP ME!
I CAN'T.
I CAN'T DO IT.
GIVE IT TO ME.
I'LL DO IT.

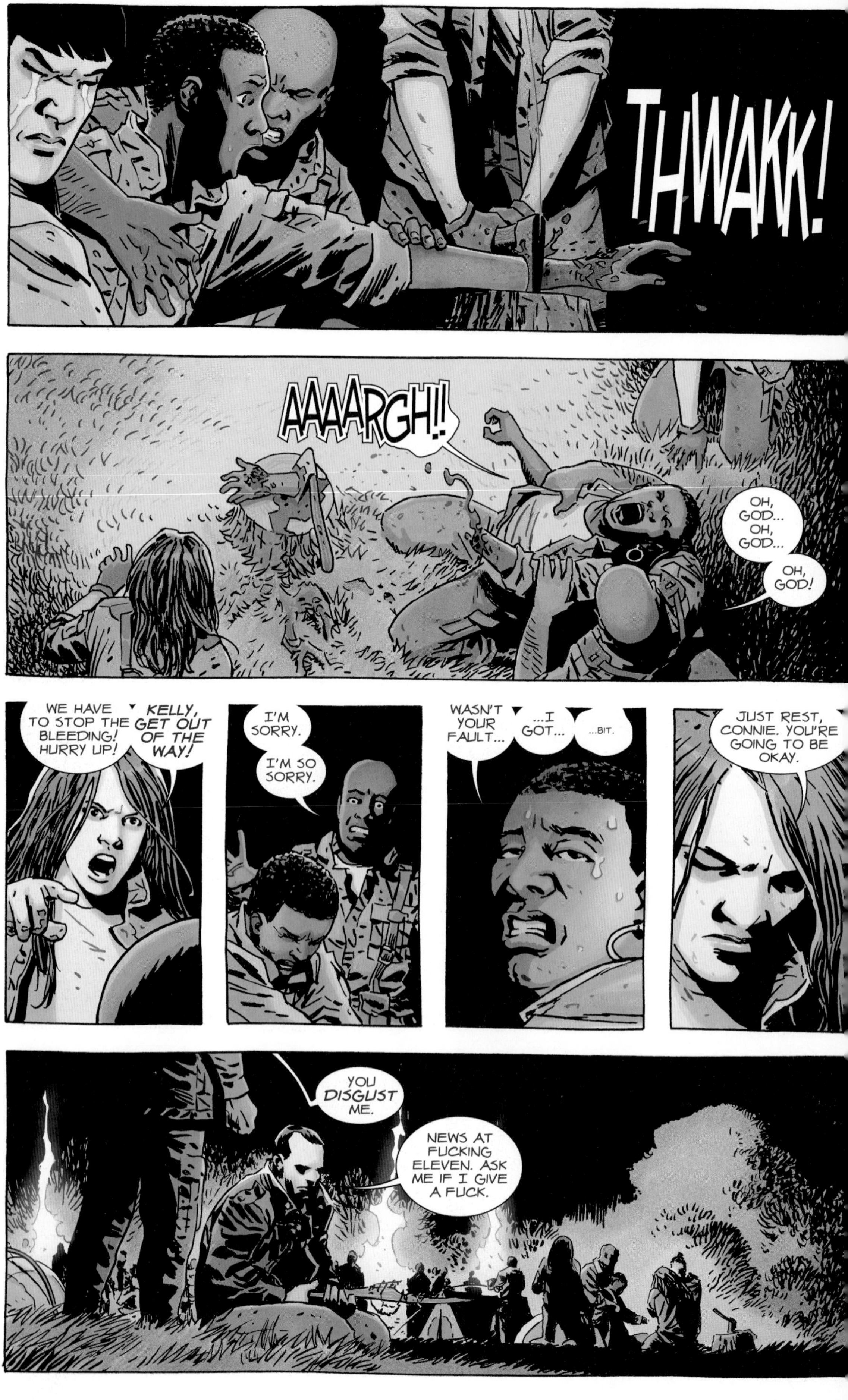
THWAKK!
AAAARGH!!
OH, GOD... OH, GOD...
OH, GOD!
WE HAVE TO STOP THE BLEEDING! HURRY UP!
KELLY, GET OUT OF THE WAY!
I'M SORRY.
I'M SO SORRY.
WASN'T YOUR FAULT...
...I GOT...
...BIT.
JUST REST, CONNIE. YOU'RE GOING TO BE OKAY.
YOU DISGUST ME.
NEWS AT FUCKING ELEVEN. ASK ME IF I GIVE A FUCK.

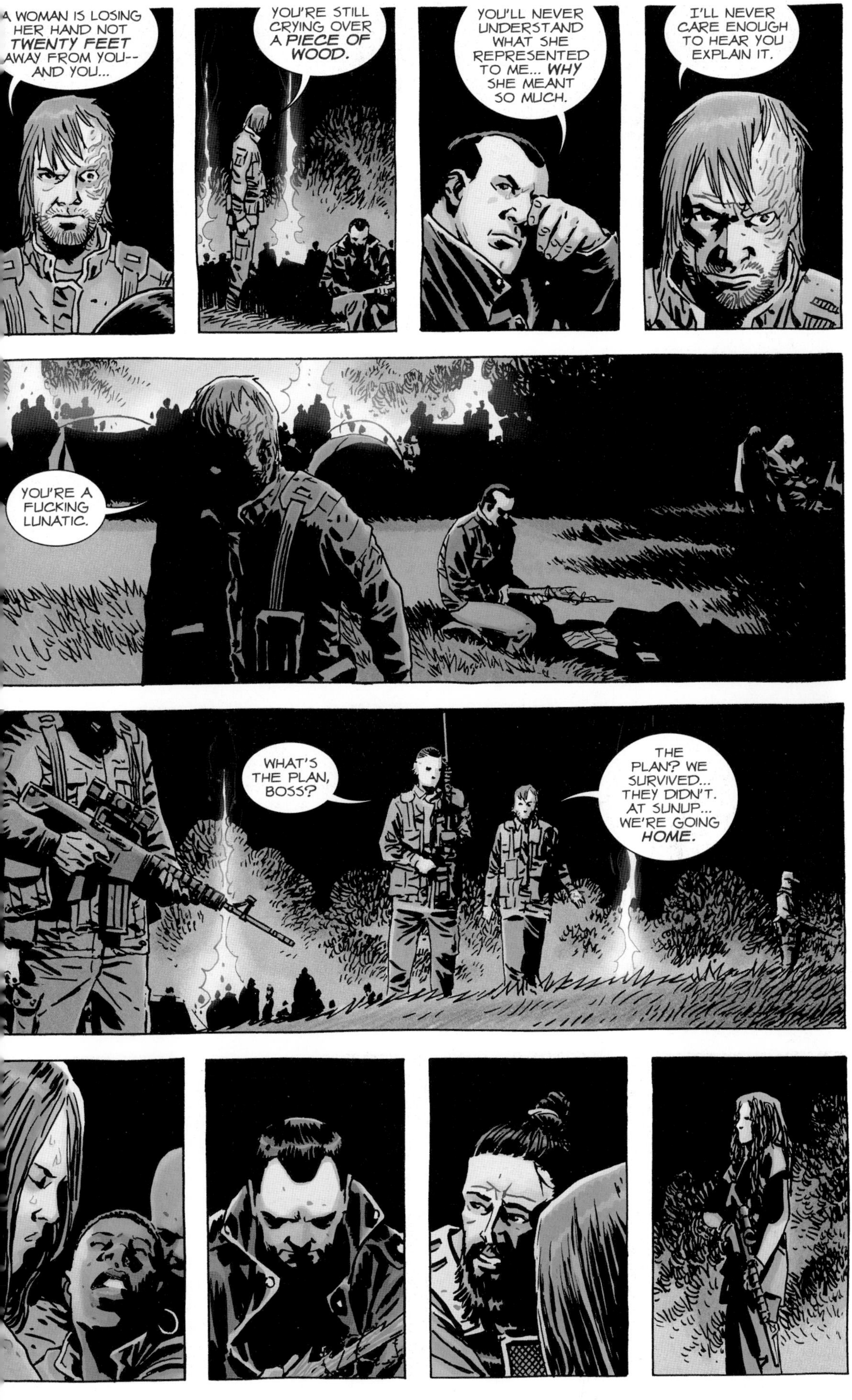
A WOMAN IS LOSING HER HAND NOT TWENTY FEET AWAY FROM YOU-- AND YOU...
YOU'RE STILL CRYING OVER A PIECE OF WOOD.
YOU'LL NEVER UNDERSTAND WHAT SHE REPRESENTED TO ME... WHY SHE MEANT SO MUCH.
I'LL NEVER CARE ENOUGH TO HEAR YOU EXPLAIN IT.
YOU'RE A FUCKING LUNATIC.
WHAT'S THE PLAN, BOSS?
THE PLAN? WE SURVIVED... THEY DIDN'T. AT SUNUP... WE'RE GOING HOME.

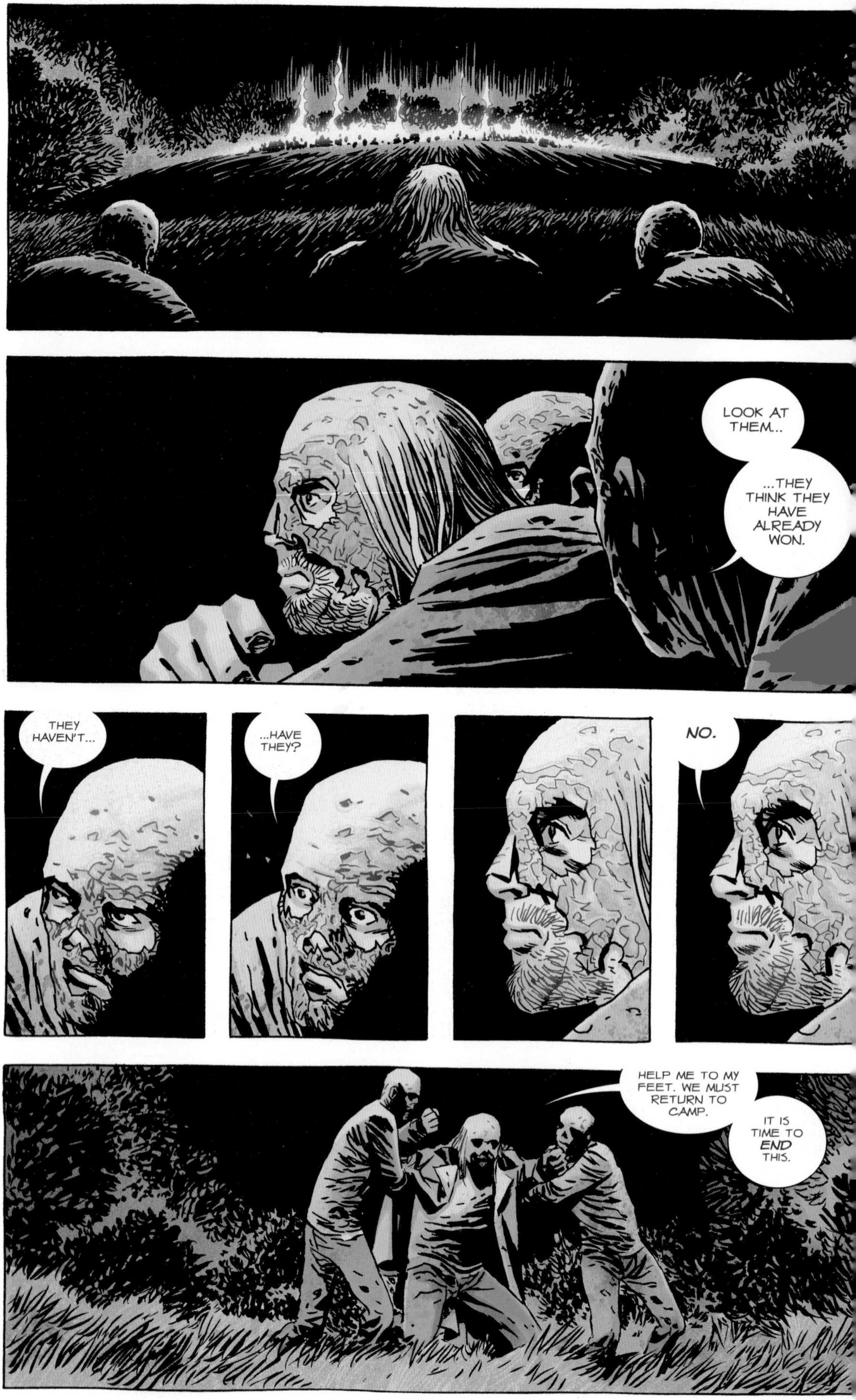
LOOK AT THEM...
...THEY THINK THEY HAVE ALREADY WON.
THEY HAVEN'T...
...HAVE THEY?
NO.
HELP ME TO MY FEET. WE MUST RETURN TO CAMP.
IT IS TIME TO *END* THIS.

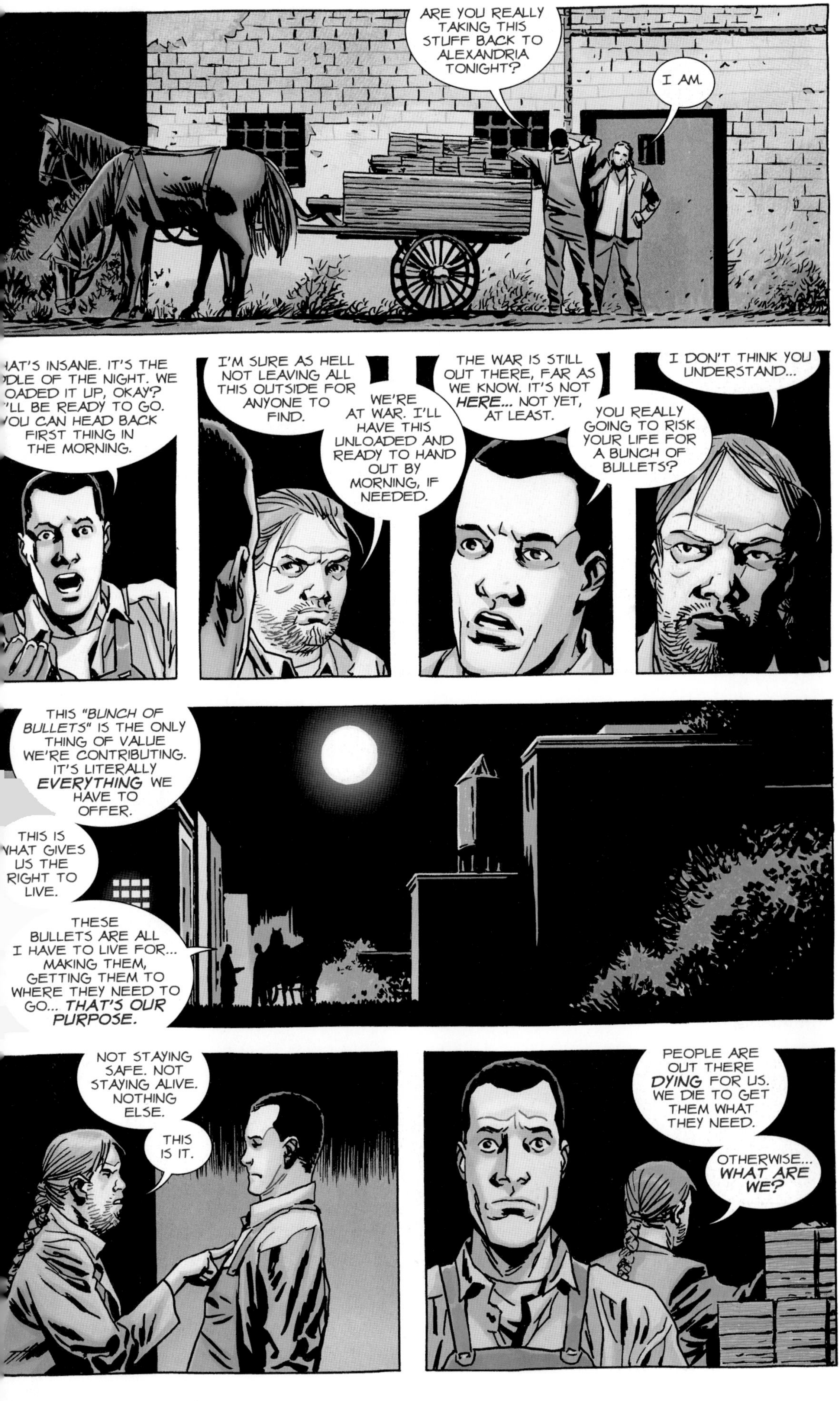
ARE YOU REALLY TAKING THIS STUFF BACK TO ALEXANDRIA TONIGHT?
I AM.
HAT'S INSANE. IT'S THE DDLE OF THE NIGHT. WE OADED IT UP, OKAY? 'LL BE READY TO GO. OU CAN HEAD BACK FIRST THING IN THE MORNING.
I'M SURE AS HELL NOT LEAVING ALL THIS OUTSIDE FOR ANYONE TO FIND.
WE'RE AT WAR. I'LL HAVE THIS UNLOADED AND READY TO HAND OUT BY MORNING, IF NEEDED.
THE WAR IS STILL OUT THERE, FAR AS WE KNOW. IT'S NOT HERE... NOT YET, AT LEAST.
YOU REALLY GOING TO RISK YOUR LIFE FOR A BUNCH OF BULLETS?
I DON'T THINK YOU UNDERSTAND...
THIS "BUNCH OF BULLETS" IS THE ONLY THING OF VALUE WE'RE CONTRIBUTING. IT'S LITERALLY EVERYTHING WE HAVE TO OFFER.
THIS IS HAT GIVES US THE RIGHT TO LIVE.
THESE BULLETS ARE ALL I HAVE TO LIVE FOR... MAKING THEM, GETTING THEM TO WHERE THEY NEED TO GO... THAT'S OUR PURPOSE.
NOT STAYING SAFE. NOT STAYING ALIVE. NOTHING ELSE.
THIS IS IT.
PEOPLE ARE OUT THERE DYING FOR US. WE DIE TO GET THEM WHAT THEY NEED.
OTHERWISE... WHAT ARE WE?

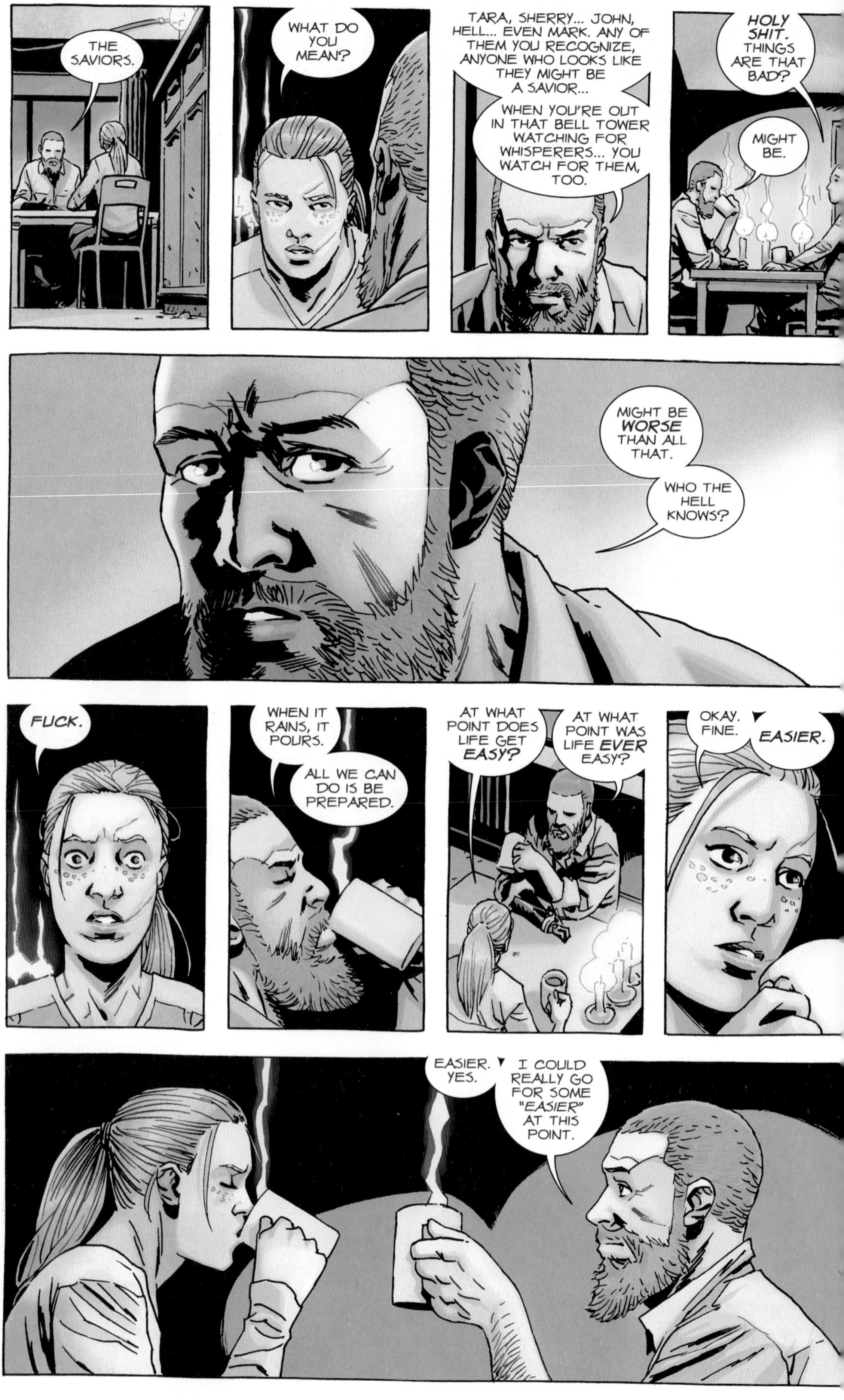
THE SAVIORS.
WHAT DO YOU MEAN?
TARA, SHERRY... JOHN, HELL... EVEN MARK. ANY OF THEM YOU RECOGNIZE, ANYONE WHO LOOKS LIKE THEY MIGHT BE A SAVIOR...
WHEN YOU'RE OUT IN THAT BELL TOWER WATCHING FOR WHISPERERS... YOU WATCH FOR THEM, TOO.
HOLY SHIT. THINGS ARE THAT BAD?
MIGHT BE.
MIGHT BE WORSE THAN ALL THAT.
WHO THE HELL KNOWS?
FUCK.
WHEN IT RAINS, IT POURS.
ALL WE CAN DO IS BE PREPARED.
AT WHAT POINT DOES LIFE GET EASY?
AT WHAT POINT WAS LIFE EVER EASY?
OKAY. FINE.
EASIER.
EASIER. YES.
I COULD REALLY GO FOR SOME "EASIER" AT THIS POINT.

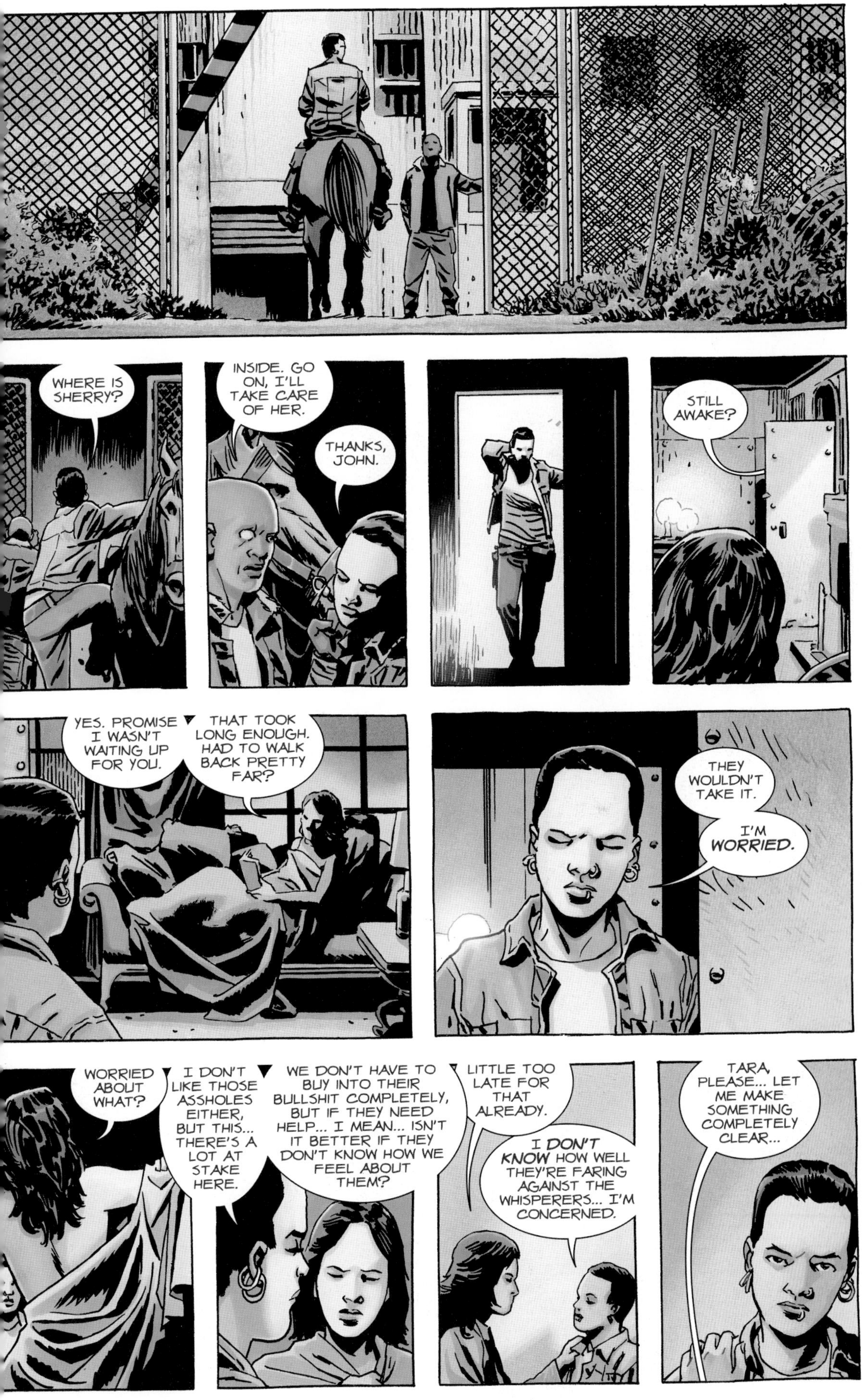

WHERE IS SHERRY?
INSIDE. GO ON, I'LL TAKE CARE OF HER.
THANKS, JOHN.
STILL AWAKE?
YES. PROMISE I WASN'T WAITING UP FOR YOU.
THAT TOOK LONG ENOUGH. HAD TO WALK BACK PRETTY FAR?
THEY WOULDN'T TAKE IT.
I'M *WORRIED.*
WORRIED ABOUT WHAT?
I DON'T LIKE THOSE ASSHOLES EITHER, BUT THIS... THERE'S A LOT AT STAKE HERE.
WE DON'T HAVE TO BUY INTO THEIR BULLSHIT COMPLETELY, BUT IF THEY NEED HELP... I MEAN... ISN'T IT BETTER IF THEY DON'T KNOW HOW WE FEEL ABOUT THEM?
LITTLE TOO LATE FOR THAT ALREADY.
I ***DON'T KNOW*** HOW WELL THEY'RE FARING AGAINST THE WHISPERERS... I'M CONCERNED.
TARA, PLEASE... LET ME MAKE SOMETHING COMPLETELY CLEAR...

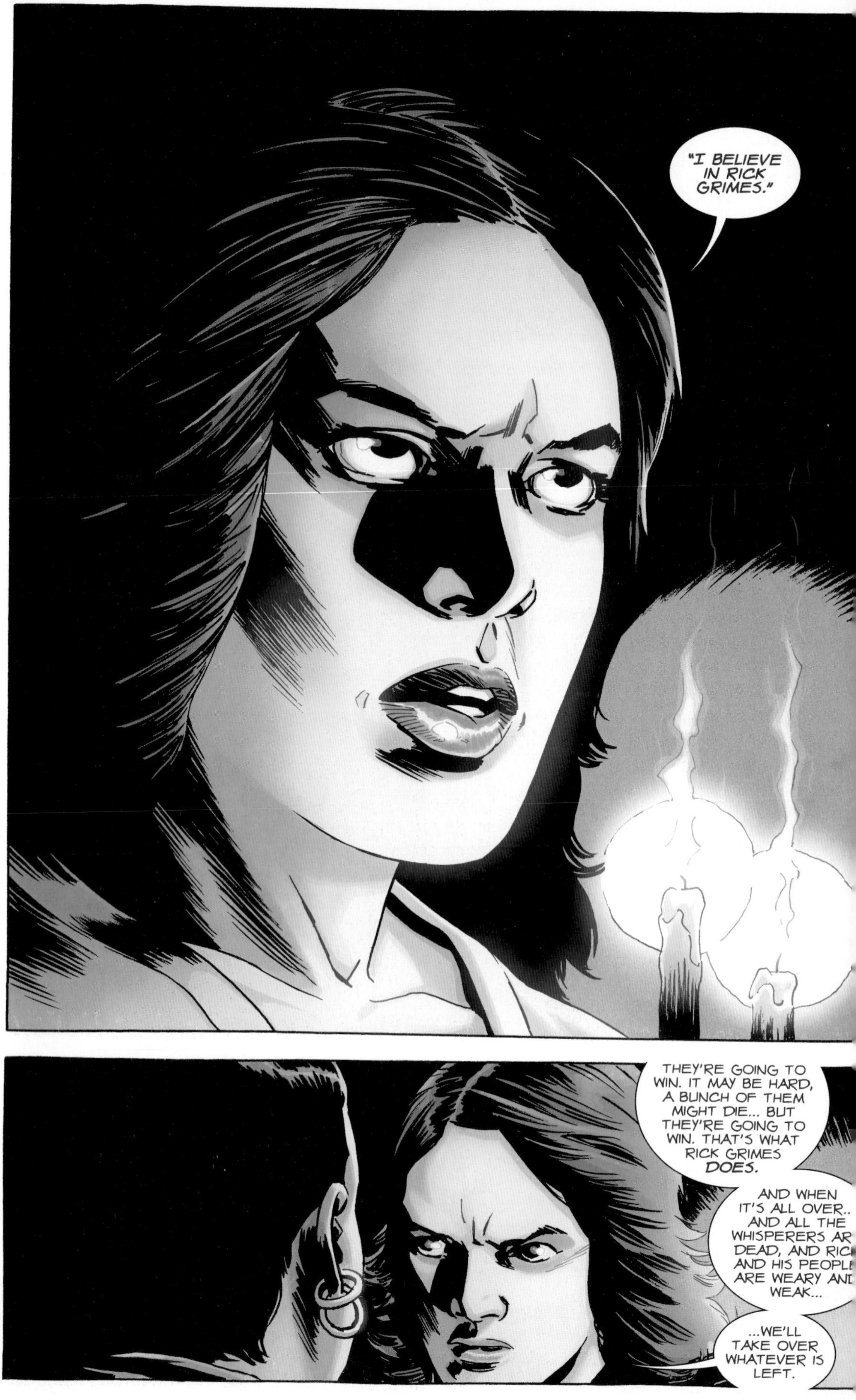

"I BELIEVE IN RICK GRIMES."
THEY'RE GOING TO WIN. IT MAY BE HARD, A BUNCH OF THEM MIGHT DIE... BUT THEY'RE GOING TO WIN. THAT'S WHAT RICK GRIMES *DOES.*
AND WHEN IT'S ALL OVER.. AND ALL THE WHISPERERS AR DEAD, AND RIC AND HIS PEOPL ARE WEARY AN WEAK...
...WE'LL TAKE OVER WHATEVER IS LEFT.

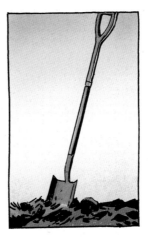

I'M SORRY.

I NEVER GOT TO BURY YOU BEFORE. I KNOW THIS ISN'T THE SAME... I'M SORRY YOU WERE NEVER *TRULY* PUT TO REST.

I'M HOPING... THIS IS THE NEXT BEST THING. THIS IS THE CLOSEST I CAN GET.

I HOPE YOU'RE AT PEACE. I HOPE YOU... I HOPE YOU'RE IN HEAVEN, AND YOU FELL IN LOVE WITH SOMEONE WHO TREATS YOU BETTER THAN I EVER DID, AND THAT THEY'RE FUCKING YOUR BRAINS OUT AND THEN FUCKING YOUR BRAINS BACK IN AFTER THAT ON A DAILY BASIS.

I'LL ALWAYS MISS YOU, LUCILLE.

I'M SORRY I NAMED A STUPID FUCKING BASEBALL BAT AFTER YOU.

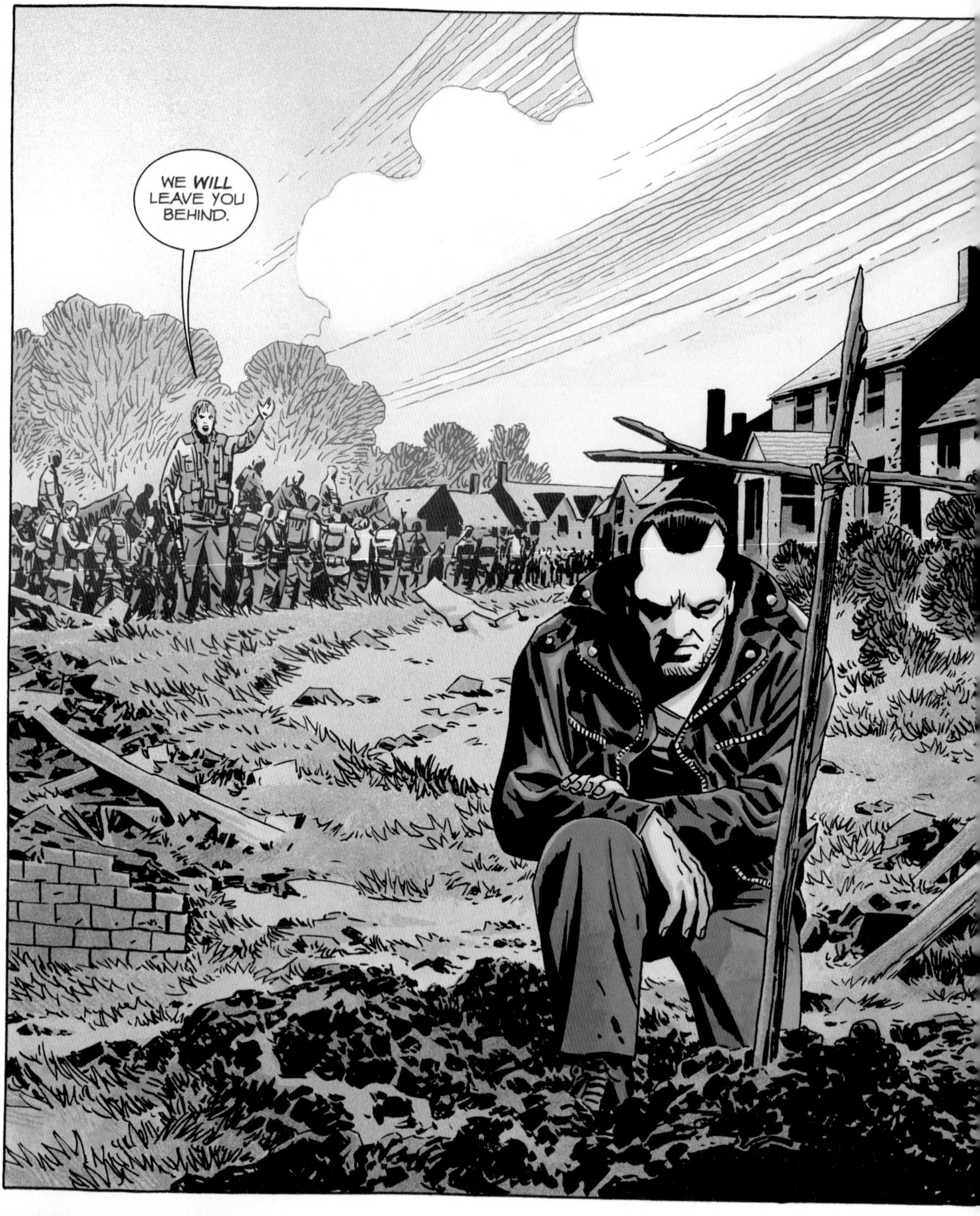
WE WILL LEAVE YOU BEHIND.

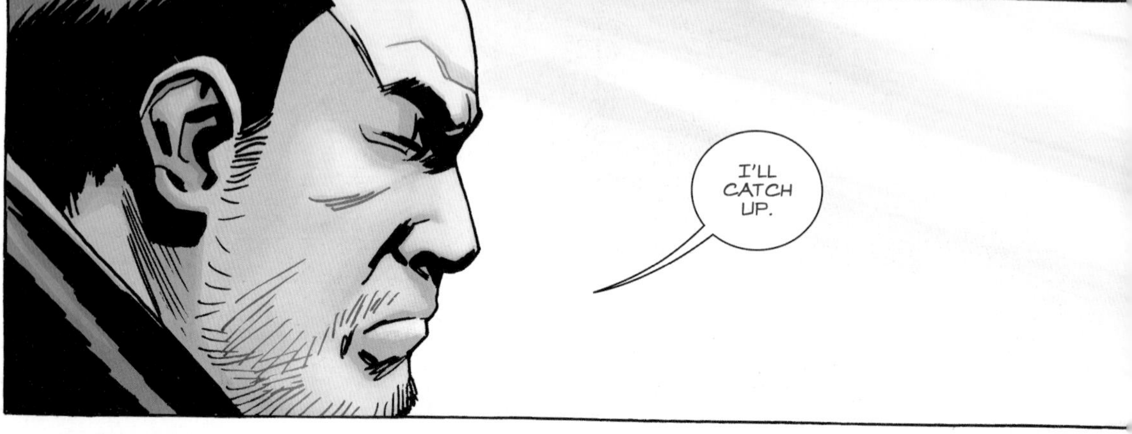
I'LL CATCH UP.

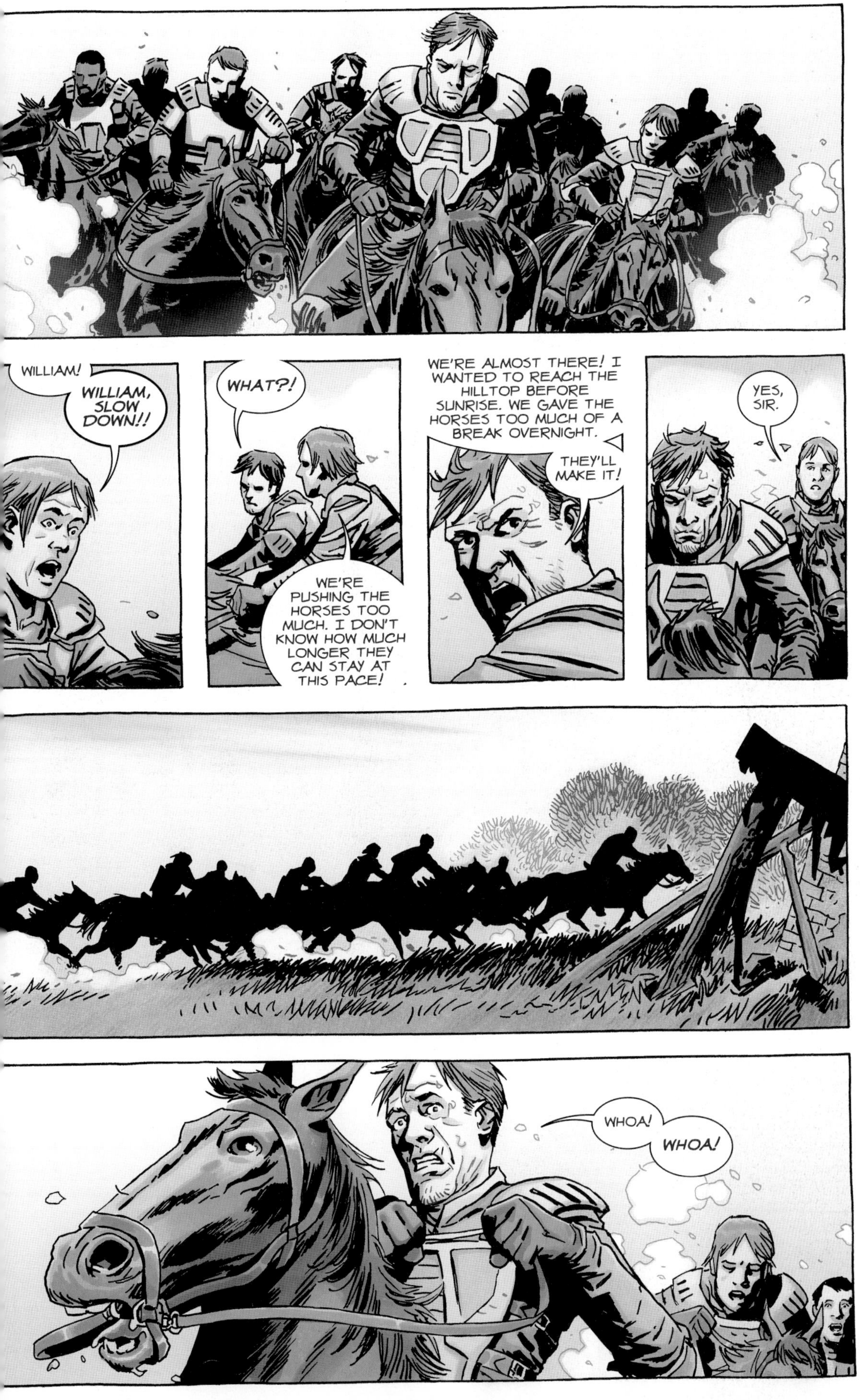
WILLIAM!
WILLIAM, SLOW DOWN!!
WHAT?!
WE'RE PUSHING THE HORSES TOO MUCH. I DON'T KNOW HOW MUCH LONGER THEY CAN STAY AT THIS PACE!
WE'RE ALMOST THERE! I WANTED TO REACH THE HILLTOP BEFORE SUNRISE. WE GAVE THE HORSES TOO MUCH OF A BREAK OVERNIGHT.
THEY'LL MAKE IT!
YES, SIR.
WHOA!
WHOA!

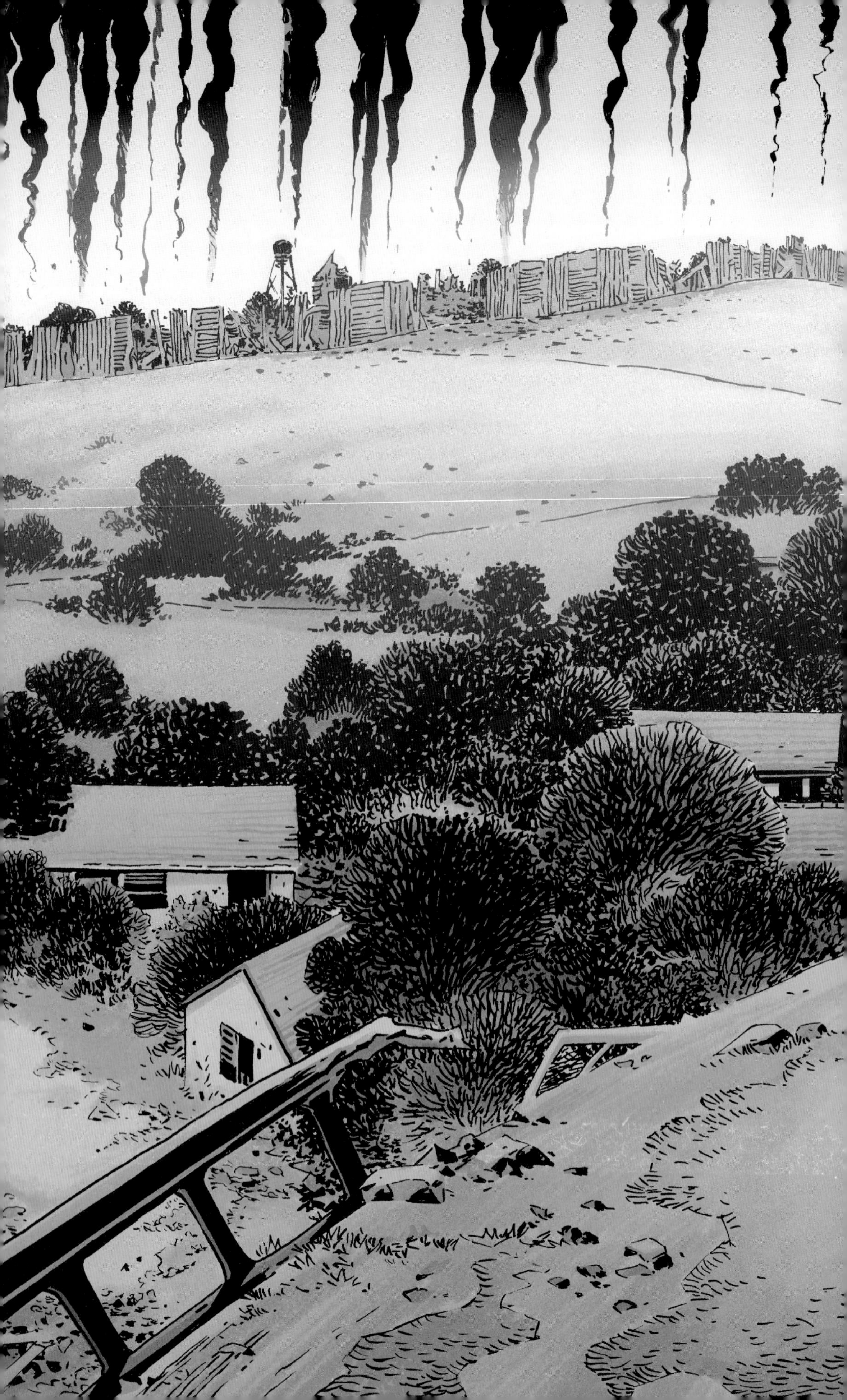

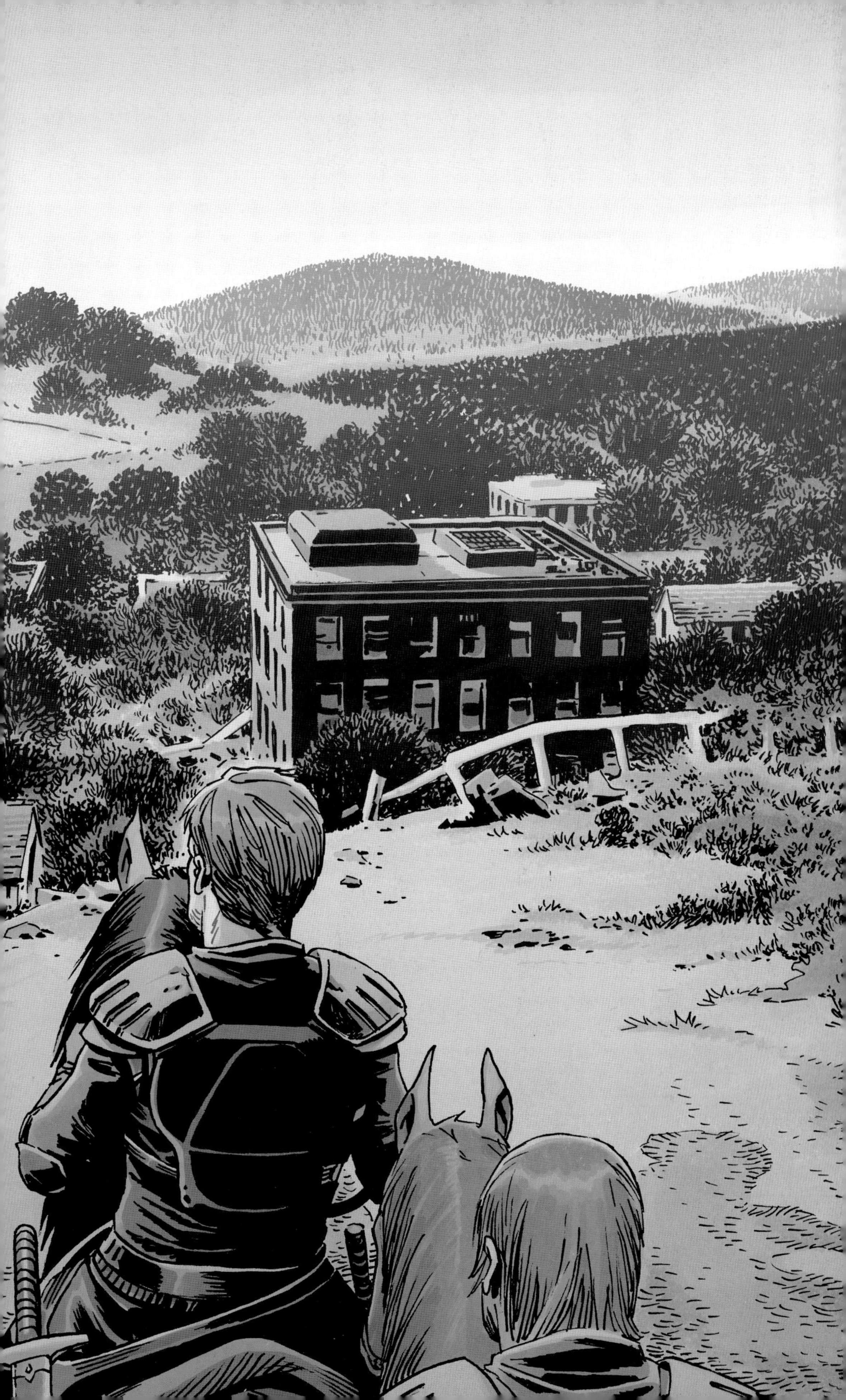

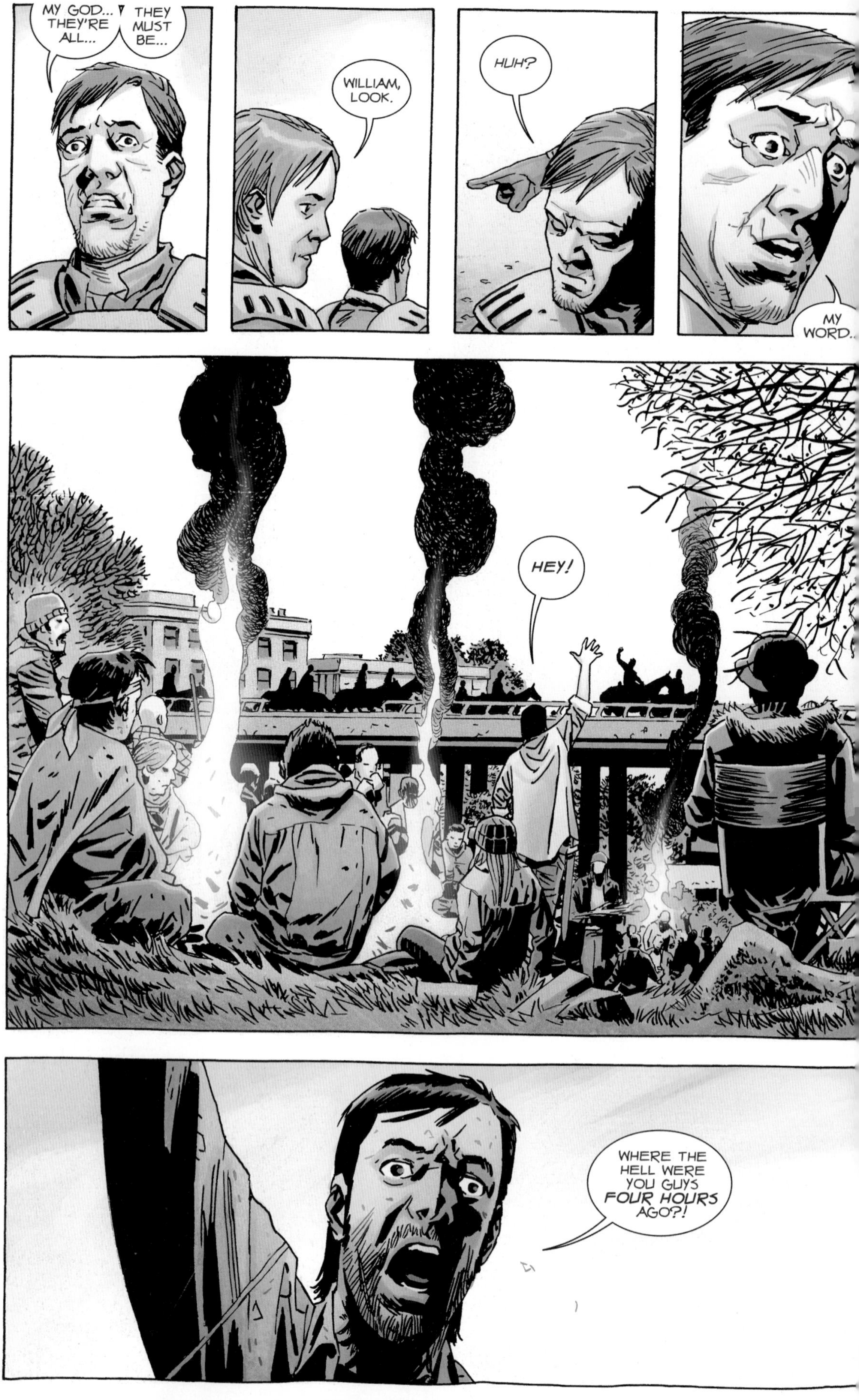
MY GOD... THEY'RE ALL...
THEY MUST BE...
WILLIAM, LOOK.
HUH?
MY WORD...
HEY!
WHERE THE HELL WERE YOU GUYS FOUR HOURS AGO?!

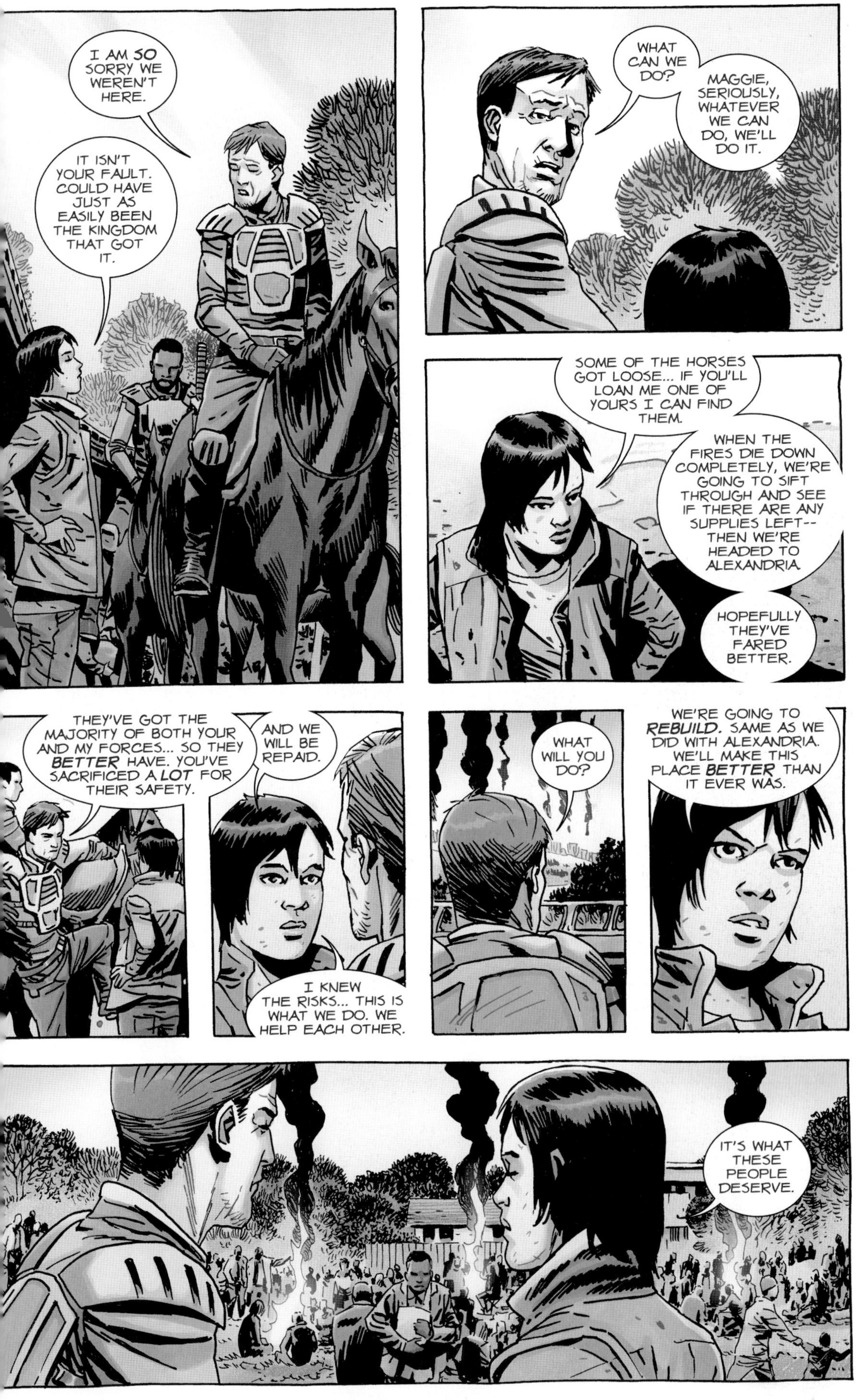

I AM SO SORRY WE WEREN'T HERE.
IT ISN'T YOUR FAULT. COULD HAVE JUST AS EASILY BEEN THE KINGDOM THAT GOT IT.
WHAT CAN WE DO?
MAGGIE, SERIOUSLY, WHATEVER WE CAN DO, WE'LL DO IT.
SOME OF THE HORSES GOT LOOSE... IF YOU'LL LOAN ME ONE OF YOURS I CAN FIND THEM.
WHEN THE FIRES DIE DOWN COMPLETELY, WE'RE GOING TO SIFT THROUGH AND SEE IF THERE ARE ANY SUPPLIES LEFT-- THEN WE'RE HEADED TO ALEXANDRIA.
HOPEFULLY THEY'VE FARED BETTER.
THEY'VE GOT THE MAJORITY OF BOTH YOUR AND MY FORCES... SO THEY BETTER HAVE. YOU'VE SACRIFICED A LOT FOR THEIR SAFETY.
AND WE WILL BE REPAID.
I KNEW THE RISKS... THIS IS WHAT WE DO. WE HELP EACH OTHER.
WHAT WILL YOU DO?
WE'RE GOING TO REBUILD. SAME AS WE DID WITH ALEXANDRIA. WE'LL MAKE THIS PLACE BETTER THAN IT EVER WAS.
IT'S WHAT THESE PEOPLE DESERVE.

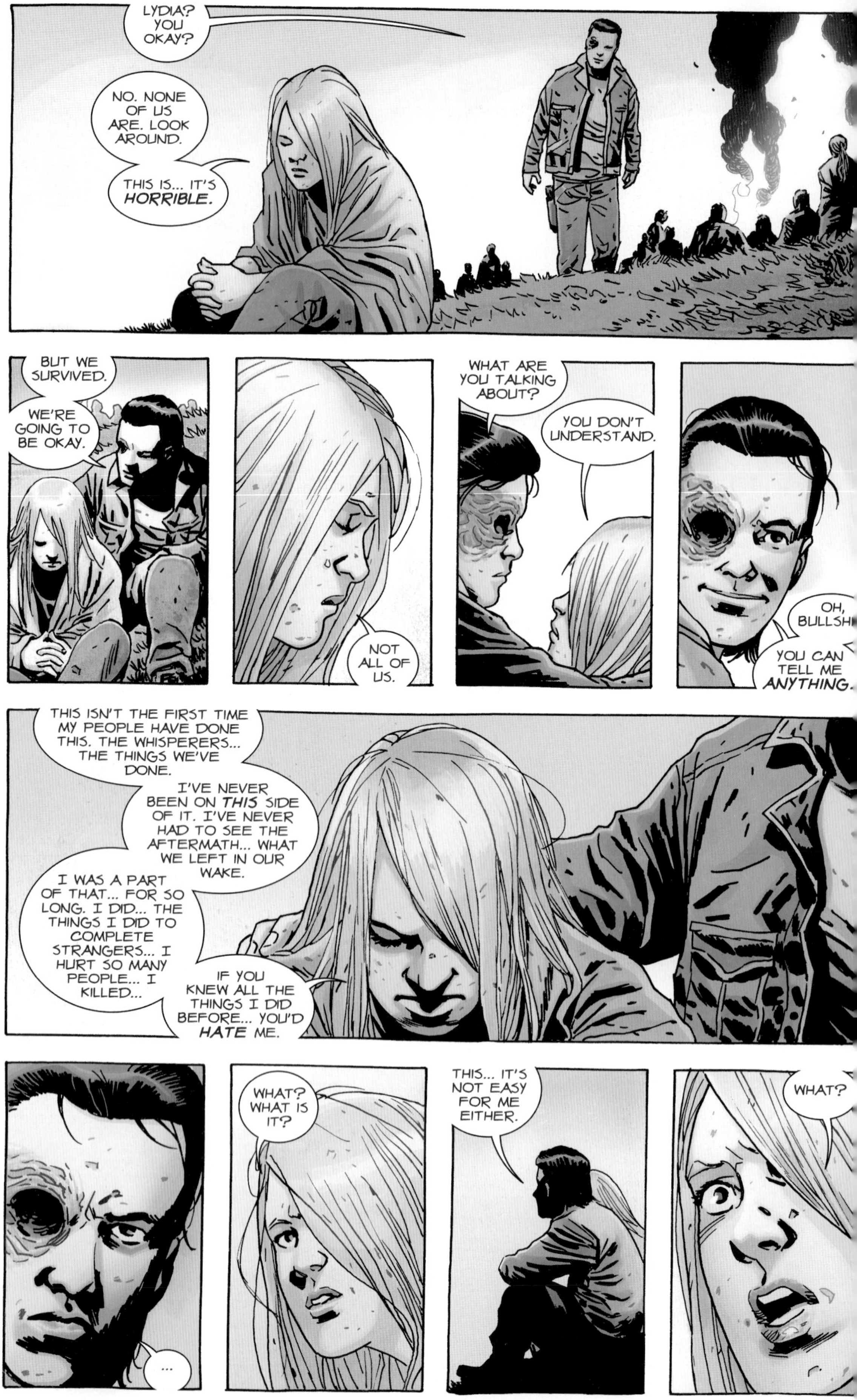
LYDIA? YOU OKAY?
NO. NONE OF US ARE. LOOK AROUND.
THIS IS... IT'S HORRIBLE.
BUT WE SURVIVED.
WE'RE GOING TO BE OKAY.
NOT ALL OF US.
WHAT ARE YOU TALKING ABOUT?
YOU DON'T UNDERSTAND.
OH, BULLSH
YOU CAN TELL ME ANYTHING.
THIS ISN'T THE FIRST TIME MY PEOPLE HAVE DONE THIS. THE WHISPERERS... THE THINGS WE'VE DONE.
I'VE NEVER BEEN ON THIS SIDE OF IT. I'VE NEVER HAD TO SEE THE AFTERMATH... WHAT WE LEFT IN OUR WAKE.
I WAS A PART OF THAT... FOR SO LONG. I DID... THE THINGS I DID TO COMPLETE STRANGERS... I HURT SO MANY PEOPLE... I KILLED...
IF YOU KNEW ALL THE THINGS I DID BEFORE... YOU'D HATE ME.
...
WHAT? WHAT IS IT?
THIS... IT'S NOT EASY FOR ME EITHER.
WHAT?

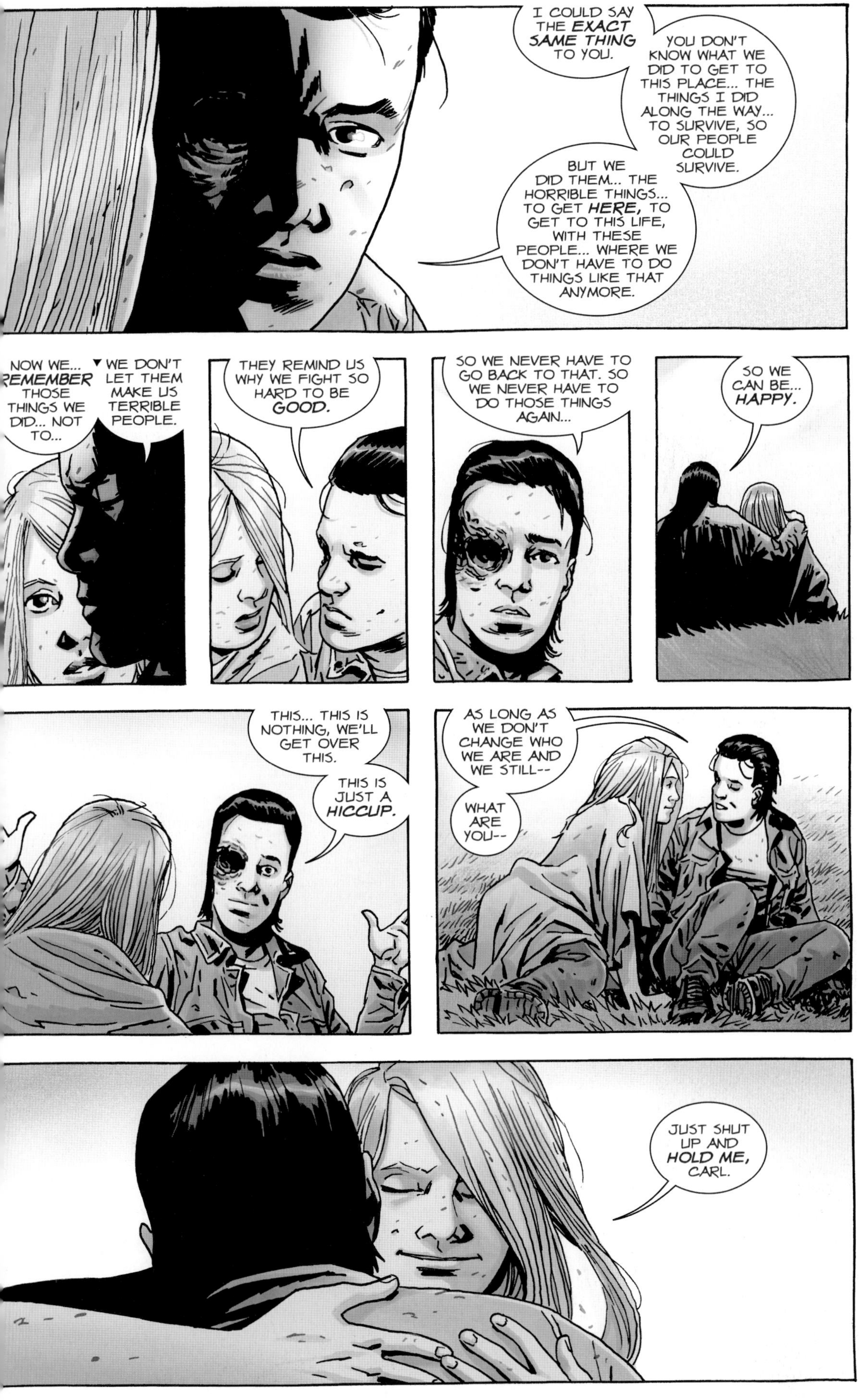
I COULD SAY THE *EXACT SAME THING* TO YOU.
YOU DON'T KNOW WHAT WE DID TO GET TO THIS PLACE... THE THINGS I DID ALONG THE WAY... TO SURVIVE, SO OUR PEOPLE COULD SURVIVE.
BUT WE DID THEM... THE HORRIBLE THINGS... TO GET *HERE,* TO GET TO THIS LIFE, WITH THESE PEOPLE... WHERE WE DON'T HAVE TO DO THINGS LIKE THAT ANYMORE.
NOW WE... *REMEMBER* THOSE THINGS WE DID... NOT TO...
WE DON'T LET THEM MAKE US TERRIBLE PEOPLE.
THEY REMIND US WHY WE FIGHT SO HARD TO BE *GOOD.*
SO WE NEVER HAVE TO GO BACK TO THAT. SO WE NEVER HAVE TO DO THOSE THINGS AGAIN...
SO WE CAN BE... *HAPPY.*
THIS... THIS IS NOTHING, WE'LL GET OVER THIS.
THIS IS JUST A *HICCUP.*
AS LONG AS WE DON'T CHANGE WHO WE ARE AND WE STILL--
WHAT ARE YOU--
JUST SHUT UP AND *HOLD ME,* CARL.

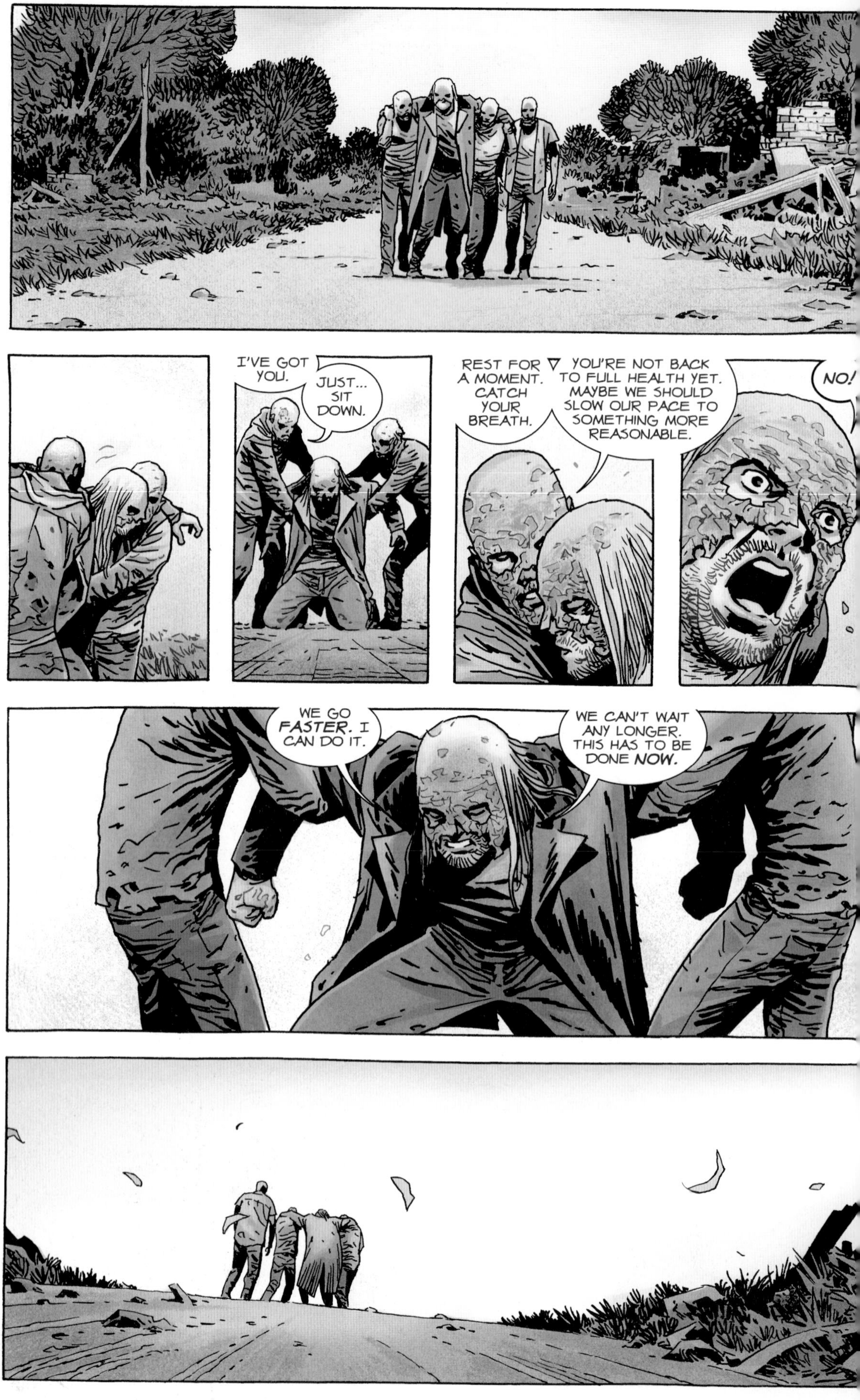
I'VE GOT YOU.
JUST... SIT DOWN.
REST FOR A MOMENT. CATCH YOUR BREATH.
YOU'RE NOT BACK TO FULL HEALTH YET. MAYBE WE SHOULD SLOW OUR PACE TO SOMETHING MORE REASONABLE.
NO!
WE GO FASTER. I CAN DO IT.
WE CAN'T WAIT ANY LONGER. THIS HAS TO BE DONE NOW.

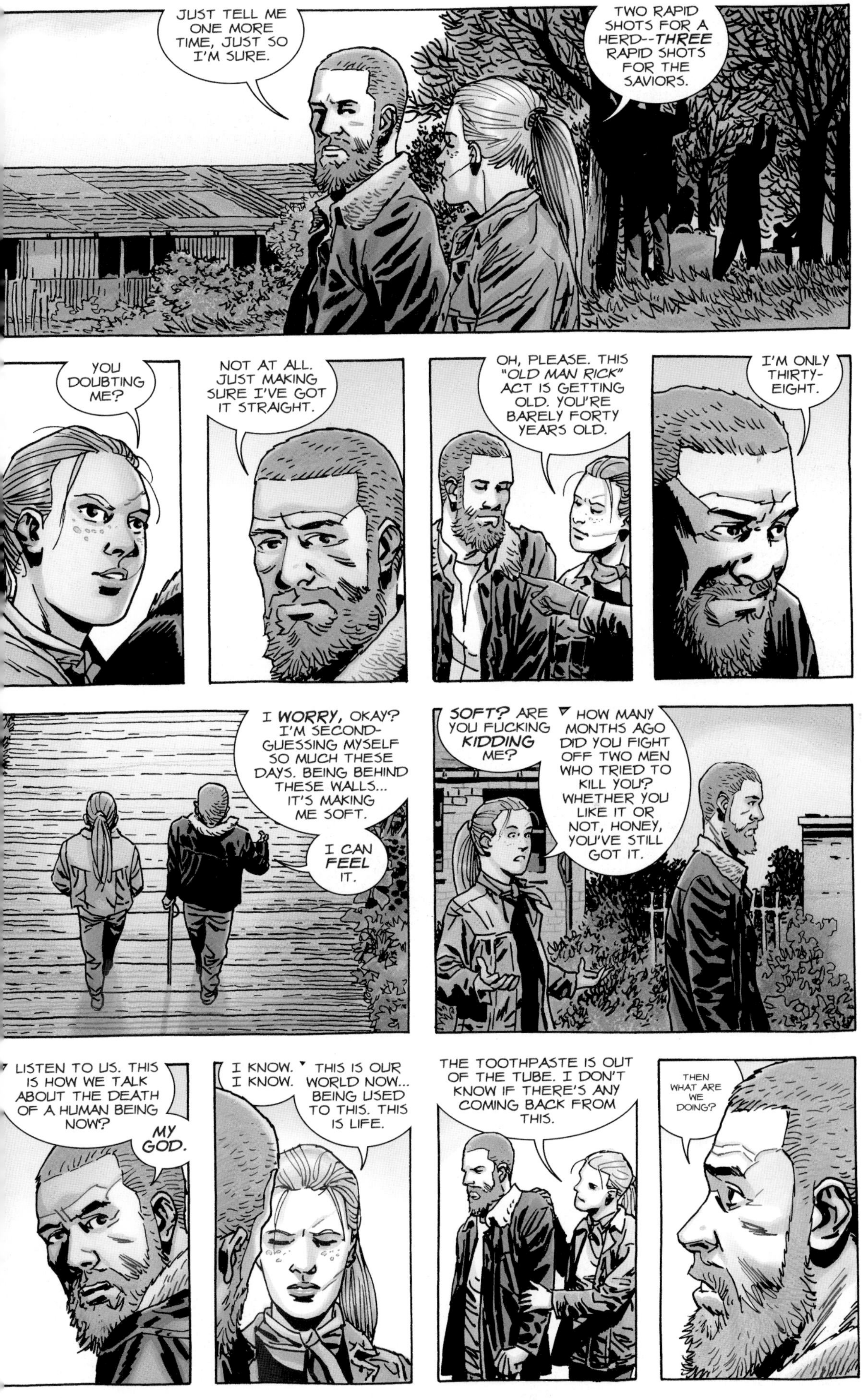
JUST TELL ME ONE MORE TIME, JUST SO I'M SURE.
TWO RAPID SHOTS FOR A HERD--THREE RAPID SHOTS FOR THE SAVIORS.
YOU DOUBTING ME?
NOT AT ALL. JUST MAKING SURE I'VE GOT IT STRAIGHT.
OH, PLEASE. THIS "OLD MAN RICK" ACT IS GETTING OLD. YOU'RE BARELY FORTY YEARS OLD.
I'M ONLY THIRTY-EIGHT.
I WORRY, OKAY? I'M SECOND-GUESSING MYSELF SO MUCH THESE DAYS. BEING BEHIND THESE WALLS... IT'S MAKING ME SOFT.
I CAN FEEL IT.
SOFT? ARE YOU FUCKING KIDDING ME?
HOW MANY MONTHS AGO DID YOU FIGHT OFF TWO MEN WHO TRIED TO KILL YOU? WHETHER YOU LIKE IT OR NOT, HONEY, YOU'VE STILL GOT IT.
LISTEN TO US. THIS IS HOW WE TALK ABOUT THE DEATH OF A HUMAN BEING NOW?
MY GOD.
I KNOW. I KNOW.
THIS IS OUR WORLD NOW... BEING USED TO THIS. THIS IS LIFE.
THE TOOTHPASTE IS OUT OF THE TUBE. I DON'T KNOW IF THERE'S ANY COMING BACK FROM THIS.
THEN WHAT ARE WE DOING?

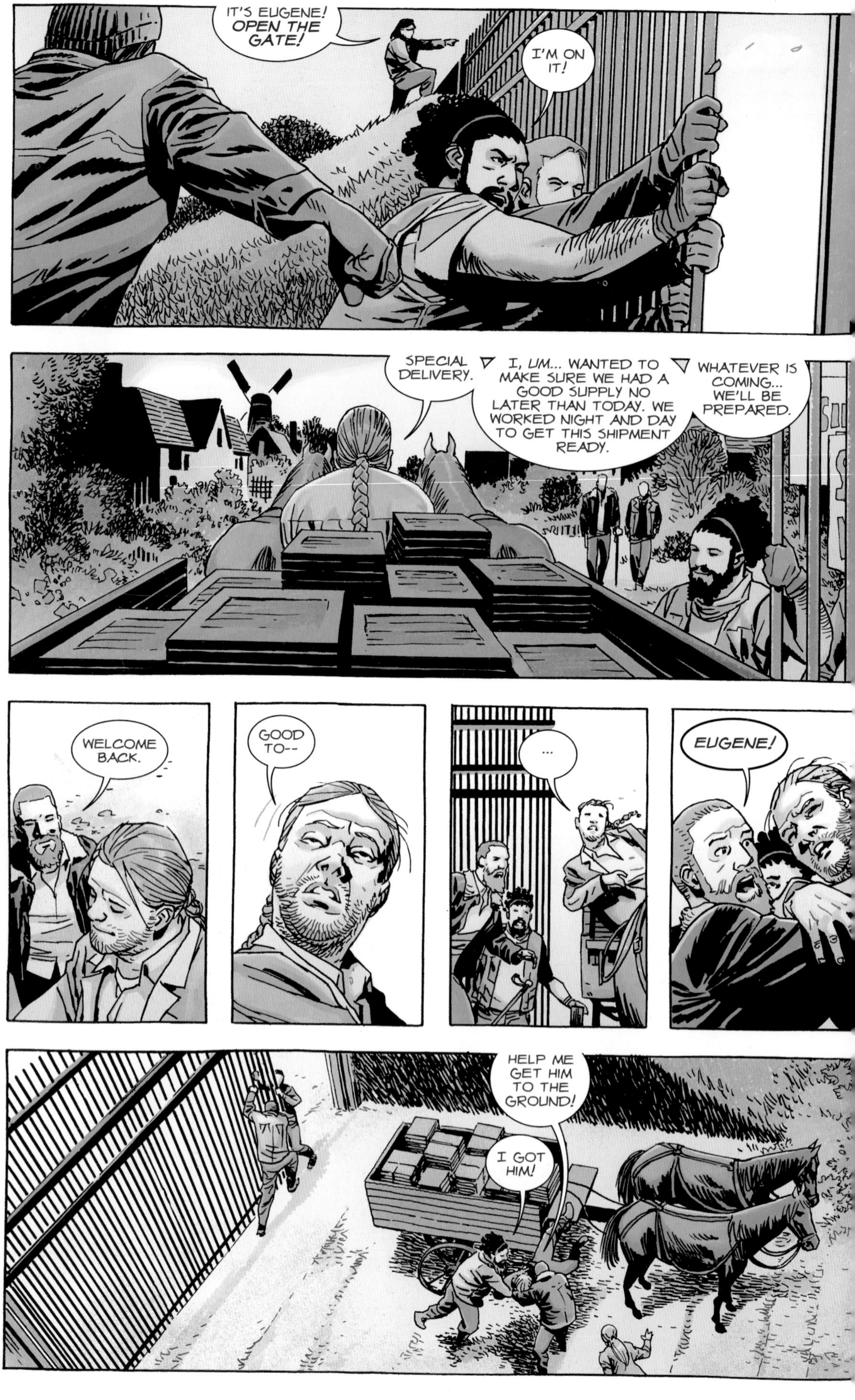
IT'S EUGENE! OPEN THE GATE!
I'M ON IT!
SPECIAL DELIVERY.
I, UM... WANTED TO MAKE SURE WE HAD A GOOD SUPPLY NO LATER THAN TODAY. WE WORKED NIGHT AND DAY TO GET THIS SHIPMENT READY.
WHATEVER IS COMING... WE'LL BE PREPARED.
WELCOME BACK.
GOOD TO--
...
EUGENE!
HELP ME GET HIM TO THE GROUND!
I GOT HIM!

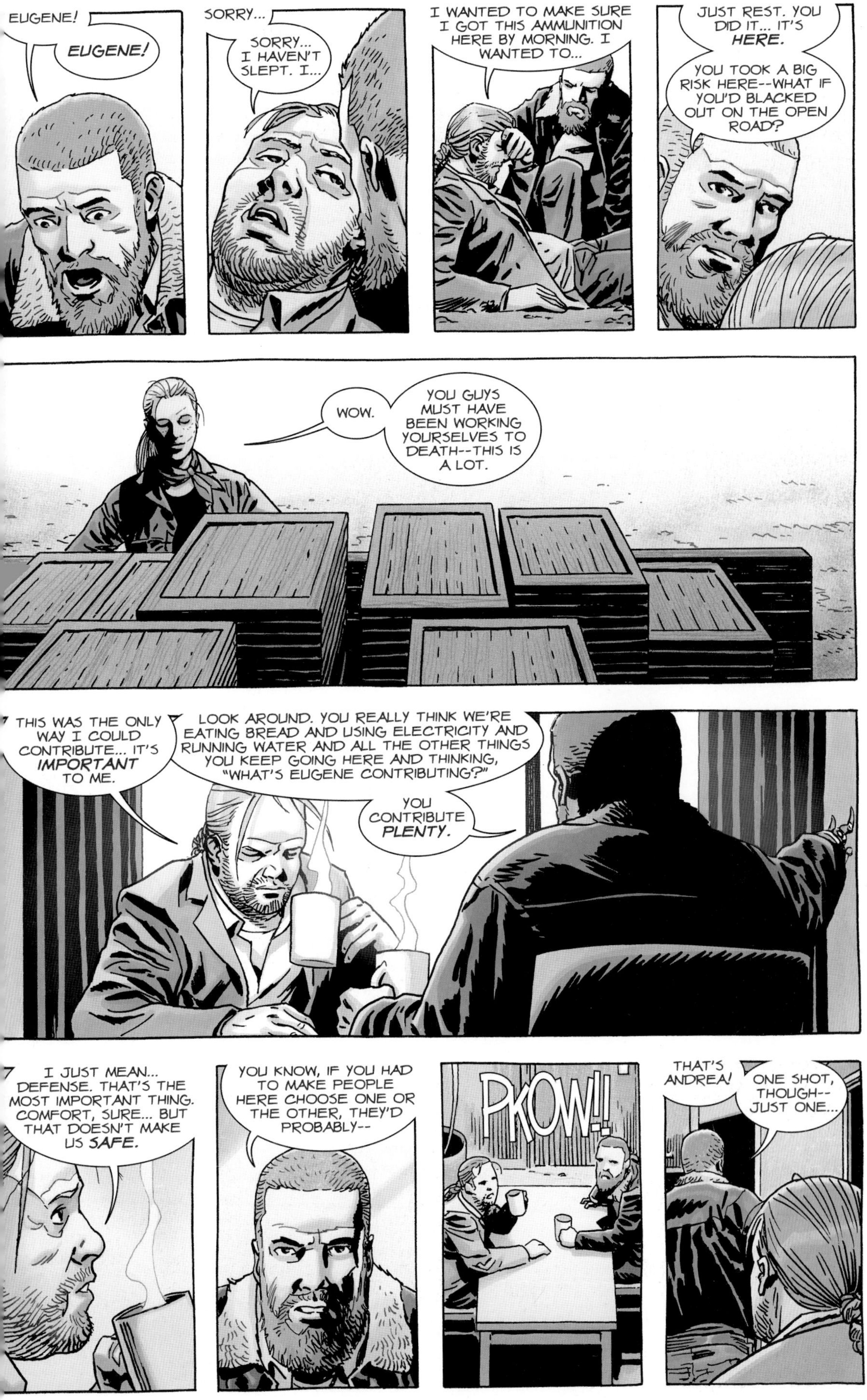
EUGENE!
EUGENE!
SORRY...
SORRY... I HAVEN'T SLEPT. I...
I WANTED TO MAKE SURE I GOT THIS AMMUNITION HERE BY MORNING. I WANTED TO...
JUST REST. YOU DID IT... IT'S HERE.
YOU TOOK A BIG RISK HERE--WHAT IF YOU'D BLACKED OUT ON THE OPEN ROAD?
WOW.
YOU GUYS MUST HAVE BEEN WORKING YOURSELVES TO DEATH--THIS IS A LOT.
THIS WAS THE ONLY WAY I COULD CONTRIBUTE... IT'S IMPORTANT TO ME.
LOOK AROUND. YOU REALLY THINK WE'RE EATING BREAD AND USING ELECTRICITY AND RUNNING WATER AND ALL THE OTHER THINGS YOU KEEP GOING HERE AND THINKING, "WHAT'S EUGENE CONTRIBUTING?"
YOU CONTRIBUTE PLENTY.
I JUST MEAN... DEFENSE. THAT'S THE MOST IMPORTANT THING. COMFORT, SURE... BUT THAT DOESN'T MAKE US SAFE.
YOU KNOW, IF YOU HAD TO MAKE PEOPLE HERE CHOOSE ONE OR THE OTHER, THEY'D PROBABLY--
PKOW!!
THAT'S ANDREA!
ONE SHOT, THOUGH--JUST ONE...

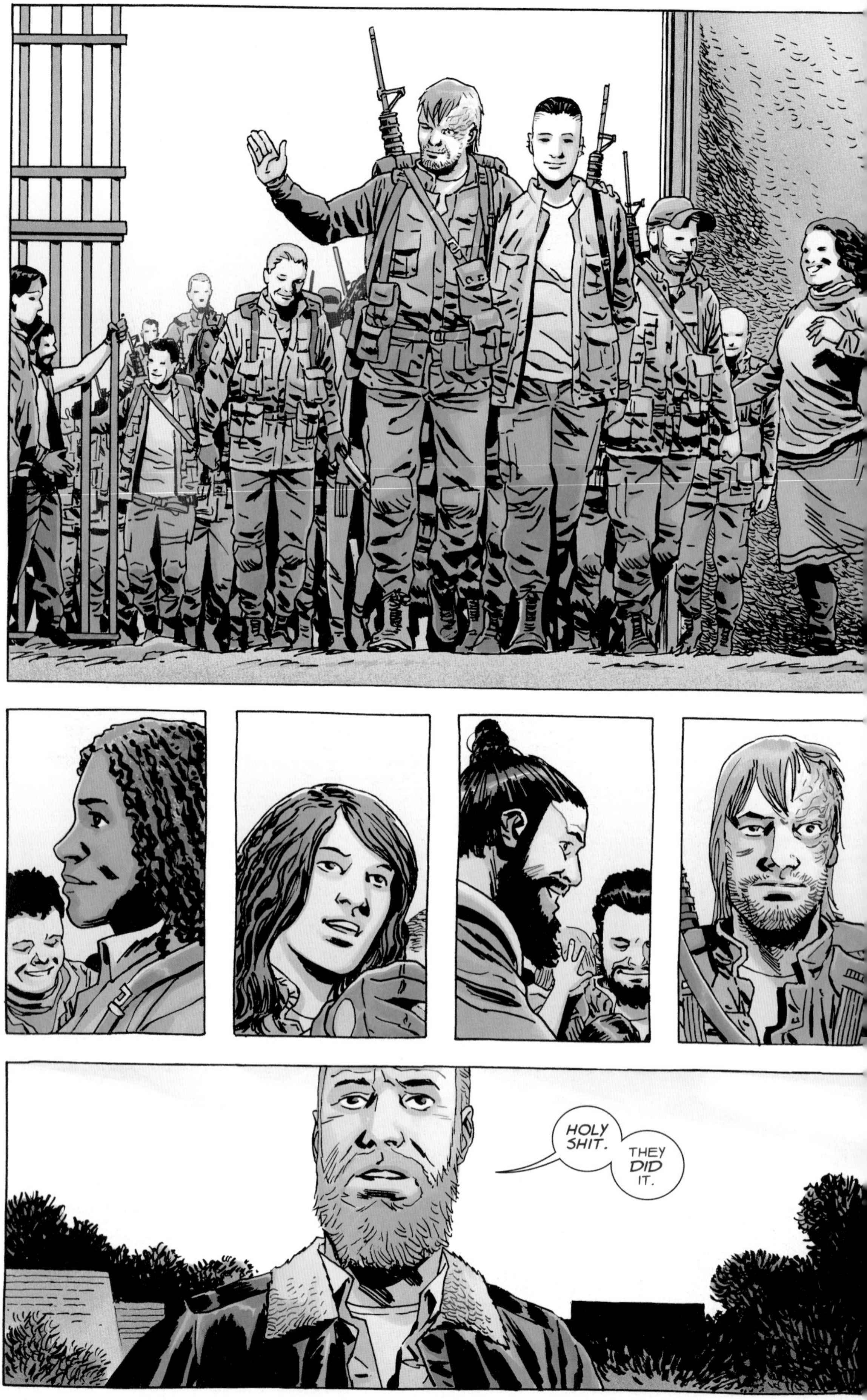
HOLY SHIT.
THEY DID IT.

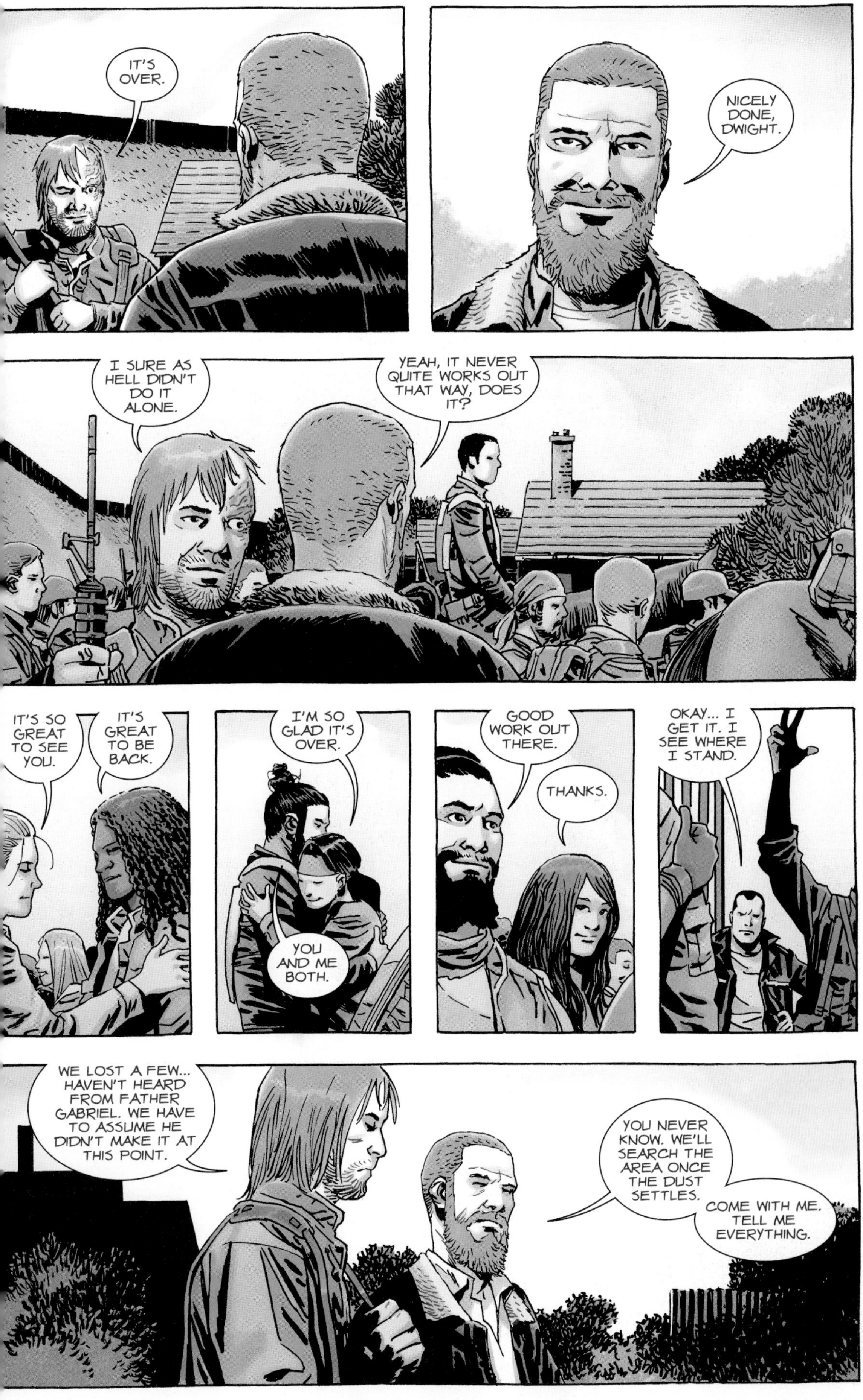
IT'S OVER.
NICELY DONE, DWIGHT.
I SURE AS HELL DIDN'T DO IT ALONE.
YEAH, IT NEVER QUITE WORKS OUT THAT WAY, DOES IT?
IT'S SO GREAT TO SEE YOU.
IT'S GREAT TO BE BACK.
I'M SO GLAD IT'S OVER.
YOU AND ME BOTH.
GOOD WORK OUT THERE.
THANKS.
OKAY... I GET IT. I SEE WHERE I STAND.
WE LOST A FEW... HAVEN'T HEARD FROM FATHER GABRIEL. WE HAVE TO ASSUME HE DIDN'T MAKE IT AT THIS POINT.
YOU NEVER KNOW. WE'LL SEARCH THE AREA ONCE THE DUST SETTLES.
COME WITH ME. TELL ME EVERYTHING.

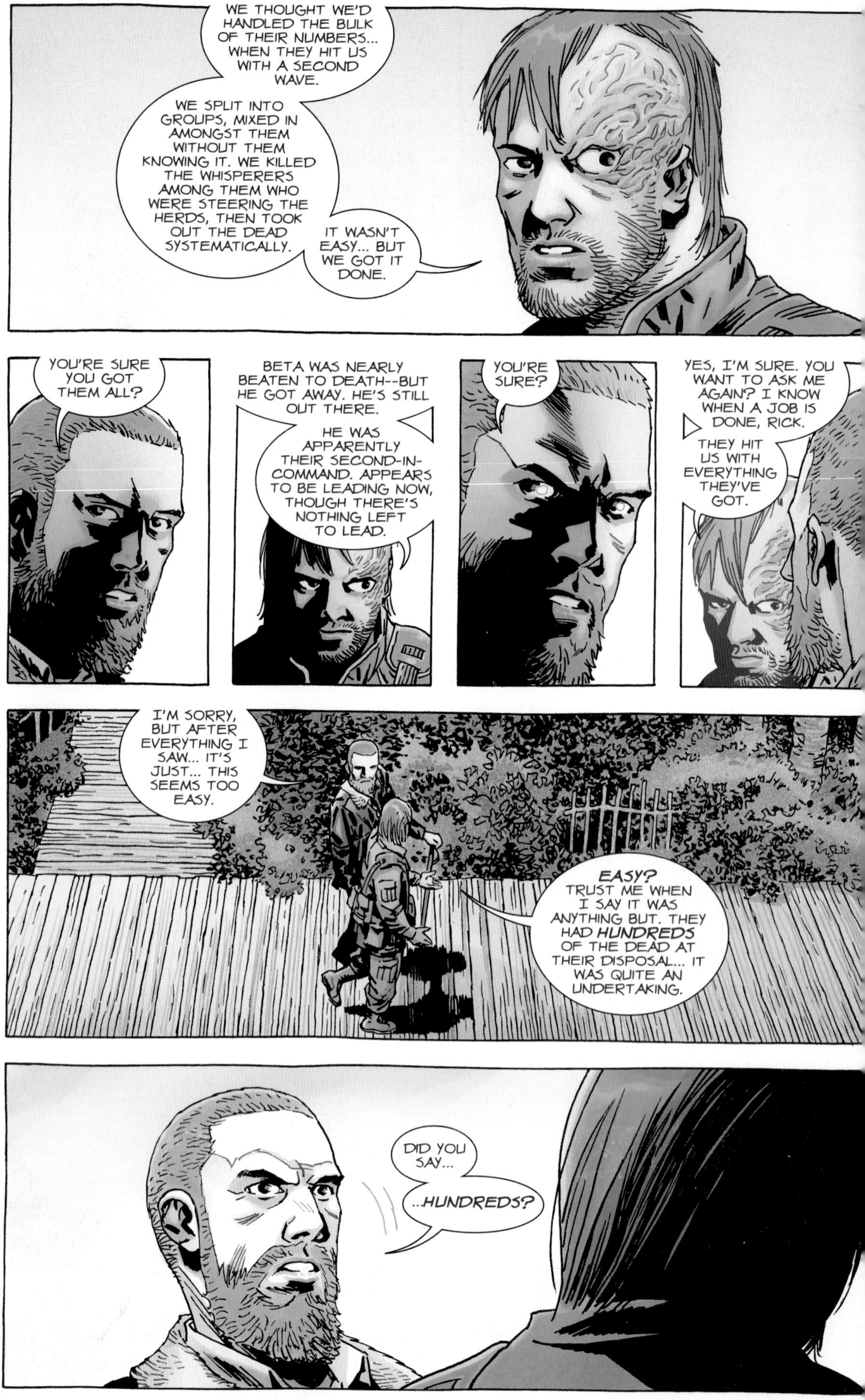
WE THOUGHT WE'D HANDLED THE BULK OF THEIR NUMBERS... WHEN THEY HIT US WITH A SECOND WAVE.
WE SPLIT INTO GROUPS, MIXED IN AMONGST THEM WITHOUT THEM KNOWING IT. WE KILLED THE WHISPERERS AMONG THEM WHO WERE STEERING THE HERDS, THEN TOOK OUT THE DEAD SYSTEMATICALLY.
IT WASN'T EASY... BUT WE GOT IT DONE.
YOU'RE SURE YOU GOT THEM ALL?
BETA WAS NEARLY BEATEN TO DEATH--BUT HE GOT AWAY. HE'S STILL OUT THERE.
HE WAS APPARENTLY THEIR SECOND-IN-COMMAND. APPEARS TO BE LEADING NOW, THOUGH THERE'S NOTHING LEFT TO LEAD.
YOU'RE SURE?
YES, I'M SURE. YOU WANT TO ASK ME AGAIN? I KNOW WHEN A JOB IS DONE, RICK.
THEY HIT US WITH EVERYTHING THEY'VE GOT.
I'M SORRY, BUT AFTER EVERYTHING I SAW... IT'S JUST... THIS SEEMS TOO EASY.
EASY? TRUST ME WHEN I SAY IT WAS ANYTHING BUT. THEY HAD HUNDREDS OF THE DEAD AT THEIR DISPOSAL... IT WAS QUITE AN UNDERTAKING.
DID YOU SAY...
...HUNDREDS?

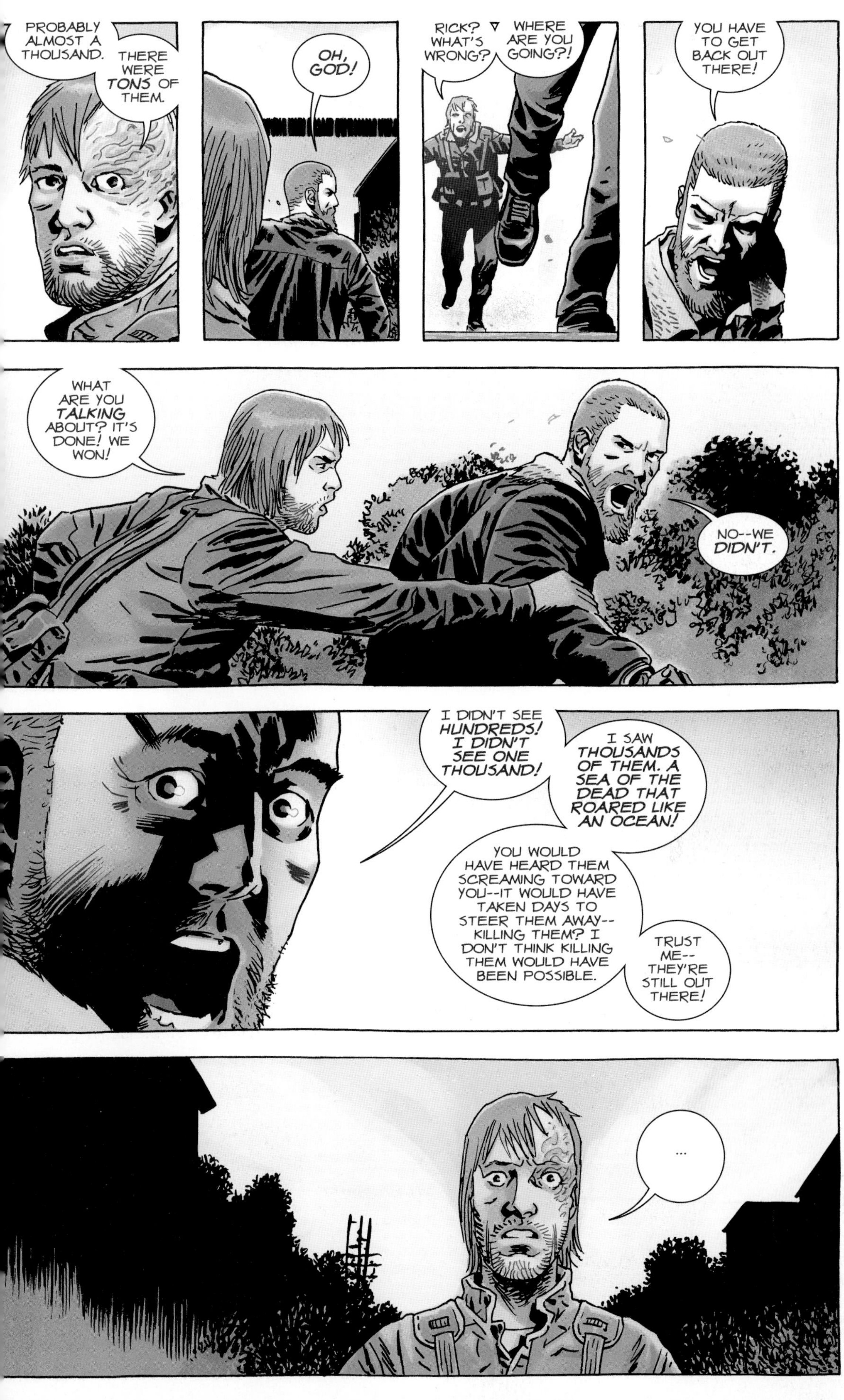
PROBABLY ALMOST A THOUSAND.
THERE WERE TONS OF THEM.
OH, GOD!
RICK? WHAT'S WRONG?
WHERE ARE YOU GOING?!
YOU HAVE TO GET BACK OUT THERE!
WHAT ARE YOU TALKING ABOUT? IT'S DONE! WE WON!
NO--WE DIDN'T.
I DIDN'T SEE HUNDREDS! I DIDN'T SEE ONE THOUSAND!
I SAW THOUSANDS OF THEM. A SEA OF THE DEAD THAT ROARED LIKE AN OCEAN!
YOU WOULD HAVE HEARD THEM SCREAMING TOWARD YOU--IT WOULD HAVE TAKEN DAYS TO STEER THEM AWAY-- KILLING THEM? I DON'T THINK KILLING THEM WOULD HAVE BEEN POSSIBLE.
TRUST ME-- THEY'RE STILL OUT THERE!
...

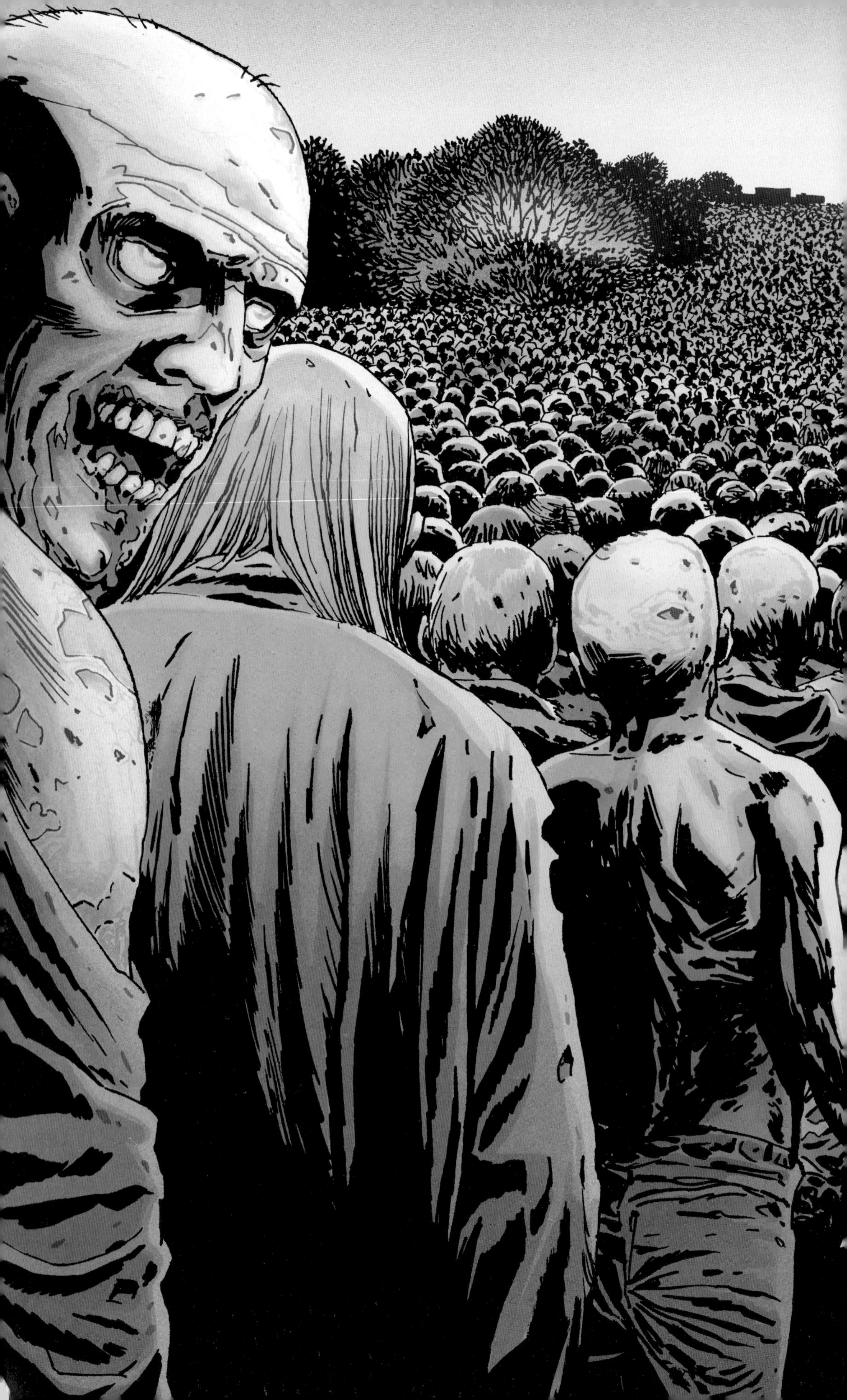

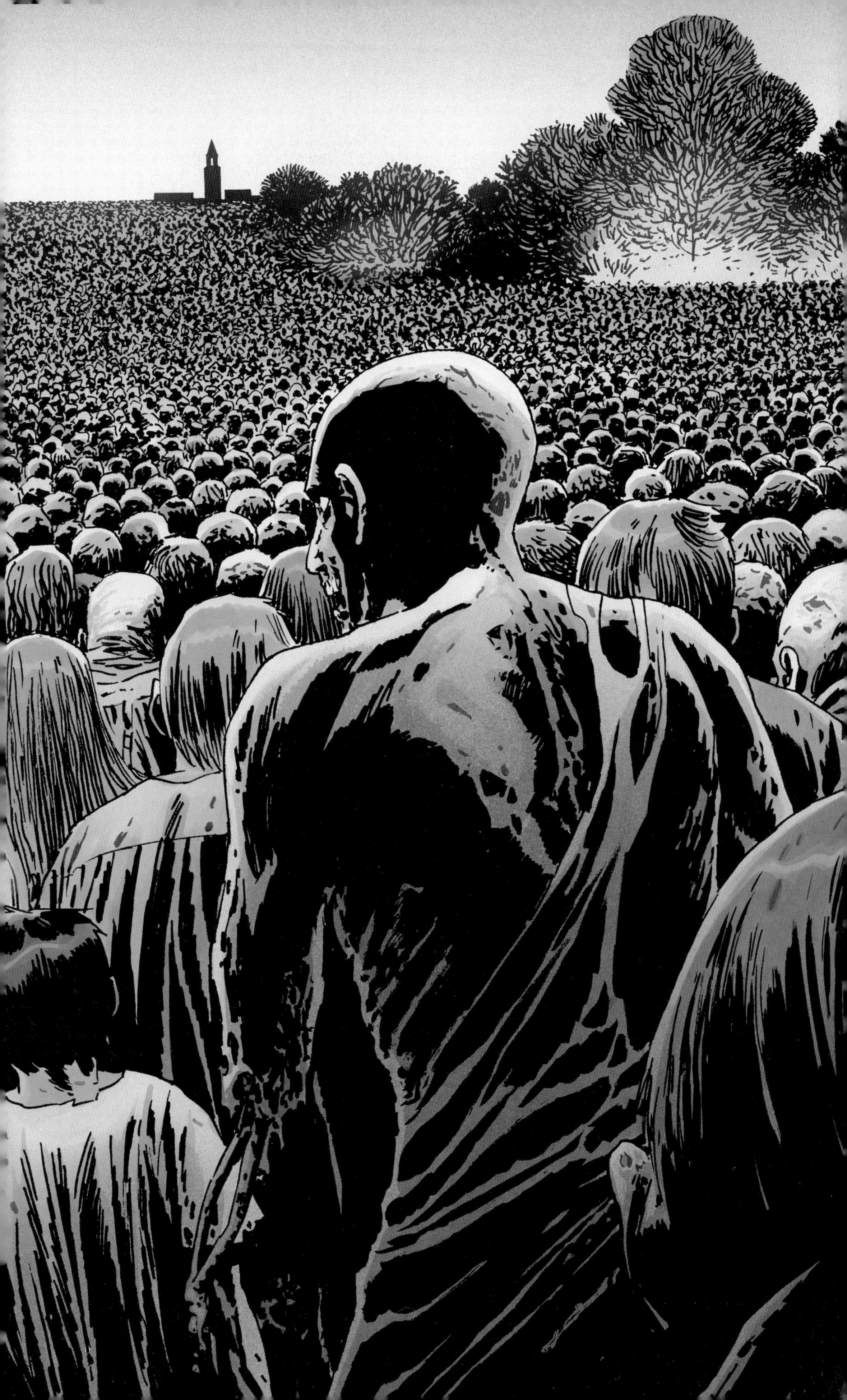

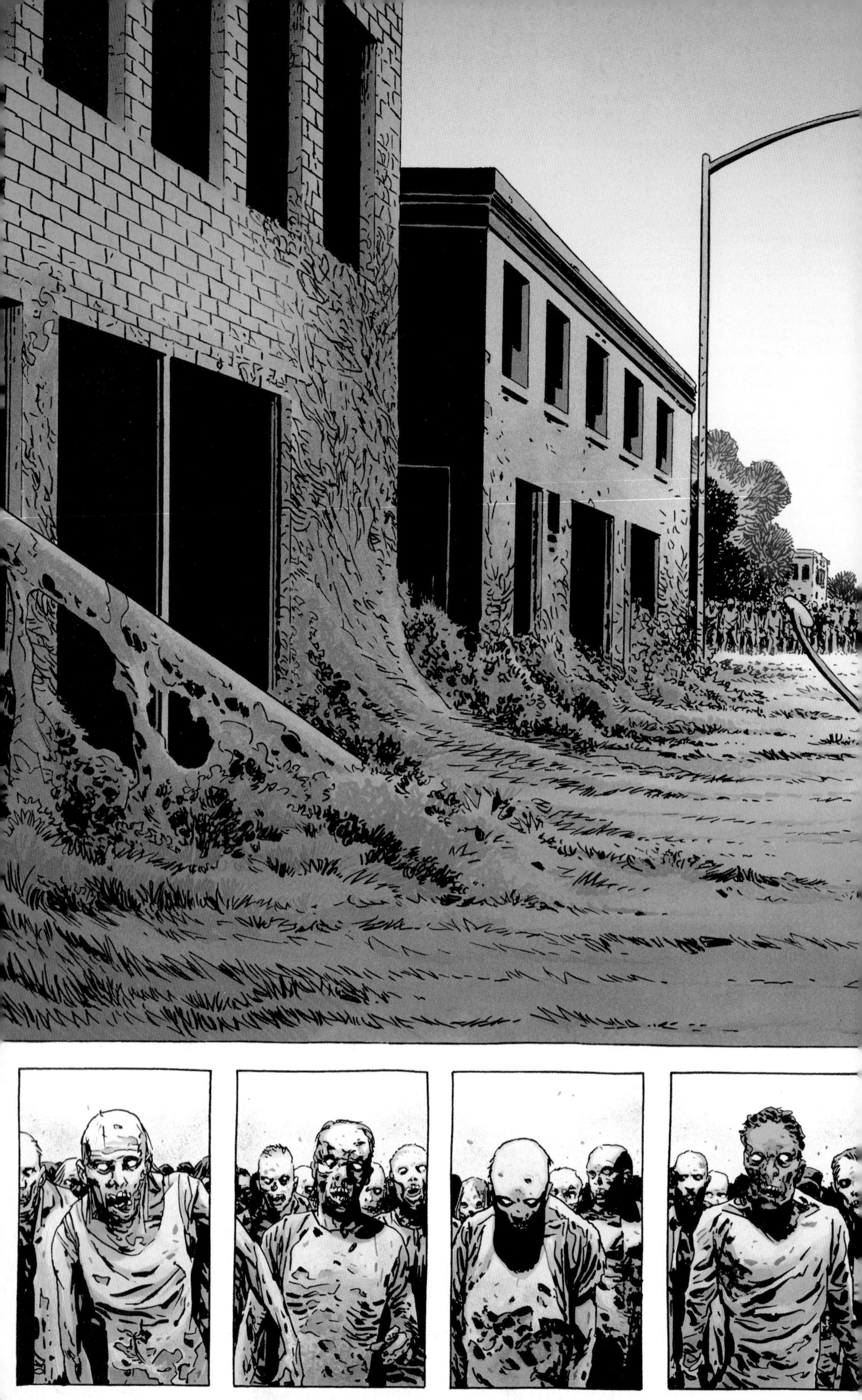

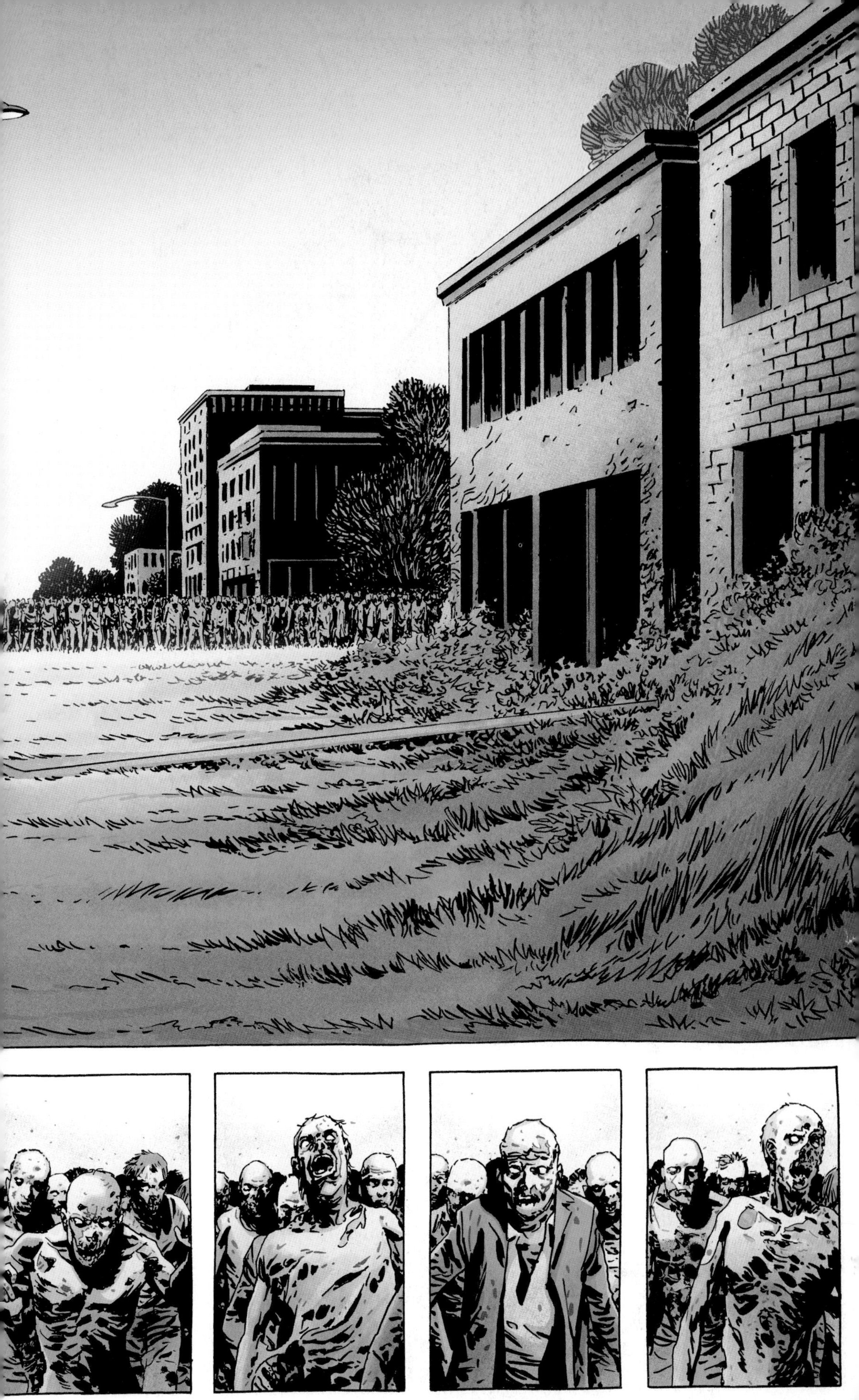

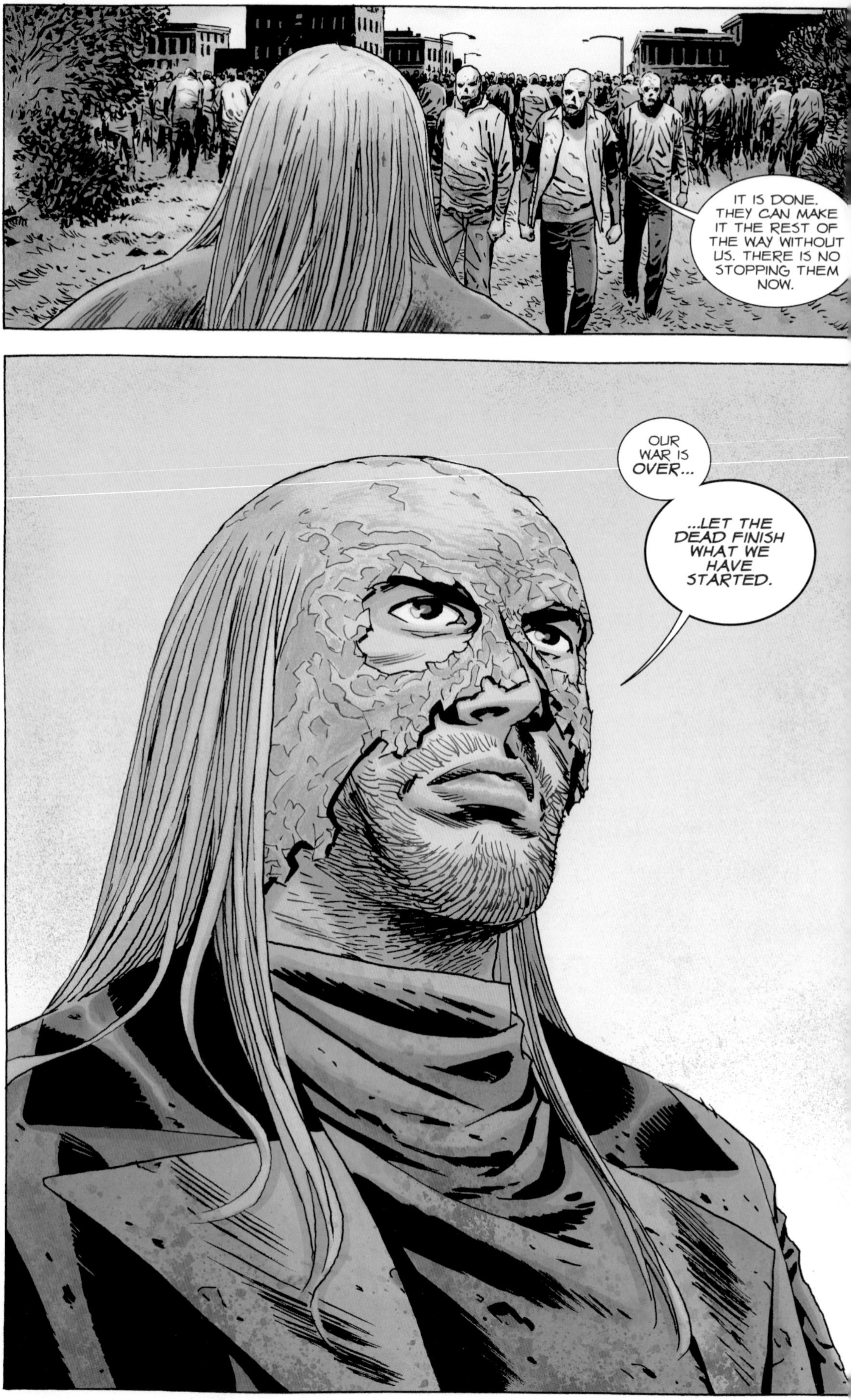
IT IS DONE. THEY CAN MAKE IT THE REST OF THE WAY WITHOUT US. THERE IS NO STOPPING THEM NOW.
OUR WAR IS OVER...
...LET THE DEAD FINISH WHAT WE HAVE STARTED.

# TO BE CONTINUED...

## for more tales from ROBERT KIRKMAN and SKYBOUND

VOLUME 3: THIS LITTLE LIGHT
OUTCAST
BY KIRKMAN & AZACETA

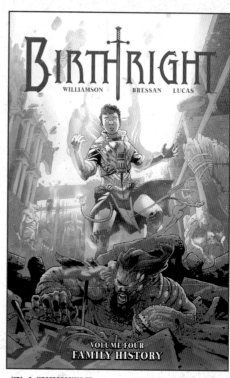

**VOL. 1: A DARKNESS SURROUNDS HIM TP**
ISBN: 978-1-63215-053-0
$9.99

**VOL. 2: A VAST AND UNENDING RUIN TP**
ISBN: 978-1-63215-448-4
$14.99

**VOL. 3: THIS LITTLE LIGHT TP**
ISBN: 978-1-63215-693-8
$14.99

BIRTHRIGHT
WILLIAMSON
BRESSAN
LUCAS
VOLUME FOUR
FAMILY HISTORY

**VOL. 1: HOMECOMING TP**
ISBN: 978-1-63215-231-2
$9.99

**VOL. 2: CALL TO ADVENTURE TP**
ISBN: 978-1-63215-446-0
$12.99

**VOL. 3: ALLIES AND ENEMIES TP**
ISBN: 978-1-63215-683-9
$12.99

**VOL. 4: FAMILY HISTORY TP**
ISBN: 978-1-63215-871-0
$12.99

CLONE
VOLUME 4
FOURTH GENERATION

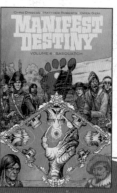

**VOL. 1: FIRST GENERATION TP**
ISBN: 978-1-60706-683-5
$12.99

**VOL. 2: SECOND GENERATION TP**
ISBN: 978-1-60706-830-3
$12.99

**VOL. 3: THIRD GENERATION TP**
ISBN: 978-1-60706-939-3
$12.99

**VOL. 4: FOURTH GENERATION TP**
ISBN: 978-1-63215-036-3
$12.99

WILLIAMSON
LACI
RYP
MIRVA
GHOSTED
VOLUME FOUR · GHOST TOWN

**VOL. 1: HAUNTED HEIST TP**
ISBN: 978-1-60706-836-5
$9.99

**VOL. 2: BOOKS OF THE DEAD TP**
ISBN: 978-1-63215-046-2
$12.99

**VOL. 3: DEATH WISH TP**
ISBN: 978-1-63215-051-6
$12.99

**VOL. 4: GHOST TOWN TP**
ISBN: 978-1-63215-317-3
$12.99

MANIFEST DESTINY
VOLUME 4 SASQUATCH

**VOL. 1: FLORA & FAUNA TP**
ISBN: 978-1-60706-982-9
$9.99

**VOL. 2: AMPHIBIA & INSECTA TP**
ISBN: 978-1-63215-052-3
$14.99

**VOL. 3: CHIROPTERA & CARNIFORMAVES TP**
ISBN: 978-1-63215-397-5
$14.99

**VOL. 4: SASQUATCH TP**
ISBN: 978-1-63215-890-1
$14.99

THIEF OF THIEVES
VOLUME 6
"GOLD RUSH."

**VOL. 1: "I QUIT."**
ISBN: 978-1-60706-592-0
$14.99

**VOL. 2: "HELP ME."**
ISBN: 978-1-60706-676-7
$14.99

**VOL. 3: "VENICE."**
ISBN: 978-1-60706-844-0
$14.99

**VOL. 4: "THE HIT LIST."**
ISBN: 978-1-63215-037-0
$14.99

**VOL. 5: "TAKE ME."**
ISBN: 978-1-63215-401-9
$14.99

**VOL. 6: "GOLD RUSH."**
ISBN: 978-1-53430-037-8
$14.99